Margaret Thornton was born in Blackpool and has lived there all her life. She is a qualified teacher but has retired in order to concentrate on her writing. She has two children and five grandchildren. Her previous Blackpool sagas, *It's a Lovely Day Tomorrow*, *A Pair of Sparkling Eyes*, *How Happy We Shall Be*, *There's a Silver Lining*, *Forgive Our Foolish Ways*, *A Stick of Blackpool Rock*, *Wish Upon a Star*, *The Sound of her Laughter*, *Looking at the Moon*, *Beyond the Sunset* and *All You Need is Love* are also available from Headline and have been highly praised:

'A brilliant read'   *Woman's Realm*

'A gentle novel whose lack of noise is a strength'
                                                 The Sunday Times

'A delightful first novel'   Netta Martin, *Annabel*

D0377973

Also by Margaret Thornton

It's a Lovely Day Tomorrow
A Pair of Sparkling Eyes
How Happy We Shall Be
There's a Silver Lining
Forgive Our Foolish Ways
A Stick of Blackpool Rock
Wish Upon a Star
The Sound of her Laughter
Looking at the Moon
Beyond the Sunset
All You Need is Love

Sunset View

Margaret Thornton

First published in 2002
by HEADLINE BOOK PUBLISHING

First published in paperback in 2003
by HEADLINE BOOK PUBLISHING

10 9 8 7 6 5 4

Cataloguing in Publication Data
is available from the British Library

ISBN 0 7553 0034 3

Typeset in Times New Roman by
Letterpart Limited, Reigate, Surrey

Printed and bound in Great Britain by
Mackays of Chatham plc, Chatham, Kent

HEADLINE BOOK PUBLISHING
A division of Hodder Headline
338 Euston Road
London NW1 3BH

www.headline.co.uk
www.hodderheadline.com

For Elaine and David, with love.

And for my 'in-laws', Tony and Linda, Betty and Don.

A special thank you to Tony Mitchell for information about the catering college and boarding-house life in the sixties.

Chapter 1

Doreen

'Gynn Square? My word, we are going up in the world, aren't we, Mum?' Veronica Jarvis nodded approvingly. 'I'm impressed, I must say.'

'What d'you mean, "we"?' retorted her sister Teresa. 'You don't live here any more, Veronica. Or are you thinking you might move back when we've got a posher address?'

'Don't be so horrid, Teresa.' Doreen Jarvis frowned at her sixteen-year-old daughter. The girl was developing a snide way of talking of late; quite nasty, she could be at times. 'Veronica's still as much a member of this family as she ever was. She just wanted her independence, that's all.'

Veronica had moved into her own flat about a year ago, but still called regularly to see her family. This balmy August evening, however, only Doreen and Teresa were at home. It was most unusual for Teresa not to be out, but the girl had stated grumpily that she wanted to wash her hair and do her nails. Doreen suspected she had had a tiff with her latest boyfriend, which happened quite regularly. The boys gathered around Teresa like bees round a jam pot, but were apt to disappear again just as quickly.

'No, I'm not thinking of moving back, Tess,' said Veronica. She smiled disarmingly at her sister. 'But it's like Mum says: I still think of myself as one of the family . . . So it's all signed and sealed, is it, Mum? When are we moving? Sorry . . .' She grinned. 'I should've said,

"When are you moving?", shouldn't I?'

'Not just yet,' replied Doreen. 'The sale hasn't been completed, and there's still this place to sell, of course, but we're getting there, gradually. Your dad and I have decided that the hotel in North Shore is just what we want, so we're going ahead with the contract and all that. The present owners want to complete the season, so they'll stay there till the Lights finish at the end of October. That suits us fine because we're nearly fully booked up here till then. And we think we've more or less sold Dorabella. A couple from Accrington are very interested. They've been back twice to look over it and they seem quite taken with everything. So it'll be all change, come the beginning of November. I'm starting to get really excited about it.' She beamed at the two girls. 'A lovely position it's got – right opposite those nice gardens at Gynn Square.'

'What's the hotel called, Mum?' asked Veronica.

'It's got a real posh name – Sunset View.'

'Sunset View?' Teresa curled her lip, sounding more than a little derisive. 'Huh! It probably overlooks a dingy back alley.'

'No, it doesn't,' her mother answered. 'I've already told you: it faces the gardens, so it stands to reason it faces the sea an' all, doesn't it? Sunset View is a lovely name. And they are the most beautiful sunsets you could ever wish for anywhere, over the Irish Sea. The pity is we've never been able to see 'em, here in Hornby Road.'

'Hm, I suppose it sounds all right then,' said Teresa, still a little grudgingly. 'Better than Dorabella anyroad,' she giggled.

'Yes, I know you've had a good laugh at the name I gave this place,' said Doreen. She smiled good-humouredly. 'But I thought it sounded . . . well, sort of distinguished, like. I really wanted to use part of your dad's name as well as mine, but it didn't seem to work.'

Veronica pursed her lips thoughtfully. 'No . . . Dor-Nor. It doesn't sound right, does it? Where is Dad, by the way?'

'He's gone to the bowling green to see if he could get a

2

game, it's such a nice evening. But he'll be back to help me with the suppers.'

'What about Dor-Man?' tittered Teresa, returning to the subject of the hotel's name. 'That would've been even sillier.'

'Well, I decided on Dorabella, didn't I?' said Doreen, a trifle huffily. 'Bella means beautiful; and I've tried to make this place as smart as I can over the years, you've got to admit that. It's always nicely painted and decorated and we've done all sorts of things to make the bedrooms comfy. All those new interior-sprung mattresses, and washbasins with hot and cold in every room. And matching curtains and bedspreads. Some of the visitors say to me, "It's like a little palace, Mrs Jarvis." That's why they come back, a lot of 'em, year after year.'

'But you wanted to go a bit more up-market, did you, Mum?' asked Veronica.

'Yes, I suppose I did, dear,' replied Doreen. 'I've always fancied the north end of the town, and your dad and I both wanted to move to a slightly bigger place when we could afford it. Well, we can afford it now, so we're taking the plunge. Central Blackpool's all very well, but . . .' She paused thoughtfully, not wanting to say anything disparaging about the area. After all, she had been brought up in a street of small terraced houses off Central Drive and had never been one to despise her roots. But time had moved on and lots of things had changed.

'But you want something a bit classier, eh?' said Veronica. 'Can't say I blame you. The centre of Blackpool's very rowdy at times, and the Central Drive area's deteriorating, not to mention that awful Golden Mile.'

'Why, what's wrong with it?' said Teresa. 'I think it's dead good. Me and Kev went there the other night. It's a real hoot, honestly. They've got a new sideshow – "The Fattest Teenager You Ever Saw. When She Walks She Wobbles". And she doesn't half wobble, an' all, I'm not kidding.'

'I think that's dreadful,' replied Doreen. 'Making fun of

a poor girl like that, putting her on show for everybody to goggle at.'

'So what?' Teresa stared back defiantly. 'Don't suppose she minds. She looked happy enough, and she's getting paid, isn't she?'

'I must say I agree with Mum,' said Veronica. 'It's not very nice to trade on people's afflictions. I never go down the Golden Mile any more.'

Teresa shrugged and pulled her mouth into a moue. 'No, you wouldn't, would you, Little Miss Prim?'

'That will do, Teresa,' said Doreen quietly. She tried hard to be patient with her second daughter, but it was not always easy. She remembered a time when she had been at variance with Veronica, but they had got on so much better together since she had left home. It was probably what the mother and daughter had both needed: some time apart to readjust after what had been a traumatic period in their lives.

Veronica had had an unhappy relationship with a young Roman Catholic priest who had been the curate at the church they attended. Doreen guessed it had been rather one-sided, with Veronica, infatuated and imagining herself in love, doing most of the running. But it had, naturally, caused something of a scandal in the parish, especially when Father Dominic had been asked to leave and Veronica had tried to take an overdose. Although that had been more of a plea for help than a real suicide attempt, her mother thought, and the girl certainly seemed to be adjusting well enough now to her new life. The abortive love affair was a thing of the past – it had happened almost two years ago and was never referred to – and Veronica, now nearly twenty, had had a couple of young men since then. But she was waiting, she said, for Mr Right. Veronica was a wee bit old-fashioned, in outlook if not in appearance, and tended to use these quaint expressions.

Now the situation had changed and it was Teresa with whom Doreen was often at loggerheads. The two sisters were very much alike in looks: small, fair-haired, blue-eyed and inclined to plumpness – like Doreen herself. But whereas Veronica's face was open and trusting – there was a look of innocence in her big blue eyes that was definitely not assumed – Teresa's expression was far more knowing. The kindness and gentleness, so much a part of both Veronica and her younger sister, Bernie, was not apparent in Teresa. Doreen told herself the girl was going through a phase, that sixteen was an awkward age, as she tried, unsuccessfully at times, to love them all equally.

There were five children in the Jarvis family, although only Bernie, aged fourteen, could really be regarded as a child any more. Veronica, the eldest, was nineteen and, to her mother's relief, seemed very contented in her position as a supervisor at the Marks and Spencer store opposite Central Station. (Or what had used to be Central Station; it was all change in Blackpool nowadays.) She had quickly been promoted from sales assistant and now was in charge of several counters, wearing the distinctive navy-blue uniform with the gilt M&S badge, rather than the paler blue worn by the ordinary shop girls. Doreen was pleased at the way she had settled down and made a go of the job, although she had been a little disappointed at first when Veronica had insisted on leaving school in the middle of her sixth-form course. She was a clever girl and had been doing very well at school; the teachers had had aspirations for her to go on to university.

'She gets her brains from her dad, not from me,' Doreen often laughingly remarked. 'Real bird-brain, I am.' That was not true, of course. Doreen was bright enough, but had not had the advantage of what they were now calling 'further education'. She had left school at fourteen and gone to work in a grocer's shop. The larger share of her wages had been used to augment the family income, Doreen being the eldest of six children. It had been a happy family; poor, undoubtedly, in material possessions and in comparison with a lot of people, but rich in the things that mattered: loving and caring and the sharing of joys and sorrows. Doreen knew that it might be said that she had gone up in the world, but the memories of that little house near Central Drive – a mite shabby and untidy maybe, but always scrupulously clean and well cared for – were precious to her. She would not want anyone to think she now looked down on her humble beginnings. It was pleasant, all the same, to look forward to the more prosperous way of life that might lie ahead.

It would be hard, though. There was nothing in life that could be achieved without a great deal of effort, at least for working-class folk such as they were; that was what Doreen believed. And work did not come much harder than that of a boarding-house keeper; in other words a seaside landlady. That was what Doreen had been at first when she and her family had moved from their home in North Yorkshire to start a new life in Hornby Road, near the centre of Blackpool. They had sold the farm near Northallerton, which Norman had run since his father's death. It was there that Doreen had first met her future husband, when she was working as a land girl during the Second World War. All the children had been born there, but Doreen had had a hankering to return to Blackpool, the town of her birth, and Norman, usually complaisant and willing to go along with his wife's plans, had agreed to the idea of the boarding house.

He had put his foot down, however, about one thing. He did not want to be thought of as 'the landlady's husband'. Music-hall jokes had long been told about such species, and cartoons of them abounded on comic post-cards. They were considered to be insignificant little men, peeling mounds of potatoes or scurrying about doing odd jobs around the house to escape from 'the wife' with her scurrilous tongue and brawny physique. The seaside land-ladies too were the target of comedians and caricaturists. They were portrayed as being well past their first flush of youth, full-busted and fat-bottomed, red-faced and broadly spoken, with hair in curling pins and feet in carpet slippers, always clad in a voluminous flowered apron.

Both Doreen and Norman had done all they could to dispel those images. Norman had found employment outside the boarding house as a gardener with the Parks Department, although he had more than pulled his weight with such jobs as painting and decorating when all the holidaymakers had departed at the end of the season, and he did not mind helping with the visitors' suppers each evening. And Doreen, still in her thirties when they first moved there some eight years ago, vivacious, attractive and with a friendly personality, did not fit the conventional image of a martinet.

But, as she often said, she had 'worked her socks off'; cooking, cleaning, changing the beds, washing up mountains of pots, although the installation of a dishwasher – a luxury, indeed – had made that chore so much easier during the last couple of years. There was no job that Doreen was not willing to tackle herself, but no boarding house could be run single-handedly. She had insisted on her daughters helping when they became old enough, and her sons as well. Her sister Vera worked there too during the summer, and seasonal jobs for waitresses and chamber maids were very quickly filled by local girls or those from inland towns who wanted a change of scene.

Doreen had tried from the beginning to set the right tone for her establishment. That was why she had given it what some people considered a fanciful name. She wanted Dorabella to be thought of as a private hotel rather than a common or garden boarding house, which, in truth, was what it was. Now, however, the term 'private hotel' was coming to be more widely used. The Blackpool Hotel and Boarding House Association, to which most aspiring landladies belonged, had now become the Hotel and Guest House Association. Several years ago this same association had expressed amusement at a decision by its counterpart in Lytham St Annes – which resort had always considered itself to be genteel and a cut above its common neighbour along the coast – to drop the 'boarding house' part of its title. 'How pretentious!' many of the Blackpool members had said. Blackpool had been built up on the boarding-house trade. Why should they be ashamed of saying so? But now the new title was readily accepted. The leaders, indeed, even rejected the label 'landlady' because of its derisory connotations, preferring to see themselves as 'hoteliers' with up-to-date premises and a businesslike approach to their occupation.

Whatever name they might give to the establishment, however, or to the person who ran it, all Doreen knew was that it was damned hard work. Until very recently she had done all the cooking herself, with a certain amount of help, of course, with the donkey work involved – the peeling of potatoes, preparing of vegetables and the inevitable mounds of washing-up. A few years ago Doreen had taken a night-school course in advanced cookery and had tried out several of the dishes on her guests. She had received an enthusiastic response from most, apart from the few die-hards who equated Blackpool with little else but fish and chips, Lancashire hotpot and jam roly-poly. This course, however, had been abandoned in a hurry after Doreen's abortive affair with another night-school student. The incident was an embarrassment to her now – it had been 'something and nothing of an affair, anyway', she always maintained – and it was never referred to by either herself or Norman. They had settled down to their family life again with a renewed affection for one another and a much better understanding.

Now, to Doreen's relief and delight, a share of the catering was being taken over by her elder son, Paul. Since the age of fourteen or so he had shown a desire to help in the kitchen that none of her other children had had. This had been a surprise to Doreen. She had considered him to be a very clever lad who, like his sister Veronica, could go far academically if he so wished. They had been the only ones of her children to pass their eleven-plus and go to grammar schools – Catholic ones, of course: the Girls' Convent School and St Joseph's College – whereas the other three had gone to the local secondary modern school. How proud she would have been and what a feather in her cap, Doreen had often thought, if even one of her children had decided to go to university. But with Paul, as with Veronica, she had learned that his happiness and following the career of his choice was the important thing. He had left school at seventeen and had now done a year of his training at Parklands, the Blackpool catering college. He would eventually be a qualified chef, ready to take up a post in a leading hotel or, indeed, to set up somewhere on his own. She hoped, of course, that he might decide to throw in his lot with his own family at their new hotel, Sunset View, but that remained to be seen. For the moment she was content that he helped out when he could.

Parklands was very near to where they lived now. Paul could foresee no problem getting to college, he said, when they went to live at the other end of town. He rode a bike, there were buses and trams, and his friend at the college, Martin, who lived at Bispham and owned a car, had offered to give him a lift should he require one. Paul was a real gem, his mother often mused – so good-natured and calm and easy to get along with. He did not have the volatile temperament said to typify many chefs, and she enjoyed working with him in the kitchen. There was a compatibility between them she did not have with any of the others, except for Bernie. Doreen's only criticism of Paul was that he was inclined to be withdrawn and secretive; sometimes the slightest bit moody. You could not always tell what he was thinking. He reminded Doreen of how Norman had been when he was younger, in looks as well as in temperament. Dark-haired, tall, slender and serious-looking, quite nondescript really until he smiled, when his luminous grey eyes and wide mouth completely changed the aspect of his face. Norman was balding now, and had worn spectacles since before she had known him, but apart from that it was easy to tell they were father and son.

Veronica and Teresa had been talking together quietly whilst Doreen was woolgathering. She was surprised now to hear Teresa say, 'OK then – I'll come round to yours.

You can make me a coffee, then you can show me . . . er . . . what you've bought . . .' Her voice petered out as she saw her mother looking at her in some surprise. It was not like Teresa, Doreen was thinking, to show so much interest in Veronica's doings. 'What's up?' the girl said. 'Why're you looking at me like that? I'm going round to Veronica's and she's going to show me some new clothes she's bought. All right?' The last two words were defiant.

'Yes, I heard what you said,' replied Doreen evenly. 'That's OK, but I thought you said you were going to wash your hair.'

'Changed my mind, haven't I?' Teresa shrugged. 'I can wash it tomorrer. Anyroad, I'm sick of being stuck inside. Come on, Veron, let's go if we're going.'

'Hey, wait a minute,' said Doreen. 'Aren't you forgetting something? You've the tables to set up for morning. It was part of the bargain; one of the things you agreed to do as part of your job.'

'Oh . . . that!' Teresa pouted.

'Yes, that!' retorted her mother. 'You said you'd set the tables, then you'd wash your hair.'

'Then Veronica came, didn't she? It's too late to wash my hair. Oh, all right then, I'll do your stupid tables when I come back.'

'Just think on that you do. I've ended up doing it myself more than once.'

'Oh, stop going on, Mum. I've said I'll set your bloomin' tables, an' I will. Come on, Veronica.'

Both girls rose to their feet and Doreen thought, not for the first time, how alike they were. Veronica was the elder by nearly four years and when her face was in repose you could see the onset of maturity there compared with Teresa's more youthful – though, it had to be said, at times more peevish – countenance. Skirts were gradually becoming shorter. The hem of Teresa's bright pink shift dress was a couple of inches above her knees, whilst Veronica, more decorous in all ways, still wore her skirts about knee-length.

'It's been nice to see you again, Veronica,' said her

mother, also getting up from her chair.

'Good grief!' Teresa chimed in. 'Anybody'd think she's been away for yonks. We only saw her last Monday.'

Doreen tried to ignore her as she smiled at the older girl. 'And I'm glad you're still enjoying your job. I must come and have a look round Marks and Sparks when I've time.'

'Yes, you do that, Mum. We've got the new autumn styles in now. They're fab.'

'And you're still sharing with Jennifer, are you? Is it working out all right?' Jennifer was another of the Marks and Spencer supervisors with whom Veronica had shared a flat for several months.

'Er . . . yes and no,' replied Veronica. 'I mean, yes, it's working out OK – we get on great together – but it won't be for much longer. She's just got engaged and she and her boyfriend . . . well, he's got a flat and I think she might be going to live there.'

'What? Before they're married?' Doreen was surprised. Even in the middle of what they were now calling 'the swinging sixties' it was rather unusual for couples actually to live together before they were married. What they got up to whilst they were courting was, of course, their own affair and anybody's guess, but they were not often so blatant as to set up house together.

'Er . . . yes, I think so,' said Veronica, sounding a little discomfited.

'So what? It's no big deal, is it?' Teresa stared boldly at her mother. 'Anyway, Jennifer's twenty-one, isn't she? She can do as she likes. It's nothing to do with anybody else.'

'Well, I don't happen to agree with you that it's no big deal,' retorted Doreen. 'And I hope I've brought my daughters up – and my sons as well – to have some sort of moral standards . . . Of course, I know we can all make mistakes,' she added, with an apologetic look at Veronica. She was not thinking entirely of her eldest daughter's indiscretion, however, but of her own fall from grace. She knew it was time to stop moralising when she saw Teresa pull her mouth down in an ironic grin at her sister. 'But I suppose you're right in a way. It's none of our business . . . So what are you going to do, Veronica? Will you be looking for another flatmate?'

Veronica nodded. 'I'll have to, Mum. I can't afford the rent by myself. I was wondering whether to ask Sandie Horsfall if she'd like to share with me. The last time I saw her she said she was thinking about getting a place of her own, now she's left school and she's working. She's only eighteen, but she's a nice kid and we've always got on quite well together. I don't really know her terrifically well, but I think it might work out OK. Do you think so, Mum?'

'Mm . . . yes, I dare say it might,' replied Doreen carefully. Sandra was the daughter of her best friend, Abbie Horsfall; now, of course, since her second marriage, Abbie Hendy. Doreen sometimes found it hard to remember that. 'I don't know that Abbie would be too happy about Sandra leaving home, though, but I think, myself, it would do the girl good to get away from her mother and stepfather. Not that they don't get on well – they do – but it would give her a bit more independence. You shouldn't think of her as a kid, though, Veronica, not any more. She's grown up a lot since that tragic accident with her boyfriend last year, poor kid.' She smiled. 'Well, you know what I mean. Poor young woman, I should have said. And she likes to be called Sandra now, not Sandie, a sign of her new maturity, I suppose. Yes, I think that would be a good idea, love. You go ahead and ask her.'

'Oh come on, for heaven's sake, Veron.' Teresa pulled impatiently at her sister's arm. 'Let's get a move on or there won't be time for anything. She says I've to get back to do the tables— Mum, I mean,' she added hastily before her mother had a chance to say, as she often did, 'Who's she? The cat's mother?'

'OK then. 'Bye, Mum.' Veronica kissed her mother's cheek. Teresa, who would be seeing her again soon, did not do so.

Doreen breathed a deep sigh when they had gone. Teresa

was getting worse. She hoped this teenage rebelliousness was not going to continue for years and years. Or maybe the girl was due for a period; that was inclined to make her more than usually difficult.

Teresa had left school a month ago with no idea what she wanted to do with her life. Doreen realised she might never have any ambitions for what might be called a career – it was doubtful that she would obtain more than the minimum of passes in the school-leaving exams – but she had hoped the girl might want to get a worthwhile job and earn some money. Goodness knows, she could spend it: she was continually borrowing from her mother at the end of the week against the next week's allowance. Apart from her spending money – which she had been given since she was a little girl, as they all had – she earned a little from doing odd jobs around the guest house, one of which was setting the tables, the chore that had been the cause of this recent argument.

This was part of what Doreen called her daughter's 'job description', because Teresa was now employed more or less full time at Dorabella. She had lounged around for a couple of weeks after leaving school, not stirring herself to look for any sort of job. It was then that Doreen, backed by Norman, had insisted Teresa either found some employment during the next week – easy enough to do in Blackpool in the height of the season – or else she settled down and worked for her mother on a more permanent basis. This had seemed to Teresa to be the more acceptable of the two propositions. Doreen tried to convince herself that it was because her daughter believed she would be happy working at home, but she suspected it was largely because the girl did not want to make the effort to find something else.

Her tasks, none of which could be called onerous, consisted of being responsible for setting, and later clearing, the tables at mealtimes; helping out in the bedrooms when required, especially on Saturday, 'change-over day'; assisting her mother with the book-keeping – bills, receipts, wages, and dealing with letters requesting accommodation – with a view to taking this job over eventually; and waitressing at breakfast time and at the evening meal. This latter duty was the one Teresa enjoyed most; it was obvious when you watched her at work that this was so. She could be very charming and friendly when she wanted to be, and she certainly made an effort with the visitors, smiling and chatting with them and dealing with their requests in a most engaging way; and receiving some very nice tips, her mother knew, at the end of the week. Doreen didn't begrudge her this and had never insisted on tips being common property. She was glad to see that Teresa did have a different side from the one she all too often revealed to her family and that there was one task she could do and thoroughly enjoy.

The evening meal at Dorabella was at five thirty – very early compared with many of the more up-market hotels, but it seemed to suit both guests and workers. At one time Doreen, along with most landladies – or proprietors, as they were now being called – had served three meals a day, as well as supper for those who wanted it: breakfast, midday luncheon (or dinner, as it was usually called in the North), and high tea. Now, it was becoming usual to provide 'Bed, Breakfast and Evening Meal'. Doreen had changed over to this system a couple of years ago and had found that it made her life comparatively easier. It meant also that the visitors were able to go out for the whole day; to take a coach trip to a different place if they so wished. Fleetwood Market, and drives round the Bleasdale Fells were popular trips run by a local company; other tours went to the rival resorts of Morecambe or Southport. Some preferred to spend the day on the beach and promenade if the weather was fine. Or if it was raining, as it so often seemed to be, to sample the delights of the Tower, not only the ascent of the Tower itself, but also visits to the ballroom, aquarium, menagerie, the roof gardens and the famous circus.

It was a great advantage to the hotel workers when the house was empty of visitors all day. It gave them time to catch their breath after the breakfast time rush, then deal with all the odd jobs that needed doing before preparing for the big event of the day, the evening meal. You couldn't stop the visitors coming back, however, if they wished to do so – after all, they had paid for the use of the room – but this was definitely frowned upon in many establishments and Doreen did not encourage it.

She tried to make the evening meal something of an occasion, a time to which the guests could look forward in the knowledge that they were going to enjoy an appetising and well-planned meal. Her cooking had become more adventurous since her sessions at night school, and even more so since Paul had started to help her, bringing home ideas from his course at the catering college. This evening, for instance, they had enjoyed potted shrimps from Morecambe Bay, fillets of pork with croquette potatoes, creamed mushrooms and glazed carrots. (Not for Paul your common or garden boiled vegetables and mashed spuds.) This was followed by a delicious pudding of summer fruits served with whipped cream. The visitors always said dining early suited them fine, giving them the chance to go to a show or to the pictures if they so wished, and it also gave the hotel staff more free time in the evening. This was particularly important to Teresa, who usually liked to rush out somewhere or other when she had finished her chores.

When they moved to Sunset View, Doreen mused, they might well have to change their meal time to fit in with what was the norm in that rather more select area. And how would that go down with Teresa? Not very well at all, Doreen suspected, but she decided she would meet that problem when it arose.

Her rambling thoughts were interrupted by the return of her husband. 'Hello there; all on your own, love?' Norman Jarvis glanced around the living room. 'I thought our Veronica was coming round.'

'She's been and gone, Norman,' said Doreen, smiling wryly. 'I think she might've stayed longer, but that was our Teresa's doing. They've both gone back to the flat to look at some new clothes Veronica's bought; at least that was what they told me. But Teresa looked as though she'd got something up her sleeve, something she wanted to tell Veronica, happen. Don't know what, but I wouldn't expect her to tell me, of course.'

'Hm . . .' Norman nodded thoughtfully. 'Finished her jobs, has she?'

'Er . . . not exactly. She said she'd set the tables when she came back.'

'Just make sure she does then. I hope you're getting your money's worth out of her, love. She's earning a proper wage, you know, not just pocket money, so she should be doing a proper job of work, not just playing at it.'

'Give her a chance, Norman – it's early days yet. She's great as a waitress and the guests seem to like her.'

'Well, that's something, I suppose. Funny how your kids change, isn't it?' Norman smiled reminiscently. 'Teresa used to do as she was told without any fuss . . . well, sometimes.'

'So long as it fitted in with what *she* wanted to do,' Doreen smiled. 'She certainly knew how to get round you, I'll say that. As crafty as a cartload of monkeys she could be when she wanted her own way.' She pricked up her ears as the front door opened and closed and there was the sound of voices. 'There's a few of the visitors coming back.' She glanced at the clock. 'Nearly half-past nine. We'd best go and see if they want any drinks. Was there anybody in the lounge?'

'Aye, just a few; then there'll be that lot as has just come in. I'll go and count heads, shall I, and see what they want?'

'OK, thanks, love. And I'll go and make a start.' Doreen went into the kitchen and filled the electric kettle, then put some milk in a saucepan and set it on the stove to boil. A few of them would want Ovaltine or Horlicks and she liked to make it with nearly all milk. There was nothing stinted at Dorabella. She was opening a new tin of Huntley and Palmer's biscuits when Norman returned.

'Four teas, three Ovaltines and a Horlicks. That's the count so far. Oh, I say, those look good. Assorted creams and choccy ones an' all. We spoil 'em, Doreen.' He picked out a custard cream and munched away contentedly as he made the tea, then set the cups out on trays.

Doreen's eyes softened as she glanced across at him. We're happy, she thought, in a sudden instant of realisation. They had had their ups and downs, but now they were very contented. She felt she could not wish for more. And to think that at one time she had moaned to her friend Abbie that her husband was dull and boring. Of course it could not be said, even now, that Norman was an exciting person – not the sort you would notice in a crowd, and on first acquaintance you might dismiss him as unexceptional. But he was, in truth, quite an interesting man when you got to know him. He could converse on a variety of topics, his chief interest, of course, being gardening, which was his job as well as his hobby.

He had not been able to pursue this activity overmuch at Dorabella as the gardens, back and front, were very small. At the rear of the house was just a concrete 'back yard', and there was only a minuscule strip of grass at the front, which by no stretch of the imagination could be called a lawn. But it was always neatly trimmed and edged with a tiny border of colourful flowers – seasonal dahlias at the moment – whilst smaller flowers – begonias, petunias and blue lobelia – bloomed profusely in window boxes and in a large earthenware pot by the front door. It was gratifying to him when visitors commented, as they so often did, on the bright and welcoming aspect to the hotel, and Doreen felt justifiably proud of him. The front garden at Sunset View was a little larger; but there was just a lawn and a couple of stunted bushes, as the present owners seemed to have no interest in gardening. Doreen knew that Norman would brighten up the front of the hotel no end – first impressions were important – and she had all sorts of ideas for improving the interior.

She watched him fondly now as he stirred the tea in the pot and refilled the milk jug and sugar basin. He always seemed so studiously intent on whatever task he was doing, large or small. Conscientious and one hundred per cent reliable – that was how one might describe Norman. Not exciting qualities maybe – Doreen remembered how she had once craved excitement – but she had come to realise that other attributes mattered so much more. When she had strayed a little from the straight and narrow – a time she tried not to think of too much now – she had discovered in Norman a strength of purpose and a dominant streak she had not known he possessed. It might have been said at one time that Doreen was the one who wore the trousers; now they were an equal partnership. It mattered little that she was, officially, the one in charge of the business, because she looked to Norman and consulted him on all decisions. She was the proprietor at the moment, with her name, Mrs Doreen Jarvis, written beneath the Dorabella sign by the front door and in the adverts in the Blackpool holiday guide, but she intended to change all that when they moved. The business would be in both their names: Mr and Mrs Norman Jarvis.

He glanced up suddenly as though aware of her watching him. His eyes behind the horn-rimmed spectacles – the type he had always worn since she had first known him as a young man – lit up with warmth and a touch of humour. He looked younger in that instant, making her forget his greying and balding head. 'What's up, boss?' he asked. That was a private joke between them. ('Your mother's the boss,' he would always say to the children.) 'Am I doing something wrong? I know I'm not as quick off the mark as I used to be. Anno Domini, Doreen love. It gets to us all. It'll catch up with you in time.'

'I wasn't thinking any such thing.' Doreen smiled at him. 'As a matter of fact I was thinking how much younger you looked when you smiled.'

He grinned. 'I could feel I was under scrutiny. In one of your thoughtful moods, are you, luv?'

'Yes, happen I am. I was just thinking . . . well, everything's going our way, isn't it, at the moment? We've had a

18

good season, and there's the new place to look forward to, and all the kids are doing OK. Teresa's a bit of a handful, I must admit, but apart from that . . .'

'Yes, everything's hunky-dory, you might say. Touch wood.' He tapped lightly on the wooden tray. 'Doesn't do to count your chickens, I suppose, but – yes – we're doing fine, luv. Come on now, stir your stumps. I've put the Ovaltine and Horlicks in the cups. It just needs the hot milk . . .'

Between them they served the guests in the lounge, then sat down in their own private living quarters to snatch a quick cup of tea before it was time for the next batch of visitors to arrive back wanting suppertime drinks. Doreen had insisted on a deadline of ten fifteen for orders or else they might well be kept going until midnight.

'You're certainly in a contemplative mood tonight,' said Norman a little while later. 'You keep staring into space, but you've just said there's nothing worrying you.'

'No, nothing wrong at all. Fingers crossed that it's all straightforward with the contract, but I can't foresee any problems. It was talking to our Veronica that started me thinking about all our children. We're very lucky, Norman.'

Norman chuckled. 'We certainly don't see as much of 'em now as we used to. I don't know whether you'd call that lucky or not, but it's nice to have a bit of peace sometimes. Where are they all tonight?'

'Teresa's gone back with Veronica – I told you. And Bernie and Michael are out with friends. They'll be back by half-past ten; I've never known either of 'em to overstep the mark. And Paul . . . well, I don't rightly know where he's gone. He's made a lot of new friends at the college.'

'A girlfriend, maybe?'

'I don't know, Norman and I don't ask. You can't always be on at your kids to account for every minute of their time. They've a right to some privacy, and Paul's a sensible lad. He's a lot like you.'

'I know he looks like me. Happen a bit better-looking than I was at his age.'

Doreen shook her head. 'Not at all; you suit me just fine, love.' She smiled affectionately at him. It was a long time since she had felt so sentimental.

'Our Bernie looks like me an' all, poor lass,' Norman continued. 'Not on the front row when looks were given out, was she? And as for the other three – well, they're the image of their beautiful ma, aren't they?'

Doreen frowned, ignoring his last few words. 'Don't say things like that about our Bernie. And for goodness' sake, don't ever let her hear you. You know how insecure she is. She'll grow into a very attractive young woman, I'm sure, give her a year or two. She's worried about her spots at the moment and her hair that won't curl, to say nothing of her teeth. She heard somebody calling her Brer Rabbit at school and she was dreadfully upset, but I said it would only be meant in fun; I know she's not short of friends. Anyway, she has an appointment at the dentist next week and he may suggest she has a brace on her teeth. Poor girl – I wish she didn't worry so much about her looks. It's no use telling her that looks don't matter; they do at her age.'

'Yes, I dare say. But she makes up for it, doesn't she, by being such a pleasant lass? She's obedient and well-mannered and she's very helpful. I know she's shy and not very sure of herself, but it's like you've just said – she seems to have quite a few friends.'

'She hadn't until that new girl, Maureen, arrived on the scene. She's taken our Bernie under her wing, I'm glad to say. She seems a nice sort of girl, but much more outgoing than Bernie. She soon made friends at school, from what Bernie says – she thinks the sun shines out of Maureen, I can tell you – and so now Bernie joins in with them as well. She used to be rather a loner – that's what her teachers always said. It wasn't that the other girls didn't like her, but they never noticed her and she wasn't one to push herself in if she felt she wasn't wanted. Kids can be very thoughtless.'

'Bernie's rather like Abbie was, you might say, until you

came along and took charge of her,' Norman observed. 'Not that I knew Abbie in those days, but you told me about her.'

Doreen smiled. 'Yes, I suppose she is. Abbie had a domineering mother, though; that was her problem. I should hate to think I was anything like that old harridan!'

'Er, no, of course you're not; not really. A mite bossy, maybe.' Norman grinned at her. 'You like to get your own way – but you're improving with age.' He laughed and ducked as she took a mock swipe at him.

She drank the rest of her tea and put the cup and saucer on the table. 'Yes, I suppose I do,' she said, after a moment or two. Norman looked puzzled. 'Like to get my own way, I mean. I was thinking about Teresa. I can't really complain too much about her because I can remember being pretty much the same at her age: wilful and rather self-centred. Most teenagers are, to a certain extent, although the term "teenager" hadn't been invented when we were young, had it?'

'You didn't have the same freedom as Teresa has, though, or the money to gad about and buy all the clothes that she buys.'

'No, that's true. We scarcely had two ha'pennies to rub together sometimes, and my parents were quite strict about where we were going and who we were with. It's different these days. You can't lay the law down too much to your kids or you may well have an out-and-out rebellion. Yes, I had to do as I was told, but I didn't always do it willingly.'

'Our Teresa doesn't know she's born.'

'No, maybe not, but the more I go on at her the worse she'll be. She and Michael are not much alike now, are they, except in looks?' Doreen smiled as she looked back across the years. 'I remember when I used to take them out in their pram. They were as alike as two peas in a pod, except that one was dressed in pink and the other in blue. People used to say, "Ooh, twins – aren't you lucky? And a boy and a girl – how nice! Are they identical?" The

21

number of times I tried to explain that they weren't identical – they both have to be the same sex for them to be identical – but they wouldn't listen. They were too busy cooing over the pram. And they're still very much alike in appearance.' Michael too was quite small with fair hair, but with a more interested, questioning, look in his blue eyes than his twin.

'But not in any other way, thank goodness,' replied Norman. 'Teresa's a flibbertigibbet. I sometimes despair of her ever settling down to anything, that one. It's a good job Michael decided to pull his socks up when he got to the secondary modern school.'

Michael, unlike his couldn't-care-less sister, had at the age of thirteen suddenly put his nose to the grindstone, showing that he was really an intelligent boy with undiscovered capabilities. 'A late developer,' they had called him at school. He had passed the entrance exam and had been admitted to the grammar school at fourteen. He had taken nine O levels and was hoping to go into the sixth form in September.

'Yes, I think our Michael'll do well,' said Doreen, 'though in what sort of a career I don't know. He doesn't seem to have any idea himself at the moment. Maybe he'll be the one to go on to university. D'you think so, Norman?'

'Happen he will,' replied Norman. 'But we can't force him, love. I know you've had great ambitions for all our children, but it's up to them to decide, you know, not us.'

'It's only because I never had the chance when I was a girl,' said Doreen. 'I might've done more with me life – who knows? – if I hadn't had to leave school at fourteen. Still, I've no regrets.'

'None at all?' Norman raised his eyebrows.

'No, not a single one.' She smiled confidently at him. 'I just hope Sunset View turns out to be all we've hoped for . . .' She cocked her head at the sound of the front door opening again, then voices in the hallway. 'Here's the next lot. They've only just made it: it's seventeen minutes past, to be precise. Still, we're not to a minute or two, are

22

we? I'll go and see what they want . . .'

An hour or so later Doreen rested her head against the cushioned back of the chair, placing her aching legs on a footstool. She and Norman took it in turns to stay up till midnight to put the bolt on the front door. The sort of visitors they had at Dorabella did not, as a rule, keep very late hours. If someone made a special request – a visit to a late night club, for instance – then Doreen was willing to relax the rules and leave the door locked, but unbolted. The door was always locked around eleven fifteen – she had secured it a few minutes ago – and visitors wanting to stay out later were loaned a key. But Doreen never felt quite safe unless both the front and back doors were locked and bolted as well. This was harking back to her childhood days, she supposed. She could almost hear her parents' voices now: 'Have you put the bolt on the back door, Harold?' 'Aye, and the front one an' all, Nancy luv. We're all safe and sound . . .'

 Nancy Miller had died of a chest complaint towards the end of the war – more than twenty years ago now, but Doreen still missed her. She knew that parents, especially mothers, cast a long shadow and you could never entirely escape from their influence. Nor did she want to do so. She only hoped she could be as good an example to her own children as her mother had been to her and her siblings. Doreen's father was still alive, now in his seventies and living with his second daughter, Vera, and her family. Doreen was very fond of him, but she had never felt the same deep affection for him as she had felt for her mother. Nancy Miller, though small in stature and often ailing, had been the strong partner in that marriage. What would her mother think, Doreen mused, about their move to Sunset View? She would probably have commented, as Veronica had done, that they were 'going up in the world', but she would have shown great interest and would not have been the slightest bit envious. When Doreen had told her father he had hardly seemed to listen to her, carrying on reading his paper and only commenting, much later,

23

'It's all right for some folk. Beats me why you want to move. You've got big ideas, I reckon.'

Yes, maybe she did have big ideas. Doreen had been hankering for a year or so now for a change of scene and a hotel that would be more of a challenge, but her resolve had been strengthened by the closure, the previous year, of Central Station. Like hundreds of others this had become a casualty of the Beeching Report and it was in November 1964 that the last train had pulled out of Blackpool Central Station. Residents were dumbfounded at the decision to shut down a terminus that was more than a century old and that had welcomed, over the years, millions of holiday-makers and day trippers, depositing them right at the heart of the town. The words of a long-serving railway worker had been reported in the local gazette: 'They have cut the heart out of Blackpool.'

It was said that Blackpool Council had bought the station and a vast amount of adjoining land for the bargain price of £950,000, and this deal was just a part of the wind of change that was blowing through Blackpool. There was another station, of course, at the north end of the town. Dorabella, though, was only a few minutes' walk from Blackpool Central; whereas Sunset View was a goodly mile away from North Station. Still, Doreen hoped that the visitors who stayed there might be a little more affluent and able to afford taxis, or else there was a good bus service or a tram along the prom. The Fleetwood trams, however, which had used to travel along Dickson Road to Gynn Square – most convenient for both visitors and residents – had been axed two years ago by the council; all, supposedly, in the name of 'progress', which was Blackpool's motto. Now the only trams running in the town were those along the promenade.

Yes, Blackpool was certainly changing, and Doreen could not believe that all the changes were for the best. She had been dismayed when, in the early sixties, the Palace building had closed down and subsequently been demolished. It was the end of an era, many Blackpudlians said, and, to Doreen, it felt as though it was the end of

24

her girlhood. In the early years of the war, before they joined the Land Army, she and her great friend Abbie Winters – as she then was – had been regular visitors to the variety theatre and the cinema and had danced in the Palace ballroom with various RAF lads who had been stationed in the town. Abbie, indeed, had married one of them a few years later. There was no doubt that Lewis's department store, now standing on the site of the old Palace, was a great asset to the town. It had been opened in April 1964, and now, with its distinctive modern architecture – a sea-green frontage in a honeycomb design – it had become quite a landmark in the town. The merchandise was good too. Doreen had bought a few items of clothing there and she often visited the household and food departments; but not without a certain feeling of disloyalty. She missed the Palace and all it had stood for in her youth.

Blackpool, in the middle of the swinging sixties, was still something of a boomtown, as it had been in the years between the wars, when thousands of trippers from the inland Lancashire towns had trooped there to spend their annual Wakes Week. Visitors came from further afield now, in addition to the old faithfuls from Lancashire and Yorkshire, although there was competition from southern resorts, such as Bournemouth and Torquay, where the weather was more congenial. Many folk, indeed, were starting to venture even further, to the Continent on cheap package tours to Spain, Greece or the South of France. But Blackpool sands were still crowded, especially on the stretch between the North and Central piers, where the sunbathers lay like boiled lobsters with scarcely an inch between them; the theatres and cinemas were full every evening; and the streets of the town centre near the numerous pubs were littered with chip papers, beer bottles and fag ends. Motorists – many more of them now – complained of the countless one-way streets and the double yellow lines appearing all over the place, making it difficult for them to park, and the dreaded traffic wardens, introduced a few years ago, were becoming ever more diligent.

The Golden Mile, that stretch of promenade between the Palatine Hotel and Blackpool's version of Tussaud's Waxworks, had long been the most bizarre, bawdy and brazen part of the town: a conglomeration of hot-dog, ice-cream and rock stalls; sideshows; slot machines; and fortunetellers. In the past it had boasted giraffe-necked women, plate-lipped savages, the ugliest women in the world, and the famous Jolly Alice, reputed to be the fattest woman in the country; and as long ago as the twenties – more respectably – various song booths where the popular music of the day was advertised. It was there, in the thirties, that the Rector of Stiffkey had starved – supposedly – in a barrel for sixty days. There was some talk now that the Golden Mile was to be cleaned up and given a face-lift by the council, but in the mid-sixties it remained, more so than it had ever been, downright decadent and dodgy.

Doreen, out of the curiosity, had taken a stroll down there at the beginning of the season, although she had not had the urge to go into any of the sideshows. As well as the Fattest Teenager, whom Teresa had mentioned, there was a plethora of other dubious delights: tattooists; striptease shows; Tarantula – part woman, part beast; Tanya, the Tattooed Girl (brought to Blackpool at enormous expense); and the Palace of Strange Girls or *Des Filles Bizarres*. An elderly lady in a booth offered to guess your age for sixpence; you could buy fish and chips, tea and bread and butter for half a crown; or purchase a hot dog and a jug of tea to take on to the sands. It was not an area generally frequented by the residents, apart from youngsters such as Teresa, to whom its garishness and vulgarity appealed. Doreen, who had never considered herself to be narrow-minded, found it a revelation.

Blackpool's shopping centre, also, at the height of the season, was not always the pleasantest of places to be, especially if you happened to be a resident, wanting to get your shopping done in a hurry. Doreen avoided it as much as she could, using instead the nearer shops on

Whitegate Drive and taking advantage of the delivery services of the grocer and butcher. Getting stuck on the pavement behind a flock of window gazers, or children trailing metal spades along the ground, or a line of carousing teenagers chanting loudly and wearing hats bearing the legend 'Kiss Me Quick' – or sometimes a more lewd invitation – only served to exasperate her. At the same time she knew that she and thousands of others in the town depended on such folk for their livelihood. Who was she to grumble about people enjoying themselves, revelling in a week of freedom and letting their hair down after the best part of a year spent doing a mundane factory or office job?

Still, she hoped the neighbourhood around Gynn Square would be a little more – what was the word she wanted? – select, refined . . . genteel? Be careful, Doreen, she warned herself; you're in danger of becoming a snob and that will never do. All the same, she intended to raise the standard of the new hotel a notch or two to attract the more well-heeled type of holidaymaker. Private bathrooms and toilets for some of the rooms, maybe. (What was the term they used? 'En suite', whatever that meant.) Perhaps a private bar; they would have to apply for a licence, of course. A more comprehensive menu . . . Doreen's ideas ran away with her at times, but at the moment they were all just in her own mind. She had not yet consulted Norman about some of her plans although she knew she would need to do so.

She glanced at the clock. Half-past eleven and still Teresa had not come in, the little madam. Paul, Michael and Bernie had all returned ages ago and retired to bed. Teresa had her own key. Doreen had had no option but to give her one especially as she was now, officially, a member of the household staff, although it had gone against the grain. Much more of this sort of behaviour and she would be losing it; Norman would say so even if she herself didn't.

She sighed and struggled to her feet. She might as well make a start on those tables although she had vowed not to do so again; Teresa really was the limit. She went into the dining room, straightening the blue and white gingham cloths, then laying out the cutlery, cups and saucers and serviettes; then lastly she placed bottles of HP sauce and Heinz tomato sauce on each table alongside the cruet. It was as she was putting the last bottle down that she heard the key turn in the lock, then the sound of Teresa's voice.

'Hi, Mum. Sorry I'm late.' The girl dashed into the dining room. 'I'll start the tables now— Oh, I say – you've nearly finished. You didn't need to have done, Mum. I said I'd do 'em, didn't I? We were so busy talking, Veronica and me, we didn't notice the time.'

Doreen found herself speechless. At least she had said she was sorry, after a fashion, and she certainly seemed to be in a more congenial mood than she had been earlier in the evening. Doreen looked at her daughter's flushed face and overbright eyes. Unless she was very much mistaken Teresa had had a drink, probably more than one.

Chapter 2

Veronica

'I say, kid, some of this gear isn't half bad. Quite snazzy, in fact. You're coming out in your old age.' Teresa picked up a rayon dress, boldly striped in pale blue and navy, and held it against her. 'This'd just suit me. A bit long, though, i'n't it?' She looked down at the hem, which came to just above her knees. 'I'd shorten it a few inches if it was mine, then it'd be just right.'

'But it isn't yours, is it?' said Veronica. 'It's mine and I like it just the way it is. I don't want folk seeing my knickers when I bend down, even if you do.'

'Oh, come on – skirts aren't as short as all that, not yet at any rate; not here. I saw a girl on the prom, though, the other day and her dress only just covered her bum, honest. And they're going to get shorter and shorter according to the magazines.'

'Well, that's short enough for me at the moment,' replied Veronica. 'Glad you approve of it. You don't think it looks too much like a deck chair? Or that it might make me look too fat with those broad stripes going across my bust?'

'No, why should it?' said Teresa. 'The stripes below the hip-line go the other way – vertical. That's the right word, isn't it, for stripes going down?' The dress in question was a simple shift, which style had been popular for a few years, with a rounded neckline and a dropped waist, finished off with a narrow leather belt at hip level.

'Anyroad, you're no fatter than me, are you? If you've got it then show it off, that's what I say. I'm proud of me bust. A 36B I am now – not bad, eh? I bet you didn't get it at Marks and Sparks, though, did you?'

'No, it was from Paige's, actually,' said Veronica. 'I do get a good discount on M&S things, but sometimes I want something a bit more – you know – special.'

'Why? Have you got a special date, then?'

'I might have.' Veronica smiled to herself, but she answered casually. She did not intend to let her sister know anything, not yet. Teresa was such a nosy parker. Veronica did not want to say too much about Richard at the moment. He might very well turn out to be 'the one'. She had a strong feeling about him. She could, of course, have denied having a date, but that was not her way. She liked to be truthful whenever possible; besides, she could not resist dropping a hint. Richard was so nice . . . It might be as well, though, to change the subject.

She hung the blue dress inside the wardrobe again, reaching for a shoe box and a carrier bag. She opened the box and took out a pair of navy suede shoes with medium-high stiletto heels and a strap fastening decorated with petersham ribbon. 'I got these to match the dress, and this bag as well.' She drew from the carrier a boxy shaped handbag also in navy suede.

'Gosh! You aren't half chucking yer money around,' said Teresa. 'They must pay you well at M&S. Where did you get 'em? Vernon Humpage's?'

'Don't be daft,' said Veronica. 'I can't afford their prices. No, they're from Stead and Simpson's, the shoes and the bag, an' all. Yes, I've splashed out a bit lately, I suppose. I hadn't bought any new clothes for ages. I took advantage of the sale at our place as well, though – and the discount. I bought this pinafore dress. Not bad, is it, for two pounds nineteen and eleven?' She laid the plain, square-necked dress on the bed. 'And these trousers and top. They call it a tabard top; all the rage, they are. We've got them in a few colours, but I liked the dark green one best.'

30

'Mm . . .' Teresa fingered the maroon pinafore dress. 'Don't reckon much to this, meself. A bit old-fashioned, i'n't it? This style's been going for yonks.'

'It'll be useful, though, to wear with all my jumpers and blouses.'

'S'pose so. If you say so. But I like this. Oh yes, this is real cool.' Teresa picked up the tabard top. 'Yes, I might go in Marks and treat myself to one of these. A brighter colour, though, for me. And you've got trousers just the same colour. That'll make you look taller, Veron. Yes, you'll look great in that. Your blonde hair'll look well against that dark green. And the blue dress is smashing an' all. I don't half envy you, being able to afford all these clothes.'

'I couldn't when I was your age. I was still at school, remember, and for a long time afterwards. And you've only just left, haven't you, so it stands to reason you haven't got all that much money to splash around yet.' Although, from what Veronica knew of Teresa, she didn't go short of much that she really wanted. She spent her money as soon as she got hold of it, and more besides if she could cadge off her nearest and dearest. Mum was getting wise to her, though, and said she was going to try and make her behave more responsibly now she had left school and was working for her living. Veronica had her doubts, however, about her hare-brained sister being employed at the family hotel. She couldn't see it working out somehow. Mum and Teresa would be forever arguing. They'd had quite a set-to tonight.

'How d'you like your job?' she asked. 'Are you sure it's what you want to do?'

'Course I'm not sure,' replied Teresa, plumping herself down heavily on the bed. Veronica quickly moved her clothes out of the way before they became all crumpled. Teresa was no respecter of persons or of possessions – other people's, at any rate. 'It was a case of having to do it, wasn't it? Mum and Dad started reading the riot act. "You've got to get a job, Teresa. You can't lounge around here like Lady Muck when everybody else is working," ' she mimicked.

31

'What would you like to do then?'

'Oh . . . I dunno.' Teresa shrugged carelessly.

'You could perhaps get a job at my place; in a little while, I mean – you're not quite old enough yet. I could put in a good word for you . . .' Veronica hesitated, realising she had spoken somewhat hastily. Her 'good word' might very well rebound on her and she didn't want to jeopardise her own position. 'Or I'm sure you could get a job at Woolie's,' she added. 'They take younger girls there.'

'No, thanks,' said Teresa. 'You wouldn't catch me standing all day behind a counter at Marks and Sparks, nor at Woolie's. I can't imagine anything more boring.' She yawned in an exaggerated manner. 'I'd die of boredom.'

'OK, then; what would you really like to do? You must have some idea.'

'I wouldn't mind being an air hostess.' The girl gazed dreamily into space. 'Or I could get a job on one of them ocean-going liners, as a hairdresser or summat. It'd be nice to travel. I've never been out of England yet, not even to the Isle of Man.'

'So what? Neither have I. More to the point, neither has Mum, and you don't hear her complaining. Oh, come on, Tess. It's all pie in the sky, talking about being an air hostess an' all that. Come down to earth, for goodness' sake.'

'Oh, you! You don't think I really meant it, do you? But it's nice to dream. Don't you ever dream about mad things you'd like to do? You're so . . . boring. A real pain in the bum, you are, sometimes, Veronica. Anybody'd think you were forty, not twenty.'

'Hey, watch it! I'm not even twenty yet.'

'Not so far off. I want to have some fun, me, before I'm twenty.'

'Why? D'you think it'll be too late afterwards?' Veronica smiled. You could not help but smile at Teresa, even though she was obstreperous and downright rude at times.

32

'It'll be too late for you if you don't watch out,' Teresa grinned. 'You haven't been anywhere since you finished with that Justin fellow, have you? Why don't you go down to that new place, the Mecca, and try and get yerself a new boyfriend?'

'Mind your own business, you!' retorted Veronica. 'How do you know where I've been or what I've been doing? I don't live at home now, as you've already reminded me tonight. As a matter of fact, I have been to the Mecca. A few of us from work went last week. We went ten-pin bowling, then we went and had a dekko at the ballroom. Not bad at all, though I still like the Winter Gardens best.' The new Top Rank Mecca ballroom and bowling alley had only recently opened on Central Drive. A boxlike, ultramodern building, it was proving quite popular with young holiday-makers and residents. It was there, last week, that Veronica had met Richard, but she had no intention of telling Teresa, or that she had a date with him on Saturday.

'What are you looking all coy about then?' persisted Teresa. 'You have got a date, haven't you? I can tell. You're grinning like a Cheshire cat. And that's why you've bought all this new gear, i'n't it? Come on – tell me. What's he called? What's he like?'

'Oh . . . honestly, you're the limit!' Veronica laughed, giving in at last. She would have no peace if she didn't; anyway, there was no reason really why she should keep it a secret. 'He's called Richard and he's twenty-four and . . . well . . . he's very nice.'

'Good-looking?'

'Yes, I suppose so, but it doesn't matter, does it?'

'It does to me. You wouldn't want to go out with anybody dead ugly, would you?'

'I don't suppose it would matter if you loved them. Anyway, Richard's not bad-looking, and he's single.'

'Are you sure?'

'Pretty sure. He was with his mates, anyway; quite a crowd of them on a night out. I met him at the Mecca, actually, and I'm seeing him again on Saturday night. But that's all I'm going to tell you at the moment, little Miss Nosy. It's all there is to tell, at any rate. Now, can we change the subject? You and this job – you will try and make a go of it, won't you, for Mum's sake? I'm sure it can't be all that bad. You're doing a lot of different things, aren't you? So it can't be boring.' This seemed to be one of Teresa's favourite words at the moment.

'I never said it was. No, it's OK really,' replied Teresa. 'In fact, I'm quite enjoying it. But you know me, it doesn't do to be too willing or folks'll put on you. I like the waitressing part best. I like chatting to people and I get some pretty decent tips an' all. They're mostly old geezers, but there was a crowd of lads in last week. Well, not exactly a crowd – three of 'em, from Bolton. One of 'em asked me if I'd go out with him.'

'And did you?'

'Course I did. Mike, he was called. He was a bit spotty, but he was the best of the three.'

'And that was your first week at the job. Goodness! Talk about getting off to a flying start. And where did he take you?'

'Oh, just on to Central Pier. Then we had a walk on the prom and ended up on the slot machines on the Golden Mile. A bit of a gambler, I reckon, that Mike. He had a go on that racing game – you know, where you have pretend horses – but he didn't win. He bought me a hot dog and a bottle of pop.'

Not exactly the last of the big spenders, thought Veronica. 'And that was it?'

'Yeah, then we came back. It was no big deal, I can tell you. And I'm dead cheesed off about it now because Kev found out – well, I told him, actually ¬ and he's gone and finished with me.'

'You can't blame him, Tess, if you were just trying to make him jealous. It sounds to me as though you were. Anyway, it doesn't matter, does it? You're only sixteen; you're too young to get serious about anyone yet.'

'And how old were you when you started getting ideas about that fellow at church?'

'That's got nothing to do with it,' retorted Veronica. She felt a twinge of shame, and of sadness too, as she always did at the memory of Dominic O'Reilly. She had been a fool and she didn't want reminding of it. 'Shut up about him, Tess. I never think about him now. I was seventeen, anyway; older than you are. You've been going around with lads since you were about fourteen. So why get upset if you've lost this latest one? There'll be another one just round the corner.'

'But Kev was different. I really liked him.'

'Well then, tell him you're sorry.'

'But I'm not sorry. I only went out with one of the visitors because I thought it'd be a laugh. There was no need for him to get his knickers in a twist about it.'

'You can't have it all ways, Teresa.'

'I know, I know.' The girl shook her head impatiently, then she looked steadily at her elder sister. There was a pensive expression on her face, most unusual for Teresa. 'Veronica . . . can I ask you something?' she said.

'I don't see why not.' Veronica smiled. 'You don't usually ask permission before you ask questions, do you, Miss Nosy?'

'It's . . . something personal.'

'OK then.' Veronica frowned a little. 'Fire away. What do you want to know?'

'Well, have you ever – you know – done it?'

'Done what?' She knew perfectly well what Teresa meant, or thought she did, but she was taken aback. What a thing for a sixteen-year-old girl to be asking. 'I . . . I don't know what you mean,' she said, stalling for time.

'Oh, come off it! I don't believe that. Not even you could be so naïve. Of course you know what I mean. Have you ever done . . . that; you know, with a feller? Gone the whole way.'

'No, of course I haven't,' snapped Veronica. She certainly wouldn't have told Teresa even if she had, but the girl had no business to ask and she was annoyed with her for even thinking that she, Veronica, would do so. 'You've no right to ask things like that. It's very personal.'

'Yeah, I know. I told you it was something personal and you said you didn't mind.'

'I didn't know you were going to ask something as brazen as that. Well, for your information, I haven't, and I wouldn't; not till I was married. And you shouldn't even be thinking about things like that; you're only sixteen.'

Teresa laughed out loud. 'Honestly! I don't believe you sometimes. You sound just like Mum. You heard her, going on about your friend Jennifer sharing a flat with her boyfriend, as though it was the most shocking thing in the world.'

'Well, Jennifer and Ted are engaged, so I suppose it might be all right if you knew you were going to be married.'

'You mean – you might do it if you were engaged?'

'Oh, goodness me, I don't know! Honestly, Tess, you're incorrigible.' In spite of herself Veronica found she was smiling.

'Oh, I say, that's a big word. What's it mean?'

'I don't really know.' Veronica burst out laughing. 'But it sounds good, and it's what you are – a damned nuisance, in other words. In any case, what's brought all this on? Why are you being so nosy about . . . what I might have got up to?'

Teresa shrugged. 'I was just curious, that's all. I wondered . . . if people did. I know they say they do. Some of the girls at school, they were always going on about how far they'd gone an' all that.'

'What? Girls of your age? Sixteen?'

'Oh, come on, Veron. Don't tell me you didn't think about it – and talk about it – when you were sixteen.'

'Not all that much, we didn't. I was at a much stricter school than the one you went to, remember. The nuns were always listening over our shoulders. I knew about it, of course, but I didn't start going out with lads when I was fourteen, like you did.' Dominic had been the first young man she had ever thought about in 'that way'. She didn't want Teresa getting on to that subject again so she hurried on to say, 'You shouldn't take too much notice of

36

what other girls say, Teresa. They're probably just showing off, pretending they know a lot more than they really
do. You mustn't try to keep up with them. You haven't,
have you?'

'Haven't what?'

'Well, let a boy . . . you know . . . touch you? Do things
that you shouldn't be doing?'

'Oh, don't be so stuffy, Veronica. I haven't gone the
whole way, if that's what you mean. But – yes – I suppose
I have . . . done what you said. Kev's older than me, y'see;
he's eighteen, an' I've been going out with him for about a
month. An' he keeps saying how much he thinks about
me and he wants me to . . . That's why I asked you about
it, because I don't know what to do.' Teresa, at that
moment, looked much younger than her sixteen years.
There were no tears in her eyes – she was not given to
crying easily – but she looked perplexed and a little
scared. Veronica felt sorry for her. She sat down next to
her on the bed, close, but not touching. They had never
been the sort of sisters that were all over one another.

'Then you say no,' she replied emphatically. 'Good
heavens, Tess – I know I keep saying it, but you're only
sixteen. If Kev really thought all that much about you he
wouldn't be asking you to . . . do things like that. Anyway, I thought you said it was all over between you and
him?'

'It is. At least it was, but I know I could get him back if
I tried. What I said to you wasn't really true. He didn't
finish with me because I went out with that lad Mike. It
was because . . . well, I wouldn't let him. He was real
mad. He got into a right tizzy. He said I was a—' She
shook her head. 'I can't say it, Veron. It was too awful. He
said he was sorry afterwards, though, and he was quite
nice again. But he just said, "Be seeing yer" when he took
me home and he never said he wanted to see me again.'

'And you're getting yourself all upset about a fellow like
that?' Veronica laid her hand over Teresa's. 'You're better
off without him, believe me. And there'll soon be someone else – a pretty girl like you. Anyway, you shouldn't try

to run before you can walk. Don't think about . . . things like that. Just enjoy yourself. Go out in a crowd if you can, with girls as well as boys; it's the best thing to do at your age. You're too young to start getting serious about anyone.' Veronica knew, however, even as she spoke the words, that she had no room to talk. It was a failing of hers to think of every man she met as a potential Mr Right. She couldn't seem to help herself. She wanted so much to be happily married and to have a family. She would like several children, like there were in her own family. But so far her prospective partners had all disappeared like snow in the sunshine.

To her surprise Teresa nodded. 'S'pose you're right,' she said. She grinned mischievously. 'I like lads, though. I always have done. And they like me an' all.'

Veronica decided she wasn't a bad kid when you got to know her better, and possibly she hadn't known her sister all that well until tonight. They had certainly never talked together in this way before. Maybe, when she got away from the bosom of her family, which was where Veronica had always seen her, she was able to shed her disgruntlement and lose the peevish expression that so often marred her prettiness. There was no sign of it at the moment and Veronica guessed that the face Teresa showed to her friends might be quite different from the one her family saw. After all, it was quite common for girls not to see eye to eye with their parents, especially their mothers, and this in turn affected relations with the rest of the household.

Veronica was even more surprised when Teresa said, 'Thanks, anyway.' It was most unusual for her to say thank you for anything. 'I needed to talk to somebody, and you're quite a bit older than me. I thought you might be more experienced, y'see, about that sort of thing, but it seems as though you're not.'

'Now don't start all that again.'

'OK. Sorry. An' I'm sorry I mentioned that Dominic chap. I know you wanted to try and forget about him. But I only thought . . .' Teresa was obviously not going to let it drop. 'I just thought you and he might have – you know – because he would want to know what it was like, wouldn't he, with priests not being able to get married and—'

'Teresa, shut up! Or I shall make you go home right now. You'll have to go soon anyway, to do those tables, or Mum'll be on the warpath. Just get this into your head – I have not had sexual intercourse, not with anyone, not ever, and I don't intend to until I meet Mr Right.'

'But how will you know when he is? I mean, you thought Justin was, didn't you? What went wrong?'

'Oh, I just realised he wasn't the one,' Veronica answered evasively. 'We both realised. Anyway,' she smiled happily, 'I've met Richard now. I didn't intend telling you about him, but you were so persistent. Keep it to yourself, though, eh, for the moment? Don't tell Mum. I'll tell her myself when there's something to tell.'

'Huh! I never tell her anything,' retorted Teresa.

'Maybe you should. Perhaps that's the trouble between you.'

'You didn't used to tell her anything when you were living at home.'

'No . . . maybe I didn't,' Veronica answered thoughtfully.

'She only goes off the deep end, whatever I say.' A slight grumpiness had returned to Teresa's face and it could be heard in her voice. 'I wouldn't care, but she pretends she's such a goody-goody, and she's not, you know. I think she had an affair once. I 'spect she's had more than one. So she's no room to talk.'

'Whatever do you mean?'

'You know that time when Mum went to stay with Aunty Janey in Preston? Well, I don't think she went there at all. I think she went somewhere else – with a feller! Don't you remember? Our Paul got hurt playing rugger and Dad was going frantic trying to get hold of her and he couldn't.'

'Yes, I do remember,' said Veronica guardedly. She too had drawn her own conclusions about that incident.

Relations between their parents had been rather strained round about that time, but whatever her mother had or had not done Veronica was sure it had only happened the once. And Teresa most certainly should not be encouraged to tittle-tattle about it. 'There might have been something going on,' she admitted, 'but it's all in the past now. We weren't supposed to know anything about it, so keep that buttoned.' She pressed her finger to her lips. 'Mum and Dad are very happy together; anyone can see that. We're very lucky, you know, to have parents who get on so well. Not all of 'em do. Jennifer says her mum and dad are always rowing. Come on,' Veronica stood up, closing the wardrobe door on her new purchases, 'let's go and make some coffee before you go home. Or would you prefer chocolate or Ovaltine? We're short of nothing we've got here.'

'Er, no, I won't bother, thanks,' said Teresa. 'It's getting late so I'd best be off.'

'You don't want a drink at all?'

'No, I don't think I've got time.'

Veronica shot her a suspicious glance. Why was it that she didn't entirely trust her? 'You are going straight home, aren't you, Tess? You're not thinking of going somewhere else?'

'Of course not.' Teresa looked indignant. 'Where else would I be going?'

'I don't know, I'm sure.' Veronica narrowed her eyes, looking searchingly at her sister. 'But you seem to be in an almighty hurry to get off all of a sudden.'

'Because I've got those bloomin' tables to do, haven't I? And you know what Mum's like. Have a nice time on Sat'day night, won't yer? He won't be able to keep his hands off when he sees you in all that new gear. But don't do anything I wouldn't do, will yer?'

'And that applies to you as well,' said Veronica sternly. 'You mustn't do anything *I* wouldn't do. I mean it, Tess. Just remember what your big sister's told you.'

'OK, OK, will do. Tara then.' Teresa waggled her fingers in an impudent sort of wave. 'Don't bother to come to the door with me. I'll see meself out. Be seeing you then, Veron.'

Veronica hurried into the living room, watching her through the window as she trotted gaily down the garden path, turning left when she went out of the gate. The flat, the ground floor of a Victorian house, was on Park Road and was about ten minutes' walk from Dorabella. She was going the right way, admittedly, but Blackpool town centre was in that direction too, and the Number Three pub on Whitegate Drive, which Veronica happened to know was a happy hunting ground for Teresa and her cronies. It mattered little to Teresa that she was nowhere near old enough to be in a pub at all. 'Oh, don't be so stuffy – everybody goes there,' she had retorted when Veronica had remonstrated with her. She was pretty sure that their mother – and certainly their father – knew nothing about it, and Veronica had decided that nothing would be gained by telling them. It was quite true, moreover, that underage drinking went on and that many landlords were willing to turn a blind eye. Not that that made it right, but Teresa would only accuse her of being a sneak if she said anything.

She decided, though, that she would keep a watchful eye on her sister, when she could. She had been quite alarmed at some of the things Teresa had said tonight. The girl, of course, loved to shock and to cause a sensation; it was all part of her quirky personality. But you could not help laughing at her sometimes, even though you were outraged at her impudence. Who but Teresa, for instance, would have dared to ask such impertinent questions about Dominic?

Veronica went into the kitchen and made a cup of Ovaltine which she then carried back into the living room with one of her favourite Penguin biscuits. Like her mother, she did not think overmuch about the extra ounces she might be putting on if she enjoyed something. The living quarters she shared with Jennifer were quite spacious. This room was high-ceilinged, in typical Victorian style, with deep skirting boards and woodwork painted in dark brown. The nondescript beige wallpaper and the shabby furniture – a heavy three-piece suite in brown chenille, an oak table and four sturdy dining chairs, and a few shelves put up at random to hold books and ornaments – did nothing to add to the cheerfulness of the room. Nevertheless, Veronica and Jennifer had made the place brighter and more welcoming with scatter cushions in vivid colours, gaily patterned curtains and a large boldly striped rug, which covered up several threadbare patches in the carpet. Their own bits and pieces – books, records, photographs, pictures and knick-knacks – had put their individual stamp on the room. Veronica knew that this flat, compared with much other rented accommodation in the town, might be considered, if not luxurious, then certainly adequate and comfortable.

The kitchen was small, with an antiquated though quite safe gas stove, which needed – but did not always get – constant cleaning. There was a tiny bathroom, with washbasin and toilet, in the space under the stairs, which, at one time, would have been the hall cupboard or 'glory hole'. There were even two bedrooms, quite small ones because they had been made by dividing the large back room into two; but both young women agreed that it was better than sharing, especially if you changed your flatmate and ended up with someone you didn't know.

The landlady, Mrs Cummings, a middle-aged widow, lived in the flat upstairs. The house had, at one time, been a large family home, a Victorian semi. After her husband had died and all her children had left home, Mrs Cummings had known she needed a much smaller place, but she had been loath to leave the home that held so many happy memories. And so she had had the house converted into two more or less self-contained flats. They shared the front entrance, and the gardens, front and rear, which, fortunately, consisted mainly of paved areas; neither Mrs Cummings nor the girls were keen gardeners.

Veronica sat down on the settee to enjoy her Ovaltine and biscuit, thinking about Teresa and Mum and her flatmate, Jennifer. She hadn't done anything yet about asking Sandra Horsfall if she would like to share with her when Jennifer moved out. She was wondering now if it might be a good idea to ask Teresa instead. The girl seemed restless, far from happy, in fact, at home. It might not be a bad idea for Mum and Teresa to see less of one another. Veronica had to admit there were faults on both sides: Mum was rather inclined to rise to the bait and let herself be upset by Teresa when, oftentimes, the girl was only trying, in her particular way, to have a bit of fun.

On the other hand – Veronica pulled herself up short – did she really want to share a flat with her sister? Besides, Mum might not be very keen on the idea. She might think that she, Veronica, was encouraging Teresa to be rebellious. And there was something else to consider that she had momentarily overlooked. The family would be moving in a couple of months to Sunset View, and that was at the other end of the town. Teresa would have been able to walk quite easily from the flat to Dorabella, but it would not be so convenient to get to the new place, especially in the early morning; Teresa had never been good at getting up. No; all things considered it would be as well to leave well alone, but she would try to take more of an interest in her younger sister. Veronica felt she had got on with her tonight far more easily than she had in the past. There had been quite a rapport between them and that was something to work on; even if it meant that she had to divulge more about her personal affairs than she had used to do. As she had seen earlier, Teresa was not easily fobbed off.

What Veronica had said to her, however, was perfectly true. She had never been with a man, not in 'that way', and, what was more, she did not intend to do so until she was married. She knew only too well that some girls were very free and easy about such things, sometimes when they had known the man for only a short time. She had heard them talking about it at work, in the canteen or the washroom. Veronica always chose not to enter into such conversations and the other girls, surprisingly, did not rib her about it. They knew she was a Catholic and seemed to respect her moral stand. It was possible that some of them thought she was a prude, but they did not say so, at least not to her face.

Veronica was determined, when the time came, that her white wedding would really mean something. That was what she wanted: a white wedding with her sisters as bridesmaids and, possibly, smaller bridesmaids and page boys as well, a celebration of Nuptial Mass in the church, and then a glittering reception and a huge, three-tiered wedding cake. A day she would remember for the rest of her life. It was what she had dreamed of for a long time, even before she had met Dominic O'Reilly.

Her feelings for the young Catholic priest, the curate at their church, had overwhelmed her. Even though she had known it was wrong she had been unable to stop herself falling in love with him. When, finally, the news of the 'affair' had become common knowledge in the parish, her mother had accused Veronica of 'doing all the running'; of leading him astray and tempting him to forget about his vows of chastity and obedience. Veronica had been hurt and angry. Such accusations were not true. She knew that Dominic felt just the same way about her, but she would never, never have led him on to commit what they both knew would be a mortal sin. All they had done was to hold hands, and he had kissed her cheek when they said good night. Afterwards, when he had gone – he had been offered a placement as far away as possible – she had wondered if she might have been deluding herself. He had never actually said that he loved her, although it had been obvious from the look in his eyes and the gentle touch of his hand. She had begun to feel ashamed, unable to face people. She had not really wanted to end her life, but at that time she had been in such a muddle that she had scarcely known what she was doing.

Both her parents, Mum in particular, had been very supportive when she had taken the overdose, and all the previous harsh words and recriminations had been laid aside. She had left school almost immediately without completing her sixth-form course and had been fortunate in finding a job with prospects and which she enjoyed at the Marks and Spencer store. Her move to this flat about a year ago, sharing at first with a friend of her Aunt Vera and then, more lately, with Jennifer, had given her the chance to develop a more independent spirit.

She had steered clear of men for a while; then she had met Shaun, a most suitable young man in every way, or so it had seemed. A few years older than herself, with a steady job in the retail trade, he worked for his father who owned several fancy goods shops in the town. Moreover, he was a Catholic and they shared many of the same ideas and interests. Not the same ideals, however. The discovery that he was married had been a great shock to her. He was living apart from his wife, admittedly, in his own flat, and he intended to divorce her for infidelity. But how could he do that? Veronica had asked. He was a Catholic, and they did not believe in divorce. His reply that many people were much more liberal in their thinking nowadays showed her they were not on the same wavelength at all.

Then there had been Justin, a trainee manager with Marks and Spencer, who had recently come to work in the Blackpool store. They had been attracted to one another from the very first day. 'What about Justin?' Teresa had asked her earlier that evening. 'What went wrong there?' Veronica had told her sister that they had both realised they were not right for one another. The truth was that Justin had seemed to get worried when she had started looking in the windows of jewellers and furniture shops. Until then he had seemed keen enough. He had told her, several times, as his kisses and embraces began to get more demanding, that he had never felt like this about anyone before. But Veronica wanted a ring on her finger before there was anything 'like that'. She had thought he would be of the same opinion. He also was a Catholic – though a lapsed one, she suspected – and he was forever going on about the lack of moral fibre in the nation today.

Looking back now she realised he had always had to have some sort of axe to grind. Not being particularly interested in politics or world affairs herself, Veronica had tended to go along with his views, or at least to pretend to do so. It was preferable to arguing. She guessed, though, as far as politics were concerned they were at different ends of the spectrum. The present Establishment, it seemed, could do nothing right for Justin. She recalled how he had been up in arms earlier this year when the Beatles had been awarded MBEs in a gesture that was considered to be bold, classless and admirably modern. Others did not agree and some previous recipients of similar honours had returned their medals to Buckingham Palace in disgust. 'And quite right too,' Justin had proclaimed. 'Whatever next? A knighthood for Cliff Richard?'

Veronica had not really agreed with him. She thought it was a fitting gesture for the four young men who had put not only Liverpool, but Great Britain, on the pop music map, and their recommendation a wise move for a prime minister, Harold Wilson, who wanted to be considered a man of the people. She was not wildly ecstatic about the Beatles, as was Teresa and her younger sister, Bernie, but she could see they had introduced a whole new concept to the musical scene. Veronica was a little old-fashioned in her musical tastes as in other ways; 'square', according to Teresa, because she preferred singers such as Frank Ifield, Nat 'King' Cole and Pat Boone. As usual, she had not argued with Justin. Things had not been going too well between them at that time, although she was still trying to convince herself that he was right for her and that they were merely experiencing a few minor hiccups, such as any couple might go through. She did not want to increase their differences by telling him she disagreed with him. However, it was soon after this that he had told her it was all over between them.

She had been dreadfully upset at the time, although not suicidal as she had been over Dominic. But she could see now that it was for the best. Justin would not have been right for her. They would have been bound to argue eventually over such things as politics and religion, and Justin, she now admitted to herself, had never been able to accept any point of view but his own. And she had never been able to get him to go to church with her despite his insisting he was a Catholic. Maybe, after all, he had only been after one thing, and that without the promise of a wedding, or even an engagement ring. No, it would never have worked out. And now she had met Richard. She smiled to herself at the thought; Richard was really nice. Whatever mistakes she had made with Justin she was determined not to repeat them this time.

Veronica was surprised to see her mother in the Marks and Spencer store the following afternoon. She had just finished sorting out a problem with a new sales assistant who had made an overring of ten shillings on the till and did not know how to make it right again, when she looked up and saw her mother standing at the side of the counter.

'Hello, Mum.' She moved across to her. 'Have you come to look at the new styles like I told you to? Or have you come to see me?' she added, noting the slightly anxious look on her mother's face.

'Er, yes, I have. Come to see you, I mean,' said Doreen. 'That is – if you can spare a few minutes. I know they don't like you chatting to people when you're supposed to be working.'

'No, it's all right,' replied Veronica. It wasn't as though she was a junior sales assistant. She had had to have words with a couple of them earlier that week – students, who were earning a bit of pin money during the school holidays and who seemed to think it was perfectly in order to entertain their chums at the counter whilst customers were waiting to be served. As a supervisor Veronica knew she was entitled to a little more leeway, but she was a conscientious worker and did not want to be seen to be taking advantage of her position. 'I can spare a few minutes.' She glanced at her watch. 'As a matter of fact I'm due for a tea break shortly. Now, what's the matter, Mum?'

'Oh, you might know. It's Teresa again.' Veronica had guessed that it might be. 'Do you know what time she came in last night? No, of course you don't; that's a silly question. Well, it was a quarter to twelve. And I knew perfectly well she hadn't been at your place all that time, had she?'

'No, of course not,' replied Veronica. 'She left my flat at – let me see – getting on for ten, I think it would be. I asked her to have a drink – of coffee, I mean, Mum – but she said she hadn't time, that she wanted to get back to do the tables.'

'The little madam! Tables indeed! I ended up doing them myself. I'd just finished when she walked in. She tried to tell me she'd been with you, that you'd got talking and forgot what time it was.' And now she, Veronica, had dropped her sister right in it. Oh dear! But it had come automatically to her to say truthfully what time Teresa had left. Perhaps she should not have been quite so hasty.

'But you didn't believe her?' she asked now.

'I tried to at first,' said Doreen. 'I'm sick of arguing with her, Veronica, so I thought, this once, I might take the line of least resistance. Then I looked at her face, all flushed and bright-eyed, and I knew she'd been drinking. I could smell it on her breath as well.'

'Oh dear! So . . . did you ask her about it?'

'Well, of course I did. She bluffed and blustered for a while and tried to deny it, then she admitted she'd met a friend on the way home and they'd gone for a drink. A friend – that's all she would say, so I don't know whether it was a boy or a girl or who the heck it was. It's supposed to be all over with that lad she was seeing, isn't it, that Kevin? Not that she's told me – she doesn't tell me anything – but I assumed it was when she said she was staying in and washing her hair, and she was in such a mood as well. I didn't like her going around with him. He's too old for her.'

'He's only eighteen, Mum.'

'Yes, I know, but two years is quite a lot at her age, and Teresa wouldn't need much encouragement to go off the rails. I know that.'

'I think it's all over with Kevin,' said Veronica. 'She said it was.' She didn't add that her sister had hinted that she thought she could get him back. Was that where she had been last night? 'I shouldn't worry about that if I were you, Mum. Nor about her having a drink now and again. I know it doesn't make it right, but lots of girls of her age do. And to make it worse, quite a lot of landlords turn a blind eye. I never used to drink at all when I was her age, but I was at a much stricter school, remember, and I didn't grow up as quickly as Teresa has. I'll try and keep an eye on her, Mum, when I can. And I'll have a "big sister" talk to her. I tried to do that last night, actually.'

'And did she take any notice?'

'I hope so,' said Veronica. 'She listened, anyway.' But she had no intention of telling her mother what they had been talking about; it would worry her even more.

'I'd be ever so glad if you could be a little more friendly with her,' said Doreen. 'I could tell last night that the two of you might get on rather well if you gave yourselves a chance. I know you've always thought of her as your kid sister, and you've got your own friends, but if you could invite her to go along with you sometimes . . . perhaps?'

'I'll try, Mum,' said Veronica. It might be rather difficult, though, she thought to herself, now Richard had come on the scene. She didn't want to spoil her chances with him by having to look after her young sister. Not that Teresa would want to be looked after, and Veronica knew also that she would not be able to act as nursemaid to her sister. The girl would have to do her own growing up and make her own mistakes, like she, Veronica, had done. For the moment, however, she must try to set her mother's fears at rest. After all, she had been thinking only last night that she should take more interest in Teresa and her problems. 'I'll do what I can. So – what was the outcome? Have you done anything about it? Said she can't go out at night or . . . anything?'

'I can't very well keep her a prisoner,' Doreen replied. 'That would only make her worse. I read the riot act, of course. I told her it was the last time I'd do her job for her and that if she didn't conform she would have to go and work in another boarding house, which might not be so congenial. And I'd make sure she did, I can tell you. I know of quite a few people who would find her a job and make her work damned hard as well.'

'Did you tell Dad?'

'No; he was fast asleep when I went to bed. And this morning he didn't enquire what time she had got in, so I didn't say. But her days are numbered, believe me.'

'Give her a chance, Mum. She's only been working full time for you for a couple of weeks, hasn't she? She's got to have time to settle down. She's only just left school, when all's said and done.'

'She knows the routine of a boarding house by now,' said Doreen, 'like you all do. She knows everybody has to pull their weight.'

'Perhaps she'll be better when you move to Gynn Square?'

'Perhaps she will, perhaps not; we'll have to wait and see. Anyway, I've got it off my chest, Veronica. I was so mad with her, and there's nobody else I can tell about it.'

'What about Abbie? You talk to her about all sorts of things, don't you? Not that she could do anything about it.'

'I haven't seen Abbie for a few weeks. They've just been away on holiday; a coach tour to Austria and Switzerland, lucky things! Then Abbie starts her new job next month. Yes, happen I'll go and see her next week and we can have a good natter. That'd be nice.' Doreen smiled. 'But I've seen you and I feel a lot better now I've told you.' Veronica was pleased to see her mother's face lighten.

'Try not to worry, Mum,' she said. 'Maybe you'll have cleared the air. Teresa needs a telling off every now and again. She may well be a whole lot different from now on.'

'Let's hope so,' Doreen sighed, then shook her head as if to get rid of the thoughts of her troublesome daughter. 'Speaking of Abbie, are you going to do what you said and have a word with Sandra about the flat?'

'Yes, I think I'll call at lunch time tomorrow and see if she's on the counter at the GPO. If not, then I could give her a ring.'

'Yes, why not? I think she would make an ideal flat-mate. Anyway, I must go, love. I've already taken nearly all your tea break, I'm sure.'

'It's OK, Mum. I've still got time for a quick cuppa. Now, why don't you go and have a look at the new dresses? Treat yourself, why don't you?'

'Yes, that's a good idea, love. I think I might do that.' Veronica was pleased to see her mother looked quite cheerful again. One good thing about her mum was that she was never down for very long.

'We've some lovely new styles in for the autumn – dresses and suits and nice blouses. You'll need some posh clothes when you move to Gynn Square, won't you? Show the visitors you're not an old battleaxe of a seaside landlady, eh?'

Doreen laughed. 'Something like that, yes, love. So long as I don't get too big for my boots. Thanks for listening to me, anyway. I mustn't take up any more of your time. See you soon then.' She gave a cheery wave as she turned towards the dress department.

Veronica stood still for a moment, watching her hurry away. She was more worried than she had let on to her mother about Teresa. She hoped the silly little fool hadn't gone chasing that Kevin again. And, moreover, that she would take heed of the warning her sister had given her.

There was only a small queue of people waiting to be served at Sandra Horsfall's position on the post office counter. Veronica took her place at the end of the line. She would buy some stamps, she decided, and a postal order she needed; she guessed the bosses at the GPO would not like their employees to chat to friends in the queue any more than they did at Marks and Spencer. And then she would ask Sandra to meet her, to come round to the flat, maybe, as she wanted to discuss something with her.

Veronica watched her dealing pleasantly and efficiently with the person at the head of the queue. Sandra was an attractive girl, one you might describe as being good-looking rather than pretty. Her bold features – a longish nose and wide mouth – precluded any claim to conventional prettiness. Her deep brown eyes glowed with warmth when she smiled, as she did when saying goodbye to the customer. Veronica remembered that this same girl had had a tendency towards moodiness a couple of years ago, and that her mother, Abbie, had had much cause to complain of her difficult behaviour. She had grown out of it, though, now. She had gone through enough trauma already, poor kid, thought Veronica, to last a lifetime. Her fairish, sandy-tinged hair reached almost to her shoulders and, to Veronica's envy, seemed to curl under of its own accord in a most attractive page-boy style. Veronica had endless trouble with her own flyaway hair, which she was forever back-combing in an attempt to make it stand up and add to her height.

'Hi there, Veronica; I haven't seen you in ages. How are you?' Sandra seemed surprised but pleased to see her, and when they had dealt with the stamps and postal order she listened, with one eye on the growing queue, as Veronica asked if she could meet her to discuss 'something rather important'.

'Sounds intriguing,' replied Sandra. 'Shall I come round to your place then? Sorry I can't talk now; you can see how it is.'

They agreed on Wednesday evening of the following week.

Before that, however, Veronica had her Saturday night date with Richard Hargreaves.

He called for her in his blue Triumph Herald at seven o'clock, as they had arranged. She was glad to see his car was not red. She was wearing her new dark green trousers and tabard top, which Teresa had assured her were 'real cool', and she was pleased to note Richard's approving glance at her, although he made no comment. He had not said where they would be going, but she guessed it would not be to a dance hall. When she had met him at the Mecca he had intimated that he wasn't much of a dancer, but had just come along with his mates to take a look at the new ballroom.

Veronica was thrilled when she discovered he had booked a meal at the River House, a small intimate restaurant, part of a country house overlooking Skippool Creek on the River Wyre. She had not been there before. The River House had a reputation for excellent food in a romantic – though rather exclusive – setting. Not everyone would be able to afford it; Veronica was impressed. She was glad she had not had much tea, only a quick sandwich after she had finished work.

Richard proved to be an interesting and entertaining companion and very easy to get along with. They found they had much in common. Like her, he worked in a store; he was in charge of the furniture department at R. H. O. Hill's, Blackpool's leading department store. He was the eldest of a largish family as she was, although she did not find out whether or not he was a Catholic. All in good time, she decided. He was twenty-four years old and had left the family home to rent a flat of his own over a shop on Dickson Road.

So far, so good, Veronica thought at the end of the evening as he drove her home. She wondered whether or not to invite him in for a coffee, but decided against it. She didn't want to appear too forward, and it was, perhaps, too soon. She could tell he liked her a lot, though, by the way he looked at her. Maybe next time . . . She certainly hoped there would be a next time.

He kissed her gently on the lips. 'Thank you for a most enjoyable evening, Veronica. May I see you again? Next Saturday, perhaps?'

They agreed that he would phone her during the week.

He said he would book for one of the season shows and maybe they could have a bite to eat beforehand. She said that sounded lovely. She wondered, though, what he was doing on all the evenings in between and why he could not have seen her sooner. She told herself, however, that she must not be too possessive this time. Some men didn't like that. Take Justin, for instance . . . It would never have been right, though, with Justin. But Richard – well, he was an entirely different kettle of fish.

Chapter 3

Sandra

'You mean . . . you're asking me if I'd like to move in with you, to share this flat?' Sandra stared at Veronica in wide-eyed surprise. 'But that's wonderful. I can hardly believe it.'

Veronica grinned. 'Then I take it that that means yes? You will?'

'Of course I will. It's just incredible.'

'What is? I can't understand why you're so surprised I should ask you, or so thrilled. Although I must admit it's quite a nice place.'

Sandra looked round admiringly. The living room where they were sitting was spacious and comfortable, though a mite shabby. It certainly could not compare with the superbly decorated home she would be leaving, but it would be a place to call her own and that was the important thing. 'I'm surprised because – well – it was just what I'd been thinking about for quite a while, but I hadn't got round to doing anything about it. You must've been able to read my mind, Veronica.'

'No, not really. You mentioned the last time I saw you that you'd like a place of your own.'

'Did I? I don't remember. It must've been just a casual remark at that time, but I've been thinking about it seriously for a month or so. It's like – I don't know – a dream come true.'

'Good. Why d'you want to get away from home then?

Don't you get on very well with your stepfather?'

'Yes, as a matter of fact I do – now,' replied Sandra. 'Duncan and I get on very well indeed. He was my music teacher – of course you know that, don't you? – before he and Mum got friendly. He's very nice . . . Well, he's a lot more than that, actually. Duncan's just great, not only with Mum but with me and Simon as well.'

'You had a few problems at first, though?'

'Yes, I dare say we did. Well, I know jolly well we did, but that was before Mum and Duncan got married. I resented him, y'see; his friendship with Mum at any rate. I liked him well enough as my music teacher, but I wanted things to stay that way. That's all I wanted him to be – my teacher, not anything else.' Sandra stopped suddenly. 'I don't want to talk about it really, about how awful I was. That part of my life is over now. I know I've got to leave it behind and step forward, if you know what I mean.' The events of the previous summer, culminating in a car crash and the death of her boyfriend, Greg Matthews, still returned quite frequently to torment Sandra. Indeed, the memories were a part of her and she knew they always would be, but, hopefully, they would fade in time and she would remember only the good things. 'Let's talk about the flat. When is your friend moving out? And when would you like me to move in?'

Veronica showed her round the flat. Sandra had been there just once before, and that time she had seen only the living room. She was pleased, now, to see that she would have a bedroom to herself; she would not have been so keen if she'd had to share. It was small, but adequate, although she did wonder, momentarily, if all her clothes would fit in the wardrobe and drawers, and what about her record player and all her records? There was certainly no room for them here, but that was a minor drawback, she supposed, compared with the advantages.

The kitchen was small, too; very small for the size of the house. Sandra knew that at the time this house was built – late Victorian era, she guessed – little consideration had been given to the room where the woman of the house would spend most of her time. Her mother had often complained about the inadequacy of the kitchen in their house in Layton. Now they had moved to a larger house in Newton Drive the kitchen was more spacious, but nothing to be compared with the spacious 'fully fitted' kitchens, all gleaming tiles and streamlined cupboards, of the contemporary homes. Sandra was used to washing up and to knocking up makeshift meals – which she had sometimes had to do for herself and her brother whilst her mother was on her teacher training course – but she was by no means an expert in culinary matters. She viewed the gas stove with some alarm – she was used to an electric one at home – but Veronica assured her it was quite safe.

'So you think you'd like to share with me then?' said Veronica, when they had returned to the living room and were enjoying a drink of chocolate and a Penguin biscuit. 'Don't be afraid to say if you've changed your mind. I know it's not Buckingham Palace or anything like that.'

'I think it's lovely,' said Sandra sincerely. 'There's just one thing . . .' She glanced speculatively round the room. Mm . . . there might be room in that corner, she thought. 'D'you think I could bring my piano with me? I need it, you see, to practise, although I don't do as much as I used to. Oh dear! I've only just realised there's only the one room; I always used to have the piano in the dining room at home. I should hate to disturb you if you wanted to watch the telly or listen to records or something. And that's another thing: there's my record player – it's a Dansette; quite small though – and all my records.'

'Don't worry about any of it,' said Veronica. 'Of course you can bring your piano, and your record player. There's plenty of room, as you can see. I'd like to listen to you, anyway. I like music, although I'm probably not as high-brow in my tastes as you are. I know you used to go in for festivals and exams and all that, didn't you?'

'Not any more, I'm afraid,' Sandra smiled ruefully. 'I passed my Grade Eight . . .' She did not add that it had been with a distinction. 'But I've decided not to go any further and sit for my diplomas. Actually, I've had it decided for me. I broke my arm, you see, in . . . in the crash, and it still aches if I try to do too much.'

'It was your left arm, wasn't it?'

'Yes, fortunately, in some ways. But it doesn't make much difference when you're playing the piano. In fact it's the left hand – and arm – that has to deal with all the crashing chords in the bass. So I'm afraid my more serious musical studies have gone for a Burton, you might say.'

'Oh dear! Poor you! So what do you play now? You said you needed to practise.'

'Yes, I do, but it's mainly light stuff that I play now; "easy listening", they call it. Songs from the shows and film music and all that. I was a bit upset about not being able to do the difficult classical stuff any more, but Duncan, my stepfather, came up with a good idea. He used to do a lot of entertaining in Blackpool, at the hotels and for civic functions and that sort of thing – he plays the organ as well as the piano, you see – and he's passed some of the work on to me. I told you he was great, didn't I? He said it was all getting too much for him. I suppose it was, really, because he teaches part time in schools and he has all his pupils as well. And then it meant he was out a lot in the evenings and he didn't like leaving Mum. But I know he's done it mainly for my sake, to give me another interest and to make sure I don't lose my technique altogether. If you don't keep on playing, then you lose it. So I'm getting acquainted with *South Pacific* and *Oklahoma!* and *My Fair Lady* and all those.'

'Great! I love musicals,' said Veronica. 'And I'm dying to hear you play. When do you start these engagements in the hotels? Or have you started already?'

'No, I've got two bookings next week. And if they like me then they'll probably book me to the end of the season, that's until the Lights finish. I'll just have to see how it goes.'

'Goodness! You will be busy, won't you, with your job

at the GPO as well? However will you manage?'

'Quite well, I hope. At least the hours are reasonable at the Post Office. We only stay late one night a week when we do the balance. And when I've finished for the day then I've finished, like it is in your job. Not like being a teacher, for instance. I know my mum will have to bring lots of work home with her when she starts at her new school next month. But she says she doesn't mind. She's trained for three years and it's what she wanted to do.'

'She may not have anticipated getting married, though?'

'Yes, that's true, I suppose. She didn't know Duncan when she first went to Chelford. But with them both being teachers it gives them something else in common, and I must admit they get on very well together.'

'What will your mum say about you coming to live here? Does she know you were thinking of moving out?'

'No, because I hadn't really started looking, had I? This just came out of the blue. I don't suppose she'll mind. I was away for a few months, you know, when I started at the Post Office, doing a training course in Manchester. I was in digs then, just coming home at weekends, so she got used to me being away. She might make a bit of a fuss at first, like she did when I said I wanted to leave school.'

'Yeah. Mums do, don't they? Mine was just the same.'

'But she'll come round in the end. Duncan'll persuade her, like he did about me leaving school. I'd only done one year in the sixth form, you see, when . . . when Greg was killed, and I knew I couldn't go back there. I knew I had to do something completely different. Greg was a brilliant pianist, you know, far better than I was. He would've been going to music college in Manchester in the September, and I'd had the idea that I'd like to do the same sort of thing. But then I realised, after he'd gone, that I didn't really want to do that at all. I knew I wouldn't be able to, anyway, because of my arm. And I doubt if I'd have got in at music college. The standard is terrifically high. You've got to be exceptional, like Greg was.'

Veronica smiled sympathetically. 'I can tell you still miss him a lot, don't you? Does it hurt to talk about him? Don't, if you don't want to.'

'Not as much as it used to,' replied Sandra. 'I couldn't mention his name, or hear it, at first, without wanting to burst into tears. I don't cry all that easily, though, and that probably made it worse. And then I found it helped to talk about him. I blamed myself, you see, for the accident. We'd been quarrelling and we were late for an engagement and I was telling him to drive faster. Nobody else seemed to blame me, though. Well, I suppose Duncan might have done at first. Duncan was Greg's music teacher as well as being a friend of their family, and Greg was his star pupil; he thought of him almost as a son, because he'd never had any children of his own. It was such a tragic waste of a life, and I felt responsible for what happened. The only consolation I could find – if you can call it that – was that Greg was rather a reckless driver.' She almost smiled. 'We'd had quite a few near misses, but of course I'd never told Mum that, not till afterwards. I wasn't making excuses. He really was quite impetuous behind the wheel, although he was so sensible in other ways. His parents knew it as well, so . . . so I didn't get blamed as much as I might have done . . . as much as I should have done,' she added.

'Try to put it behind you,' said Veronica kindly. 'You know what you were telling me earlier, that you have to step forward? So – you left school and got a job instead of finishing your sixth-form course? That's just what I did; I left school and went to work for Marks and Spencer when . . .' she paused, then: '. . . when I had all that trouble with Dominic,' she added quickly.

'Yes.' Sandra looked at her guardedly. 'I remember.'

'My parents were disappointed that I wasn't going to take my A levels and go on to a college or university,' Veronica continued, 'but they can see now that it was the best thing for me to have done. I needed a fresh start, and I've got a good job that I enjoy. I'm very happy there. You like it at the GPO, do you?'

'Yes, I like it well enough,' replied Sandra. 'I don't know that it's the job I want to do for evermore, but, yes, I'm quite happy there. Mum wasn't keen on the idea at first. Like your parents, she thought I should stay on and take my A levels, and that by that time I might have changed my mind about going to college. It was Duncan who convinced her that I might be making a wise move in leaving school, that it would help me with . . . everything if I had a proper job of work to do. And then I heard they were taking trainees at the Post Office . . . So there we are.'

'And you've got a boyfriend now, haven't you? Your mum was telling my mum.'

'Oh yes?' Sandra grinned. 'She would, wouldn't she? Yes, I've been seeing Ian Webster. Mum would like to think he was my boyfriend, but I'm not too sure myself. Mum hasn't said it in so many words, but I'm sure she thinks it would be rather fitting. She used to work with Ian's father, Jim, when she was a land girl, yonks ago, of course. Jim's father owned the market garden then, and now Jim has taken it over. It's on Marton Moss. They were rather friendly, actually, at one time; that was when she thought my dad had been killed in a bombing raid.'

'But it was a mistake, wasn't it? My mum told me the story, about what a miracle it was – so romantic – when they discovered your dad wasn't dead, that he was a prisoner of war.'

'Yes, that's right. Except that he wasn't my dad then, of course, just my mum's fiancé. They got married after the war, and Jim Webster just sort of faded into the background. Then she met up with him again, quite by chance, and I was introduced to Ian.'

'But you're not all that keen, eh?'

'He's a very nice lad – well, young man, I should say; he'll be twenty next month.'

'Same age as me then,' Veronica remarked. 'I'll be twenty in September.'

'I like him very much. The trouble is, he reminds me of Greg. I don't mean because of how he looks, although Ian

61

is tall and slim – and quite handsome too, I suppose – like Greg was. But they were at school together, you see, in the same sixth form, so whenever I see Ian I'm reminded of Greg.'

'They were friends, were they?'

'Not close friends, but they knew one another quite well. Greg was in the Arts section of the sixth form and Ian was in the Science. He's at Leeds University at the moment. Well, not right at this moment, of course, because they're on holiday. He's done a year there.'

'And what's he going to do? Will he take over the family business, the market garden?'

'No; his dad would have liked him to go into partnership with him, but Ian has other ideas. He's studying to be a pharmacist. He's not like Greg at all really. He's much more practical and down to earth than Greg was. Greg was a bit of a dreamer, but Ian sees things just the way they are. He's great fun to be with, and he's been very good to me – and good *for* me, I suppose. It's just that he knew Greg, and so it brings it all back.'

'You won't be able to see him all that often, though, with him being away at college?'

'No, only at holiday times, or the occasional Saturday night if he's over for the weekend. I've been seeing him since January. He called to see me when I came out of hospital last summer. He asked me if I'd like to go to the pictures, but I said no, not yet, it was too soon after Greg; and he understood perfectly. He's very nice . . . kind and understanding.' She smiled a little sadly. 'He's always had respect for how I'm feeling; that's one of the things I like about him. Anyway, he popped up again just after Christmas.'

'So he must've been keen?'

'I suppose so. At least he hadn't forgotten me. And so we went to the pictures, and I've been seeing him, on and off, ever since. I think he'd like things to be a little more definite, but I'm not sure. I don't know what I want to do with my life, not yet.'

'Give him a chance, Sandra. He sounds lovely; just

what the doctor ordered, in fact.'

'It's too soon, Veronica. He has his university course to finish anyway, and we're far too young to think of getting serious.'

'Is that what you thought about Greg? That you were too young?'

'No, I don't suppose so. We just . . . well, we loved one another very much, I know we did, even though we were very young and we used to fall out sometimes. We hadn't talked – or even thought – about what might happen in the future. And now I'll never know, will I? But we hadn't . . . you know what I mean. Greg was a very trustworthy sort of young man, and so is Ian. So I haven't been tempted to do anything that I shouldn't.'

'I'm very glad to hear it,' said Veronica, rather primly, Sandra thought. 'Neither have I. I was talking to my kid sister Teresa the other night and she seemed amazed that I hadn't . . . er, gone the whole way. I told her I was saving myself for marriage, or at least until I'm engaged to my Mr Right.'

'Marriage? Good heavens! I'm not thinking of that just yet awhile!' exclaimed Sandra.

'But I'm older than you, aren't I?' said Veronica, just a trifle smugly.

'Only – what?' Sandra counted on her fingers. 'Only about a year and four months older.'

'But it's enough to make a difference.' Veronica smiled serenely.

'Why?' asked Sandra. 'Has your Mr Right, as you call him, come along then?'

'He might have done.' Veronica looked down coyly at her pink painted nails, then up at Sandra, smiling in a self-satisfied manner. 'As a matter of fact, I met this gorgeous fellow a couple of weeks ago – Richard, he's called, Richard Hargreaves – and we've started going out together.'

'Early days, though, isn't it?'

'Yes, but I have a feeling about this one. This might be *it*.'

Sandra sat and listened as Veronica talked, first about the virtues of Richard – who sounded quite a Superman – and then about the various men who had preceded him. First of all there had been Dominic, the Catholic priest, whom the girl had fallen for in a big way. Sandra remembered how she had tried – or half tried – to commit suicide after that episode although Veronica didn't mention that now. Sandra felt sure her new friend was a much better balanced person now. But she seemed to be incredibly naïve about men and her relationships with them.

After Dominic there had been Shaun, then Justin, and now Richard. And Veronica had believed that each of them would turn out to be 'the one'. She had believed they were falling madly in love with her, as she was with them, only to see them, for one reason or another, fall by the wayside. Sandra came to the conclusion, as she listened, that Veronica tried too hard, that she wanted to get a ring on her finger too soon, and so the men took fright and disappeared. She seemed desperate to be married, to belong to someone – Veronica was certainly no feminist – and Sandra feared that it showed a certain insecurity. But Sandra would not dream of telling her what she thought – at least not yet. Perhaps when they were flatmates she might be able, tactfully, to air an opinion.

She decided, however, that she liked Veronica Jarvis very much indeed and she was sure they would get on famously as flatmates. Sandra remembered how, in the past, she had looked up to Veronica as a more sophisticated 'woman of the world', whereas she, Sandra, had been only a schoolgirl. She recalled the occasion – it must have been about three years ago – when Veronica had told her, confidentially, about her blossoming friendship with the young priest at her church. Sandra had thought that was ever so daring and cool, although she had sensed too that it could lead to trouble as, indeed, it had. But Veronica had seemed then, to the fifteen-year-old schoolgirl, to be very grown up and worldly wise.

It was she who had encouraged Sandra to use a touch of green eye shadow to highlight her brown eyes, and shown her how to apply her make-up more skilfully. Veronica had moaned about her own hair, blonde and wispy and flyaway, compared with Sandra's shoulder-length hair, which had golden highlights and was abundant enough not to require a perm. Veronica still wore her hair in a bouffant style to add to her height, as she had done three years ago, and now, as then, Sandra was the taller by a few inches.

Sandra realised that the other girl, far from being a sophisticated woman of the world, was, in some ways, quite immature and lacking in confidence. She felt of the two of them that she herself, in spite of being some sixteen months younger, was the more mature. All the same, she thought that Veronica was a very sweet, warm-hearted person and she was looking forward already to sharing her home.

Veronica promised to let her know the exact date that Jennifer would be moving out; it would probably be towards the end of September. When they parted they both felt that it was the beginning of a good friendship.

Her mother's reaction was predictable, when Sandra broke the news to her the following morning. There were only the two of them at the breakfast table. Sandra, at the moment, was the only one in the household who was going out to work, although the long summer holiday from school would come to an end next week. Her mother insisted on getting up early every morning to make her breakfast even if she only wanted cornflakes and toast, a task she would very soon have to do for herself.

'Oh dear, I thought you were settled here, Sandie, love,' said Abbie Hendy. She still had difficulty in remembering that her daughter preferred to be called Sandra now and not Sandie, as she had been when she was little. 'We've decorated your room just the way you wanted it, and you've even got your own piano up there as well.' There were two pianos in the household. Duncan had brought his own with him, a Steinway baby grand, when he and

Abbie had moved to the house, and this was in the lounge where he taught his pupils.

'Yes, I know, Mum,' said Sandra. 'And I love my room, honest I do. But didn't you think I might want to get a flat now I'm working? I've been working for a year now. And if I'd been going to college when I was eighteen, like you wanted me to do, I'd be going anyway now, wouldn't I?'

'That's different, dear. You have to live away from home when you're at college, unless you travel there every day like I did.'

'But you got used to me being away, Mum, when I was on that Post Office training course. You didn't seem to mind then.'

'I wouldn't say I got used to it, love. I missed you – we all did – but you were home at weekends and I knew it was only for a few months anyway. It's so convenient for you, living here. We're quite near to the town centre and it's easy for you to get to the post office.' Sandra sometimes walked to work if she was feeling energetic; it took her about half an hour. Or, more frequently, she made use of the handy bus service.

'Not as easy as it would be if I was living on Park Road,' replied Sandra.

'Mm, that's true, I suppose,' said Abbie, sighing a little. 'I shall miss you, love. I can't pretend otherwise, but I'm not going to stand in your way. I can see you've made up your mind that it's what you want to do.'

'Good heavens, Mum! You'll hardly notice I've gone, you'll be so busy with your new job. And I'll come back and see you. Did you really think I wouldn't? Like Veronica goes to see her mum; she goes at least once a week.'

'Yes, that's something in its favour, you sharing with Veronica. I wouldn't have been happy about you moving in with a complete stranger, love. But Veronica's a very nice sensible sort of girl. She seems to have settled down since she got over that silly business with the priest. I know she's had a few boyfriends – Doreen told me – but I think she's quite – how can I put it? – prudent.'

Sandra smiled. 'She's not likely to lead me astray, I can assure you of that. It isn't that I'm dying to get away from home, you know. I just think it would be a good idea for me to have a little more independence. And it will give you and Duncan more of a chance to be on your own, won't it?'

'Not really. We'll still have Simon with us.'

'It'll be one less for you to look after though, Mum.'

'That isn't why you're going, is it? Because of Duncan?'

'No, of course not. You know it isn't. It might have been at one time, but not now. We get on famously together, but I'm growing up, Mum. So is Simon. Only another couple of years and he'll be off to university.'

'Who's taking my name in vain?' Simon came into the dining room at that moment. He narrowed his eyes and glowered at his sister, although she could see he only meant it in fun. It was not often that his dark brown eyes lost their glint of good humour. 'Trying to get rid of me, are you, Sissy?'

'Don't call me that!' she snapped, frowning at him. 'Yes, maybe I am. But it's me that's going, not you.'

'What are you on about?' He sat down, placing his hand on the brown earthenware teapot. 'Is this fresh tea, Mum, or shall I make some more?'

'I'll see to it in a minute,' replied Abbie. 'Duncan should be down any time now and I'll make a fresh pot. Just listen to what Sandra's got to tell you.'

Simon raised his eyebrows quizzically. 'So . . . ?'

'I'm going to share a flat with Veronica Jarvis,' said Sandra. 'I'm moving there in September.'

'Good show!' said Simon, a grin spreading all over his rounded face. 'Can I have your bedroom then?'

'Well, you cheeky so-and-so!' Sandra exploded. 'Of course you can't have my room. Is that all you can think of? Won't you miss me?'

'Yeah . . . I might,' replied Simon, casually tipping a large helping of cornflakes into his cereal bowl. 'Like I'd miss a pain in the . . . er . . . head.' Sandra stuck out her tongue at him and Simon retaliated by grinning fatuously, then crossing his eyes.

'Honestly, you two!' said Abbie, laughing. 'What was that you were saying, Sandie, about you both growing up? Can't say that I've noticed.'

'I'm Sandra, Mum,' she replied calmly, 'not Sandie or Sissy. Please try to remember, both of you.' The latter was a silly nickname that Simon had adopted for her over the last year. She knew, of course, that it was only meant as a joke. He pretended that he liked to annoy her, just as she made a pretence of being annoyed. Deep down they thought the world of one another, as much as any brother and sister two years apart in age could do. Sandra knew he had really tried, this past year, to be nice to her and to treat her normally, which she appreciated. He knew how much she had agonised over Greg and this was his way, by cheerful bantering and friendly teasing, to show that he cared. He too had been very shaken by Greg's death; he had admired the older lad and thought him a really decent guy, considering he was his sister's boyfriend.

Sandra looked across at her brother now. He had matured quite a lot over the past year and if you didn't know you might think he was more than sixteen. He was a little taller than Sandra now – their father had been tall – although he resembled his mother in looks. He had the same fresh-complexioned roundish face, brown eyes and dark brown hair, whereas Sandra had inherited the features and colouring of Peter, their father. Peter had died ten years after the war, when Sandra was eight years old, having never entirely recovered from wounds he had received in his plane crash. She had been very much her 'Daddy's girl' and she had missed him acutely and gone on grieving for a long time. This was why, at first, she had resented her mother's friendship with Duncan Hendy. No one would ever be able to replace her father. Now she knew that Duncan had no intention of doing that; he just wanted to be their friend and helpmate when needed, hers and Simon's, and he had proved to be that and more.

'Yes, I'm sorry, love,' her mother said now. 'I must

remember to call you Sandra. I keep forgetting. It just comes naturally to say the name we used when you were a little girl.'

Sandra smiled. 'You used to call me Sandra when you were annoyed with me. I always knew I'd displeased you when you used my proper name.' She reflected, as she said it, that those occasions had occurred quite frequently. She had been something of a trial to her mother and she knew it only too well. The situation was very different now and she wanted to keep it that way.

'Yeah . . . I suppose Simon could have my room,' she went on, with a show of nonchalance. 'It makes sense 'cause it's bigger than the one he's in.' She was still wondering how she would find room for all her belongings in the small room at the flat. She could leave some of them here, she supposed – her winter clothes, for instance – and collect them when she needed them, swapping them over with her summer gear. 'He'll have to put up with my choice of décor though.' At least the walls were not shocking pink, the colour she had favoured at their previous house. Pale mauve and lime-green walls and a heather-toned carpet, which was what she had now, should not be objectionable to her brother.

'Don't talk about me as though I'm not here,' retorted Simon. 'I couldn't care less what colour the wallpaper is. It can be sky-blue pink with yellow dots for all I'm bothered, so long as I have a bit more room for all my stuff. And the walls'll soon be covered up with posters, anyway.' His sporting heroes, she guessed, and the pop groups he favoured at the moment.

'Hey, wait till I've gone,' she said.

'I didn't mean I was going to do it right now, did I? Yeah, I'll wait till you've moved out. Thanks anyway, Sissy . . . I mean Sahn-drah.' He elongated the vowels in a teasing way. 'When did you say you were going?' He grinned.

'Who's going where?' Duncan came in and sat down at the table. Abbie immediately jumped to her feet.

'I'll make a fresh pot of tea. This one'll be stewed by

now.' She made towards the kitchen, but Duncan pulled her back.

'Hey, what's the hurry? The tea can wait a minute. Sit down and tell me who's going. It's not you, I hope?' He grinned at her, then winked at Sandra and Simon.

'Don't be silly, Duncan. As if I would,' replied Abbie. Sandra mused, as she had done many times, that her mother did not possess a great sense of humour. Duncan had done a lot to lighten her earnestness, and so had her great friend Doreen over the years, but she remained a little unsure of herself, the result of a girlhood in which she had been suppressed by a domineering mother. She did smile, however, now. 'I was going to make some tea, anyway, before you came down. We're all ready for some. I shan't be long. It's Sandra that's going. She'll tell you all about it.'

'So what's all this?' asked Duncan. 'Got a job in another town, have you?'

'No, nothing like that,' she replied. 'Nothing so drastic. I'm going to share a flat, that's all, with Veronica Jarvis. I went round to see her place last night and we got on very well together. So I'm going towards the end of September, when the other girl moves out.'

'Yeah, terrific, isn't it?' said Simon. 'And I'm going to have her room. There's bags more space there than I've got in mine.'

'Yeah, terrific,' repeated Duncan, grinning. 'We'll have a bit of peace and quiet, eh, Simon? Can we help you pack your bags?'

'Hm . . .' Sandra grimaced at them, her mouth set in a firm line. 'I might've known what sort of a reaction I'd get from the males in the family. Typical!' She knew, though, that Duncan was only having her on, as Simon had been. There might have been a time when Duncan would have been glad to see the back of her, but not any more. 'There's only Mum who's sorry I'm going.'

Duncan laughed. 'You know we're only kidding, don't you? Of course you do. We'll miss you. It'll be strange, not having you around. But I think it's a jolly good idea, all the same. Veronica's a nice girl and it'll be good for you to have more independence.' He lowered his voice. 'What did your mother say?'

'Oh – you know – the usual. She thought I was settled here and that there was no need for me to move. How convenient it is living here, and all that. It isn't that I want to go, Duncan, that I'm dying to leave home or anything. But, well, I think I'm ready for a change, after . . . everything, you know.'

He nodded gravely. 'Yes, I know. Don't worry about your mother, I'll have a talk to her,' he said quietly, raising his voice when Abbie returned with the tea. 'Yes, that was quite a surprise, wasn't it? I've just been telling Sandra that we'll miss her, but I think she's making a wise move.'

'Yes, in some ways. I know she's growing up.' Abbie looked at her daughter fondly. 'But it won't be as easy for you, Sandra, love, as it is living at home. Have you thought about your washing, and ironing, and making meals for yourself? And, don't forget, you'll have two jobs to think about soon: the GPO and your engagements at the hotels. I don't want you wearing yourself out.'

'She's young and strong, Abbie,' Duncan interpolated.

'Yes, so I am,' said Sandra. 'Thanks, Duncan. I've thought about all those things, Mum, and I still think it's no big deal. I'll manage. Look, I'll have to dash now, or I'm going to miss my bus. Cheerio; see you later . . .'

Sandra's first musical booking was to take place the following week at one of the sea-front hotels in North Shore, on the stretch of promenade known as Lansdowne Crescent. It had always been considered one of the more select areas of Blackpool. In the second half of the last century it had been part of Claremont Park, a private enclosure with laid-out walks, flowerbeds and shrubberies. A toll of a penny had been charged to walk there, which people had preferred to pay rather than risk walking along the crumbling cliffs. All that, of course, was long ago. There was now, and had been for more than fifty years, a fine promenade – a three-tier promenade, indeed, on that stretch of land – with strong sea defences. But this was still thought of as the more salubrious part of the town, away from the noise and boisterousness of the Central Beach area.

Sandra found, to her slight surprise, that she was nervous at the thought of facing an audience again after an interval of well over a year so she had invited Ian to go along with her as moral support. He was an unflappable sort of young man and she hoped his sanguinity might rub off on her. Besides, he might well be annoyed if she did not invite him. He liked to think of the two of them as a couple, and Sandra would go along with this when it suited her.

He called for her in his little Morris Minor, a recent acquisition. She had been pleased to note, on the few occasions she had been with him in the car, that he was a much steadier driver than Greg had been. Ian had not long ago passed his driving test, but he was quietly confident as well as being careful and observant.

'I don't think your stepfather's any too keen on your friendship with me, is he?' Ian said as they drove along Church Street en route for the promenade.

'Why do you say that?' asked Sandra, although he had made the remark before. 'I'm sure you're imagining it. Of course he likes you. Why shouldn't he? Duncan gets on well with most people; I've never known him to fall out with anyone.'

'I'm not saying he doesn't like me. Nothing as strong as that. He just seems to – you know – look at me askance whenever I come to pick you up. I do know why, though, and I suppose I can understand it. He's thinking about Greg, isn't he?'

Sandra gave an inward sigh. It was always the same whenever she was with Ian. At some time during their outing together Greg's name would be sure to crop up. She wished it didn't have to be so, and she made up her mind now that it was not going to continue like this. Ian wasn't being fair to himself, and neither was she getting a chance to forget. No, she reminded herself; she would never forget, but she was not being given the opportunity to discover whether or not she really cared enough for Ian to carry on seeing him. He was a person in his own right, not just someone who had known Greg and gone to the same school.

'Yes, Duncan thinks about Greg,' she agreed. 'He's bound to. He thought as much of him as he would have done of a son of his own. I suppose it might remind him when he sees us together. But, Ian, you and I don't need to talk about him – Greg, I mean – not any more. It helped at first, but now, well, I'd rather try and move on a bit further.'

'With me, you mean?' Ian glanced away from the wheel for a second, looking at her intently.

'Maybe,' she said. 'At least, let's give ourselves a chance and not keep harking back to the past. Agreed?'

'Agreed, yes.' He squeezed her hand briefly as it lay on her lap, then returned his hand quickly to the wheel. 'That's great, Sandra.' The smile he gave her lit up his blue-grey eyes, transforming the expression on his usually serious face to one of sheer delight. 'Duncan's a good sort, I can see that,' he continued in a more matter-of-fact tone. 'He and your mum seem very happy together, don't they? Good-looking fellow for his age, isn't he?'

Sandra laughed. 'He's not all that old. Fifty last birthday, actually, and my mum's forty-four. Yes, he's a handsome chap; I always thought so.' Duncan Hendy was quite tall, with aristocratic features that could look stern in repose, belying his amiable personality. His silver-grey hair, which waved slightly, was showing no signs of thinning. 'Of course he's aged quite a bit since . . . you know.' It was hard not to mention Greg, but they had agreed. 'Yes, he and Mum are very happy. They don't go hitting the high spots or anything, but they're content just to be at home together or to go away for the occasional weekend. And they've never stopped talking about their coach trip to the Continent. But I'm afraid Mum's come down to earth with a jolt this week. She's started her new job.'

'Oh yes, of course. How does she like it?'

'She's not said very much. I think she's OK. She says she likes the headmaster, and the staff are quite friendly. But she's got a big class – thirty-six of them. She looks rather tired.'

'I'm not surprised. Duncan'll understand, though, won't he, with him being a teacher himself?'

'Yes, a peripatetic one, though. He goes around to a few schools, teaching music, so it's not the same as having a class of your own. But it's something they've got in common. He's a great help to my mother. He made the meal tonight because she was tired, and they'll share the washing up.'

'What about you?' Ian grinned at her. 'Don't you help?'

'Of course I do, when I can. I didn't get in till six, though, tonight, and I've had to dash out again so I got out of doing any chores. Mum keeps reminding me that I'll have a lot more to do when I go to live at Veronica's, but I'll meet that problem when I come to it.'

'You don't really see it as a problem, though, do you?'

'No, I'm looking forward to it.'

'I think you're right. It's good to get away from home – from the apron strings, you know – when you're eighteen. I'm sorry I missed out on National Service, in a way. I think everyone should have to leave the nest when they're eighteen.'

'You can't generalise, Ian. Not all girls are alike, or all lads, for that matter. Some are more inclined to be home birds than others. It's easy to say you would have liked to do National Service when you know you'll never have to do it.' The last call-up had been in 1960.

'True enough. I didn't find it all that easy at first at uni, I must admit. I missed my home comforts. The grub isn't as good as my mum's cooking and the room's a bit spartan. But you feel you've got more freedom and it does you good to have to fend for yourself a bit more.'

'What are you on about?' Sandra laughed. 'Fend for yourself, indeed! You're in a hall of residence. All laid on for you.'

'Not entirely. We have to change our own beds, and see to the washing of our own clothes; I go to the launderette. And we've got a kitchen, so we do make meals for ourselves now and again.'

'Big deal!' Sandra grinned.

'But I may well move into a flat for the final year; sharing, you know, with two or three others.'

'Sounds like fun,' said Sandra.

She really meant it and she may well have sounded regretful, because Ian asked, 'Don't you sometimes wish you'd stayed on at school? You'd be going to uni yourself now, or to college.'

'No, Ian . . . no,' she replied. 'I did what I thought was right when . . . at the time. Anyway, we've agreed not to talk about certain things, haven't we?'

'Yes. Sorry.' He pressed her hand again.

'It's OK. I'm quite happy at the post office, for the moment, and I've got these bookings . . . Oh heck! D'you know, Ian, I feel frightened to death. I never thought I would. I never used to.'

'You'll be fine; just great,' he replied, smiling at her encouragingly. 'When you get in front of an audience all your nerves'll vanish. It isn't as if you're not used to an audience, is it? What time are you on?'

'I'm not sure. About half-past eight, I think, when the visitors get back from their evening stroll or whatever, but I wanted to get there early to get acclimatised, to sort out my music and everything. It's largely a matter of playing it by ear tonight, finding out just what's expected of me. And that's another thing I'm rather anxious about – playing by ear. I'm not good at that – I usually have to use the music – but Duncan's brilliant. He could play anything, request numbers and all that sort of thing. Oh, Ian, supposing I make a mess of it?'

'Hey, that's not like you at all.' He glanced concernedly at her. 'Come on, love. I've never known you to lose your cool before. Look, we're here now. You'll feel better when we get inside. I'll just find somewhere to park.'

'The car park looks pretty full,' said Sandra, trying to

get a grip of herself. The forecourt of the hotel, at one time a lawn, had recently been tarmacked to accommodate the increasing number of cars that many holidaymakers now used instead of travelling by train or coach. 'Let's try round the back in Dickson Road. I don't mind walking a few yards . . .'

'I'm OK now,' she smiled as Ian took out her music case and locked the car door. She tried to sound confident. 'Just a fit of the collywobbles. It'll pass.'

'Of course it will. Chin up, love. No, I'll carry this,' he said as Sandra reached for her music case. He put his other arm round her, the first time he had done so in the street, and they made their way to the front entrance.

The Allenbank dated from the mid-Victorian era, as did most of the hotels in the area. It was a three-storey building, plus the attic rooms. These originally had been used for servants, but at the height of the season all possible rooms were made available for the visitors. The aura of the place, as Sandra and Ian entered, was pleasant and welcoming: the cherry-red and gold carpet; the highly polished hall table on which stood a colourful arrangement of flowers, artificial, to be sure, but pleasing to the eye all the same; gleaming white paintwork and Regency striped wallpaper echoing the gold colour in the carpet. There was an unmistakable aroma of cooking, which was hard to disguise in any hotel or boarding house. It was quite pleasant, however – roast meat, chicken, maybe? – with none of the whiff of overcooked cabbage.

The proprietress, Mrs Pollard, whom Sandra had met briefly beforehand, appeared from the bar area to greet her. She was a plumpish middle-aged woman with bright auburn hair arranged in sausage-like curls. Her salmon-pink dress, embossed with silver beads on the bodice, was very modish; it might have clashed with her hair colour, but, oddly, it didn't. She was a very elegant woman who knew how to make the best of herself.

'Hello there, Miss Horsfall – Sandra, isn't it?' She shook her hand. 'Nice to see you again. And this is . . . ?'

She glanced at Ian in a friendly manner.

'This is Ian Webster, my . . . friend,' replied Sandra. The two of them shook hands. 'He's come along to give me a bit of moral support. I was feeling a little . . . well, not exactly nervous . . .' it would not do to let Mrs Pollard know how keyed up she was actually feeling, '. . . but rather apprehensive. Duncan, my stepfather, he has a very unique style, hasn't he? And he's so versatile he can play practically any sort of music. My presentation might be rather different, not quite what you've been used to.' She could see Ian looking at her rather anxiously and she decided she'd better shut up. Why on earth was she prattling on like this anyway? Nerves, she supposed, something she was not used to experiencing.

'So, what does that matter?' said Mrs Pollard, patting her arm in an encouraging way. 'We're all different, aren't we, and all the better for that. You'll develop your own style as you go along. Duncan had nothing but praise for you, and I loved the pieces you played for us when you came here a couple of weeks ago. Not that I'm any judge, I must confess. I can't play a note and I can't sing for toffee, but I do like a nice tune.' Sandra had played some excerpts from popular classics: 'The Warsaw Concerto', 'The Cornish Rhapsody', and 'The Dream of Olwen'. It had not been exactly an audition as she had been offered the job on Duncan's recommendation, but Mr and Mrs Pollard had been well pleased at her performance.

'Anyway, I'll leave you to sort yourselves out. And whatever you do, don't start getting all het up. They're a lovely crowd we've got in this week, all nice and friendly. They'll be drifting back soon; I told 'em we'd got summat special on – a nice musical evening. We had bingo last night and tomorrow we're having a TV quiz. Now then, I'll fetch you a drink from the bar, then I'll leave you in peace. What would you like, both of you?'

Sandra settled for an orange juice – even though she felt more like downing a double brandy – as she wanted to keep a clear head, and Ian a light shandy. The bar area where the piano was situated was really the back end of the visitors' lounge. At the front end, overlooking the sea, there was an arrangement of comfortable chairs and settees with small coffee tables interspersed among them. A few visitors were sitting there, quietly chatting or reading a newspaper or magazine. There was a small dance area at the bar end with a gleaming parquet floor, whilst the lounge part was carpeted in the same cherry-red and gold as the hall. There would not be much peace and quiet, Sandra reflected, for those who preferred not to join in with the musical entertainment or the other various evening activities. It was only in the larger hotels, such as the Imperial or the Cliffs, where they had separate ballrooms, lounges, bars and dining area. In the small establishments, like this one and the one Doreen would soon be moving to, strategic use had to be made of the somewhat limited space. Still, there was not much point in coming to a jolly place like Blackpool if you weren't prepared to muck in and enjoy yourself with your fellow guests.

'What are you going to begin with?' asked Ian as she started to take her music out of the case. She had already put it in some sort of order, although she knew she would have to be flexible. ' "The Dream of Olwen"? That's still a popular favourite, isn't it? Everybody knows the tune.'

'Yes, I thought I'd begin with that.' She had put it at the top of the pile. 'It goes down well with audiences. Mrs Pollard said she liked it, didn't she? And I know I can play it quite well.' She laughed. 'It's not terribly difficult, but it sounds good.'

'And which songs are you going to sing?'

'Sing?' Sandra looked at him in surprise. 'I'm not going to sing. I've been booked to play the piano, that's all. That's what Duncan did. Just light incidental music to listen to, and some to join in with – a bit of community singing – if they want to. I've got a few selections from musicals and some songs from the last war. But I didn't intend singing.'

'Why not? I took it for granted you'd be singing as well as playing. You used to sing, didn't you, when you were in that group The Blue Notes with— Oh heck! I'm sorry, Sandra. We said we wouldn't mention him, didn't we? I'm really sorry.'

'That's OK, Ian.' She smiled at him, just a little sadly. 'That's perhaps why I don't want to sing. I haven't done, you see, not since The Blue Notes packed in.' The group had been formed by Greg and three of his pals, Dave, Mike and Tony, a few years ago. They had played guitars and sung, and Tony had played the drums. Their followers in the Fylde had considered they were just as good as the Beatles. Then, later on, they had invited Sandra – Sandie, as she then was – to be their female vocalist. They had been on their way to their final concert, somewhere over the River Wyre, when Greg's car had crashed. The group had fallen apart. It would have done so in any case when Greg had gone to college. He had been the leader, and without him they could not – or did not have the heart to – survive. Sandra had hardly seen the other three lads at all since Greg's death.

'You don't have to sing the same songs that you used to sing,' said Ian. 'It was the Top Twenty sort of stuff, wasn't it, with The Blue Notes? I was thinking of something . . . you know . . . more nostalgic, that'll go down well with the other folk. I take it they'll all be older than us?'

'I should imagine so,' said Sandra. 'Oh, I don't know, Ian. I'm out of practice.'

'Don't you ever sing now, not at all?'

'Only in the bath,' she laughed, 'and in the church choir, occasionally, if I happen to be there on a Sunday morning.' Her friend Paula, with whom she had joined the youth club and youth choir, was now away at training college, and Sandra had found she had outgrown both these activities. There had been quite a long period when she had not felt like singing at all. She still attended the Methodist church, however, and had been cajoled into singing with the choir, an assorted bunch of people, mostly ladies who were considerably older than herself, whenever she went to the service.

'Well, there you are then,' said Ian. 'Do you know, I've

never heard you sing, and I would love to.'

'I would have to accompany myself,' said Sandra. 'No mean feat. Oh, I don't think so, Ian. Perhaps next time, when I've practised at home, I might.'

The lounge was filling up now. There were several people ensconced in the easy chairs and more in the bar area, seated round the small tables with drinks in front of them, casting interested looks in the direction of the attractive sandy-haired girl who was seated at the piano, playing very quietly as if to amuse herself.

She had found, as soon as her fingers touched the keyboard, that her nervousness had largely disappeared; not entirely so, but she hoped that as soon as she got into her stride she would gain in confidence. When a goodly crowd had assembled Mrs Pollard appeared from behind the bar to introduce her, quite informally, Sandra was pleased to note.

'Listen, everybody. This is Sandra – Miss Horsfall – but I know she'd like you to call her Sandra, and she's come along to play the piano for us. I know you're in for a lovely evening with all sorts of nice music. I'm not sure exactly what, so I'll leave it to Sandra to tell you herself. Give her a big hand, everybody. I expect she's feeling a bit shy.' There was a round of enthusiastic applause from the audience, many of whom were smiling encouragingly at her.

'Oh, and that's her friend Ian, who's come along to keep her company,' added Mrs Pollard. 'Isn't he lovely? I wouldn't mind him keeping me company. What do you say, ladies?'

There was a ripple of laughter and Ian blushed, but Sandra felt herself beginning to enter into the carefree spirit of the evening. Come on, she told herself. There's nothing to be worried about here, nothing at all.

'Ladies and gentlemen, good evening,' she began, 'and thank you for such a warm welcome. I'd like to start with one of my favourite piano pieces, and, I hope, one of yours too – "The Dream of Olwen".'

She knew she played it well and the audience responded

wholeheartedly. She had chosen, to follow, selections from Ivor Novello's *The Dancing Years* and Noel Coward's *Bitter Sweet*, favourites of an earlier generation, which made up the larger part of her audience. 'Don't feel you have to sit in silence,' she told them. 'Talk if you want to; go to the bar and get your drinks – don't mind me.' This, she knew, was one of the main objectives of the evening, to add money to the bar coffers. 'Enjoy yourselves, and if you feel like joining in with the songs then please do so.'

A few of them, mainly the women, joined in, though a little timorously, with 'Waltz of my Heart' and 'I'll See You Again'.

'And now for something a little more up-to-date,' said Sandra, as she started on a selection from *South Pacific*, then *My Fair Lady*. She was well into her stride by this time, but decided she had deserved a break. She paid a visit to the cloakroom, then accepted gratefully the chilled pineapple juice that Ian brought her. Her cheeks were flushed and her eyes were bright. She had been surprised to see in the cloakroom mirror how vivacious and happy she looked.

'Well done,' said Ian. 'You're enjoying yourself, aren't you, love? I thought you would once you got started. Now, what's next?'

'Oh, another piano piece, I think. "The Golliwog's Cake Walk" – that goes with a swing. And then some wartime songs. They're very nostalgic, and it's long enough ago now for the unhappy memories to have receded. D'you think so, Ian?'

'Yes, I'm sure,' he replied. 'Those songs Vera Lynn used to sing, and Anne Shelton. Not that I remember them, but my parents do. They're still very popular.'

After her rendition of the Debussy piece she introduced, 'A wartime medley. Sing along, please, ladies and gentlemen. I know you'll recognise them all.' She did not intend to let them ask for requests, which might well leave her floundering – she needed the security of the music in front of her – and so, without further ado, she plunged straight into 'Bless 'Em All', followed by 'This is the

Army, Mister Jones' and 'Run, Rabbit, Run'. Then some gentler, more wistful songs, destined to bring tears to the eyes of more than a few of the women: 'The White Cliffs of Dover', 'It's a Lovely Day Tomorrow', 'A Nightingale Sang in Berkeley Square', and 'We'll Meet Again'.

'And now, ladies and gentlemen,' she said, when the applause had died down. 'I'd like to perform for you a very special wartime song. Actually, it's my mum's favourite. I wasn't around, of course, during the war, but my mum was engaged to a flight sergeant in the RAF. He became my dad, and this was "their song". And, if you don't mind, I'd like to sing it for you.' She smiled, rather shyly, across at Ian, who grinned broadly and stuck his thumb in the air.

'I'll Be Seeing You' was the song, the one about looking at the moon and remembering a loved one. Her voice was vibrant and melodious while her gentle piano accompaniment provided the perfect backing. When she had finished, the audience was silent for a moment, before they all burst into ecstatic applause.

What a girl! thought Ian as he gazed at her in admiration and wonder. It was at that moment he knew he had fallen in love with her.

Chapter 4

Teresa

'Oh, I say, Mum, that's not fair, is it? You begged me to work for you, and now that you don't need me no more you're telling me I've got to get a job.' Teresa scowled at her mother, feeling very hard done by. She knew it was not strictly true that her mother had begged her to work at the hotel. It had been more of an ultimatum from Doreen: find yourself a job or else you'll have to come and work here. 'I think that's dead mean. You didn't tell me I'd be sacked at the end of the season.'

'Teresa, don't be so melodramatic,' Doreen sighed. 'You're not being sacked. Your dad and I have already told you that we'll carry on paying you a small wage; a retainer, they call it, which means that we'll promise to take you on again full time as soon as we can.'

'Huh! Big of you, I'm sure,' Teresa muttered, but Doreen went on speaking as though she hadn't heard the insolent remark.

Teresa knew she was being cheeky and was surprised her mother didn't tell her off, but she was feeling fed up with herself and everything and everybody. Nothing seemed to be going right since they'd moved here. 'You know we don't employ staff to carry on from one season to the next,' her mother was saying. 'All our workers are seasonal and they know that, apart from your Aunt Vera, of course. She's family and she knows she's got a job here any time she wants it, and so have you. It stands to reason we can't pay you a full wage – that's why we want you to get a part-time job – but we will expect you to help with getting the hotel ready for Christmas. It'll be all hands on deck; your Aunt Vera'll be helping an' all. There's a lot to do to get it shipshape; giving the place a thorough cleaning, top to bottom, then painting and decorating.'

Teresa decided she didn't like the sound of that at all. Cleaning! She had enjoyed her work during those last few weeks at Dorabella in spite of her initial grumbles. She had liked the waitressing best of all, but she had not minded as much as she thought she would the setting of tables – she had begun to take a certain pride in getting them just right – or even the Saturday stint as a chamber-maid, preparing the rooms for the next set of visitors. It was also her mother's idea that Teresa should eventually take over the book-keeping, but that was the job she found the most boring. Since they had moved to Sunset View last week, however, it was the only job that remained for her to do. The season had finished with the ending of the Lights and they were now dealing with letters that were arriving for next year's reservations, few and far between though they were at the moment. They had had a few requests, also, for the four-day break, which her mother had decided to open for at Christmas. Teresa hated writing letters, but even that would be preferable to scrubbing floors and washing down paint-work and tiles. And as for painting and decorating . . .

'Er, what sort of a job do you think I should look for?' she asked now, very tentatively.

'Oh, changed your mind, have you?' said her mother with a shrewd glance at her. 'Well, that would be entirely up to you, wouldn't it? Part-time work in a shop, maybe, or an office?'

'Oh no; not a boring office.' Teresa pulled a face. 'A shop might not be so bad. I wouldn't be much good at decorating anyway, Mum. Yes, I can see maybe it's not a bad idea for me to get a job.'

'Mm, I thought you might come to that conclusion,' said her mother with a decided twinkle in her eye. 'As far as the painting and decorating's concerned your dad and I thought we might get a proper firm in. Quite a few rooms need doing and it would be quicker, with us deciding to open for Christmas. I'm quite a dab hand meself at paper hanging, and happen I could do the smaller jobs. We'll want some help with the cleaning, though, so don't think you're going to escape scot-free. They'll all have to help, not just you: Michael and Bernie, and Paul when he's got time to spare from college. Goodness, you wouldn't believe the cobwebs I've found already, or the amount of dust on top of the wardrobes and under the beds.'

'So Sunset View's not the palace you thought it was, eh, Mum?'

'We always knew it wasn't a palace, love, but your dad and I thought it had potential. Well, it has; there's no doubt about that. We had a survey done and it's structurally sound, but I can't pretend there aren't any snags because there are. All the mattresses need renewing. It's all very well for them to say they were leaving the beds, but they didn't tell us all the spring interiors were shot. Those at Dorabella had a lot of life left in them, but that's the way it goes.'

'You've not been diddled, have you, Mum?'

'No, of course not. Your dad and I are too canny to have the wool pulled over our eyes – well, not entirely – but there's a lot that they didn't tell us. Still, we got it at a good price, so we can't grumble. And by the time we've finished with it, it will be a little palace, I can tell you . . . just like Dorabella was,' she added, sounding a mite regretful.

Teresa, for once, had the good sense not to ask her mother if she was having regrets. She decided, instead, that it made a nice change for her to be sitting here chatting with her mum in quite a normal way instead of going at it hammer and tongs as they so often did. She even offered to make a cup of tea, and though her mother looked at her in surprise she agreed it would be a nice idea. Teresa came to the conclusion as she went into the kitchen and switched on the electric kettle that maybe all that was the matter with her was that she was bored. It had been hard work during those few weeks at the end of the Illuminations and now, since they had come here, there was very little to do but write the same boring old letter time and time again. She suspected, though, the letters were not as plentiful as her mother might have wished. There had even been a few cancellations for next summer when it was discovered that the previous owners had left. Teresa thought that was disgraceful. In a sudden attack of loyalty that had surprised her, and Doreen too, she had told her mother that these folk must be off their heads, that there was nowhere in Blackpool where they would be looked after better than under her mother's roof.

She nodded to herself now as she spooned the tea into the pot and got out the cups and saucers. Yes, that was what was the matter with her: she was bored and she hadn't realised it. A job might be a great idea after all. She visualised herself, perhaps, in a record shop where she could listen to the Top Twenty all day long, or a shoe shop – there was an abundance of them in Blackpool – where she could try on all the latest styles.

And there was, also, her present lack of male company. That was not doing anything to improve her mood. Since Kev there had been no one, and her last meeting with him still hurt when she allowed herself to think about it. She had gone to find him, that night after she had been to Veronica's, in spite of the promises – well, half-promises – she had made to her sister. She had almost thrown herself at him, she now recalled to her embarrassment, but he had made it all too plain that he thought of her as nothing more than a child. He had humiliated her in front of his friends by openly flirting with that brassy-haired, brazen-faced barmaid. She had decided she hated him and she would never forgive him.

'Do you really think we'll be able to open for Christmas?' she asked her mother a few moments later as they sat drinking their tea. Like two old biddies at a women's meeting, thought Teresa, who could not remember ever having done this before. 'Supposing we're not ready?'

'Supposing doesn't come into it,' replied Doreen. 'We've got to be ready and that's a fact. I've already put adverts in lots of local papers – Preston, Chorley, Bolton, Bury, Oldham, Rochdale; even Halifax and Todmorden. We get quite a lot of folk from Yorkshire, at least we used to at the other place. And I've said as how Sunset View is under new management, and made a lot of the Cordon Bleu cookery an' all that. I'm hoping our Paul will pull all the stops out at Christmas. Yes, we'll have to make sure we're ready. And you know me, love: when I make me mind up about something, then that's it. I make sure it happens.'

'And which rooms are you thinking of having decorated? Not all of them?'

'Not at the moment, no. We'll start with the second-floor rooms; some of them are pretty bad. And the dining room and the visitors' lounge; they would do at a pinch, but I want summat a bit more . . . classy, you know. And I want a bigger telly in the lounge. It's a must these days. And then . . . well, I've got big ideas, I must admit, for the first-floor rooms. I want to go real posh and have a bathroom and lav for each room; en suite, they call 'em.'

'Gosh! That'll take some doing,' said Teresa. 'There's already a bathroom on that landing and two toilets.'

'You're supposed to have more these days. The Hotel and Guest House Association's getting very particular.'

'So that means you'll have less bedrooms, if you're going to have all them bathrooms?'

'I don't know exactly, not yet. Happen only one less bedroom. Some of the rooms are quite big and can easily be divided. I know it'll need quite a lot of mucking around with, so we're going to get a firm of builders to come and give us an estimate. Then they can start straight away after Christmas, we hope.'

'Does Dad know about all this?' asked Teresa, somewhat bemused. It was the first she had heard of all her mother's grandiose schemes.

'Of course he does,' Doreen grinned. 'You don't think

I'd go ahead without his say-so, do you? We're a team, your dad and me. Oh yes, and there's summat else we want as well. Actually, this was your dad's idea. We're going to apply for a licence so we can serve drinks. We'll have a little bar at the end of the lounge. I'm hoping that'll be ready before Christmas.'

'Wow!' said Teresa. 'The times they are a-changin', eh, Mum?'

'You could say that, love. You've got to move with the times and Blackpool's motto is "Progress", isn't it? Well, it can be ours an' all. This'll be the best hotel in Gynn Square before we've finished, take it from me. Small hotel, I mean, of course. We can't compete with the big 'uns like the Savoy, but we'll get our own clientele – sounds posh, eh? – in spite of the cancellations.'

The Savoy was the large hotel on the promenade at the corner of Gynn Square, and there were several well-known and well-patronised hotels a little further to the north, including the Cliffs, and Uncle Tom's Cabin, which had been rebuilt on the other side of the tramtrack after the original building, teetering on the eroding cliff edge, had been demolished in the early years of the century.

'Yes, the Jarvis family will make their mark here if we all pull together. Team work, Teresa, that's what's needed.' Doreen smiled at her daughter and it seemed, at that moment, as though they were the best of pals. Teresa decided it might not be a bad idea to humour her mum now and again. It was certainly pleasanter than being at one another's throats.

Doreen, for her part, wondered how long this change of heart would last. It was a long time since she had known her middle daughter to be so biddable; only half an hour ago she'd been grumbling and pulling her face at the idea of getting a job. Her mother was not fooled, however. She knew Teresa of old and was well aware that the girl, by hook or by crook, would endeavour to do exactly what she wanted at the time she wanted it. Still, it was good to be experiencing the sunnier side of her nature for a change. It was more often like being caught in a thunderstorm when Teresa was around.

'Tell me about these posh bedrooms then,' Teresa said now. 'The ones with their own bath and lav. You'll have to charge more for them, won't you?'

'Oh yes, it might all be rather complicated, actually. There'll have to be a list of the various prices to send to prospective clients. You can help me to work it out and we'll get it printed. Of course they'll have to pay more if they want a bath and WC; private facilities, they call it. And the front rooms ought to be a bit more expensive than the back ones. They're the ones that have the view of the sea. "Sea view extra"; that's what it says in the ads, doesn't it? We never had to worry about that before, when we lived in Hornby Road. And I know it's usual to charge a little more for a single room. Not that we get many requests for singles. Folk who come to Blackpool are usually only too willing to share a room; to share a bed, even, in the olden days. I've heard some of the older landladies talking about the times when they used to pack 'em in like sardines, three or more to a bed sometimes, and two families sharing a bedroom with just a curtain down the middle. Yes, as you say, love, times are changing. You wouldn't get away with it today. You'd soon have the Association on to you.'

'Supposing somebody wants a room with a sea view and a private bathroom?' asked Teresa. 'Will that be the dearest of all?'

'Oh, goodness me, that'll take some working out,' said Doreen. 'Yes, it would have to be, I suppose. Don't let's worry our heads about it at the moment. I'll leave it to your dad – let him decide, eh?'

The youngest member of the family, Bernie, looked somewhat surprised when she came in from school a few moments later to see her mother and Teresa chatting together over a cup of tea as though they were best mates. 'Hello, Mum.' She stooped and kissed Doreen on the side of her face and her mother put up her hand and patted her cheek.

'Hello, dear. Have you had a nice day?'

'Yeah, not bad.' Bernie grinned. 'As nice as school can ever be, I suppose.'

Teresa agreed with her sister about that. She had disliked school, if anything, more than Bernie did. Her young sister, like herself, was not academic, but whereas Teresa had not cared and had wasted her time, Bernie was prepared to work to the best of her limited ability. To what end Teresa could not imagine, because it seemed as though the height of Bernie's ambition was to work in the hotel on leaving school. Probably because she was scared of letting go of her mother's apron strings, thought Teresa. Bernie had always been very much a 'Mummy's girl' – her mother's favourite of the five of them, maybe, although, to give Mum her due, she didn't openly show any favouritism. Perhaps it was because Bernie was the baby and still, to Teresa's way of thinking, behaved like a child. She didn't go in for all that kissing and lovey-dovey nonsense herself, not with her mother, for goodness' sake. Mum and Bernie had only seen one another a few hours ago; anyone would think they'd been parted for yonks.

'Can I have a cup of tea? Is there some left?' said Bernie, plonking herself down on a sagging easy chair. It was one that Doreen had removed from the visitors' lounge as she considered it too shabby, but it would do well enough as an extra chair for the family, especially when it had been re-covered. All the odds and ends of furniture, in fact, that the previous owners had left behind had seen better days. Their own furniture they had brought with them from Dorabella looked quite splendid by contrast.

'This is cold, dear,' said Doreen, leaping to her feet. 'I'll make a fresh pot. No, stay where you are,' she said as Bernie – not Teresa – with 'I'll go . . .' on her lips started to get up from the chair. 'Michael will be in soon and he'll perhaps have a cup as well. You stay and talk to Teresa.'

Teresa had no intention of waiting on her kid sister. Why should she? It was one thing making a cup of tea for Mum, but she was not going to be at everybody's beck and call. Talk to Teresa, her mother had just said to

Bernie. What about, for heaven's sake? The two of them very rarely conversed. They had got out of the habit, somehow, and Teresa hadn't a clue what to say to her young sister now.

'I'm going to get a job,' she said baldly, after there had been a few seconds' silence. 'Mum says I've got to 'cause there's nothing to do here in the winter, apart from cleaning. And we've all got to help with the cleaning, she says, you and Michael, and Paul as well when he's got time.' She grimaced. 'At least if I get a job I'll be out of the way. I can't clean windows and polish furniture if I'm not here, can I?'

'I don't mind,' said Bernie cheerfully. 'I like polishing. I like seeing the wood all nice and shiny when I've finished. I don't mind doing your share as well.'

'Hm . . .' Teresa grunted, a little nonplussed. Really, Bernie was too good to be true sometimes. In fact, all her brothers and sisters seemed to be so. Why was she, Teresa, the only one who was rebellious? Veronica had had her moments, but now she seemed to be settled, boringly so at times. 'There'll be other things to do that won't be as nice as polishing,' she continued. 'Scrubbing floors and cleaning the lavs. D'you fancy doing that as well?'

Bernie shrugged. 'Don't mind. Have you got a job then? What are you going to do?'

She leaned forward eagerly as though she was ready to hang on to her sister's every word, and Teresa felt rather mean. Bernie was a pleasant, easy-to-get-on-with kid. You couldn't help but like her. Teresa was sorry for her at the moment. That brace she'd got on her top teeth had done nothing to improve her unremarkable looks, although it was hoped it would eventually cure her slightly protruding front teeth. Teresa hoped she had not been teased about it at school. Girls could be dreadfully cruel, she knew, as one who had more often been on the giving, rather than the receiving, end of mockery. But Bernie had been happier, she recalled, since her more out-going friend, Maureen, had come on to the scene. Bernie didn't appear to mind too much now about her teeth, or her straight dark hair and high forehead, or her lanky build.

Michael, also, when he came in a short while afterwards, seemed surprised at the family gathering. 'What's all this then?' he chuckled. 'When shall we three meet again . . . ?' he added in a lugubrious tone.

'Don't be so cheeky,' laughed his mother. She looked happy at having so many of her children with her at the same time, thought Teresa. It didn't often happen. Three out of five was not bad going.

Teresa decided she would be really magnanimous now. She did not intend to make a habit of it, but she would make an exception for her twin brother. 'D'you want a cup of tea, Michael?' she asked cheerily. 'I'll go and get you a cup from the kitchen.' She did so, then poured his tea, adding milk and sugar. 'There you are, Twinny.'

He looked at her in some amazement. 'What's got into you?'

'Oh, nothing. Why?'

'Well, you're not usually all sweetness and light, are you?'

She scowled at him. 'Then you'd better make the most of it, brother. You don't know how long it'll last, do you?'

Doreen glanced at her a little anxiously, then at her son. 'We were all having a nice chat, Michael,' she said, 'about our plans for Sunset View. Your dad and I have decided to apply for a drinks licence and have a little bar. And we're going all out to make Christmas a real slap-up occasion. I'll ask Paul to think up some appetising menus, happen something a bit different from roast turkey, although we'll have to have that as well, of course . . .'

Michael showed a polite interest in his mother's chatter, although Teresa got the impression his thoughts were far away. She and her twin had been as close as peas in a pod, and as alike, too, when they were younger. They had been a couple of little imps, she recalled, into all sorts of mischief. She remembered how they had once sent a whole rack of shoes flying in Stead and Simpson when they had been playing tig round the shop; their mother had never really been able to control the pair of them. They had scribbled on the wallpaper, flicked food at one another across the table, trailed mud and sand into the house and been generally unruly, egging one another on, though without any real malice.

They had fooled around a bit at school too, when they were younger, until, at the age of thirteen, Michael had decided it was time he mended his ways. He was now in the sixth form after a very creditable performance in his O levels. The twins had gradually grown apart and Teresa felt she no longer knew him very well at all. He was much too studious for her liking, forever poring over his books and homework. Pious, too; he had been an altar boy for several years and would never dream of missing Mass or confession. Teresa still attended church from time to time, as they all did, partly to stop her mother from having something else to nag about, and partly because . . . well, it had become a habit, she supposed, one that was hard to break.

As for Michael, though, his devotedness was altogether too much of a good thing. She had seen the most incomprehensible, boring-looking tomes in his bedroom, inches thick and weighing a ton, dealing with doctrines she couldn't even be bothered to think about: transubstantiation, papal infallibility, saints and martyrdom, and so on. A lot of Catholics were very much like herself, she guessed, believing what they were told with only the occasional query or doubt. Her parents, and Veronica too, had always been pretty faithful in worship – Mum went less frequently during the holiday season – but she couldn't imagine they had ever done a great deal of soul-searching about what they believed. Veronica, of course, had been more interested in the fellow wearing the dog collar than in what he was preaching.

She found herself half smiling at the thought. Veronica was the one with whom she got on best of all. They had discovered a new rapport of late, and Teresa, encouraged by her sister, quite often popped round to the flat to see her. It was further to go since they had moved, but a promenade tram took her within reasonable walking distance. She would go and see Veronica this evening, she decided. It was possible her sister might be going out with Richard, but if she went early enough she might be able to catch her before she went out. She might see Richard as well. Teresa had decided she approved of her sister's new boyfriend; well, not all that new now; she had been going out with him for more than two months. Sometimes she thought, however, that he might prefer a girl who was a little more spirited than her goody-goody sister.

It was Sandra Horsfall who opened the door to Teresa early the same evening. She had been living there over a month now. Teresa like Sandra very much. She had not known her all that well until recently. Their mothers had always been friendly, and so the two families had met together from time to time, for Boxing Day tea, for instance. The children had always been polite and quite agreeable with one another, but without the ease or intimacy they would have shown to their real pals. Now, since they had shared a flat, Veronica and Sandra had become quite close friends. Teresa would like to think that Sandra was her friend too. She admired the older girl; not in any daft sort of way, she told herself, like those idiots at school who had developed silly crushes on senior girls – hockey captains and the like. She admired Sandra's boldness of outlook and the confidence she had shown in leaving a nice comfortable home and coming to live here. Teresa knew she had gone through a personal tragedy that she was trying hard to put behind her; how awful to have been in the crash that killed your boyfriend.

'Hi there, Teresa,' said Sandra. 'Nice to see you. Come in. Veronica's getting ready to go out with Richard.' She raised her eyebrows, grinning significantly. 'She's been ages already.'

'Oh, that's still going on then?'

'Not half! Going from strength to strength, from what she says.' She pushed open the door of the living room, standing back to let Teresa go in first. 'My brother's here.

94

He arrived a few minutes ago. You know Simon, don't you? Simon, here's Teresa, Veronica's sister.'

'I know who Teresa is,' said the tall lad, rising to his feet as she entered the room. 'I should do, seeing that we've been meeting up since we were nine or ten years old. Hello there, Teresa.' He smiled at her in a friendly way and she found herself smiling back at him with real warmth.

'Not all that often, though, Simon,' she replied. 'I haven't seen you for ages; well, it seems like ages. I wasn't prepared for . . . You've grown,' she added, looking up at him. He was several inches taller than she was. His brown eyes twinkled and he burst out laughing.

'That's what my mum's friends say: "Ooh, isn't he a big lad; hasn't he grown?" You're not much taller, though, are you? But I must say you've grown . . . up.' He looked at her appraisingly – admiringly, she thought. 'The last time we all met was when my mum married Duncan, wasn't it? More than a year ago. Gosh! Haven't I seen you since then?'

'No, p'raps not,' she said airily, sitting down on the settee. Simon immediately sat down beside her. He doesn't need to start getting any ideas, she thought, because he's much too young for me. He was actually the same age as herself and Michael, sixteen last February, but everyone knew that girls matured much more quickly than boys. He was a good-looking lad, though, she had to admit; tall with dark glossy hair like her Aunt Abbie – not her real aunt, but that was what she had always called her. He had his mother's fresh complexion too, and his rosy cheeks, which were inclined towards chubbiness, gave his face a boyish look that he would possibly never lose. She knew he was a clever lad, though she guessed he might not be as studious or as sanctimonious as Michael. He too was in the sixth form after gaining good passes in all his O levels; not the same school as her brother, though. She didn't know what career he wanted to pursue, just as she didn't know what Michael's ambitions were.

'So, what do you do with yourself, Simon,' she asked

casually, 'when you're not at school, I mean? I know you're dead brainy – sixth-form student, aren't you? I say! But I'm sure you do other things as well.' He half smiled at her, quizzically, as though he was unsure whether or not she was taking the mickey.

'Yes; I do all sorts of . . . other things,' he answered in the same casual, slightly teasing tone. 'I go to the pictures now and again. I collect records—'

'What sort?'

'Oh, all sorts, really. The Beatles, Rolling Stones, Manfred Mann, Gerry and the Pacemakers; I like mod music, but I like some of the classical stuff as well. Beethoven, Wagner, and I've just discovered Prokofiev; he's really cool.'

'Never heard of him.'

'Oh well, never mind . . . And I go to youth club, sometimes, for a game of table tennis or badminton.'

Teresa made a moue. 'I've never bothered much with youth clubs meself. I think they're rather childish.'

'I only go to get a game,' he answered quickly. They looked at one another challengingly. 'Well – yes – I suppose I do find it a bit childish now,' he added. 'I've joined a cycling club as well. And I do cross-country running, but that's at school.'

'My goodness! You are a busy bee. I thought you played football at school.'

'No, they play rugger at my school, like they do at most grammar schools – secondary schools, I mean,' he corrected himself, so as not to sound too boastful, she supposed. 'I've always preferred soccer, with me being a keen Blackpool supporter, but you don't find many schools that play the game. So I opted for the alternative, cross-country running, when I got the chance. I see something of the Fylde countryside, like I do when I'm cycling, and it gives me a chance to be on my own now and again.'

'Oh, you like to be alone then, do you?'

'Occasionally,' he grinned. 'Most of the time I prefer to be with other lads . . . Not always with lads, though,' he added slyly. She wondered if he was hinting that he had a girlfriend, but if he was waiting for her to ask, then he would be disappointed. She couldn't care less whether he had a girlfriend or not, but he was pleasant enough to chat to.

'D'you still go to watch Blackpool?' she asked now.

'Yeah, whenever I can. Jimmy Armfield, Alan Ball; they're fantastic. They're in the England squad as well, you know.'

'They're your heroes then?'

'Well, I wouldn't exactly say that,' he replied with an attempt at nonchalance. 'I admire their skill.'

Teresa nodded. 'So . . . what're you going to do when you leave school?'

'Go to college, I hope. I've decided I'd like to be a teacher.'

'A teacher?' Teresa gasped, knowing she sounded as incredulous as she felt. 'You've got to be joking!'

'No, I'm not.' He laughed easily. 'Why, what's wrong with being a teacher? My mum's one. Although I must admit I was rather astonished when she first told us she was going to college.'

'There's nothing wrong with it,' said Teresa, realising she might have been rather tactless, although she didn't usually care how much she offended people. Simon was different, though. He was a nice lad and she was beginning to discover, to her amazement, that she wanted him to think well of her. 'It's just that . . . well, I couldn't wait to leave school; and to think that somebody would want to spend their whole life there . . . What d'you want to teach, then?'

'PE,' he answered, 'and games, in a secondary school. I'd have to take another subject as well, though. History, I thought . . . I was a bit fed up with school myself,' he added confidingly, 'when I was in the fifth form. Too many rules and regulations, aren't there? But it's different in the sixth. Anyway, that's quite enough about me. What about you? You're working for your mother, I believe? How are you all settling down at the new place; Sunset View, isn't it?'

'Yeah, that's right. It's OK, I suppose.' She shrugged. 'We haven't had any visitors in yet, 'cause it's the end of the season. But my mum wants to open for Christmas. She's got all sorts of weird and wonderful ideas for bars and private bathrooms and goodness knows what.'

'I bet that's Mum you're talking about,' said Veronica, appearing suddenly in their midst. 'Hi, Teresa; hello there, Simon. I thought I could hear a lot of voices.'

Sandra laughed. 'It's these two you could hear. I haven't been able to get a word in edgeways. What time is Richard picking you up?'

'Oh, in about five or ten minutes.' Veronica sat down and looked across at her sister. 'You were talking about Mum, weren't you? She's surely not planning to do all that before Christmas, is she?'

'No, only some of it,' said Teresa, 'but we've all got to help, she says, with the cleaning an' all that. Lucky you! You're the only one who'll get out of it. I was mad with her at first 'cause she said I'd got to get a job for the winter, but I'm thinking now it might not be such a bad idea.'

The doorbell rang and Veronica sprang to her feet. 'That'll be Richard now.'

She entered a few minutes later – Teresa guessed they'd been having a quick snog in the hallway – hand in hand with Richard. She seemed loath to let go of him. Teresa noticed it was Richard who released her hand, sitting down on the one remaining easy chair. 'Quite a crowd, eh? Hello, everyone.' He smiled at the two girls, whom he had met before several times, then raised his eyebrows quizzically at Simon. 'Hello. I don't think we've met, have we?'

'This is Simon, Sandra's brother,' said Veronica. The two young men nodded at one another. 'Come on, Richard.' She pulled at his arm. 'We'll have to be going or else we'll be late.'

'No, we won't. It doesn't matter what time we get there.'

'Why? Where are you going?' asked Teresa in her usual blunt manner.

'We're going to the Gaiety Bar,' said Richard, turning to give her his full attention. Teresa had noticed before how his eyes, of such a deep blue that they were almost black, seemed to look right into the depths of her own. His wide mouth turned up slightly in a quirky smile, giving him a roguish look. His features were thin, narrowing to an almost pointed chin; like a pixie, she thought, especially as his ears tended to protrude a little. 'You should go sometime; it's all the rage. Have you never been?'

''Fraid not,' said Teresa. 'Not old enough, y'see,' she added, smiling at him coyly.

'More's the pity. Never mind; your day will come.' His lips curled in a slow grin and he closed one eye in an almost imperceptible wink. 'We're meeting a few friends for a drink, that's all, so I don't know why she's in such a hurry. Relax, honey. The night's still young.' He patted Veronica's arm in an avuncular way, and she sat herself down on the arm of his chair.

'All right then; if you say so.' She seemed a little put out, glancing uneasily at Richard before turning to her sister again.

'What was that you were saying about getting a job? You might as well tell me, seeing that Richard seems to think we've got all the time in the world. What sort of a job are you looking for?'

'Well, I haven't started looking at all yet. But shop work, I suppose.'

'You've changed your tune,' said Veronica, a mite snappily. 'I remember you dismissed it as boring at one time.'

'Well, p'raps I've changed me mind then,' retorted Teresa. 'I can if I want. An interesting shop, I mean, not one where you're all regimented like Marks and Sparks, and Woolies.'

'What about a newsagent's – sweets and tobacco and that sort of thing?' said Richard.

'No, thank you very much,' replied Teresa. 'I don't fancy getting up at five o'clock in the morning to see to the papers, 'specially not in the winter.'

'The owners see to all that,' Richard went on. 'They don't expect the assistant to do it. It's just that I know of a job that might interest you. It's where I have my flat, as a matter of fact. They're looking for an assistant.'

'Why?' asked Veronica, looking at him sharply. 'Why are they looking for an assistant? The season's over. I should have thought they'd be wanting to get rid of staff, not take more on.'

'They have got rid of some,' said Richard. 'The seasonal staff they had for the summer and the Illuminations have gone now. They were all part-timers, and now they want somebody more permanent to deal with the regular trade. They're getting in more fancy goods lines and toys now it's getting near Christmas and Mrs Ashcroft – that's the owner – wants somebody reliable to help out.'

'Reliable!' said Veronica, almost under her breath. She did not add, Well, that rules you out, Teresa, but her sister could imagine what she was thinking. Right, I'll show you then, she thought to herself. Veronica was behaving very oddly; you might almost think she was jealous.

'Would it be a full-time job?' Teresa smiled sweetly at Richard. 'My mother said I'd to look for something part-time, but I dare say she wouldn't mind if—'

'The hours would be negotiable, I should imagine,' said Richard. 'Why don't you go along and see? Mr and Mrs Ashcroft are very obliging. It would be convenient for you as well. It's not all that far from Gynn Square.'

'It's not all that near either,' Veronica broke in. 'Your flat's nearer to North Station than Gynn Square. It's a fair walk, I can tell you, Teresa. It must be a mile or more.'

'So what?' said Richard easily. 'Teresa's young and fit, isn't she?'

'And I can always get a bus along Dickson Road,' added Teresa.

'You're talking as though the job's already yours.' Veronica sounded decidedly piqued.

'It's as good as,' snapped Teresa, 'especially if I've got Richard to vouch for me. What's up with you, anyroad?'

'Nothing . . . nothing at all.' Veronica sighed. The look she gave her sister was wary, more than unfriendly. 'It's just that . . . well, you haven't had a proper job before, have you? Not in the outside world; you can't really count working for Mum. So I don't want you to think you can walk straight into it. They might want references and . . . and all that.'

'Mr and Mrs Ashcroft are quite free and easy,' said Richard. 'Anyway, let's not make a big issue of it, eh? There's no harm in Teresa coming along to have a look at the shop, is there? Anytime you like.' He nodded at her before turning to Veronica. 'Come on then, let's make tracks. I know you're anxious to be off. Cheerio, everyone. Be seeing you.'

'Yes, cheerio . . . See you,' echoed Veronica.

Oh dear! thought Sandra. That's put the cat among the pigeons all right. Oh, Veronica, she pleaded silently with her departing friend; don't make the same mistake again, please! Don't start getting all possessive and jealous; men don't like it. She guessed that Richard would not like it at all. She fancied he was already starting to get a bit edgy, although they had seemed OK as they left. He had put his arm round Veronica in a protective way and Sandra had watched through the window, with half an eye, as he had opened the car door for her and settled her in the passenger seat as though she was very precious cargo.

Her friend certainly looked stunning tonight, as she always did when she was going out with Richard. Her blonde hair was piled high in an elaborate bouffant style and her make-up immaculately applied – blue eyeshadow (possibly a shade too much of it), eyeliner, and mascara to darken her pale lashes, and glossy ice-pink lips – all set off by the blue striped dress she had bought earlier in the year and which had become a firm favourite. She was wearing it tonight with a three-quarter-length navy jacket with a stand-away collar.

That sister of hers really was the most dreadful little flirt. It was not surprising that Veronica had been getting uptight. She was inclined to be insecure at the best of times, something which Teresa did not appear to suffer from in the slightest degree. Sandra had watched with some amusement as the girl, in a teasing way, had chatted up her brother, although she was pleased to see Simon was giving as good as he got. She had then turned her attention to Richard, who had been encouraging her more than a little, and now she was concentrating on Simon again. What were they talking about? She started to listen. Teresa was asking Simon if he had been to see the new Peter Sellers film, *What's New Pussy-cat?*, which was showing in Blackpool this week. He replied that he hadn't.

'Have you, Sandra?' asked Teresa sweetly, bringing her into the conversation. Sandra could not make up her mind whether the girl really was ingenuous, as she appeared to be at times, or whether she was just a crafty little minx. She decided to give her the benefit of the doubt. Teresa had never been anything but nice and pleasant to her, although she had heard reports from Veronica about what a terror she could be and how she tried to run rings round her mother. Sandra could empathise with that, however. She had not always behaved well herself, which was why she made an effort to befriend Teresa.

'I don't get a great deal of time to go to the cinema,' she replied. 'I go with Ian now and again, when he's home from college. But I'm working, you see, at two of the hotels, playing the piano and singing a bit.' She laughed rather deprecatingly. 'It was Ian who persuaded me to start singing again. I used to sing with a group, you know, at one time, but I thought I might not be much cop on my own. Anyway, they seemed to like me, so now I put in a singing spot a couple of times each night.'

'Which hotels?' asked Teresa. 'Veronica said you were an artiste at some of the hotels – clever you! – but she didn't say which ones.'

'The Allenbank's one of them,' said Sandra. 'That's quite near that shop Richard was talking about. I think

I know the one he means, not far from the Imperial cinema. And the other one's down on the central promenade; a slightly younger clientele down there.'

'The season's finished, though, hasn't it?' said Teresa. 'I know we've no visitors in at our place. It's dead along the prom at this time of year. So who are you performing for now?'

'Blackpool residents and the odd weekenders,' said Sandra. 'I'm at the Mountjoy – that's the central prom hotel – on Friday evenings, and they're still getting the odd weekend guests, Friday to Sunday. The proprietors at both the hotels decided to keep me on, and they're encouraging the local people to drop in. At the Allenbank it's more of a sing-along, easy-listening evening – you know, the songs that the older folk like: bags of nostalgia. And they serve a nice supper for those who want it: sandwiches, sausage rolls and cakes, coffee and tea as well as the usual drinks. At the Mountjoy they're rather more with it. They get the younger folk in because there's a slightly larger dance floor. Not all that much room, of course; not like the Tower,' she laughed, 'but they can jig about a bit.'

'And do you play for the dancing as well?'

'No, they've got records and a disc jockey. I alternate with him. I play some piano pieces that are a bit more up to the minute. D'you know "Walk in the Black Forest"?'

'Yeah, I think so,' said Teresa, a little doubtfully.

'Well, that sort of thing. And I sing – or attempt to – usually a couple of songs from the hit parade. I accompany myself, of course, so I can cover up my own mistakes.'

'I'm sure you're fantastic,' said Teresa, looking at her with admiration. 'Gosh! Aren't you clever? Have you been to listen to her, Simon?'

'What, me? Not on your life!' He chuckled, pulling a face at his sister. 'I can hear her any time – at least I could until she left home. She was forever caterwauling and thumping on the joanna. We get a bit of peace now.'

Sandra pulled out her tongue at him. 'You can't come

103

and listen to me anyway, little brother, 'cause you're not old enough to be in a bar. So there! And neither are you, Teresa,' she added as an afterthought.

'Pooh! I don't take any notice of that; neither do my mates,' said Teresa. 'OK, OK . . .' She lifted up her hand. 'I know we're not supposed to drink beer an' all that, but if you stick to lemonade then they don't refuse to serve you.'

'And do you always stick to lemonade?' asked Sandra, grinning.

Teresa wagged her finger playfully. 'Ah, that would be telling, wouldn't it?'

'Hey, hang on a minute,' said Simon, with a sly glance at his sister. 'Correct me if I'm wrong, but don't I recall an occasion where a certain *sixth-form student*,' he emphasised the words, nodding his head meaningfully towards her, 'was suspended from school when she was discovered in a – public house!' He gave an exaggerated gasp of horror as he uttered the last two words. He winked at Teresa then turned back to Sandra. 'You remember, don't you, Sissy?'

Sandra forced herself to smile back at him – at least she made her lips move – although she felt more like throttling him. Honestly, Simon was the limit at times and not always as tactful as he might be. He had probably forgotten – as she never would – that the incident to which he was referring had occurred only a couple of weeks before . . . before the time when she believed her whole world had come to an end. However, she smiled bravely at him, not wanting to fall out with him in front of Teresa, something the old Sandie Horsfall would not have hesitated to do.

'OK, Simon,' she said. '*Touché*. I didn't mean to sound all prissy and prudish, as though I'd forgotten what it's like to be young. Good heavens, I'm only eighteen myself, aren't I? Sometimes I feel more like thirty,' she added in an undertone which she did not intend them to hear. They probably didn't because Teresa was laughing out loud and goggling at her.

'I say, what a hoot! Were you really expelled from school? What happened?'

'Not expelled, just excluded for a time,' said Sandra. 'I left school soon after that anyway. I'd got in with a giddy crowd, although it isn't fair to blame them entirely; I was just as bad myself. We thought it was a great joke to sneak out of school at dinner time, change our clothes and have a quick half at the local pub. But we got caught, didn't we?' She shrugged. 'It was no big deal, honestly. Let's forget about it, eh?'

'OK.' Teresa was still regarding her with a touch of hero worship. 'Suits me. You used to be quite a girl, though, didn't you?'

'What d'you mean, "used to be"?' smiled Sandra. 'I still am.'

'Yes, of course you are. And I really would love to come and hear you sing an' all that. I'm sure Simon would too; he's just having you on.' Teresa suddenly threw out her arms in an impulsive gesture. 'Listen, listen everybody.' She shook her hands wildly as if to attract the attention of a crowd, although there were only two others in the room. 'I've just had the most marvellous idea. Why don't you come and sing at our place, Sandra – at Sunset View? I'll ask my mum, but I know she'll say yes. Don't you think it would be a terrific idea? Oh, go on – say that you will.'

Sandra stared at her. 'What, now? Soon? But you're not even open yet, are you?'

'No, but we will be for Christmas. My mum's got all these big plans, and they'll be having a bar an' all that. It would be a great idea to get people in. We could put it in the adverts – "Cabaret acts every night" . . . or summat like that.'

Sandra laughed. 'Steady on a bit. Don't let's get carried away. We don't know that your mother will agree.'

'She's sure to.'

'And I haven't said I'll do it.'

'You will, though, won't you? I know you will.'

'Well, I must admit it sounds promising.' In fact, the

more Sandra thought about it, the more she liked the idea. She had been wishing she had a few more bookings. 'In the meantime you must come and see my performance; make sure you're not getting a pig in a poke. I didn't really mean it about you being under age – I was just getting my own back at him!' She grimaced at her brother. 'It's OK in the hotels, so long as under-eighteens stick to soft drinks . . . well, officially, you know. Yes, you can come and listen to me. Perhaps you could bring your mum as well – Aunty Doreen.'

'Not likely!' said Teresa. 'Not with me, anyroad. I'd rather go with Simon. You will go with me, won't you, Simon?' She opened her eyes wide as she looked at him, then blinked once or twice. Her eyelashes were not long enough to flutter, but she made a good attempt. 'You were only joking, weren't you?'

'Oh, I suppose so.' He shrugged one shoulder in a couldn't-care-less manner. 'Don't mind all that much really.'

'Good, that's settled then,' said Teresa. 'Simon and me, we'll come and see you at that more swinging place down central prom; what did you call it? Mount . . . summat or other.'

'The Mountjoy.'

Teresa nodded. 'And my mum could go to that place you said was more for old codgers, the Allenbank. P'raps your mum could go with her, and Duncan . . . and my dad an' all. Yeah, the four of 'em could have a real rave-up, couldn't they?'

Sandra burst out laughing. 'Teresa, honestly! They certainly wouldn't like to be called old codgers, and they might not appreciate you organising their social life either.' The girl really was naughty and disrespectful, but you couldn't help but laugh with her. 'Maybe I could suggest it to them . . . a little more tactfully, eh?' Her mother and Duncan had been to listen to her, just once, but their presence tended to embarrass her. Come to think of it, though, they didn't have much of a social life, not now.

'When shall we go then?' Teresa was asking Simon. She certainly didn't intend to let the grass grow under her feet.

'Oh, I don't know; I'll think about it,' he replied, a trifle grudgingly. Perhaps he won't agree after all, thought Sandra, but then her brother went on to say, 'I tell you what, Teresa. I'll walk you home and we can talk about it on the way there. How about that? You didn't want to stay any longer, did you?'

'No, ready when you are.' Teresa jumped up eagerly. 'I only came to see our Veronica, to tell her about the job and everything. But it's been nice seeing you an' all, Sandra. What are you going to do when we've gone? Will you be all on your own?'

'Yes,' Sandra nodded. 'But I don't mind. I've some practising to do. I must get up to scratch if I'm going to have talent scouts in the audience!'

'Oh, that's all right then; don't want you to be lonely.'

'Don't worry, I won't be. It's a heck of a way to Gynn Square, Teresa. What sort of shoes have you got on?'

They were black patent-leather ankle-straps, very fashionable, with open sides and thickish heels. 'Oh, these are OK.' Teresa stuck out a shapely leg. 'I can walk miles in these if I have to. And Simon'll be there for me to hold on to if I get tired.'

'We can always hop on a tram,' said Simon, 'if you think it's too far.'

'No, of course it isn't. It's lonely on the prom, though, now all the visitors have gone. Lonely and dark. I wouldn't like to be there on my own.' Teresa gave him a half-fearful, half-mischievous, grin.

Sandra watched them thoughtfully. Teresa was a terrible tease, though it was hard to know whether she was teasing or whether it was for real, this hint of fearfulness. As for her brother, he seemed a little nonplussed, as though he might be out of his depth. Sandra did not know whether he had had any thoughts, as yet, with regard to the opposite sex. Surely at sixteen he must have done, but she did not think he had ever had a girlfriend.

She remained thoughtful after they had gone. She saw

Teresa get hold of his arm as they reached the gate, turning to wave with a grin of what might be termed triumph on her face. She remembered how Veronica had remarked, only a short while ago, that it might be nice for Simon and Teresa to become acquainted, that the lad might be a steadying influence on her sister. Sandra had had her doubts, although she had not expressed them. Now the two youngsters had met, quite by chance, and she was even more doubtful. Simon was a sensible enough boy, or so he had always seemed, but she was not sure that it would be a good idea for him to have Teresa Jarvis for his first girlfriend.

And she hoped she had only imagined the look that Richard Hargreaves had levelled at Teresa – his girlfriend's sister. Veronica was still insisting that everything in the garden was lovely, but Sandra could not help but wonder if Richard was cooling off a shade. As Justin, his predecessor, had done; as all Veronica's young men seemed to do. Again, Sandra hoped she was wrong.

As for herself, she was glad she had no such problems. There was only Ian, faithful Ian, whom she was growing more fond of every time she saw him. The thought that he would soon be over for a weekend, towards the end of November, filled her with a warm glow.

Chapter 5

Abbie

Abbie Hendy slumped in an armchair without even bothering to take off her coat. She could not remember ever having felt so tired, not since she was in the Land Army. Whatever had she been thinking about, she often asked herself, to embark upon a three-year teacher training course at the age of forty-one? And to believe, as she had so naïvely done, that she would now be able to cope with her first teaching post with as much vim and vigour as a youngster of twenty-one. Like Jacquie Holt, for instance, the girl who had started at Park Gates Junior School at the same time as Abbie. It was her first job too, but she did not appear to be as thoroughly whacked as Abbie was. Jacquie, of course, lived with her parents and there was always a meal ready for her when she arrived home at the end of the day. She didn't have to start cooking for herself and a husband and teenage son.

Abbie pulled herself up sharply as she felt the disgruntled thoughts entering her mind. This was not like her at all. Whatever was the matter with her? If anyone were to ask her she would say, and truthfully, too, that she was very, very happy. She had one of the best husbands in the world, a loving son and daughter and a comfortable – in fact quite luxurious – home. What woman could wish for more? You're tired, that's all, she told herself, deciding to make a cup of tea and try to snap out of it.

She got up, took off her coat and threw it over the

chair – she would put it away later; that was what Simon always said when she admonished him about the selfsame thing – and went into the kitchen to switch on the kettle. She really was lucky, she mused, as she looked around her half-tiled kitchen complete with all mod cons: fully fitted cupboards and gleaming Formica working surfaces, refrigerator and automatic washer; and, though not over-large, with lots more room than she had had in the previous house. The wallpaper above the pale yellow tiling was new, a colourful design of grapes hanging on the vine, orange and lemon trees and bottles of Chianti, a constant reminder of sunnier climes. She and Duncan had chosen it together and, very bravely, had decided to tackle the decorating of this room themselves; with highly satisfactory results, she thought.

They had been living here for just over a year and she knew it had been one of the happiest of her life. She would never have believed she could find such happiness again, not after the love she had had for Peter. He had been a wonderful husband and father, and when he had died in 1955 it had left a gap in all their lives.

The last year had been a hectic one, with Abbie in her final year at Chelford Training College. She had driven each morning to the station, parked the car, and then taken the train for the forty-minute journey to Chelford. And back again at the end of the day to the demands of her home and family. The three of them were very good, though, she had to admit. Duncan was quite a modern sort of husband who was not averse to helping in the kitchen, and Sandra and Simon were not bad kids; now, of course, there was only Simon here. They had fitted everything, somehow, into their busy schedule: her own lectures and home study; Duncan's pupils – all day Saturday and the occasional early evening; Sandra's piano practice; Simon's homework and out-of-school activities . . . Yes, it had been an extremely busy year, but, fortunately, the holidays were long. That was what everyone said about teachers, particularly those who were not actively involved in the job: 'Just look at all the holidays they get!'

Would she have started on the course, Abbie sometimes wondered, if she had known what was going to happen in her life? When she had started at Chelford she had not even met Duncan. She had been looking upon her teacher training and subsequent career as something useful she could do for the next twenty years or so, which would fit in well with her family commitments; she had to admit the long holidays were a blessing! She smiled to herself as she popped a tea bag – a very new innovation, which she had recently been persuaded to try – into her china beaker. It was futile to imagine what she might, or might not, have done if she had known in advance about Duncan. You could not see into the future, and sometimes – probably most times – it was best that you couldn't. At least Duncan understood about the challenges and occasional trials of being a teacher. And he understood that his wife, at the moment, was possibly more tired than she ought to be.

Abbie carried her mug of tea into the living room and sat down again. She would allow herself a few minutes before she started to think about what they might have for their evening meal. She knew she was very lucky to have been given a teaching post, not only in her home town, but so very near to where she lived. Park Gates School, a red brick, two-storey, forbidding-looking establishment, had been built towards the end of the Victorian era. There were two buildings that made up the primary school – one for the juniors, where Abbie now taught, and, across the tarmacked playground, a separate one for the infants. Built into the brickwork above two of the entrances there were still the signs saying 'Boys' and 'Girls', dating from the time when the sexes were taught in different classes; it seemed to have been a question of never the twain should meet. A separate sign declared that it had been a 'Board' school, although Abbie was not sure exactly what the term meant. Nothing to do with boarding there, certainly. It probably meant that it had been under the jurisdiction of the Blackpool Corporation, as it still was; what they were now calling a 'state' school. The whole area was surrounded by iron railings, some seven feet high, which must, somehow, have escaped the scrap metal drive during the war. Abbie remembered how iron railings had been taken away from houses and parks in those early, dark days; maybe schools had been exempt from making this sacrifice? At all events, the railings only served to make the place look even more like a prison, and the stunted bushes growing – or, rather, hanging on to life – in the dry soil behind them heightened the grimness of the surroundings.

Abbie's heart had sunk at her first real sighting of the school. She had seen it, briefly, in passing, when in the car or on the bus, but never at close quarters, and her interview for the post had been at the Town Hall along with several other candidates for various teaching posts. She had been invited to go along to the school for a preliminary staff meeting at the end of August, a few days before the term was due to start. She was full of trepidation as she went through the door, but she soon learned that the old saying was true, that you should not judge a book by its cover, because the inside of Park Gates Junior School was vastly different from the exterior.

The walls of the corridor and of the large hall through which she passed were half-tiled in green; old-fashioned tiles which, again, were an indication of the school's age. But much had been done to bring the décor more up to the minute and welcoming. The walls above the tiling were painted a pale apple-green shade, the woodwork was of a gleaming white, and the classroom doors opening off the corridors and hall were a bright pillar-box red. Abbie could see, through the glass-panelled doors, that the classrooms were painted in various pastel shades and in each room there were large display boards, empty at the moment, which would hold the children's work and the teacher's visual aids. There was a pleasant smell of furniture polish and disinfectant, and everything was shining with a recent cleaning.

The staffroom too had quite a welcoming aspect, with large windows on two sides overlooking the playground, a carpet of green, red and black checks, and various arm-chairs, some rather dilapidated and others appearing much more comfortable, and a few upright chairs. Abbie opted to sit on an upright one. She had been warned, at college, about older members of staff who resented it if anyone sat in their particular chair. And it seemed to be the same here; the older teachers, more noticeably the women, made a beeline for certain seats.

All the staff, that first day, however, had seemed agreeable enough and Abbie had gone home feeling much less apprehensive than when she had first set eyes on the school. She felt she would be happy there and she was determined to make a go of her first teaching post.

Now, only two months later, she was not so sure. It was not just that she was tired, although she tried to tell herself that that was all it was. It was the feeling that she did not fit in at Park Gates School. It was not the children; she had already grown rather fond of her class of seven- and eight-year-olds. Teaching them was not too difficult provided she kept up with the marking and was well prepared in advance for the lessons, and she had had very few problems with discipline. This was probably because she was an 'older teacher' – as some of the children on her last school practice, used to twenty-year-old students, had reminded her – not a youngster they felt they could run rings round.

No, it was the staff that were the stumbling block at Park Gates. To be fair, not all the staff, not even several of them; just one in particular. Namely, Mrs Bell, a fourth-year teacher who had been at the school longer than any other member of staff, with, occasionally, a couple of her cronies agreeing with her, probably because it was easier than arguing. Usually, though, Mrs Bell's was a lone voice, which she raised whenever Abbie was within hearing distance, or so it seemed to her.

Abbie had been astounded, and more than a little upset, too, on hearing the strident voice outside the staff cloakroom door during her second week at the school. Abbie and Jacquie Holt, the young teacher with whom

113

she had become quite friendly at the preliminary meeting, were washing their hands. The two of them, both 'new girls', had felt drawn together. It was Mrs Bell speaking, although to whom, Abbie did not know.

'These mature students are all the same,' she was saying. 'D'you remember, we had one of them on supply last term? Cocky madam she was! And now there's another one: that Mrs Hendy. They think because they come into teaching when they're older that they know it all. I've been here nearly twenty years and never once has a headmaster made a fuss of me like Mr Knighton made of her. Just because she raised that point about playground duty at the staff meeting. What's it got to do with her? The children have always taken the teacher's cup back to the staff room. It's a little job they like doing and no one has ever fallen and cut themselves. Her and her safety regulations! Who does she think she is? But it's, "Oh, thank you, Mrs Hendy; yes, yes, I'll look into it; a very good point." ' She mimicked the headmaster's way of speaking. 'Huh! When I was a young teacher I knew my place. I knew when to shut up . . .'

'Pity you can't shut up now, you old cow!' said Jacquie very loudly at Abbie's side.

'Shhh . . . She'll hear you!' said Abbie, almost in tears.

'Don't care if she does, and don't let her upset you.'

'Ah, but Mrs Hendy's not such a young teacher, is she?' Abbie recognised the other voice as that of Mr Dalton, a fourth-year teacher who also taught PE and games, and was usually to be found dressed in a tracksuit. 'You said so yourself, Mrs Bell, and times have changed since you came out of college. Give her a chance. I think she seems a very nice person and she needs our support. Anyway, what she was saying was quite right; we have to make sure the children don't hurt themselves in any way. Have you forgotten what it's like to be in your first job? Aye, happen you have, it's so long ago.'

Abbie noticed the chuckle he gave. Len Dalton was a good-humoured fellow, on friendly terms with everyone. He would not be making a dig at Mrs Bell, just having a joke and trying to make her change her uncompromising attitude.

'Take no notice of old Ding Dong Bell,' Jacquie said to her at playtime as they sat together on two of the less comfortable, sagging armchairs. That was what the children called Mrs Bell, supposedly behind her back, but there was not much that their teachers were not aware of. Fortunately, the said person was on playground duty that afternoon. 'She gets her knife into everybody in their turn, so that nice Mrs Goodall was telling me, but the others are used to it and they take no notice. She was getting at me as well the other day, talking in a loud voice about youngsters of twenty-one straight out of college and what can they possibly know about reading books? That's because she knows Mr Knighton has asked me to help out in the library. She's bitter because she's never got promotion, that's what Mrs Goodall says, although I would say she doesn't deserve it. She spends most of her time sitting on her behind in that chair, doesn't she? When she's not in the classroom, I mean.'

'Shhh,' said Abbie. 'Don't let the others hear you. We are newcomers, after all. We mustn't be heard running the rest of the staff down.'

'You're too nice, Abbie, that's your trouble.' Jacquie smiled warmly at her. 'You really are thoughtful and kind. I'm ever so glad you're here as well as me. It would have been awful if I'd been on my own.'

'Thank you, that's nice of you,' smiled Abbie. 'I'm glad that you're here too. But like you say, Mrs Goodall seems friendly and helpful; in fact, most of them are OK.'

'Just a bit set in their ways. They've been here too long. Need a bomb behind them, some of 'em.'

'Shhh! Don't talk so loud.'

There had been other snide remarks that Abbie had overheard – or, sometimes, had been meant to overhear, as well as that first one. Like the time when Abbie, with Jacquie helping her, had set to and washed a sinkful of dirty beakers in the staffroom, some of which had been kicking around unwashed for ages, and then had cleaned the sink and draining board. Most of the staff had smiled and expressed their thanks. Teachers could be a surprisingly feckless bunch at times, forever waiting for someone else to clean up after them, not because they were lazy, but because they couldn't be bothered with something so unimportant. Mrs Bell, however, had announced, to anyone who would listen, that it wasn't up to young upstarts straight out of college to start showing them what they should do; that the two young women would be better employed keeping their classrooms tidy and teaching their children to behave.

Abbie knew also that Mrs Bell disapproved of her teaching methods. The woman had come into her classroom earlier that week, ostensibly to pass on a notice from the headmaster – which she could just as easily have sent with a child – but in truth, Abbie felt, to do a bit of snooping. The whole of the class had been painting, the desktops covered with newspaper on which were placed the palettes of paint and jars of water. It was an example of Sod's law that a water jar should be knocked over just at that moment, soaking a little girl's painting and palette and then dripping on to the floor. Abbie, desperately reaching for a cloth and trying to comfort the tearful child, could have done without Mrs Bell's comment that the class would be better employed learning their tables or doing a spelling test.

'It says art on the timetable,' Abbie had replied, 'so that's what we're doing.'

'Oh, I see . . . Yes, of course; we must obey the timetable,' the older teacher had muttered in a disparaging tone as she left the room.

One might have thought that an old-fashioned teacher such as Mrs Bell might have obeyed the timetable to the letter; but Abbie had gathered that the woman paid scant regard to it, except for those subjects of which she approved, namely 'the three Rs'. The other aspects of it, relating to the more creative pursuits such as art, music, poetry and drama, she largely ignored. The time spent on these subjects had increased, Abbie had learned, during

116

the reign of the present headmaster, Philip Knighton, who believed in a well-balanced and wide-ranging education for the children in his charge. The children in Mrs Bell's class, for the larger part of each day, were made to keep their noses to the grindstone and the time they were allowed for creative and artistic pursuits was minimal. The reason she gave was that these children had to be schooled for the eleven-plus examination to the exclusion of everything else. It was a point of honour with her that she should get more passes from her class than the other two teachers of the parallel classes managed to achieve.

Mr Knighton did not believe in streaming – grouping children according to their ability – as was the norm in many schools. It had to be admitted that Mrs Bell's results, year after year, were good, and it was said that more ambitious parents made a special request that their children should be put into her class. Philip Knighton, however, had grave doubts about cramming for this particular examination. Sometimes children taught by Mrs Bell scraped through by the skin of their teeth, only to find when they got to the grammar school that they could not cope with the pressure or compete with the much cleverer children from other, more privileged, areas of the town. The pupils at Park Gates were, by and large, of very moderate ability. There were the occasional high fliers, and several who were what was termed 'slow learners', but on the whole they were pleasant, ordinary kids of average intelligence. Mr Knighton wanted them to enjoy their days at school and to be able to look back on them as a happy time.

Changes were afoot in the education scene; at least the winds of change were to be felt drifting across the country. The Labour government was in favour of comprehensive education, where pupils of all abilities would be taught under the same roof; there would be no selection at eleven, which was thought to be demoralising for those children who did not pass. Some authorities were already making moves in that direction, but Blackpool, a staunchly Conservative borough, still had its grammar

117

schools; and Mrs Bell was of the belief that as many of her children as possible should go there.

All these thoughts were passing through Abbie's mind as she sat there with her cup of tea. The longer she sat the more in control she started to feel, her tiredness and lethargy dwindling away. Duncan had told her to stand up to Mrs Bell and she was determined she would do so . . . eventually. It was difficult at the moment, though, as a new teacher with only a few weeks' experience behind her. The woman's antagonism had upset her more than it might have done because Abbie was a peace-loving person and was not used to being disliked. She knew that she usually got on well with people; everyone, in fact, seemed to like her. Maybe the woman's feeling was not strong enough to be termed dislike, but it was certainly resentment and Abbie did not know why she should incur such rancour. Her latest dig had been only that afternoon . . .

'Hello, love. Getting your feet up for five minutes, are you? Can't say I blame you.' Duncan, who must have entered the house so quietly she had not heard him, interrupted her reverie, stooping to kiss her gently on the lips. 'I'll come and join you. No, don't get up. I'll get myself a cup of tea.'

Abbie swung her legs off the pouffe – really, she was getting like an old woman of seventy – and patted her hair and straightened her skirt. The last thing a husband wanted when he came home from work was a weary, woebegone wife. She put a smile on her face as he came back from the kitchen, but it came naturally to do so. She was pleased to see him and she never stopped marvelling at how happy they were together.

'How's it going then?' he asked, sitting down beside her. 'I know you must be feeling tired again.' He glanced at her discarded coat and her shoes she had kicked off which were lying on the hearthrug. His smile was one of concern. 'Have you had a hard day?'

'No, no more than usual,' she replied. 'In fact I think it's getting easier as I get more used to it. It's sure to, isn't it? I can't go on being tired for ever.'

His blue-grey eyes were regarding her anxiously. 'And how is old Ding Dong Bell today?'

Abbie felt her smile fade for a moment, but she answered quite brightly. 'Oh, you don't want to know. Let's forget about her.'

'No, tell me. I know there's something on your mind, and you always feel better when you've shared it with me. What is it now?'

Abbie knew she would, indeed, feel better when she had told Duncan about Mrs Bell's latest snide remark, and then she would let it drop and enjoy their evening. They would only be watching television, but they were very contented together. *The Man from UNCLE*, which they both enjoyed, was on tonight, and later there was what seemed like a good play on *Armchair Theatre*. 'I suppose it's nothing much really,' she began. 'Just a dig about my piano playing, that's all.'

'What! How can the woman possibly criticise that?' Duncan sounded most indignant. 'You're a very good pianist.'

'No, not the way I play,' replied Abbie. 'Though I say it myself, there's nothing wrong with that.' She knew she was a very competent pianist, although not of the standard of either her husband or her daughter. 'It's more the fact that I play at all. I know she resents Mr Knighton asking me to do it.'

'Why? What did she say?'

'Oh, the usual. Jacquie and I were sitting together in the staffroom, minding our own business, and we heard her say – we were meant to hear her, mind you – that it was all very well being able to play the piano, but it was far more important, in her opinion, to be a good class teacher. She said they were even giving Special Responsibility posts in some schools for playing the piano and she didn't agree with that at all.'

'Who was she talking to?'

'Anyone who would listen. Not that anyone takes much notice of her.'

'But you haven't got a special post for music.'

'No, of course not. How could I have? I've only just started teaching.' But Abbie knew that one of the reasons she might have been given the job at Park Gates was because of her musical ability as well as her good results at Chelford Training College. The young woman who had acted as their pianist had left quite recently and Philip Knighton had been glad to find someone who could take her place. 'It wouldn't be fair for me to have an SR post, and I don't want one either, but maybe Mrs Bell resents it because I'm too much in the limelight – you know, playing for assemblies and all that. She likes newcomers to know their place.'

Duncan burst out laughing. 'Oh dear! Women teachers can be so petty. Sorry, love, but it's true.'

'Well, let's hope I never get like that then.'

'You won't, you won't. I sometimes think they've nothing else in their lives; at least that's the impression they give. I've come across several women like that in my travels, like your Mrs Bell. Trivial little incidents are blown up out of all proportion and they can talk about nothing but school, school, school, as though there's nothing going on in the outside world. Teaching can be such an insular sort of profession. That's the main trouble with it, I think.'

'Yes, I'm just beginning to realise that,' replied Abbie. 'You get so bogged down in your own little world with your own trifling little concerns. But I think infant-school staffrooms are far worse than the juniors for being petty and narrow-minded. At least having a few men on the staff does help to lighten the atmosphere. They're usually far more free and easy in their approach than us womenfolk. They help us not to take things quite so seriously.'

Duncan was regarding her steadily. 'Do you know what I think, darling? I think we're not getting out and about enough, you and me. Ever since you started this new job we haven't been anywhere; well, only to church or to see Frank or Faith.' Frank Horsfall was Abbie's former father-in-law, with whom they were on very good terms. Her mother-in-law, Lily, had died a couple of years previously. And Faith was the second wife of Abbie's father, Dr Winters, who had died a year ago following a series of strokes. Faith, several years younger than her husband, was a very active person in her early sixties with whom Abbie had always had a close relationship.

'It's occurred to me,' Duncan went on, 'that we're in danger of getting into a rut. A real old Darby and Joan,' he added, smiling.

'But we're happy, Duncan. You know we are.'

'Of course we are, but we're still only quite young and we mustn't get set in our ways. I know you've been extra busy with your school work, and starting a new job isn't easy. But maybe you're feeling tired because you're bored.'

'But I'm not bored. How can I be?'

'Well, not exactly bored then, but in need of a change. And I've decided that's what we're going to have. There's that new film on at the Palladium, *The Sound of Music*. Everyone says how good it is.'

'Is it still running?'

'Yes, it's been on since the summer season and it's still going strong. We'll go there, and we must listen to Sandra again at the Allenbank. You heard what she was saying, didn't you, about the possibility of playing at Doreen's place at Christmas? She's spreading her wings is our Sandra, and I think she deserves a bit of encouragement. There was some talk of Doreen and Norman going to the Allenbank as well, wasn't there? Well, don't let's talk about it – let's get on and do it. Go and see Doreen, why don't you? You haven't seen her for ages.'

'No, not since she moved to Sunset View,' replied Abbie. 'It really is dreadful of me, but I don't seem to have had the time.'

'We're going to make time, you and me, for what we really want to do,' said Duncan. 'I think you'll find you're a lot less tired if you have something else to occupy your mind apart from school. It sounds as though Sandra's making quite a name for herself with her playing and singing – in a quiet way, you know. She's finding her own little niche. She's taken it a step further than I did. I only used to play the piano or organ – incidental music to a background of chatter, I sometimes thought – but Sandra's singing is making them sit up and take notice. It's something I can't do; I've never had much of a voice.'

'You have lots of other talents, dear,' said Abbie, looking at him fondly. He really was a handsome man, so very aristocratic-looking, and she did not think she was prejudiced. She had thought so the first time she had seen him, at Blackpool Musical Festival, when she had had no idea who he was. He had aged somewhat since then, the shock of Greg Matthews' death having turned his hair even more grey and increased the lines across his forehead and round his eyes. But his blue-grey eyes still glowed with the same alertness and warmth, and there was still a spring in his step, an eagerness about him that made him rebel against advancing middle age. He was right, she thought; they had been settling themselves into a comfortable little rut of far too much television and too many cosy nights by the fireside. It was what they enjoyed, but there were other pleasures in life and maybe it was time they sampled them.

'Sandra must be good, mustn't she, if Simon admitted it?' Duncan went on. 'Younger brothers are not usually so lavish with their praise.'

'If I remember rightly he wasn't exactly lavish,' Abbie smiled. 'He said she was, "OK, yeah . . . not bad", not "fab" or "wizard" or whatever else they say. But I suppose that was praise indeed, coming from Simon.'

'And that little girlfriend of his seemed quite impressed,' said Duncan. 'Nice girl, isn't she?'

'Teresa . . . yes,' replied Abbie slowly. 'I don't know that I'd call her a girlfriend, Duncan. He's only seen her a time or two, as far as I know. Anyway, he's very young; so is she . . .' But she was thinking that Teresa Jarvis was far older in her ways than Simon. An old head on young shoulders was the rather old-fashioned phrase that such as Abbie's mother might have used.

'They're too young, that's what you're thinking, isn't it?' laughed Duncan. 'I can read your mind. You're thinking about that song Jimmy Young used to sing. Don't worry about it, love. They're only a couple of kids. Simon will no doubt have lots of girlfriends before he's much older. Now, you stay just where you are, and I'll make the tea tonight. How about that?'

'Oh, Duncan, you really shouldn't. You spoil me.' All the same, Abbie did not protest too much. She knew he liked to feel he was sharing the workload with her. 'What are you thinking of making?'

'Oh, pasta and whatever else I can find. I know we've some cheese and some tinned tomatoes.'

'There's a tin of minced beef too.'

'OK then. Leave me to it. I'll see what I can conjure up.'

Abbie was still thinking about Simon and Teresa Jarvis. It had been quite a surprise when Simon had arrived home with the girl a few weeks ago. She learned that they had met at Sandra and Veronica's flat when they had both been visiting their sisters.

'We're going to my room, Mum, to play some records,' he had said. Not 'May we?' or 'Would it be all right if . . . ?' But Abbie had not embarrassed him by refusing to allow them to go to his bedroom. It would have looked as though she was accusing them of improper conduct and, as Duncan said, they were only a couple of kids. All the same, she knew Teresa a lot better than Duncan did. She had known her since she was a tiny girl, and she knew also what Doreen had said from time to time about the girl's wilfulness. Not that she wasn't perfectly polite and respectful, calling her Aunty Abbie, as she had always done, and going out of her way to be friendly. It would have been churlish of Abbie to put the damper on their no doubt innocent plans. But she hoped Simon would not start getting any silly ideas about the girl. He was in the sixth form and had excellent prospects, whereas Teresa had already left school and was working in a shop, when she was not helping her mother in the hotel.

Abbie rebuked herself now for being a snob. What did it matter if Simon was the cleverer of the two? But she suspected that Teresa's whole outlook was different from that of her son. Teresa was what you might call a 'good-time girl', whereas Simon was a hard-working studious lad ... at least she presumed he was.

They had not seen Teresa, however, for more than a week. Abbie knew the two of them had been to listen to Sandra and also, at least once, had been to the cinema; but Simon had been evasive the last time she had – casually – mentioned the girl. Maybe the friendship was already fizzling out?

Chapter 6

An Invitation

Teresa had decided that Simon Horsfall was OK as far as he went, but that was not very far. He was a friendly lad whose company she enjoyed, but he was so young in his ways. He was still at school, and who wanted to talk about school, for goodness' sake, which was what he did some of the time? Not all the time, admittedly, but the mere mention of the place bored Teresa rigid.

She guessed, from the tentative way he had behaved that first night, when they had walked home along the prom, that he was not used to the company of girls. Or, more relevantly, to the company of one girl on her own. He had, rather shyly, taken hold of her hand and then, even more hesitantly, put his arm around her when they had reached the seclusion of the middle promenade, near to the Metropole Hotel. From here up as far as Gynn Square stretched the colonnades, a favourite haunt of courting couples. If she had been with Kev he would have guided her – not unwillingly – into one of the dark corners behind the serried ranks of stone pillars; as he had done many times, until his amorous antics had become too much for her. She would not have expected such behaviour from Simon, of course, especially on their first time together, and she had to admit he would have gone down in her estimation if he had tried anything on.

He did not even try to kiss her, but she could sense him plucking up courage to ask her to go out with him.

Eventually, when they had nearly reached the Gynn, he blurted it out. 'Will you go to the pictures with me? You know, to see that film you mentioned? I thought – you know – that we could go . . . together.'

'You mean *What's New Pussy-cat?* Oh, I'd love to, Simon,' she replied, nudging him playfully. 'I thought you'd never ask.'

'Well . . . that's . . . that's great then.' She heard a relieved sigh escape from him. He had appeared to be full of confidence when they had been talking to his sister, but now he was almost at a loss for words. She decided they wouldn't get anywhere unless she helped him out.

'We were talking about going to hear your Sandra an' all, weren't we?' she said. 'D'you want to? When shall we go?'

'Dunno. Next week if you like. I think it's Fridays she performs down there. But we'll go to the pictures first. Er . . . is this Friday OK?'

'Yeah, suits me. Then you don't have to get up for school the next day!'

He looked at her sharply, obviously noting her bantering tone. 'I do go out at night, you know, and I don't have to be in by ten o'clock! And I'm not really at school – it's the sixth form college.'

'Oh, sorry! It's just that I've never been out with a sixth-former before.' She looked up at him, smiling coyly; but she could feel his slight exasperation and decided she'd better stop her teasing. 'I'm glad we've met, Simon,' she said, much more seriously. 'Honest, I am. Met properly, I mean, not just with our families. Funny, isn't it? Our mums have been friendly for yonks, but we've never really got to know one another.'

'Yeah, I'm glad too,' he replied. He smiled at her, all traces of his huffiness gone. They had reached the Gynn gardens and he took his arm away from her as they drew near her gate. 'Oh, this is where you live, is it? Sunset View, very nice. Quite posh, eh?' He shuffled his feet, looking down at the ground, not quite sure how to take his leave of her. 'Er, I'll see you on Friday then, Teresa.

126

Where shall I meet you? Outside the cinema or—'

'Don't dash away, Simon,' she said. 'You've told me you don't have to be in early. Come in and see my mum. It isn't as if you don't know her.'

'Oh, d'you think I should? Well, all right then. It'll be nice to see Aunty Doreen again. I always liked her.'

And it was obvious from her mother's reaction that she liked Simon too. She seemed surprised at first at seeing the two of them together, but she made a great fuss of him, plying him with cups of hot chocolate and her best selection of biscuits. In fact Simon and Doreen spent most of the evening chatting together, to Teresa's annoyance, and when he said he had better be going her father had insisted on running him home in the car. Her mother had left them alone for a couple of minutes, at last, and it was Teresa who had then put her arms around Simon, kissing him – though very gently – on the lips. He had seemed a little discomfited, but she decided it was because her mother was hovering in the hallway.

Since then Doreen had never shut up about how wonderful he was. She had been thrilled to bits that they were going to the pictures together and already seemed to be regarding him, if not as a future son-in-law, then certainly as a regular boyfriend for her daughter. 'He's a nice steady lad, Teresa,' she said. 'You couldn't do any better than Simon Horsfall . . . for now, I mean,' she had added. 'You're both very young, of course.'

They had enjoyed the film and Simon had been much more daring, holding her hand in the darkness of the cinema, then kissing her on the lips, quite briefly, when they said good-night at her gate. He refused her invitation that time to go in for a drink. No doubt her dad would offer to run him home again and he wanted to be independent. It would look daft, he said, as though he were a little kid, and he could easily get a bus.

Teresa had offered to pay for herself, however, at the cinema, but Simon would not hear of it. He had seemed a little piqued at the suggestion, so she had given in graciously and not argued. She was working, though, and he was not; but she knew it would not be very tactful to remind him of that.

She had been working at the newsagent's shop for more than two weeks now and, to her surprise, she was enjoying every minute of it. Mr and Mrs Ashcroft, the owners, had taken to her at once, especially as she had been recommended to them by Richard, who rented their upstairs flat. And Teresa knew how to give a good impression when she felt like so doing. It was not an act, though; she had known as soon as she went into the shop that she would like to work there. There was still something of the child in her, although she liked to think she was grown up and sophisticated.

It was often said that it was every little girl's dream to work in a sweet shop, and Teresa could feel her mouth watering the moment she set eyes on the rows of colourful jars. Pear drops, black and white humbugs, jelly babies, sherbet lemons, coconut ice, caramels, marshmallows . . . She was quite greedy about sweets and could easily demolish a quarter of jelly babies while she was watching television.

They sold other things as well: newspapers, magazines, Mills and Boon and other light romantic novels; cigarettes and tobacco; toys and fancy goods; and greeting cards and postcards. During the summer months and right up to the end of the Illuminations season, the postcards – both the scenes of Blackpool and the comic ones – were displayed on a rack on the forecourt of the shop – when fine – together with a selection of buckets and spades, fishing nets, sunhats and sunglasses. Now, as Christmas approached, they were concentrating on the festive season. It was discovered that Teresa had quite a flair for window dressing, and having admired a display of chocolate boxes she had arranged in the window and on the shelves, Mrs Ashcroft had decided to give her more of a free rein, not only with the window dressing, but with the ordering as well.

And so, as the year crept on towards December, Teresa

was finding herself more and more at home there. She remembered what a silly fuss she had made when her mother had first told her she must get a job. Of course, it was second nature to her to raise an objection to any suggestion of her mother's – she always did – but she knew now that working for the Ashcrofts was far, far preferable to slaving away at Sunset View. Her job in the shop was only on a part-time basis, the hours staggered to fit in with the requirements of both her employers and herself. But she was finding it worked to her advantage to put in an extra hour or so at the shop whenever she felt there might be an unpleasant job looming at the hotel. They were up to their eyes in decorating at the moment, and a small firm of workmen was employed in modernising the lounge and fitting a small bar. Her mother hadn't appeared to notice Teresa was skiving. Well, she wasn't, not really, she told herself. She was working jolly hard at the shop and she wondered if her mother might be turning a blind eye to her not pulling her weight at Sunset View because she, Teresa, was happy. And she knew that when she was 'sunny side out', as her mother called it, then everyone around her breathed a sigh of relief.

With Mrs Ashcroft's permission she had ordered from the commercial traveller a selection of toys and small gifts. Nothing too pricey: jigsaw puzzles; model cars by Corgi and Dinky; doll-dressing books – Teresa had loved these when she was a little girl; boxes of crayons and paints; stocking fillers rather than expensive presents. And inexpensive gifts for casual friends or such as children might buy for their relations: pottery vases; cute animal figures; photograph frames, letter racks and paper weights. All of quite a good quality, however; Teresa was learning to differentiate between quality merchandise and what she thought of as 'tat'.

It was now the first week in December and Mrs Ashcroft said that next week they would put up some trimmings and tinsel to make the shop look festive. The inviting window display and the array of chocolates on the shelves had attracted not only regular customers, but

129

also many casual passers-by. There were the old favourites: Quality Street, Black Magic, Milk Tray and Dairy Box, in fancy boxes with pretty pictures and ribbon bows, as well as a few newcomers: Macintoshes Weekend and Good News assortments, New Berry Fruits and After Eight Mints. Teresa had already reserved boxes of chocolates for her mother and her sisters: a large casket of Black Magic for Mum and Cadbury's Roses for Veronica and Bernie.

Already she was feeling excited about Christmas; it was always a fun time. She would be working, though, at the hotel, not at the shop. The thought fazed her momentarily, but she decided it might not be too bad to get back to waitressing. There were all those lovely tips and, maybe, some interesting visitors.

It was a Tuesday afternoon and Mrs Ashcroft had left her in sole charge whilst she attended to a workman at home, and Mr Ashcroft had just popped out to the wholesaler's. They would both be back before long, but it was a quiet time, the hour between one and two o'clock, and they had both assured her that they knew she would manage just fine. She felt pleased they had such confidence in her and she sang happily to herself as she straightened the display of magazines at the front of the counter.

She glanced up at the ping of the doorbell, then gave a gasp of surprise. 'Richard – what on earth are you doing here? It's Tuesday; shouldn't you be working?'

'Half-day, sweetheart.' He rolled his eyes, grinning at her. 'Yes, I know we used to close on Wednesdays, but we're staying open now 'cause it's getting near Christmas – new idea this year, so they say – so our half-days are staggered. I was hoping I might find you here . . . What's the matter? Aren't you pleased to see me?'

'Yes, yes, of course I am,' she replied, meeting his half-smile with what she hoped was a confident stare. She had hoped she might see more of her sister's boyfriend whilst she was working at the shop, but it had not worked out that way. They both, as a rule, did not work on

Wednesday afternoons, the customary half-day closing in Blackpool; and Richard left before she arrived in the morning, and arrived home at night after she had gone.

She had seen him a couple of weeks ago when she and Simon had gone to listen to Sandra at the Mountjoy Hotel, and who also should be there but Richard and Veronica. It had been evident to anyone watching them closely – as Teresa had been doing – that there was a certain edginess between her sister and her boyfriend. Veronica, in fact, had been bravely trying to control her irritation as Richard began to flirt with both Teresa and, at the interval, with Sandra. Sandra was not having any. Her own boyfriend, Ian Webster, had been there too, and it was quite clear that the two of them had eyes only for each other. But Teresa had not been averse to the odd wink and suggestive remark. And she had been tickled pink when Richard had actually asked her to dance with him. The look on Veronica's face had been like a thunder cloud, but it was only meant in fun and she had been getting a bit fed up with Simon. Maybe if he thought someone else was interested in her he would buck his ideas up. It had not worked like that, however. Simon had been decidedly cool with her afterwards and as for Veronica . . . well, Teresa had steered clear of her from that day to this. They were not right for one another, though, Veronica and Richard, and she hoped her sister was beginning to realise it.

And now here was Richard, looking her up and down appraisingly with that half-amused, half-suggestive glint in his eyes. She had planned how she would behave if she ever came face to face with him on their own. She would be bold, she had decided, and suave; she would let him see she was not just a kid, a silly teenager. But in the face of his tantalising smile she found, to her annoyance, that she was blushing. She looked away hastily, her hands moving once more to the task of straightening the books.

'All on your own, I see?' Richard observed.

'Er . . . yes. Mr and Mrs Ashcroft won't be long, either of them, and we're quiet at the moment.'

'So I see. What time do you finish?'

'Three o'clock or thereabouts. I only work part time, you know.'

'Which is lucky for me or I might never see you. What do you say, Teresa?'

She didn't say anything; she just grinned foolishly at him.

'How about coming up to my flat when you've finished here? For a cup of tea or . . . whatever you like. How does that sound?'

'It sounds . . . very nice,' she said. Then, more boldly: 'Yes, Richard. I'll look forward to that.'

'That's good then; that's very good.' He started to laugh, although she couldn't see there was anything all that amusing. 'And may I say how very charming you look in your pink overall. Very demure. Yes, it's very "you". Or is it? I wonder . . .' He narrowed his eyes, looking at her speculatively. 'See you soon then, sweetheart. I'd better go. You've got a customer, see.'

He went out through the door to the stockroom. There was a staircase there that led to the upstairs flat. There was also a separate entrance at the back, which made the flat self-contained, but she knew he had come in through the shop in order to see her and to arrange a meeting. Did he really like her, she wondered – or fancy her, which was more to the point? Or was it just a spur-of-the-moment thing to invite her up for a cup of tea? Was that all it would involve – a cup of tea? And should she tell Mrs Ashcroft where she was going? It would seem sneaky to go out of the shop door and then round to the back entrance to the flat. After all, why shouldn't she go and see Richard? He was her sister's boyfriend and there was no harm in going to his flat for a casual visit.

Her mind was in a turmoil as she served her customer, and as three o'clock drew near she started to feel more and more bewildered. And that, indeed, was a very unusual state of affairs for the normally happy-go-lucky Teresa.

Chapter 7

Richard

Veronica knew that Richard was cooling off. She had not admitted this to anyone else, not even to Sandra, to whom she confided most of her secrets. In fact she was only just beginning to admit it to herself. What was wrong with her that she could never keep a boyfriend for more than a couple of months? And what would her friends and family think of her, knowing this to be the case? Veronica was always very conscious of what other people were thinking.

It was for this reason she decided she would make an all-out effort to keep this friendship going until after the Christmas period. Christmas was such an awful time to be on your own and she did not want anyone feeling sorry for her. She made up her mind she would laugh and joke and be vivacious, all the attributes Richard seemed to admire in the opposite sex, and she would try her hardest not to be jealous or possessive. She would show him what a lot of fun she could be, and then, perhaps, she would be able to keep him all to herself . . . that was, for as long as she wanted him.

Because Veronica knew, deep down, that she too was cooling off, but she wanted to be the one who finished the relationship this time. It was so humiliating to be ditched, and this had happened to her twice already, three times if she counted Dominic. Or, maybe, if she managed to rekindle Richard's interest in her she might find she was still in love with him.

They had got on so amazingly well at first. They enjoyed the same films and music and had spent several evenings ten-pin bowling at the new Top Rank Mecca building. When and why had it all started to go wrong, she wondered. She knew the answer only too well, though, if she were honest. Veronica was still set on 'saving herself' for marriage, whereas Richard . . . well, it seemed as though he was turning out to be just like his predecessor, Justin, interested in only one thing. They had, inevitably, spent quite a lot of time alone together, either in her own flat, on the evenings that Sandra was out, or at Richard's place over the shop on Dickson Road. She had to admit that she enjoyed his lovemaking – or partial lovemaking, because she had allowed him to go so far and no further. When he had suggested, as he had done a couple of times, that they should adjourn to the bedroom her answer had been a definite no. The last time she had refused his advances he had sulked a little, but had managed to laugh it off and they had parted that evening on reasonably good terms.

The next time they had met had been at the Mountjoy Hotel. Veronica had been insisting for a while that they must go and listen to Sandra, and who should be there, also, but Teresa, with Simon Horsfall. Veronica had been delighted when she found out that the two youngsters were going out together. Simon was such a nice steady lad and he would be a good influence on her sister. Sandra, however, had seemed doubtful about the friendship.

Not without cause, because it was clear as the evening progressed that Teresa was not content to have just one young man in attendance: she was determined that the other males in the party should notice her as well. She didn't get anywhere with Ian Webster, nor did she really try very hard. It was obvious that he and Sandra were very much a twosome now. It was Richard on whom the little minx had set her sights, although, to be fair to the girl, it was his doing just as much as hers, if not more so. Veronica had known why he was doing it, of course – openly flirting first with Sandra, with whom he got absolutely nowhere, and then with her sister. It was because of her, Veronica's, refusal to let him have all his own way with her.

She felt herself getting crosser and crosser, and humiliated too, as the evening went on. Everyone must have noticed he was making a fool of her, but she tried not to let her hurt and anger show. Whilst Richard was dancing with Teresa, and Ian with Sandra, on the postage stamp of a dance floor, she had gone across to sit with Simon, who was looking very down in the dumps.

'Don't worry about Teresa,' she said as they both watched the girl grinning up at Richard, whilst his hand strayed far too near her neat little bottom. 'It's just the way she is. I don't think she can help it. She's always been like that. Anything in trousers . . .' She gave what she hoped was an unconcerned laugh, then, at the stricken look on Simon's face, she went on to say, 'Oh, sorry. I didn't mean to suggest that was why she's going out with you. She really likes you. I know she does – she said so.' It was a white lie, but what did it matter? 'And I'm ever so pleased you've got friendly with her, Simon. Nice, isn't it, that you've got together at last when our families have known one another for so long?'

'Yeah, I thought so at first,' replied Simon, 'but I didn't really know what she was like. Don't you mind?' He nodded in the direction of the couple who were giggling together, although Richard's hand was now placed more decorously on her waist.

'No, course I don't,' said Veronica, although she was feeling all hurt and sick inside. 'I know Richard, you see, and I know that what we've got . . . well, we would never let something as trivial as that come between us. He's just having a bit of fun, that's all. Why haven't you asked Teresa to dance?'

''Cause I can't dance, that's why. I've never learned.'

'You've been to youth club, surely? They have dances there, don't they?'

'Yeah, but it wasn't much in my line. I was more interested in table tennis and snooker and darts. I can't dance properly, only jig around a bit. Seems as though there's a lot of things Teresa can do and I can't.' He sounded very fed up.

'Rubbish!' said Veronica. 'She's lucky to have met a nice clever lad like you. That's not proper dancing anyway.' She motioned towards the couples on the dance floor. 'They're only shuffling around to the music; they're not even keeping in time to it.' That was true of all the couples – only six of them on the small dance floor. It was supposed to be a slow foxtrot, but it was just an excuse for most of them to do a bit of smooching. To be fair, Teresa and Richard were not kissing and messing about, just giggling and appearing to enjoy one another's company. No doubt Richard was wondering just how far he'd dare to go before she, Veronica, exploded with rage; and as for Teresa, the naughty little madam, surely she must have some qualms about flirting with her sister's boyfriend?

'Take her on for a dance yourself when they come back,' Veronica said. 'You can do as well as that lot.' She fully intended to make Richard dance with her again. They had shared one dance, but it had been a sort of rock and roll where they didn't touch one another.

'I might,' said Simon. But, as it happened, they were both disappointed. That was the end of the dancing session and it was time for Sandra's next spot.

Veronica could not help feeling a slight pang of envy as she watched Ian kiss Sandra, not passionately, but so very tenderly, on the side of her mouth and squeeze her hand as she took leave of him to go back to the piano. Richard and Teresa returned, sitting down again with the partners with whom they were supposed to be spending the evening. It had been taken for granted when Veronica and Richard had arrived at the hotel that they should sit with the younger couple. It would have been discourteous not to do so. It was quite a coincidence that they were there as well, but not a very happy one. The evening was turning out to be such a disappointment. Veronica felt as though she could have strangled her sister. She was sitting there now as though butter wouldn't melt in her mouth, opening her big blue eyes wide and smiling coyly at Simon. It looked as though she were trying to make up to him again, but Veronica guessed she might have a tough job on her hands.

Sandra was well into a piano medley of Beatles hits to which some people were singing quietly along, or half listening whilst they chatted with their friends. Veronica turned to Richard, who had had the cheek to put his arm around her as though there was nothing amiss.

'What d'you think you're playing at with my sister?' she hissed. 'Just watch what you're doing. She's only sixteen, you know.'

'Oh, I know perfectly well how old she is. Plenty old enough, I'd say,' he added, with a tantalising smile. 'What's up? Are you jealous?' He glanced across at Teresa, but she was not looking in his direction. Simon was, however, and he narrowed his eyes, giving his rival a look that could kill. Veronica felt like hitting Richard, but she clenched her fists into tight balls and tried to answer in a casual voice.

'Course I'm not jealous – don't be silly. But she's only a kid and she's rather impressionable; easily led, you know.' In truth, Teresa was nothing of the sort and Veronica knew it; the girl was quite capable of doing the leading herself. 'You don't want to egg her on and then find you've got in so deep that you can't get rid of her. I know it's only a bit of fun, but she might not realise that.'

'Don't worry, my pet, I can handle it. As you say, it's only a bit of fun. I know she's a girl who likes a laugh, and that's all it is.' He nuzzled at her ear. 'She's only a kid,' he whispered, 'and you know I go for older women.' He paused, then continued, more pointedly, 'I don't like them too old though, nor too old-fashioned either. You'd better watch out, darling, or you'll be turning into a nag.'

He behaved casually towards Teresa for the rest of the evening. She and Simon appeared to be friends again – at least they were holding hands – but they were not talking very much. They departed with Ian and Sandra when the evening came to an end. Ian had offered them both a lift home in his car. It was out of his way, but he was a friendly, helpful young man, ready to do anyone a good turn.

Richard kissed her good night as she got out of the car, and Veronica almost convinced herself that everything was back to normal. She tried to convince herself, too – as she had insisted to Richard – that Teresa was only a kid. Besides, this was her sister, and surely not even Teresa would stoop so low as to pinch her sister's boyfriend.

Teresa was decidedly peeved. What did Richard think he was playing at? She had worked herself up into a right old state that afternoon he had invited her to his flat. And then, what had happened? Nothing at all. Well, practically nothing.

He had made a cup of tea and they had sat on the settee drinking it and eating chocolate biscuits. He had asked her if she was enjoying her work at the shop and she had said yes, it was wizard, and she was ever so pleased he had put in a good word for her with Mr and Mrs Ashcroft. He had laughed easily and said, 'Anything to oblige, sweetheart.' Richard was always laughing in that half-teasing manner. She didn't know whether he found her amusing or just thought of her as a kid or . . . what.

He had put a Bob Dylan record on his up-to-the-minute stereogram; a recent acquisition, he told her – with the usual staff discount, of course – from R. H. O. Hill's, where he was in charge of the furniture department.

'Your sister doesn't care for Dylan,' he said. 'She doesn't understand him. He's a bit too deep, too . . . Bohemian for someone with her ladylike tastes. She likes the Beatles. She says they seem like nice lads now we're getting more used to them.' He laughed again. 'What about you, Teresa? What turns you on, eh? Are you a Beatles fan?'

She agreed that she was, very much so, and that she

liked the Rolling Stones too; another group that she knew her sister found too loud and 'different'. If Teresa were honest she didn't understand Bob Dylan's songs either, but she tried to look as though she were listening intelligently, nodding her head in time to the music as he sang about the times a-changin', and homesick blues.

'It seems as though we have a lot in common, you and me, Teresa,' Richard remarked with a sideways glance at her.

'Oh, and what might that be?' she asked pertly.

'Well, our taste in music, for one thing . . . and who knows what else there might be?' He turned then and looked straight at her. 'But don't tell your sister.'

'There's nothing to tell her, is there?' she retorted. 'We're only sitting here and listening to a record. What's wrong with that?'

'Why, what else do you want to do?'

'Nothing.' She began to feel a little uneasy then, but excited too, as he put his arm around her.

'Nothing?' he repeated. 'Are you sure?'

'Well . . . not really sure.'

'How about this then?' He put both arms around her, then brought his lips down to hers. He kissed her just once, but very slowly and deeply. It was a kiss that left her gasping and desperately wanting more, but she knew, at the back of her mind, that it was a kiss that was more calculating than passionate.

'You're a great girl, Teresa,' he said as he drew away from her. 'Now, don't you think it's time you popped off home? It's beginning to get dark and your mother will be wondering what's happened to you.'

'She won't bother. She doesn't know what time I finish work today.'

'All the same, it might be best, eh?' He winked at her. 'Perhaps we could do this again sometime. It's been fun, hasn't it?'

'Yeah . . . great,' she replied, feeling suddenly deflated.

'Cheerio then, Teresa. Be seeing you.'

'Yeah . . . See you, Richard.'

She went out of the flat the back way. He did not kiss her again, nor did he offer to drive her home as she had thought he might do. On the other hand, she tried to tell herself that that might not have been a very good idea. Supposing her mother had seen them and told Veronica? Besides, Richard did not use his car for work; it was becoming impossible to park in Blackpool town centre and it was easier for him to walk. She could hardly expect him to fetch his car from his parking spot in a nearby side street just to run her home, could she? It would have been a kind gesture, though – 'gentlemanly', as Veronica might say – if he had done so. But Teresa was beginning to suspect that Richard Hargreaves was, alas, no gentleman.

Dickson Road was quite busy with late afternoon shoppers hurrying home for their tea. Teresa was not worried by the darkness, or twilight as it was at that moment. The lights from the shops and the streetlamps shone out cheeringly and she was used to the mile or so walk to Sunset View at any time of day.

Nevertheless, she felt very disillusioned as she strode along through the gathering darkness. Richard had said it would be fun to 'do it again', whatever that meant, but he had not suggested when that might be. Moreover, he had seemed almost glad to see the back of her, hurrying her out of the flat like that. She was hurt that he had shown no concern about her long walk home alone. She was a big girl and could look after herself, but that was not the point. He wouldn't have let Veronica walk home on her own; but Veronica, of course, was his proper girlfriend, or was supposed to be.

Her sister and Richard were not right for one another, though, Teresa argued with herself. Surely Veronica must have realised this by now. Richard needed someone more carefree and jolly, someone less inhibited, a girl, in fact, very much like herself.

She wondered if Richard, also, had the same idea, that she, Teresa, was much more fun than Veronica? If that was the case then he really ought to finish with one sister before starting to see the other one. Maybe that was why he had kissed her and then, so suddenly, had seemed to change his mind. Or maybe he was trying to make her keener and more willing by pretending to hold back. Oh, what a puzzle it all was! She wished she could see into his mind.

Deep down, though, she guessed that, if she could do so, she might not like what she saw there. Whichever way she looked at it she was forced to admit that Richard Hargreaves, no matter how attractive he might be, was a dreadful flirt. And maybe Veronica, eventually, might come to the same conclusion.

As for Veronica . . . To Teresa's credit, her feeling of remorse was getting the upper hand now as she realised she had not set eyes on her sister since that night at the Mountjoy Hotel. She had been avoiding her, and Teresa knew that this was because she was the teeniest bit ashamed of the way she had flirted with Richard. She made up her mind there and then that she must go to see her again very soon. If she didn't, it would look as though she had something to hide; which, of course, she hadn't. She and Richard had only had a cup of tea and listened to a record. As for that kiss . . . Teresa decided she must try to push all thoughts of it to the back of her mind.

Veronica was a little cool with her at first when she went round to the flat later that week. That was only to be expected, but Teresa had decided she would behave quite normally, just as though nothing had happened. She had been on pins in case Richard should be there, but Veronica told her as soon as she arrived that she was on her own that evening. It was her night for washing her hair, and Sandra was out, visiting her mother and Duncan.

Veronica's head, bulging with large-size rollers, was wrapped in a colourful turban and she was wearing a frilly apron. 'I've just finished washing up,' she said, 'and I was going to start making some shortbread biscuits. Richard loves them,' she added, with a meaningful look at Teresa, 'but it'll have to wait now you're here.'

Quite the picture of cosy domesticity, Teresa reflected, but she decided it might be best not to make a snide comment as she would normally have done. She was not altogether sure of her welcome; but she could not help thinking, yet again, that a homely little 'wifey' figure might not fit into Richard's scheme of things; not yet awhile at any rate. Was Veronica living in cloud-cuckoo-land, she wondered, or was she trying to hang on to something which had, in truth, run its course?

'Anyway, you'd better come in and sit down – that is, if you're staying. Or are you on your way somewhere else?'

'No, I just thought I'd come and see you. I've missed you both times when you called to see Mum and Dad.' That had been Teresa's intention, of course. She had felt she couldn't face her sister and had made sure she was out when she knew that Veronica was coming round.

'Yes, so I noticed,' said Veronica, giving her a knowing look. 'And what brings you here now?'

'Nothing much. I just thought it was a long time since we'd had a chat. So . . . here I am,' she finished brightly.

'Mm, so I see.' Veronica was still regarding her suspiciously, but after a few seconds Teresa was relieved to see her sister's eyes soften and a hint of a smile curve her lips. 'OK then, Tessie, sit yerself down and I'll make us a cuppa. Take your coat off – just sling it over the chair – or you won't feel the benefit when you go out.'

Teresa breathed a sigh of relief. Veronica seemed to be back in her 'looking after the little sister' mood, something that irritated her at times, but which she was glad of now. Her use of her childhood name – hardly anyone called her Tess or Tessie nowadays – showed that Veronica was not, after all, too annoyed with her.

'That's nice. New, is it?' asked Veronica, coming back with the tea tray. She nodded towards Teresa's bright yellow mini-length raincoat, which was hanging over the chair arm. 'Shouldn't imagine it's very warm, though, is it? What's it made of – plastic?'

'Yeah, sort of,' said Teresa. 'I'm not bothered about it being warm – I've got me big sweater on underneath, see

– but it looks good, doesn't it? I got it last week from Paige's. It wasn't all that expensive. I've got a bit more money to spend now, y'see. I love it at the shop,' she added a little tentatively. 'It's dead good, and Mr and Mrs Ashcroft are ever so nice.'

'Er, yes, I'm glad you've settled down there,' said Veronica, just as cautiously. 'Richard said they were very pleased with you. Good for you, Tess.'

Teresa breathed again. His name had been mentioned without, it appeared, any embarrassment or rancour. 'Yes, it was really because of Richard that I got the job. Will you tell him I'm ever so pleased? You're still seeing him, are you?'

'Of course I am.' Veronica looked at her steadily. 'Why shouldn't I be?'

'No reason . . . I didn't mean . . .' Teresa was trying not to sound flustered.

'Haven't you told him yourself how pleased you are? He said he'd seen you in the shop.'

'Yes, I did see him. And I've said thank you, course I have. But . . . Veronica . . .'

'What?' Her sister looked at her sharply.

'I just wanted to say I'm sorry, for that time at the hotel – you know – when I was dancing with him and . . . and chatting him up a bit. I didn't mean anything. It was dead mean of me. And – well – I'm sorry.' Teresa was surprising even herself by her confession, which had been a spur-of-the-moment thing, brought about partly by guilt and partly because of her affection for her sister; Veronica was certainly the best of the bunch. She didn't intend confessing to everything, however.

'It takes two,' Veronica replied easily. 'And Richard's a terrible tease; I know that. He was just playing a game with both of us. I was annoyed at the time, but,' she smiled a little smugly, 'what Richard and I have going . . . well, it won't be hurt by a bit of flirting. It's all right, Teresa; you're forgiven.'

Teresa swallowed hard. 'It's . . . it's still going strong then?'

'Not half,' Veronica grinned. 'We went to the pictures last night, to see *West Side Story*. Have you seen it?' Teresa shook her head.

'It's good – you'd enjoy it; lots of catchy songs. Get Simon to take you; it's on for two weeks. And next Tuesday we're going Christmas shopping, Richard and me. We've got the same half-day, so we thought we'd get some lunch in town and then go round the shops.'

'Bit of a busman's holiday, isn't it?'

'Yes, I suppose so, but I haven't done any Christmas shopping at all yet, and Richard wants me to help him choose presents for his parents and sister. Honestly! Men are hopeless, aren't they?'

'Will Richard be coming to our place for Christmas Day?'

'Don't know.' Veronica gave a slight shrug. 'We haven't talked about it yet. We'll be lucky if we get any dinner at all at Sunset View. Mum's got twelve guests coming for Christmas, hasn't she? How's it going? Is the decorating nearly finished?'

Teresa told her it was all going along very nicely. There had been panic stations a few days ago when the decorator had run out of paper for the lounge, but he had managed to find some more; and now all was, hopefully, on schedule again for the opening of the restyled Sunset View in just over two weeks.

The sisters were the best of friends again by the time Teresa left. She had answered evasively the questions about Simon. He was still rather cool with her, but she was determined to make it up with him, for the time being at any rate. She didn't want to be without a boyfriend at Christmas and, if Veronica was to be believed, it was still very much on between her and Richard. Teresa felt a stab of pique which was partly hurt pride, partly remorse and partly righteous indignation. If Richard Hargreaves tried anything again she'd tell him where to get off!

Simon didn't want to know when she phoned him a day or two later to suggest they should go and see *West Side*

Story the following week. He was busy, he said. It was his mum's Christmas concert at school and she'd asked him if he'd go and help with the scene shifting. He couldn't let her down. Teresa had slammed the phone down in annoyance. What a lame excuse! Well, see if she cared! There were much better fish in the sea than ever came out of it; far bigger and better than Simon Horsfall.

She felt cross all weekend, mooching around miserably at home until her mother set her to work sorting out Christmas decorations and washing crockery and glasses in readiness for the opening of the hotel. Strangely enough, she didn't mind, especially as Bernie was helping too, and had offered to do the far more tedious job of wiping the pots. Well, she hadn't exactly offered; Teresa had plunged her own hands into the soapy water straight away, giving her sister no choice in the matter.

She was still a trifle peeved on Tuesday, a day on which it had been arranged she should leave the shop at lunch time and have the afternoon free, especially when she envisaged Veronica and Richard playing at being a happy couple, doing their Christmas shopping. She stayed later than she needed to have done, as some very choosy customers came in just before one o'clock. They took ages to decide between the various boxes of chocolates, and then the toys and books and knick-knacks on display. Teresa didn't mind because she knew they would buy a lot of items in the end; and Mrs Ashcroft was watching her approvingly, not offering to take over, though, as she knew it was her assistant's sale. It was half-past one before they left and then there were all the goods to put back in their right places.

'Leave that, Teresa love,' said Mrs Ashcroft. 'Off you go home. You're very late already.'

'No, it's OK,' replied the girl. 'I don't mind, honest.' She had nowhere to go, anyway, and her mother would only find her a job if she went back to Sunset View. She was feeling happier now. She enjoyed serving and trying to please the customers. It brought out the best in her, especially in this cosy, friendly shop, now tastefully decorated with tinsel and streamers and images of Santa Claus and snowmen. 'I'll just put these back, then I'll go.'

'Very well, if you insist. You're a good girl, Teresa. I tell you what – come in an hour later tomorrow. We're not usually very busy after the early morning rush, and Jack and I can manage. Have a bit of a lie-in, eh?'

'OK – thanks.' Teresa grinned.

'I'm just going through to the back to put the kettle on. We might as well have a cup of tea while you're still here.' Mrs Ashcroft disappeared into the stockroom and Teresa carried on arranging the shelves. She glanced up a few moments later at the sound of the doorbell. She gave a gasp of astonishment.

'Richard! What are you doing here?' She remembered having said the self-same thing before, a week ago. 'It's Tuesday. Veronica said you were going shopping. It's your half-day and hers . . .' Her voice petered out as she noticed his quirky grin and the gleam of devilment in his eyes.

'Quite right, sweetheart; so we were. It still is my half-day. But not your sister's, unfortunately. Some mix-up at Marks and Sparks. One of the girls had an urgent appointment and there was no one else who could change. I only found out an hour ago when Veronica rang me. So I decided to come straight home.'

'What about your Christmas shopping?'

'Oh, it'll get done some other time. I can't be bothered today. It's, er, it's not your half-day, by any chance? No, it can't be, or else you'd have gone.'

'As a matter of fact, it is. I was supposed to finish early, but I got tied up with some customers. I'm just going to have a cup of tea with Mrs Ashcroft, and then I'm going home.' She spoke decisively, but Richard continued to stand there grinning at her.

'Come and have one with me instead. I'm going to make some lunch as well. Beans on toast, perhaps. Why don't you join me?'

'No! No, thank you very much for the offer,' she said,

with what she hoped sounded like polite sarcasm. 'I'm going home – I've told you – in a few minutes. So you don't need to start—' She stopped speaking abruptly as Mrs Ashcroft came back with a laden tray.

'Oh, hello there, Richard,' she said. 'I thought it was your voice I could hear. Teresa and I were just going to have a cup of tea. Will you join us?'

'I'd love to, Mrs Ashcroft.' He smiled disarmingly. Richard was Prince Charming personified when he chose to be, and Teresa guessed this was the only side of his personality that his landlady had seen. 'As a matter of fact, I was trying to persuade this young lady to come and have lunch with me, but she seems reluctant. I can't imagine why. If I'm making beans on toast for one, then I might as well make it for two.'

'Oh, Teresa's a good girl, that's why,' said Mrs Ashcroft. 'She's probably worried about what her sister might say, with you being her young man an' all that.' She turned to Teresa. 'Your Veronica would be only too pleased that Richard's looking after you. She's a lovely young woman, your sister, and they make such a nice couple.' She beamed fondly. Mrs Ashcroft was the sort of person who saw the best in everyone. 'Off you go with Richard, dear, when you've drunk your tea. You must be as hungry as a hunter after all that hard work. She's worked like a Trojan this morning, Richard.'

Teresa decided she had no choice but to go along with the plans they were making. She smiled weakly. 'OK then . . . Thanks, Richard.'

'She's quite right, you know,' Richard said when they had adjourned to the flat above. 'Your sister wouldn't mind; at least she wouldn't mind me making you some lunch. But the point is, she won't know, will she? We're not going to tell her. And what the eye doesn't see—'

'But Mrs Ashcroft might tell her I was here.'

'Why should she? There's nothing to tell. Anyway, Mrs A. doesn't see her all that often. She's not here in the evening, is she?' Mr and Mrs Ashcroft had a nice detached bungalow on Warley Road, not too near, but

147

not too far away from the shop. 'Sit down and make yourself comfy and I'll get on with making the toast. Beans, I said, didn't I? Or would you prefer spaghetti?'

'No . . . no thanks – beans'll be fine.'

'Take off your overall, then you'll look as though you're staying a while. You will, won't you?'

'Just until I've eaten my lunch, that's all.' Teresa glanced at him warily as she took off her pink nylon overall, then tossed that and her shoulder bag over the back of the settee. She sat down, perching a little uncomfortably on the edge.

'Relax, sweetheart,' said Richard. 'You're all tensed up and I'm sure I don't know why. You've got a half-day and so have I. Why shouldn't we spend it together? We enjoy one another's company. We'll have a bite to eat, then we'll listen to some records and . . . well, we'll see how it goes, shall we?'

'Oh, I don't know about that. I told you, I'm going home as soon as—'

Richard sat down on the settee next to her and put his arm round her shoulders. He leaned back, causing her to do the same.

'And I've told you that what the eye doesn't see . . . I think you're a great girl, Teresa, and if I'd met you before I met Veronica, then who knows what might have happened?'

'Don't say that! You mustn't!' She put her hands against his chest and pushed at him, but he was holding her firmly. When he brought his lips down to hers she found she couldn't struggle any more. He was much bigger and stronger than she was; besides, it would be very undignified and childish to try to fight him off. What harm was there in a kiss anyway?

Or two or three kisses . . . Teresa soon realised that whereas Simon was an inexperienced boy who needed a helping hand and maybe a bit of a push – although they hadn't gone any further than kissing – Richard was a man who knew exactly what he was doing and had been here many times before. With her sister, moreover . . . But that no longer seemed to matter as his hands stole beneath her sweater, fondling her breasts in an experimental way before starting to unhook the waistband of her skirt. She put a hand over his at that point. No, she couldn't; she mustn't; she hadn't intended it to go so far. But Richard was kissing her more fervently now and she knew she must wait until he, momentarily, released her. Then she would tell him no – that was enough. If he intended finishing with her sister, however, it might be different . . .

They were both brought up short in their thoughts and their actions by the sound of footsteps coming up the stairs, then a voice. 'Hello, Richard. Surprise, surprise, eh? It's me. I managed to get away.' Veronica! They stared at one another in horror.

'Be with you in a minute,' she was saying. 'I'm just going to your loo . . .' Which was in the cubbyhole of a bathroom at the top of the stairs.

'Quick! Get into the bedroom,' Richard whispered, almost manhandling her off the settee and through the bedroom door, which opened off the living room.

'But why? There's no point. She'll know anyway. She'll have seen Mrs Ashcroft. And how will I get out?'

'Shut up and do as you're told.' Richard closed the door behind her, only just in time because a few seconds later she heard Veronica's voice again as she entered the living room.

'That's better. I was dying to go. I dashed straight here as soon as I could. Lisa got someone else to change with her at the last minute, you see. I know it's too late now to go back to town to do the shopping, but I thought . . .'

Teresa was listening in fear and panic. She had realised, too late, that she had left her shoulder bag and overall on the settee – unless, of course, Richard had managed to hide them under the cushion or something. It was all his fault for pushing her out of the way so hurriedly. She should have stayed and brazened it out; and he didn't need to have been so rough.

'Have you seen Mrs Ashcroft?' she heard Richard ask. 'Is she . . . is she still in the shop?'

'Mrs Ashcroft? No – why d'you want to know? Mr Ashcroft's there now. Richard, what's the matter with you? Why are you just standing there? Why don't you come and—' There was a pause, then Teresa heard Veronica's voice again, shriller and several decibels louder. 'What's that doing there, that overall? It's Teresa's, isn't it? And . . . and her bag. What the hell's going on? Where is she?'

'Wait a minute, Veronica. Just listen, darling. I can explain—'

'Don't you darling me, Richard Hargreaves! I might have known. She's in here, isn't she?' Veronica flung open the bedroom door, lunging herself forward at her sister, her arm upraised. 'Yes, just as I thought! You little trollop! You sneaky little minx—'

'Stop it, Veronica.' Richard got hold of her from behind before she could strike out at her sister. She tried to free herself from his grasp, but, as Teresa had realised a few moments earlier, he was too strong for her. Teresa felt benumbed and, for the moment, speechless. She was sorry too, as she noticed the tears forming in Veronica's blue eyes.

'How could you?' her sister breathed. 'How could you do this to me?'

Richard winked at Teresa from behind Veronica's back. 'Listen, love, you've got it all wrong. Don't you think you might be jumping to conclusions? Honestly, you are. You tell her, Teresa.'

'Yes, he's right, Veronica.' Teresa managed to find a small voice, of sorts. 'There's nothing . . . going on, honest. It's my half-day and Richard said he'd make me some lunch . . . while he's having his own, see.'

'And I'd just gone into the kitchen to make a start when we heard you coming,' Richard went on. 'And I suppose – well, I thought it might be better if—'

'We panicked,' said Teresa. 'That's what we did. Honest truth, there's nothing going on, but I suppose we thought you . . . you might be mad.'

'Why should I be,' Veronica looked at her sister keenly,

'if there's nothing "going on"?'

'Because . . . because that's what you're like, isn't it?' Teresa persisted. 'You get all upset. You know you do. Like that time when we went to listen to Sandra—'

'And I happened to have a dance with your young sister,' Richard continued, smiling at her so very reasonably. 'That's all it was; a dance and a bit of a laugh together. I told you so at the time and I thought you believed me. Good gracious, darling! This is your sister. Do you honestly believe that she would . . . ? Or that I would . . . ?'

He's a plausible devil, I'll say that for him, thought Teresa, relieved to see that Veronica was now looking doubtful; not completely convinced, but not so blazing mad.

'Of course we wouldn't,' said Teresa in a small voice. 'Come on, Veron – you know that's just silly.'

'Is it? Then why were you hiding?'

'Richard's told you, and so have I. We got in a panic. Anyway, I'm going home now. I'll leave you two to enjoy your half-day.'

'Oh, come on, there's no need for that,' said Richard. 'Is there, Veronica?' He turned and smiled at her so beguilingly. 'Teresa's welcome to stay and have lunch with us, isn't she? It'll be beans on toast for three now.' How could he appear so calm, Teresa wondered, and so credible?

'No, thank you.' She shook her head. 'I'd rather not. Er . . . see you soon, Veronica?' she asked tentatively.

'Perhaps, but I don't know when,' Veronica replied in a quiet voice. There was still that look of doubt, almost of distrust, in her eyes.

'Cheerio, then.' Teresa dashed out of the bedroom, where they were all still standing, grabbed her overall and bag and made off down the stairs to the shop.

Whew! That was a narrow escape! But one thing was certain, she told herself as she strode purposefully along, scarcely aware of the fine rain and the chilly wind stinging her cheeks and tangling her hair: she would never, never again have anything to do with Richard Hargreaves. She was angry with herself, and a little ashamed too of what had happened, although it had not been her fault, not her fault at all. It was him, that Richard; he was so glib, so persuasive. How could she have believed that he was really interested in her, Teresa, when, no doubt, all he was doing was playing some devious game, just to amuse himself. It was her opinion that Veronica would be well rid of him, but her sister was so gullible, willing to give even the most unreliable characters the benefit of the doubt.

She was realising now that the sudden appearance of her sister, although it had been very embarrassing, had saved her bacon. Richard had become too much for her to handle and she had been getting into a situation for which she knew she was not ready. She should never have let him kiss her in the first place. Goodness knows what might have happened if Veronica had not arrived on the scene just when she did. She, Teresa, might have done something she would regret for ever. She had little doubt that Richard might have forced her; he had seemed very strong and determined. And her sister's boyfriend, of all people! She was feeling very ashamed now; ashamed but at the same time very relieved. What about Veronica, though?

She felt herself quaking a little at the thought of meeting her sister again. Veronica had been so angry. Teresa had never seen her in such a frenzy, and even when they had told her there was nothing untoward going on – what else could they have done but lie? – she had still looked at her coolly and with a good deal of mistrust. It might well be Christmas before she came face to face with her again. And would Richard still be with her? Teresa certainly hoped not, and that was no longer because she wanted him for herself. As far as she was concerned Richard Hargreaves could go and jump in the sea.

She found her thoughts drifting towards Simon. She was sorry now that she had fallen out with him. She was realising, belatedly, what a decent sort of lad he was, in spite of his being rather young; a much better person in every way than Richard Hargreaves. She knew she would far rather be with Simon than with Richard. Christmas was coming and she would very much like to see him again, but she feared she may have messed things up there. It was worth a try, though. Surely he could not go on being evasive and making excuses that he was 'too busy'. Maybe she would go round and see him; that would be better than a phone call and there was no reason why she should not do so. Their families had been friendly for ages, especially her mum and Simon's mum. She liked Aunty Abbie very much. She was old-fashioned, of course – even more so than her own mother – but what could you expect when they were both well into their forties?

'Honestly, Veronica, it was nothing. Why can't you believe me?' Richard was still waving his arms about and protesting wildly – too much, Veronica thought – after Teresa had gone.

'So you keep saying. Then why was she hiding?'

'We've told you, both of us. We panicked. We know what you're like, you see.'

'Oh, and what am I like? Jealous and suspicious? Possessive?'

'You said it, not me. All right then, if the cap fits.' Richard's eyes narrowed and the tone of his voice changed. 'As a matter of fact, Veronica, that's just what you are like. I told you a while back you were in danger of turning into a nag, and that's all you do. Nag, nag, nag, the whole of the time. I can't even speak to another girl without you putting on that damned martyred expression, and as for you flying off the handle like that at your sister . . . Poor Teresa!'

'Poor Teresa my foot! She's a crafty scheming little minx.'

'She was tired and hungry. The poor kid had been rushed off her feet all morning and I was making her some lunch.'

'Oh really? My heart bleeds for her, I'm sure.'

'Oh, what's the use? If you don't believe me then that's that, isn't it?' He looked at her coldly. 'You'd better go.'

'Don't worry – I am going. Right now. And I won't be coming back. And you don't need to come chasing after me either—'

'Huh! There's no chance of that. You're not only a nag, you're frigid as well.' His last remark hurt, but she went on as though she hadn't heard it.

'Because I never want to set eyes on you again, as long as I live.'

'Then that makes two of us!'

Veronica slammed the door and dashed down the stairs. She went out the back way as she didn't want to encounter either Mr or Mrs Ashcroft in the shop. She found she was trembling as she stood in the backyard at the rear of the premises. She hadn't meant to say all that; she certainly hadn't meant to lose her temper. Her fists were tightly clenched and her breath was escaping in short gasps, whilst tears, more of anger than of hurt, welled up in her eyes. After a few moments she pulled herself together, wiping her tears away and wondering what she was to do with the rest of the afternoon. It was a miserable rainy sort of day and it might have been a good idea to go and see her mother, but Teresa would be there and there was no way she could face that little madam, not yet. She was not sure what she believed. Surely even Teresa could not be so duplicitous as to steal her sister's boyfriend? But whatever the pair of them had been doing it could not have been entirely innocent. She, Veronica, was not so green, not nearly so much as people imagined her to be.

She felt a new resolve as she turned into Dickson Road, heading back towards the town. She was reminding herself that she had been very doubtful about continuing her relationship with Richard, certainly once Christmas was over. Well, it had happened rather sooner than she had wished, but what did it matter? Christmas was a family time anyway and her parents would make her very welcome at Sunset View when they were not involved in looking after their guests. She decided she would do some Christmas shopping as it was a shame to waste the rest of the afternoon. Then she suddenly realised she had not yet had lunch and in spite of her upset she was hungry. She would go to the Lobster Pot. Why not? She deserved a treat after all that had happened, and as for Richard Hargreaves, well, he could jump from the top of Blackpool Tower for all she cared.

Veronica was very thoughtful as she sat on her own at the small table, enjoying her scampi and chips. She knew now that she had been deluding herself about Richard, and for quite a while too. It had seemed so right when they had met, or so she had believed. Or had she only been convincing herself that this man was the one for her . . . as she had done several times before? Now, possibly for the first time in her life, Veronica was starting to take a long hard look at herself, and at her attitude towards the men she met. Was she guilty, she wondered, as Sandra had sometimes hinted she might be, of imagining herself in love with every man she met? She felt herself blushing a little at the thought although there was no one there to see it. She had realised a while ago that it had been she who had done all the running with the young priest Dominic. Had she been equally to blame with all the others: Shaun and Justin . . . and Richard? What a fool they must have thought her! She made up her mind never to behave so stupidly again.

To hell with both of them, thought Richard, as he scraped the black crumbs from his toast before piling the full tin of beans on the top. Prissy Veronica and her kid sister an' all. Pity – the young one had seemed promising, but he was pretty sure he had blown it there. Blood was thicker than water and he guessed that the kid, when it came to the crunch, would have had continual guilt feelings about doing the dirty on her sister. As for Veronica, he was well rid of her. He knew her game. No sex without a full commitment on his part. Well, he was not ready for that, not for ages yet, and there were others he knew that would not be so unwilling. It was a pity, though. Veronica was a smashing-looking bird, blonde and blue-eyed and curvaceous, and he knew too, if he were honest, that she was a very warm-hearted, kind and friendly girl. He had liked being seen with her and had been gratified by the admiring glances of other men.

Ah well, he would, perhaps, leave it a day or two – a week, even – and then give her a ring and see if she was willing to forgive and forget. No, he corrected himself; not forgive; he must not put himself in the wrong. He would ask if she was ready to come back to him. He knew she would be unable to resist him.

Chapter 8

Christmas

Abbie had always known, ever since she decided to become a teacher, that Christmas time was the most hectic and tiring time of all in a teacher's year, at least for those in primary schools. The secondary schools might give a token observance to the season with a festive concert or a carol service, but, on the whole, school life went on pretty much as normal. It was not so in the infant and junior schools. From the end of November, or even earlier in many schools, Christmas was the subject that loomed large on the horizon in most of the teachers' minds, monopolising the conversations in the staffroom and, to a certain extent, disorganising the timetable.

Park Gates Junior School was no exception. Probably, in the infant school, the separate establishment across the playground, things were even more frenzied. But surely it could not be much worse than this, thought Abbie, up to her eyes in paint, paper, paste and glitter. She was enjoying it, however. Christmas had always been one of her favourite times and now that her own children were growing up and well past the age of wonderment and magic, it was good to see it all once more through the eyes of a child. Each class was expected to decorate its own classroom, as well as make a large frieze or picture depicting some aspect of Christmas to fill a section of the wall in the corridor. This was for the benefit of visitors who would come to watch the Christmas concerts and, at the same time, admire the festive appearance of the school. The younger the children, the more help they needed, and Abbie's class of seven- and eight-year-olds were among the youngest of all. Art and craft had never been exactly her forte, she thought wryly as she struggled, surrounded by a horde of excited children, to put the finishing touches to the scene depicting 'The Twelve Days of Christmas'. Why on earth had she chosen something so complicated? she asked herself, looking critically at the lopsided lords-a-leaping and pipers piping, and the swans-a-swimming, which looked more like ducks and almost identical to the three French hens. Ah well, at least it was the children's own work, unlike the efforts of some of the classes, which were obviously the teacher's handiwork, with the minimum of help from the children.

Mrs Bell, for instance, was known to produce the same frieze of three wise men, plus camels and palm trees, every year, and no one, not even Mr Knighton, dared to suggest she should come up with something different. She might condescend to add a little more gold to Melchior's crown or give Balthazar a new turban to disguise the shabbiness of years, but, in her opinion, there were far more important things to do. Her class continued to struggle with long division, intelligence tests and the intricacies of the English language whilst much of the rest of the school was involved in the making of Christmas cards and calendars, or rehearsing the plays to be performed for the parents, or painting the makeshift scenery, or deciding what the characters in the plays must wear. Mr Knighton, the headmaster, believed that it did not matter overmuch if the school routine was disorganised for a couple of weeks. The most important consideration was that the children should enjoy themselves and be thoroughly involved in all the aspects of the festive season. There would be time enough to buckle down to work again in January; the spring term was always the one when there was least interruption by extraneous events and the major part of the work was done.

Abbie, as well as coping with the art work, had found

herself catapulted into the job of pianist, at least for the lower half of the school, a task which she found much easier to tackle and more to her liking. The school performed two Christmas concerts, one put on by years one and two, and the other by years three and four. The upper school, unfortunately, had no pianist, apart from an older member of the staff who played, but only when she was forced to do so, rather timorously and inaccurately, so they were forced to rely on taped music and records. Not so in the lower school. The other teachers of the first and second year classes, three in each year, had expressed their delight at having a 'real pianist' in their midst. Abbie had been put in charge of the 'choir', which consisted of all those children who were not acting in the play; whether they could sing or not was irrelevant.

This year the lower school was performing a traditional nativity play. The script, devised some years ago by members of staff, was still in existence, so there was no problem there. The leading lights – usually the best readers – from the six classes took the parts of Mary and Joseph, the angel Gabriel, King Herod, shepherds, wise men and innkeepers. There was a very large 'multitude of the heavenly host', taking care of many of the girls, whilst the boys loved wearing masks and being animals in the stable: the donkey, cattle and a few stray sheep who had accompanied their shepherds down the hillside. Not forgetting the travellers to Bethlehem, which involved a goodly number of children who were assumed to be capable of doing little else. Mr Knighton insisted that every child in the school should be involved in the performance, not just the high fliers. If they were not chosen to act, then they must be part of the choir.

Abbie had given up several dinner times to the task of training them. Her charges had learned and could now sing, reasonably tunefully, many of the old favourites: 'Once in Royal David's City', 'Away in a Manger', 'How far is it to Bethlehem?' and the 'Rocking Carol'; plus a few unfamiliar ones she had introduced from *The Oxford Book of Carols*. She had even added a percussion backing with triangles, cymbals, tambourines and drums.

The concert of the younger children was to be performed in the afternoon and evening of Wednesday, the week before the final breakup from school. This was to accommodate both the parents who worked and those who were at home. Abbie, proud of her achievement, had invited Duncan along to watch the evening performance, and then, on an impulse, Simon. They were in need of a scene shifter to make sure the various props were in place at the right time: the square houses and palm trees that comprised the Bethlehem flats; the manger – making sure the baby was inside – and the straw to scatter on the floor; the shepherds' fire, lit from inside by a red bulb; and King Herod's throne – an important task, one which the teachers had said they could not undertake as they were far too busy seeing to the dressing-up and make-up of the children and making sure they behaved themselves, both off and on the stage.

Simon, to Abbie's surprise, had agreed that he would 'give it a whirl'. She did not tell him, of course, that she had an ulterior motive in inviting him. Her friend Jacquie Holt had said she had invited her younger sister, Melanie, to come and watch the play and to help out if needed. Abbie had met her on one occasion when she had come to meet Jacquie after school. She was a very pleasant girl, quiet and well-mannered, but very friendly too. Attractive as well, with auburn hair, like that of her sister, and warm brown eyes. Simon had been like a bear with a sore head just recently. Abbie guessed he might have split up with Teresa, or else they had had a quarrel, but she knew better than to ask outright. Not that she was trying to matchmake, but it would do him no harm to get around and meet other girls. Teresa, of course, was not suitable for him as he would no doubt realise himself eventually. As for Melanie, she was a year or so older than Simon, in the upper sixth at the school Sandie had attended. Apparently she was a clever girl and was going to teacher training college in September . . .

★ ★ ★

The school hall was filling up rapidly by the time Simon and Duncan arrived, although it was still quite early; only just turned seven o'clock and the concert was not due to start until half-past. Abbie had been there for ages. She had had a quick meal and then dashed out again as there was so much to do, she had told them. There were the children from her class who were acting in the play to be dressed and made up. One of her boys was playing King Herod and that involved a great deal of messing about to make the beard stick adequately to his face. At the dress rehearsal he had kept losing it, although it had stayed pretty well intact at the afternoon performance. Then there were the members of the choir, Abbie's responsibility, who had to pass muster. They must all be wearing the correct school uniform – Mr Knighton insisted on this: no party dresses or jazzy sweaters – with ties knotted correctly and hair neatly combed. There was her music to sort out and place on the piano in the correct order and the percussion instruments to be handed out to the 'instrumentalists'.

Duncan had been forced to suppress a smile, though a very affectionate one, as she enumerated all the tasks that had to be done. He was sure, in Abbie's eyes, that even Harold Wilson would not have more on his plate at that moment, but he did not tease her about her enthusiasm and dedication to duty. He was only too pleased to see she was throwing herself into the proceedings with such vigour. It had worried him a while back when she had seemed so down in the dumps and depressed about her new teaching post, feeling she didn't fit in and that some of the staff resented her. She hadn't mentioned the notorious Mrs Bell recently, so maybe the woman was realising that Abbie was an asset to the staff and not, as she had seemed to think, a pushy newcomer. Duncan knew his dearly loved Abbie could not be pushy if she tried, but he was glad this new job was helping her to grow in self-confidence and act more assertively. He had had his doubts – unspoken – as to how she would fare as a teacher. It was not a job for anyone who was insecure or self-effacing; but her stint as a Tupperware rep, before and during her college training, had helped to a certain extent, as had her experiences at Chelford College. It was a different matter, however, to be faced with a class of thirty-odd, not always obedient, children.

Abbie had told them not to be late, although there was a seat reserved for Duncan on the first row and Simon, of course, was to help with the props. Duncan sat down, noting he was the first of the 'VIPs' – husbands and wives of the teachers, and school governors – to arrive, whilst Simon went over to greet his mother, who was already at the piano, sorting through her music in a businesslike manner.

Her face lit up as she saw him. 'Oh, hello there, love; you're nice and early.' She glanced across, smiling and raising a hand to welcome her husband. 'I've just about finished here,' she placed the carol book, open at 'Once in Royal David's City' on the music stand, 'so I'll show you where all the props are. And here's a list to tell you in which order they come on. It's all quite straightforward really.'

Simon had noticed that the stage was a portable one, only erected at those times when concerts were to be performed, quite often as it happened at Park Gates, and that there were no curtains. 'I say, Mum, do I have to walk on to the stage in front of all those people?' he asked. 'I thought there'd be a curtain, like, at the end of each scene.'

'No, it's all very simple and spontaneous,' replied his mother, laughing. 'Why? Don't tell me you're shy. Nobody'll take any notice of the scene shifters anyway. They'll be too busy talking about how well their little Linda or Jimmy's doing.'

'Is there going to be somebody to help me then?' He looked at the two flats of the Bethlehem scene which, with the manger and the straw and all the rest of the paraphernalia, were stored in the classroom opening off the hall, nearest to the stage. They did not look heavy, but rather cumbersome. 'Not that it matters,' he added. 'I can manage.'

'Er, I think I might be able to find you an assistant,' said Abbie. She turned to speak to a young auburn-haired woman who was busy adjusting a shepherd's headdress. 'Miss Holt, this is my son, Simon. He's come to help with the scenery, like I told you.'

'OK, Gavin, off you pop,' said the auburn-haired girl to the shepherd. 'You'll do.' She turned to Simon, holding out her hand and smiling broadly. 'Hi, Simon. I've heard a lot about you. I'm Jacquie. Your mum was only using my Sunday name 'cause the kids are here. We're not usually so formal. Melanie, come and meet Simon, Mrs Hendy's son.'

Another auburn-haired girl, very much like the first one, but rather younger and slimmer, left her task of fixing an angel's wings and came over to them. 'Hello, Mrs Hendy,' she said. 'Nice to see you again. And to meet you, Simon.' She smiled a little shyly and as he shook hands with her he noticed she was quite pretty, though rather thin and pale, with nice brown eyes.

'Hello, Melanie,' he said. 'I'm glad I'm not the only one who's been dragged along to help.' He grinned at her, then pulled a face at his mother. 'Mum insisted, but I was beginning to feel like a fish out of water. You're helping with the props as well, are you?'

'I'm helping to dress the children,' she replied, 'but then I'm supposed to be watching the performance. Jacquie's reserved me a seat at the front – with the VIPs, you know.' She laughed, then went on rather hesitantly, 'But I don't mind helping with the scenery as well, that is if you'd like me to help?'

'Yes, of course I would. But don't feel you've got to, not if you've come to watch the concert.'

'Oh, you'll be able to see it just as well from the side of the stage,' said Jacquie. 'Yes, you go and help Simon, Mel. I think that's a great idea. Don't you, Mrs Hendy?'

'Yes, it is,' replied Abbie. 'Simon was worried about the audience staring at him, but they'll be far more likely to be looking at Melanie.'

'Oh, don't say that, Mrs Hendy,' replied the girl,

tugging anxiously at her miniskirt. 'You don't think . . . ? It's not too . . . ?'

Her sister laughed. 'No, you'll be fine, Mel, so long as you don't bend down with your back to the audience.'

'Take no notice of her,' said Abbie. 'You look very nice. I wasn't thinking about your skirt at all; I've seen far shorter ones than that, believe me. I only meant they'd look at you because you're so pretty.' The girl blushed, smiling uncertainly. 'Simon'll look after you, don't worry.' Simon glanced suspiciously at his mother, but she was smiling guilelessly at Melanie.

He discovered as the evening progressed that Melanie was not as shy as she appeared to be on first acquaintance. She was quiet, however, and not at all pushy, and he found he was enjoying her company very much. She was a pretty girl in an inconspicuous sort of way and she was dressed quite modestly, in spite of her worries about her short skirt. It was a miniskirt, to be sure, but nowhere near as short as the ones Teresa wore. He guessed it was Teresa's apparel to which his mother had been referring in her remark. He knew she didn't entirely approve of his friendship with the girl; erstwhile friendship as it might well be; he hadn't seen her for a while and was not at all sure what he wanted to do about it.

Melanie's green skirt and her paler green sweater enhanced the colour of her hair and eyes, although she was not nearly so curvaceous and did not fill up the sweater as well as Teresa would have done. Simon had not known many girls and could not help making the comparison. But she was easier to get along with; that was certain.

'They're good, aren't they?' she whispered to Simon as they watched the play, between their bouts of sceneshifting. 'For such young kids, I mean – I'm very impressed.'

There had been the usual, only to be expected, hitches, when the angel Gabriel had forgotten her lines, to her obvious consternation, a shepherd had lost his teatowel headdress, and a member of the 'orchestra' had dropped his tambourine with a loud clatter, earning him a severe look from his own teacher as well as Mrs Hendy, and reducing his fellow musicians to fits of giggles. Now they were watching King Herod shouting menacingly from his throne, his beard, mercifully, still clinging to his chin.

'I don't remember the nativity play being such a big performance when I was at school,' Melanie continued, later. The concert had finished and all the more privileged guests had adjourned to the staffroom to partake of tea and biscuits. Simon and Melanie sat quietly together in a corner whilst Abbie and Jacquie circulated, talking to the governors and other members of staff. 'I never had much of a speaking part anyway. I was one of the angels, and another time I was the first innkeeper's wife. I just had to agree with my husband that there was "no room".'

'I actually rose to the dizzy heights of third wise man,' laughed Simon. 'Balthazar – I remember having my face blacked; it was a devil of a job to get it off and my mum went mad when it got on the sheets. I think the headmaster here likes to make a big thing of the play, according to my mother. She's got quite carried away with it all.'

'She's a good pianist, isn't she?'

'Yeah, not bad. Ours seems to be a musical family, except for me. My sister's very good; she plays at some of the hotels, and sings as well. And Duncan's a music teacher. He's my stepfather, of course, not my real father. But my own dad was a pianist too. It seems as though I was at the back of the queue when that talent was handed out.'

'You can do other things, though, I'm sure?' They had already found out that they were both sixth-form students.

'Mebbe; this and that,' he shrugged. 'I'm not bad at games – some games. I'm quite a whizz at table tennis, though I say it myself, and I enjoy running. What about you?'

'Oh, I'm no good at games,' said Melanie. 'Art's my thing. I draw and paint reasonably well; that's why I decided to go in for infant teaching. I like watching football, though.' She gave a giggle. 'I know you might not think so to look at me, but I'm a real football fan. I usually go to watch Blackpool when they're at home.'

'You're kidding! Well, fancy that. So do I. Er . . . perhaps we could go together sometime. What d'you think?'

'Yes, that would be lovely,' Melanie replied, looking down at her cup of tea and seeming shy again. 'Don't you go with your friends, though? I mean to say, I wouldn't want to—'

'Sometimes, but I can go with you instead, can't I? I wouldn't have said so if I didn't mean it—' He broke off as his mother and Melanie's sister came up to them.

'Hello, you two,' said Abbie. 'Thanks for all your help. We couldn't have managed without you, could we, Jacquie?'

'We sure couldn't,' agreed Jacquie. 'And you seem to be getting on very well, the pair of you.' She raised her eyebrows expressively.

'Er, yes; so we are,' said Simon. He quickly changed the subject. 'Quite a crowd here, Mum. Is the dreaded Mrs Bell here? Which one is she?'

'Shhh,' said Abbie, although there was such a hubbub in the room no one else would hear. 'She's not here tonight . . .'

'Thank God!' put in Jacquie.

'She teaches a fourth-year class and it's their turn tomorrow. Not that she takes much interest in this sort of carry-on. Anyway, never mind about her; she's not been too bad lately as it happens. Oh, look out – here's the boss himself. He'll want to say thank you.'

The headmaster was a smallish man with a shock of dark hair springing back from a high forehead. He was in his late forties, still a bundle of energy, and ever since he had taken over the reins some six or seven years ago he had pretty well revolutionised the school. Some of the staff had become complacent, almost apathetic, during the regime of the previous, elderly head, but Mr Knighton had stirred them up – the majority of them, at any rate –

injecting them with a new enthusiasm. Abbie, to Duncan's secret amusement, was always singing his praises. His grey eyes, which looked as though they missed very little, shone with fervour as he shook hands with Simon and Melanie, thanking them for their efforts. Then he was off again like a jumping jack to the other side of the room, to have a chat with Mr Holdsworth, the deputy head, and Duncan, who were deep in conversation.

'So, you've enjoyed yourselves, you two, have you?' asked Abbie. 'I know it's only a kids' performance, but we're quite proud of them, aren't we, Jacquie?'

Jacquie nodded agreement, but rather wearily, whilst her sister was fulsome in her praise. 'It was terrific, Mrs Hendy, and . . . and I'm pleased to have met Simon,' she added, a trifle diffidently.

'I don't know about you,' said Jacquie, trying to suppress a yawn, 'but I'm ready for my bed. D'you think we might be allowed to go now, Abbie? We don't need to stay any longer, do we?'

'I shouldn't think so,' said Abbie. 'The PTA women'll wash up and some of the teachers have already gone. Yes, we'd better be off. I'll just go and rescue Duncan. What about you, Simon? Are you coming back with us in the car, or . . . ?' She was trying not to look too pointedly at Melanie.

'Er, no – I don't think so,' said Simon. 'I'll . . . er . . . I'll walk home with Melanie.' He had already discovered that she lived with her parents and sister near Stanley Park, not all that far from the school or from his own home. He smiled a little unsurely at the girl. 'That's if . . . if you'd like me to?'

'I came with Jacquie in the car,' she said, 'but – yes – that would be nice . . . if you want to.'

'Oh, for heaven's sake, you two, stop faffing about!' said Jacquie. 'Of course he wants to go with you, Mel. Don't be such an idiot! I'm off anyway – I'm nearly dropping with exhaustion. See you later, Mel. See you tomorrow, Abbie. Cheerio, Simon – nice meeting you. See you again, maybe . . .'

'Come on,' said Simon, tapping Melanie's arm. 'We'll be off as well. See you, Mum.' He gave a quiet smile and the merest suggestion of a wink at his mother as they left the room.

'You're matchmaking, aren't you?' Duncan said to Abbie, with a twinkle in his eye, as they sat drinking a late night cup of cocoa before retiring to bed. 'What's more, you're encouraging Simon to two-time.'

'Indeed I'm not!' retorted Abbie. 'It was just a coincidence that Simon and Jacquie's sister both happened to be there tonight; it was nothing to do with me. Although they did seem to be getting on well together, didn't they?'

'I thought you said he was too young to be interested in girls?'

'So he is, really. But you can't interfere, can you, when they do start showing an interest?'

Duncan laughed out loud. 'Honestly, Abbie, you're priceless! If he's too young to go out with Teresa Jarvis, then he's too young for Melanie.'

'But she's a very different sort of girl from Teresa, isn't she? You must admit that, Duncan. Far more . . .'

'More suitable?' He lifted his eyebrows, his face more serious now. 'Yes, maybe she is, although I've hardly met the lass; I've only said "How do you do?" to her. But I'd leave well alone if I were you. Simon won't thank you if he thinks you're interfering. It's far more likely to make him do just the opposite. He'll sort it all out for himself, don't worry; he's a sensible lad. Come on, love – we'd best get off to bed. We don't want him to think we're waiting up for him.'

They heard the front door open and close again soon after they had settled down. Duncan hugged his wife. 'There you are, you see; he wasn't long. I know you never settle until he comes in. Just let things take their course, love. What will be, will be . . .'

Abbie had taken Duncan's advice about the two of them getting out and about more. She agreed with him that much of her tiredness might well spring from being in a rut – albeit a comfortable one – as well as from over-work. They had had a few little jaunts out together recently. In addition to hearing Sandra sing and play at the Allenbank, they had been to see *The Sound of Music*, which had filled them both with nostalgia, having visited Salzburg earlier that year; although Abbie had insisted that the film was not strictly accurate.

'If they crossed the mountains north of Salzburg, they'd be in Germany, wouldn't they?' she said. 'The very last place they would want to be. They said they were going to Switzerland.'

'Poetic licence, my love,' Duncan told her. 'Never mind, it was a lovely film even though their geography might be a bit shaky.' They had decided, on the strength of it, to visit the country again the following year, maybe venture as far as Vienna. It was something to daydream about on the dark winter evenings, although, as Christmas drew near, there was little time for dreaming.

Abbie knew she was not the world's best cook, but she liked to make her own Christmas cakes and puddings; mince tarts, too, although she cheated a little there by using Robertson's mincemeat instead of painstakingly making her own. She had discovered the ready-made pastry from Redman's was very handy too, and it was doubtful that any of her family would notice the differ-ence. When she went to visit Doreen at Sunset View she found that she had been similarly occupied, but on a much larger scale. Doreen proudly showed her the larder, overflowing with cakes, puddings, pickles and jams, whilst dozens of mince tarts were tucked away in the freezer. This was a necessary appliance in the hotel, Doreen told her, although in domestic households, such as Abbie's, a refrigerator was thought to suffice.

'Goodness me!' exclaimed Abbie. 'You have been a busy bee. It makes my little efforts seem pathetic, and I thought I'd been so clever.'

'Don't forget I'm catering for visitors,' said Doreen. 'Anyway, you've quite enough to do with your teaching, haven't you?' she added loyally. 'I'd die if I had to teach all those kids like you do. Each to her own . . . We've twelve guests coming for Christmas, you know, and with the family going at it as well this lot'll soon disappear. Anyway, I'm glad you've managed to pay us a visit at long last. Come on and I'll show you round. It's in rather a mess at the moment with decorators and everything, but we'll be straight by Christmas . . . hopefully.' She crossed her fingers. 'Well, we'll have to be – it's no use just hoping – even if we have to stay up all night to get ready.'

Abbie was very impressed by her friend's new venture. The double-fronted hotel – which had at one time been two smaller premises – overlooking the Gynn gardens had a pleasing aspect. It had been freshly painted in a not-too-garish shade of green, and the sign with the name Sunset View had been touched up as well, with the addition of the new proprietors' names, Doreen and Norman Jarvis. Abbie was pleased to see that Norman was now being given credit for all the jobs he did behind the scenes. Doreen could certainly not manage without him. The hotel was rather larger than Dorabella, and Doreen hoped, eventually, once all the renovations were complete, to have fifteen bedrooms, a few with their own baths and toilets.

'That won't be until after Christmas, though,' she told her friend as they sat together in the small family living room. 'At the moment we're concentrating on the visitors' lounge and dining room and the little bar. We've been jolly lucky to have been granted a bar licence so quickly, I can tell you; but Norman knows somebody on the council, with him being well in at the Parks Department. It's all wheels within wheels, you know.' She tapped her nose. 'But it's best to say nowt.'

The rooms were in the process of being decorated now in gold and green Regency striped wallpaper. Doreen had ordered a toning green carpet with a small fleur-de-lis motif in gold; then the joiner would come in last of all to fix the bar and shelving.

'New chairs too,' she enthused. She sounded like a child

with a new doll's house, but Abbie did not doubt her friend's capabilities. 'Some comfy bucket-shaped ones, and some modern bar stools for the youngsters to perch on. And then we'll have to draw our horns in; we've spent a small fortune, honestly, kid!'

'It sounds like it,' said Abbie. 'But I'm sure you'll do well. You deserve to, and it's all going to look lovely when it's finished. Our Sandra was thrilled to bits, by the way, that you've asked her to sing here at Christmas. That should bring in a few extra customers, shouldn't it, having a music licence?'

'Oh, it's only for the hotel guests and personal friends,' replied Doreen. 'What I mean is – when we put on a musical evening we can't throw it open to the general public, the non-residents. They don't want the smaller places like this going into competition with the big boys – you know, the cabarets and nightclubs and the larger hotels. So they'll only grant you a licence if the bar and the entertainment's just for your own guests.'

'Oh, I see; I didn't realise that. But what about the hotels where Duncan used to play, and the Allenbank that Sandra's taken over from him? They have people in the bar who are non-residents, don't they, and no one seems to bother?'

'Well, I dare say it's all wheels within wheels, like I was saying. Some of the sea-front hotels are very old-established concerns and they probably get away with a lot more – provided there's no rowdiness or drunken behaviour. Anyway, we hope you'll come along to listen to your Sandra on Christmas night; you and Duncan, and Simon as well. I expect Simon will be here whether or not, won't he? Isn't it lovely that he's got friendly with our Teresa? I was tickled pink when she brought him home that first time. He's such a nice boy, Abbie.'

'Er . . . yes,' replied Abbie. 'I know they're . . . seeing one another, but I wouldn't read too much into it if I were you, Doreen. They're very young and I'm sure they'll both have lots of other friends before . . . well, before they decide which is the right one.' She knew she must be careful not to make it sound as though she considered Teresa unsuitable for her son. 'We were pleased to see Teresa as well,' she added brightly. 'She's a very friendly girl, isn't she? She was telling me all about her job at the shop and how she's enjoying it.'

'Our Teresa's OK when she's right side out,' commented Doreen, 'and she seems to be at the moment. Let's hope it lasts. Your Simon's done her a world of good.'

'Mm . . . yes. That's . . . great,' replied Abbie.

It was soon after her meeting with Doreen that she began to notice a change. Things appeared to be not quite so rosy between their children. Abbie did not ask her son what, if anything, had gone wrong. As she had told Duncan, she would not dream of interfering. All the same she was secretly delighted when Simon met Melanie Holt and seemed to take a shine to her. She was even more delighted the following week when Simon revealed that he was going to the cinema with Melanie to see the new Beatles film, *Help!*, which was showing at the Opera House. She was surprised he had told her where he was going and with whom, and very pleased he had not tried to be secretive about it.

It was about eight o'clock the same evening when Duncan went to answer a knock at the door, and came back looking decidedly ill at ease. He cast a worried look at his wife as he said, 'We've got a visitor, love. It's Teresa.'

Abbie jumped to her feet. 'Teresa! How . . . how nice to see you, dear. Do come in and sit down. Duncan and I were just going to have a cup of tea. Perhaps you'll have one with us? Oh, Duncan – turn that off, love. I don't think either of us is really watching it, are we?' It was Benny Hill on the television, a comedian that Abbie found she could take or leave, but whom Duncan, surprisingly, found very amusing. They certainly would not be able to talk, though, with the cheeky comic's face grinning at them all the while.

Duncan obediently turned off the set. 'I'll . . . er . . . go and put the kettle on,' he said, quickly disappearing in the direction of the kitchen. Leaving me to face the music, thought Abbie. Oh heck! What on earth was she going to say to the girl? Unless . . . unless, of course, Simon had already told her. That would have been the decent thing to do, but Abbie would bet her bottom dollar that he had not done so.

'Sit down, dear,' she said again, because Teresa was still hovering uncertainly. The girl perched on the edge of a chair.

'Actually, I've come to see Simon, Aunty Abbie,' she laughed, 'as you've probably guessed. Is he in? Can I see him, please?'

'Well, he's not in at the moment, dear,' said Abbie, 'but I'll tell him you've called. I'll ask him to phone you. I thought he might have done, actually.'

'Why? Why did you think that?'

'Well, we haven't seen you for a while, and I was wondering if he'd said anything to you about what he's been doing lately.'

'He said he was too busy to see me. He said he was going to your school, to do some scene-shifting or summat.' Teresa was looking at her challengingly, as well she might.

'And so he did, dear. He was a big help at the play. He's been . . . very busy.'

'So where is he now? Where's he gone?'

Abbie was longing to say, It's none of your business, you cheeky little madam! Nevertheless she bit her tongue and replied, 'He's . . . he's gone to the pictures.'

'Has he now? Has he indeed? And who has he gone with, may I ask?'

'Oh, just a friend.'

'One of his school friends – from the sixth form?' She sounded rather scathing.

'Er, no. Actually it's somebody he met the other night, when he came to help with the play.'

'It's a girl, isn't it?'

'Well . . . yes. She's the sister of one of my colleagues, you see, and they were doing the scene-shifting together. That's all. They both wanted to see the film, so they decided to go together, that's all. There's nothing to it, honestly, Teresa love.'

'Which picture?' the girl asked boldly.

'The Beatles' new film, I think: *Help!*' Abbie, indeed, felt like crying for help.

'Oh, so that's all, is it?' Teresa sprang to her feet. 'Well, you might like to know that that's what I came for – to see if he'd go with me. He knew I'd been looking forward to seeing that film. Thank you for telling me, Aunty Abbie. He hasn't had the courage to tell me himself.' Abbie was surprised and horrified to see tears forming in the girl's eyes; she had thought she was such a tough little madam. 'I'll go now. I don't want any tea, thanks. Perhaps you'll tell Simon I've been.' She dashed a hand across her eyes as she fled out through the door, almost colliding with Duncan returning with the tea tray.

'Oh, Abbie, you didn't tell her, did you?' He put the tray on the table, looking at her rather sternly, she thought.

'Well – yes. But what else could I do? She wanted to know where he was and . . . and she got it out of me somehow. It's Simon's fault; he should have told her.'

'Yes, maybe he should.' Duncan sighed. 'But he's only a young lad, you know, and he hasn't had the experience yet to deal with this sort of thing. I know you always insist on being truthful, so I suppose I shouldn't be surprised the poor girl's found out. But sometimes a white lie can be kinder, Abbie. Well, I suppose you've got what you wanted, haven't you? That'll no doubt be the last we'll see of Teresa.'

Abbie felt no satisfaction at the thought. The sight of the girl's stricken face had made her feel all mean and horrid inside. And now Duncan was annoyed with her. That would only be a temporary phase, she knew, but she hated it when they were out of step with one another.

'Well, this is going to be a very merry Christmas, I must

say,' Doreen remarked to her husband as they sat at the breakfast table on the morning of Christmas Eve, 'with our daughters at loggerheads.' She recalled how you could have cut the tension in the air with a knife a couple of nights ago when Veronica had come round to see them. She hadn't spoken a word to Teresa, and then the younger girl had stuck her nose in the air and walked out of the room. 'And they won't say what's wrong, neither of them,' Doreen went on. 'I asked Veronica and she said, "Oh, nothing much; we've had words, but it's nothing serious." And Teresa's got a right cob on her just now. She as good as told me to mind my own business.'

'Boyfriend trouble, I dare say,' said Norman complacently, 'with the pair of them.'

'Yes, happen it is,' replied Doreen, 'but that's no reason for the girls to fall out, is it? Mind you, I'm not sorry that it's over between Veronica and that Richard fellow. I realised he was rather a bighead once I got to know him better. Poor lass, she doesn't seem to have much luck with men, does she? I wish she could find a nice steady fellow who was right for her.'

'Give her a chance, love,' said Norman. 'She's young enough. She's not twenty-one yet.'

'I know, but she's what you might call the marrying kind, isn't she? I know she'd love to settle down and have a husband and children of her own.'

'She's not like Teresa and that's for sure,' Norman chuckled. 'She's a flibbertigibbet if ever there was one. I reckon it won't be long before she's got another poor lad in tow.'

'Yes, happen she will. I'm sorry she's split up with Simon, though. She hasn't actually said so, but I know she's not seen him for a while. I'm surprised at how upset she is about it – if that's what it is that's upsetting her. I wonder if he'll still come with Abbie and Duncan tomorrow night? Oh, it's going to be a real jolly occasion, I don't think!'

'For goodness' sake, stop worriting, love,' said Norman. 'We're going to be too busy before long to be bothering our heads about the kids and their petty little squabbles. Anyway, I'm sure it'll all turn out OK. Our Veronica and Teresa will have made it up before then. I mean – Peace on earth and goodwill towards men, and all that. They won't want to let it spoil Christmas, will they? You know we've always tried to make it a happy family occasion. And we will this year, in spite of having visitors here. Thank goodness the decorating and everything was finished in time, eh, love? It all looks grand, doesn't it?'

'Yes; I'm very pleased, and I'm getting very excited too,' replied Doreen. 'Our first guests in our new place, Norman. It's actually going to happen.'

Norman nodded, smiling fondly at her. 'And it's all down to you, love. I thought it was a big step when we moved here, and when I saw the work that had to be done I thought, Gosh! We'll never make it, not in time for Christmas. But we have done. You always had the faith that we'd get there in time, didn't you?'

'It's taken more than faith, Norman. It's been hard graft as well, and you've done more than your fair share, stripping walls and papering and painting, on top of your gardening job.'

'We're partners, love, aren't we?' He grinned at her. 'Always have been and always will be. We pull together.'

'Yes, that's right.' Doreen regarded him steadily. She was wondering now how she could ever have thought he was so dull and boring that she had considered being unfaithful to him. He was still, in truth, the same old Norman: not terribly exciting, to be sure, but loving and steadfast and loyal. The crux of the matter was she had rediscovered how much she loved him. 'We've weathered the storms, haven't we, love? And you're right: I'm not going to worry about the girls. They'll have to sort themselves out. I'm sure everything's going to be just fine and dandy . . .

'And I'd best get cracking. Sitting here chatting won't buy the baby a new bonnet. Our Paul's been busy in the kitchen this last half-hour, bless him! He's a real good lad.' She stood up, quickly piling together the remainder of the breakfast pots. 'I'll just bung this lot in the dishwasher, then I'll get on with preparing the lunch. Just a cold buffet today, Paul and I thought, for the visitors who arrive early. They'll be coming in dribs and drabs all day I suppose, so we'll put the main meal on tonight.'

'And I'll go and make sure everything's shipshape in the bar,' said Norman. 'Fancy that, eh? I never thought I'd end up being a landlord. I'm looking forward to playing the part of "mine host". Makes a change, doesn't it, from tea and coffee and Horlicks?'

'Oh, they can still order those if they like, Norman. Some of the guests might be teetotal, you know. Our Bernie has said she'll give a hand with the suppers when we need her. It'll be all hands on deck for the next few days, that's for sure . . .'

In a family-run hotel all members had to pull their weight for the business to be a success, and Doreen was confident that all the children would rise to the occasion. This did not apply, of course, to Veronica, who had her full-time job at the store and no longer lived 'at home' anyway; but she would be coming to stay at the hotel for a few nights over Christmas, making the family complete. Teresa was working a couple of hours at the newsagent's on this Christmas Eve morning, and Doreen was hoping she would be in a more amiable mood when she returned. Michael and Bernie, on holiday from school, would help out when required, and as for Paul, he was busy at work in the kitchen, as he had been for most of the time since the term finished at Parklands.

He turned and smiled as his mother entered the room, nodding briefly, then turning back to his task of rolling out pastry. Doreen was proud of her elder son; his quiet competence and the way he always dedicated himself wholeheartedly to the job in hand. She loved to see him too in his whites. The students at Parklands all wore the chef's full white uniform whilst doing their training, including the tall white cap, and Paul wore it at home as well, to Doreen's delight. It would be so good for the prestige of the hotel if any of the guests were to catch sight of him, as she was determined they would do. He was not a fully trained chef as yet, as he would be when he had completed his two-year City and Guilds training, but he was already just as good, his mother was convinced, as the ones who were qualified.

'Sausage rolls, dear?' she enquired, eyeing the bowl of sausagemeat on the table. 'Those should go down well at lunch time. And what else have you planned?' She had left the organisation of the menus for the four-day Christmas break to Paul. He had such good ideas, although she would do her share with the preparation and the cooking.

'Puffed pastry for the sausage rolls,' said Paul, not pausing in his task. 'I think it's nicer, and they're always best when they're fresh from the oven. Nothing too fancy this lunch time, Mum, but we're not having sandwiches – they're too ordinary. We'll put on a selection of cold meats – ham and beef and luncheon meat; not turkey – there'll be quite enough turkey eaten tomorrow – with potato salad, coleslaw, onions, beetroot . . . you know, a "help yourself" buffet. The presentation's the main thing. We have to make sure it all looks attractive and appetising.' He put down his rolling pin momentarily, gesturing with his hands, a mannerism he seemed to have affected since he had started at the college. 'Oh, and big bowls of chips; they'll be hungry no doubt. And individual trifles for afters, then coffee or tea.'

'A banquet for a king, in fact, or a queen,' smiled Doreen. 'Now, what's to be done? You're in charge in the kitchen. I don't mind taking my orders.'

'Right – you can make a start on the trifles, Mum. We got some ready-made Swiss rolls, you remember, and I think we'll add a touch of tinned fruit. That's not strictly correct, you know, for an authentic trifle, but it makes it taste better.' He turned back to his work whilst Doreen happily set about her task of cutting up the Swiss rolls and soaking them in cooking sherry. All was peaceful in the kitchen. There was never any friction when she was working along with Paul.

The first guests arrived at about twelve o'clock.

Doreen, hearing voices, quickly took off her apron and hurried out into the hallway. 'Mr and Mrs Taylor, from Preston,' said Norman, ushering in a middle-aged couple and beaming all over his face.

'How do you do?' said Doreen, holding out her hand. 'You're the first to arrive. Our very first guests, in fact,' she said, smiling broadly. 'I'll show you to your room and my husband will bring your case up. We'll be serving lunch at one o'clock today when a few more of the guests have arrived.' She took a deep breath to control the excitement – and the feeling of panic too – that had seized hold of her. 'We do hope you'll enjoy your stay with us . . .'

It had finally happened. Sunset View was on its way.

It was not until late on Christmas Eve that Veronica and Teresa made up their quarrel. The family always exchanged their gifts on Christmas Day when breakfast was over, and both girls had known that this would be an awkward time, not only for the two of them, but for the rest of the family as well, if they were still at loggerheads.

Teresa had already bought a box of chocolates and a scarf for Veronica. On Christmas Eve, on an impulse, she chose for her, in addition, a leather bookmark tooled in gold, one of a selection they had for sale in the shop. 'Make new friends but keep the old; One is silver, the other gold', read the inscription on it. It was not like Teresa to be so sentimental, but she put it in an envelope with a Christmas card, 'To my sister', on which she had scrawled, 'Sorry – hope we can still be friends.'

Veronica had come to Sunset View as soon as she had finished her work on Christmas Eve; her father had gone to the flat in his car to pick her up. What made things even more difficult was that the three sisters, Veronica, Teresa and Bernie, had to share a room because the hotel was full. Teresa decided to see her sister as soon as she arrived. She followed her up to their attic room, closing the door behind her and watching as Veronica took off her coat.

'Hiya,' she said, her meek little voice sounding not much like the old Teresa.

'Hello, Teresa,' Veronica answered in a not-too-friendly tone. She was not smiling and for a few seconds the two girls regarded one another uncertainly.

'I . . . I want to say I'm sorry . . . for everything,' said Teresa. 'I didn't mean it – honest, I didn't.'

'You said that before,' answered her sister, 'when you were flirting with Richard at the Mountjoy that time. It seems to me that you never mean what you say.'

'But I do; honestly, this time I do. Please, please forgive me, Veron.' Teresa took hold of her sister's arm. 'I didn't mean it to happen. And nothing did happen; nothing . . . like that anyway. I hate it when we're not friends . . . and I know it was my fault.'

Veronica looked at her steadily for a moment or two, then she half smiled and put an arm round her. 'OK, Tess; it's all right, honest. I was as mad as anything when . . . when I saw the two of you together. Well, you would've been, wouldn't you? But . . . well . . . I know what he's like. I think I've always known, but I wouldn't face up to it. It's all over between us. I shall never go back to him, even if he goes down on his bended knee – and he's not very likely to do that!'

'I'm ever so glad,' said Teresa, also putting an arm round her sister. They hugged one another, something they did very rarely. 'He's not nearly good enough for you, Veronica. In fact he's an absolute rotter, and I'm glad you've found out.'

'So am I.' Veronica stood back, regarding her sister a little sternly. 'And I hope you've learned your lesson too. I know he could be very charming and persuasive, but he's not to be trusted. Goodness knows why I didn't realise it sooner. I've been a stupid idiot.'

'We both have,' said Teresa. 'Here – I've got you something.' She gave Veronica the envelope she had been holding in her hand. 'It's not your real present – I'll give you that tomorrow – but I saw it and I thought . . . well, you'll know when you open it. I'll go now and let you sort

180

yourself out. Tara. See you later.'

Veronica's eyes misted over a little when she saw the motto on the bookmark. Who would have thought that Teresa could be so tender-hearted? She was a good kid at heart and she was glad they had made friends again. Veronica was pleased to be with her family at this Christmastime. She had lost her boyfriend – once again – but the warmth and friendship of a loving family more than compensated for the unhappiness she had experienced. She made up her mind to be happy and to face the future with confidence – and not to get hurt ever again by wearing her heart on her sleeve.

Sandra was feeling more nervous than she had felt for ages at the thought of performing at Sunset View, although Doreen had told her there was nothing to worry about. Her performance was to be just a friendly, intimate sort of occasion, for the hotel guests and the members of the family; her own family and the Jarvises. It was the idea of her own family being there, and Doreen's too, that fazed her the most. In some ways it was far easier to perform for strangers, but she told herself not to be so silly; she would be amongst friends. And, of course, Ian would be there.

She found she was missing him whilst he was away at college and was looking forward, more than she would have thought possible, to him coming home again. His last visit home had been in November, when he had gone with her to her performance at the Mountjoy Hotel. Veronica and Richard had been there, as well as her own brother, Simon, and Teresa. That evening had turned out to be quite a watershed for the two couples, from what Veronica had told her; the beginning of something that seemed to have hurtled away out of control. She was glad her friend had had the good sense to send Richard packing when he had come back expecting her to fall into his arms again. The tender-hearted Veronica might so easily have been ready to forgive and forget; but that, apparently, was what had riled her. Richard did not admit that there was anything to forgive. Well, good for you, Veronica, thought Sandra. It was about time the young woman rebelled against being treated as a doormat.

She was not sorry, either, that her brother was no longer seeing that little minx Teresa. Who would have believed she could be guilty of such sneakiness as to pinch her sister's boyfriend? Veronica was inclined to think it was mainly Richard's doing, but Sandra was not too sure. She would not trust that little madam as far as she could throw her. Simon was well rid of her. As for herself and Ian, their relationship had undergone a change that weekend. There was a different light in Ian's eyes. She had always known he was fond of her, but this look seemed to be deeper and stronger, a look of longing and of . . . love? He had not yet told her that he loved her, but it was there in his glance and in his embraces although they were, still, just affectionate and undemanding. As for her, Sandra, she was not sure how she felt. She was afraid to fall in love again, and yet she knew she was almost there.

'Close your eyes, for we're almost there . . .' Sandra finished her rendition of the recent Andy Williams hit song to appreciative applause from the audience. It was a small audience: no more than two dozen, which included the guests at the hotel, and her own family as well of that of Doreen and Norman. And Ian. She had chosen this song for Ian and she stole a look at him as she finished singing and playing. He was gazing at her with the same look in his eyes that she had seen several times lately. Her own eyes softened and she knew there must be a glow of tenderness there, and longing too, as she smiled back at him. Was she now ready to admit to herself that she was falling in love with Ian? She looked away, not wanting the others in the audience to be aware of her self-discovery before she had even acknowledged it to herself.

It was turning out to be a lovely evening. Doreen was obviously over the moon about her new hotel, and from the comments Sandra had overheard she had good reason to be. The guests were full of praise for the excellent food and service and the 'home from home' atmosphere which greeted you as soon as you stepped over the threshold, becoming even more apparent as they met the friendly Jarvis family, who could not do enough for them.

Doreen was looking particularly attractive in a green velvet dress with gold edging on the bodice and cuffs. Her rounded cheeks were rosier than usual and there was an excited sparkle in her blue eyes as she circulated amongst her guests. Sandra wondered if she had chosen the dress to match the décor of the hotel. It was all very elegant: green and gold tones in the carpet and curtains and the newly papered walls; and the baubles and tinsel decorating the large Christmas tree, which stood in a corner of the lounge, were of the same colours. There were golden streamers, too, looped around the walls, and floral decorations with holly, ivy, sprays of evergreen and Christmas roses – artificial, to be sure, but all so very tasteful.

Norman looked as pleased as Punch, enjoying the evening's entertainment, but nipping back to the bar whenever anyone required a drink. Sandra was pleased they had wanted her performance to be a casual sort of thing. The audience could talk if they wished to do so whilst she played background music, but they gave her their full attention during her solo singing spots.

She had put together a programme of melodies and songs that she hoped would appeal to everyone: some old-fashioned seasonal standards, of course, 'Silent Night', 'Have Yourself a Merry Little Christmas' and 'White Christmas', as well as a few carols with which the audience could join in. Come tomorrow, Boxing Day, they would not be sung again until another year had passed. She had also entertained them, to their obvious enjoyment, with some numbers The Seekers had made popular: 'A World of Our Own', 'The Carnival is Over', and 'I'll Never Find Another You'. It was strange, she thought as she sang, how the words of the songs tonight seemed to echo her own feelings. Or was she just feeling sentimental, affected by the warmth and the happy ambience of the surroundings, and the loving feelings to one another that Christmas always generated? Last Christmas had been marred by memories of Greg who had been killed only a few months beforehand. Sandra had been almost afraid to look to the future, but her eighteenth birthday at the beginning of the year had proved to be a turning point. Since then she had been on a training course for her job at the GPO – her first taste of life away from home; she had started 'singing for her supper', as she sometimes called her hotel bookings; she had moved into her own flat – well, hers and Veronica's, to be accurate; and she had decided, not without a certain amount of soul-searching in the beginning, to start 'seeing' Ian Webster.

She had not forgotten Greg and she knew she never would; but the nostalgia that Christmas always evoked had not been so painful this time as memories of him returned. She remembered him with warmth and affection, but the hurt had almost gone. She knew that Ian, if encouraged, would be only too willing to take their friendship a stage further. She was still not quite nineteen, however, uncertain as to how far she could commit herself and what her future with Ian might be. But she felt increasingly sure as the evening progressed that she was falling in love with him.

He held her hand as they sat side by side on one of the new green plush settees that Doreen and Norman had bought to match the chairs. Gosh! The décor must have cost a bomb, thought Sandra as she looked around. She had finished singing and playing now and was able to enjoy the supper that Doreen and Paul had placed on a side table for everyone to help themselves. It was amazing how much food some of the folk had piled on to their plates, considering they must already have enjoyed a hearty Christmas lunch and high tea as well. Sandra had not eaten since lunch time, for which her mother had cooked the usual giant-sized turkey and all the trimmings, and so she was ready to tuck into the delicious supper with relish. Faith, her Granddad Winters' widow, and Granddad Horsfall had come to join them for Christmas dinner, but Ian had spent the day with his own family. Simon too had been on his own, although he had appeared to be unconcerned about the recent girl trouble he had been experiencing. In fact he was very cheerful.

'It's all over with our Simon and Teresa,' her mother had whispered to her in the kitchen as they put the finishing touches to the meal. Sandra could tell that this fact was not displeasing to her mother. 'As a matter of fact, he's met another girl. Melanie, she's called; she's Jacquie Holt's sister – you know, one of our staff. Melanie's ever such a nice girl.'

'Well, fancy that!' Sandra replied. 'My little brother is growing up, isn't he?'

He was sitting with Teresa now, however, and they appeared to be getting on well enough. They were not holding hands, but they seemed to have plenty to say to one another. Probably they had had no option but to sit together, thought Sandra, both of them having felt in honour bound to be there at the family gathering, and a dose of the Christmas spirit would do the rest. Sandra wondered how her mother felt about it, but Mum and Duncan were chatting together confidingly, holding hands beneath the table like a courting couple.

'You're very quiet, darling,' whispered Ian. 'Deep in thought, are you?'

'Not entirely,' she replied. 'As a matter of fact, I was just savouring every mouthful of this delicious pork pie. It's home-made, you know – Paul made it – what they call a "hand-raised" pie. Doreen was telling me he's won an award at the college for his pie making.'

'I'm not surprised,' replied Ian. 'It's certainly tasty. He's a very talented chef already, isn't he? Doreen's very fortunate that her elder son is willing to throw in his lot with the family business. They very often want to go their own way.'

'Like you did, you mean?'

'Yes, I suppose so, although I think Dad gave up long

ago on the idea of me going into the market garden. Janet's all set to do that, so it suits him fine.'

'Mm . . . Actually, Veronica was telling me that Paul might have other plans. He told Veronica on the q.t., but he hasn't said anything to his parents yet. He and Martin have the idea they might set up in business together. Not yet, of course, but eventually.'

'You mean in the hotel business?'

'I'm not sure. A restaurant, possibly. I suppose it would depend on how much capital they had.'

'Doesn't it always? I'd like my own chemist's shop eventually, but you have to learn to walk before you can run, as they say. Paul and Martin appear to be close friends, don't they? So that's a good start.'

'Veronica seems to be getting rather friendly with Martin too,' said Sandra, smiling knowingly. Paul had invited his pal from the catering college to join in the Christmas evening festivities at the hotel, and it hadn't taken Veronica long to latch on to the two of them. When Paul went to do his stint in the kitchen Martin seemed quite happy to stay and talk to Veronica. Sandra recognised the familiar gleam in her friend's eye. Is Martin to be her next conquest? she wondered, watching Veronica's face light up and her blue eyes sparkle at a remark he was making.

'At least she's getting over Richard,' said Ian. 'There was something about that bloke that I didn't like.'

'Yes, she's well rid of him,' said Sandra, although she hadn't told Ian about Teresa's perfidy. She had gathered, however, from a whispered remark of Veronica's, that the two sisters were now friendly again, but with a certain amount of reservation on the elder girl's part.

'Anyway, never mind about them, eh?' said Ian, moving closer to her. 'What do you say to a walk along the prom, just for a little while? I'm sure you're ready for a breath of fresh air after all that singing, and we can get back in time for "Auld Lang Syne" – no, that's New Year, isn't it? – well, for whatever they do.'

'Yes,' said Sandra. 'Let's go. No one will miss us.'

'It doesn't matter if they do, does it?' Ian's secret smile made her heart turn a somersault.

'No, it doesn't matter at all,' she said softly, taking his arm as they rose from the table and made their exit without any explanation. Except to her mother, to whom Sandra whispered, 'We'll be back soon, Mum. Just going to blow the cobwebs away.' Abbie smiled and nodded understandingly.

In the shelter of the Gynn gardens Ian drew Sandra into his arms and kissed her, gently at first, then with an urgency he had not shown before.

'Do you know what, Sandra?' he whispered. 'I love you. I knew I did quite a while ago, but it didn't seem to be the right time to tell you. It is now – the right time, I mean. I love you, my darling.'

She drew back from his embrace, looking at him steadily. 'And do you know what else, Ian?' she asked.

'No. Tell me.'

'I love you too.' As he kissed her again there was no doubt in her mind. She did love Ian; she was sure of that. But as for the future, Sandra knew she did not want to look too far ahead.

Chapter 9

Paul

'I've something to tell you!' Sandra noted the elation in her friend's voice and the gleam of excitement in her eyes. Aha! she thought. This, unless I'm very much mistaken, is something to do with a member of the opposite sex.

'Go on, then – fire away,' she said, taking off her coat and flopping down in a chair.

Veronica had arrived home before her on this February evening. They both finished work at five thirty, unless it was Veronica's half-day or the day on which Sandra was 'balancing'. It was agreed that the one who was home first should make a start on the meal, then they would both 'muck in', doing whatever was necessary and then sharing the washing-up. The system worked very well. They both had a good midday meal at their respective canteens, so the evening meal usually consisted of something quick and easy to prepare. Today, however, it did not look as though much preparation had been done. Veronica was wearing her frilly apron, which she always donned whenever she entered the kitchen, but the table was not set and there was no smell of cooking or any sign through the open kitchen door of food waiting to be cooked.

Veronica also sat down in the chair opposite her friend, leaning forward eagerly. 'We've had an invitation to a party. It's next Thursday at the Belmont.' That was one of the larger hotels on the central promenade. 'You will be able to go, won't you, Sandra? It's not one of your singing nights, is it?'

'Er, yes; I mean no – it's not one of my singing nights. I suppose I'll be able to go. But hadn't you better tell me whose party it is and who's invited us?'

'Oh yes, silly me!' giggled Veronica. 'Our Paul came into the shop on his way home from college, and he said that he and Martin – you know, Martin Wade, his friend – would like you and me to go with them to this party.'

'Whose party?'

'Oh, it's one of the students at the college. It's his twenty-first and he's invited a lot of his friends along – with partners, of course. So, you'll be Paul's partner and I'll be Martin's.'

'Mm, yes, I see.'

'What's the matter? You don't sound very pleased,' said Veronica. 'Oh, I get it,' she went on without waiting for an answer. 'You're thinking about Ian, aren't you? And what he might say about you going out with somebody else. Well, it isn't really somebody else, is it? It's only Paul, and I expect he only decided to invite you because Martin wanted to invite me.'

Sandra was forced to suppress a smile, not just at her friend's lack of tact, but because she was so naïve. If Martin had really wanted to invite her to this party, then why hadn't he issued the invitation himself? That was what had concerned her when Veronica had told her about it. The fact that Ian might object had not entered her head. Ian would not mind at all. They had discovered that they loved one another and were very happy and secure in this knowledge. She missed him when he was away, but he now came home for weekends more frequently. While they were apart, however, neither of them behaved like a hermit. Their relationship was founded on trust and they always told one another what they had been doing whilst they were separated.

'Er, yes,' she said, deciding a white lie might be best. 'Of course I was thinking about Ian. I don't like going anywhere like that without him. But, as you say, I don't

189

think he will mind. And it is only Paul. I've known him for ages, haven't I? Have you . . . er . . . have you seen much of Martin lately? I was just wondering, you see,' she was trying to be tactful, 'why he didn't ask you himself?'

'Oh, he's very shy.' Veronica was ready with an answer straight away. 'He's been there, at the hotel, a few times when I've called to see Mum. We always have a nice long chat, him and me, but, like I say, he's shy. I can tell he likes me, though – well, fancies me, I suppose.' She laughed a little self-consciously. 'I know he does; it's the way he looks at me.'

Oh dear, I hope you're right, thought Sandra. Martin Wade had not seemed at all shy to her on the couple of occasions she had seen him. She felt that if he had wanted to see his friend's sister, apart from when they happened to meet at the hotel, then he would not have been afraid to do something about it. She did so hope that Veronica was not about to get hurt again. For that reason, if not for any other, Sandra knew she must go to this party with her friend. Veronica was so vulnerable.

'Yes, it should be great,' she said, forcing a note of enthusiasm into her voice. 'It'll be nice to have a night out. Now, we'd better see to our tea, hadn't we? All this excitement is making us forget we're starving. Let's see – there's half a steak pie in the fridge and we can make some chips . . .'

'I've been thinking,' said Veronica a little while later as they ate their hastily prepared meal, 'it would be nice, though, wouldn't it, if you and Paul were to get friendly – I mean, really friendly? Of course I know you don't think of him in that way, because of Ian, but if you did—'

'No chance,' said Sandra decidedly. 'Don't start getting any crazy ideas in that direction, Veron. Don't get me wrong – I like Paul, he's a nice bloke and he'll make somebody a wonderful husband one day. But not me; definitely not me.'

'No, I suppose not . . . But it would have been nice, wouldn't it? You and Paul, me and Martin—'

'Forget it,' said Sandra, a little abruptly. 'Anyway,

haven't we had enough pairing off in our families with Simon and Teresa? And that wasn't a great success, was it?'

'Is he still seeing that other girl, Melanie?'

'Yes, I believe so. What about Teresa?'

'Oh, I don't know. Mum was worried she might have started seeing that Kevin again, but I don't really think she will. I'm hoping she's learned her lesson there. I tried to advise her – to keep a sisterly eye on her, you know – ages ago, but then she threw it all back in my face with what happened with Richard. Still, that's all forgiven and forgotten, thank goodness! She's still at that shop, you know, the one where Richard lodges, but she steers clear of him. Mr and Mrs Ashcroft have taken her on permanently. They say she's such a hard worker and so pleasant with the customers. At least, that's what Mum says.'

'Well, that's good, isn't it?' said Sandra. 'She's not a bad kid at heart, your Teresa. There must be some good in her; there is in everyone if you look for it.'

'So long as you keep her away from your boyfriends,' said Veronica, laughing. 'I shall make jolly sure she doesn't go anywhere near Martin. That is, if . . .'

A very big if, thought Sandra.

The party at the Belmont, towards the end of February, consisted of food, drink, chat and a little dancing. It was all very informal and Sandra feared that Veronica had overdressed for the occasion, but it did not seem to worry her friend. Veronica loved pastel shades, especially pale blue and pink, despite Teresa having told her, quite bluntly, that they made her look fat. Sandra, also, had tried to advise her – more tactfully – that darker colours were more sophisticated and, possibly, more suited to her figure, but Veronica had insisted on an ankle-length dress in powder blue, bought specially for the occasion. The length, admittedly, was flattering, but Sandra thought the boat-shaped neckline and elbow-length sleeves made her look like a bridesmaid, especially as she had fastened a blue satin bow on the back of her bouffant hairstyle.

Sandra was wearing a green trouser suit, not new, but one which could be dressed up or down according to the occasion. She had chosen a white satin blouse to wear beneath it, whereas for daytime wear she would have opted for a black polo-necked sweater.

Martin, who had collected Paul from home first, had come for them in his Morris 1100 car. A fairly new model, Sandra noted, wondering how a student could afford such a vehicle. She was to learn as the evening went on, from her conversations with Paul, that his friend's parents were 'loaded' and the car had been a present for his twenty-first birthday the previous year. She had already guessed he was a few years older than Paul who was, roughly, her own age – nineteen.

Martin had greeted both girls cordially, but had not paid any more attention to Veronica than he did to Sandra, and it was Paul who still occupied the front seat next to his friend. Sandra had already asked about a present for the – as yet – unknown young man whose birthday it was, but Veronica had said that Paul and Martin were taking care of that. They had bought something from the two of them and they would put all four names on the card. It turned out to be a silver cigarette lighter inscribed with his name, Gary, which the said young man put to immediate use. Paul told Sandra later that Gary smoked like a chimney, but as for himself and Martin, that was not one of their vices.

'Gosh! That's great. Thanks a million,' said Gary on receipt of his present. 'Good to see you here, you two.' He slapped both young men on the back in a companionable way. 'And these are your lady friends, are they? Wow! Very nice too.' His words, however, did not sound suggestive, just friendly and welcoming. Sandra had already decided, on a first acquaintance, that she liked Gary Newby.

'Well, lady friends for the evening, at any rate,' replied Martin in a quiet voice. Oh dear! thought Sandra, hoping against hope that Veronica had not heard him, but she did not appear to have done so. Her friend was staring round at her surroundings, possibly thinking that this place was nowhere near as posh as Sunset View.

'Yes, these are our friends,' Paul broke in quickly. 'Actually, Veronica is my sister, and this is her friend Sandra. My friend as well, of course.'

Gary shook hands with them both, telling them they were very welcome and sounding as though he meant it. 'And this is my girlfriend, Susan,' he said, putting his arm around a small dark-haired girl who was standing near him. 'I should really say my fiancée, shouldn't I, darling? We've just got engaged, you see. That's another reason for the party.'

There were exclamations of 'You dark horse!' and 'You've kept that quiet, mate,' from the young men, whilst the girls enthused over the dainty diamond and emerald ring, which Susan blushingly displayed.

'Oh, how lovely,' gushed Veronica. 'You must be so thrilled. I do hope you'll be very happy, both of you.'

'We already are,' said Gary, smiling down at his fiancée.

'When are you getting married?' Veronica went on. 'Is it soon?' Her friend was not noted for her tact, thought Sandra, feeling rather embarrassed, but the couple did not seem to mind.

'Next spring, we thought,' replied Susan, looking up at Gary, 'Didn't we, darling? Next year, I mean, not this year. Perhaps April or May.'

'Oh, I've always thought how nice it would be to have a spring wedding,' said Veronica. Sandra took a deep breath, hoping her friend would not be so foolish as to cast her eyes in Martin's direction, but, thankfully, she did not do so. Martin, anyway, was deep in conversation with Gary and Paul. When some more guests came towards their host, bearing gifts and cards, the two young men joined the girls and escorted them to one of the tables near the dance floor.

'What are you drinking?' asked Martin. 'The first round's on me,' he said to Paul.

'OK. Thanks,' said Paul. 'There'll be a free drink later, I expect, and perhaps some bubbly with the toast.' He grinned at his sister. 'I mean a toast to Gary and

Susan, not toast and marmalade.'

Veronica bristled. 'Shut up, Paul! I'm not as stupid as all that. I do know what a toast is. Whatever will Martin think? You're making out I'm a dimwit!'

'OK, OK.' Paul held up his hands. 'Only joking, sis.'

'Take no notice of your brother,' said Martin, smiling at Veronica so appealingly that Sandra could imagine her friend's heart turning a somersault. 'We all know you're certainly not a dimwit. Come on now, what would you like to drink?'

The girls decided on a lemonade shandy each and Paul and Martin went to join the crowd that had already formed round the bar.

'Martin's lovely, isn't he?' said Veronica, casting adoring eyes in his direction. She had obviously been bowled over by his last remark and winning smile, although Sandra had noticed it was almost the only remark he had addressed to her individually so far that evening.

'He's very charming,' Sandra replied. 'Yes, I think he's very nice and easy to get on with. He and Paul get on very well together,' she added, watching the two of them with their heads together, laughing and sharing a joke about something or other.

'And so handsome too, isn't he?'

'Yes, I suppose he is.' If you like that sort of thing, Sandra added to herself. Martin Wade was a touch too suave and sophisticated for her liking, but he probably seemed so because he was a few years older than the rest of them, and she had already gathered his family were not without a bob or two. He was quite handsome, she supposed, although she did not see him in the same light as did her friend. He was tallish, about the same height as Paul, but whereas Paul was dark-haired, Martin was fair with, she had to admit, very attractive luminous hazel eyes, more green than brown, and with longer lashes than it was fair for any male to have. Many girls would give anything to have eyelashes like that. Martin, like Veronica, appeared a little overdressed for the casual sort of evening it was, in a grey suit with a dazzling white shirt and red silk tie, while Paul wore grey flannel trousers and a sports jacket. She regarded them closely, thinking they were a contrasting, yet complementary, couple of young men. She wondered . . .

'What's up?' said Veronica, nudging her. 'You're miles away. Don't say you fancy him yourself,' she giggled.

'Don't be silly, of course I don't.' Sandra nudged her back in an affectionate way. 'I was just thinking,' she went on quickly, looking around, 'about this place. It's a lot bigger than your mum's hotel, isn't it, but it's nowhere near as classy. A bit run-down, in fact.' You could not have said it was dirty or even shabby, but the red carpet was rather worn in places and the sagging armchairs had seen better days.

'Oh well, I expect it's a bit of a struggle to keep up this sort of hotel, especially in the winter,' said Veronica. She could be very sensible and prosaic at times and she knew what was what, having been brought up in a boarding house herself. 'I mean, it's not like the huge places – the Imperial and the Savoy and the Cliffs and all those – that keep busy all year round, with functions and trade fairs and goodness knows what. It's these medium-sized places that find it hard to keep going. They're neither one thing nor the other. Sunset View is quite small really compared with some hotels and that can be an advantage. Mum's setting her stall out at the moment, trying to attract new visitors, whereas this place . . .' She looked around. 'Yes, I suppose it could do with a bit of a face-lift. Never mind, though; it's comfortable and friendly and I'm enjoying myself. I'm sure we're going to have a lovely time.'

The young men came back with the drinks and sat down, Paul next to Sandra and Martin next to Veronica.

'Cheers,' said Martin, raising his glass.

'Cheers,' they all replied.

'Here's to a lovely evening,' Veronica added, her cheeks flushed and her blue eyes shining as she looked at Martin. Sandra felt her heart plummet right to the soles of her feet.

★ ★ ★

'Whatever's the matter with him?' said Veronica, her eyes bright with unshed tears. It was now just turned midnight and they were sitting drinking a comforting cup of tea by the warmth of the gas fire, Martin having driven them back to the flat and then left them, to take Paul home. 'I mean to say, he did invite me, didn't he? And then all he does is ignore me.'

'Oh, come on, you can't say that,' replied Sandra. 'That's not true. He did dance with you, didn't he? And I saw the two of you sitting there chatting away twenty to the dozen. You looked as though you were getting on really well together.'

'So we were; at least I thought we were. But I thought . . . I suppose I thought he'd say something. Ask if he could see me sometime, just the two of us. But he didn't. He just ran us home, and then off he went with Paul.'

'Well, you and I share a flat, don't we?' said Sandra. 'So he had to bring the two of us back here. He didn't have the chance to say anything – just to you, I mean.'

'There was plenty of opportunity all evening if he'd wanted to. But he didn't. He's gone off me, Sandra, and I don't know why. I don't know what I've done wrong. I was sure he liked me . . .'

Sandra was in a quandary. It was tempting to take the easy way out, to tell her friend he might ring tomorrow, or next week, but she knew in her heart that this would not happen. And she knew, somehow or other, she would have to tell Veronica what she had guessed and feared was the truth. Martin would never ask her, or any girl, to go out with him. Neither would Paul. She had watched the two of them surreptitiously throughout the evening and realised she could come to only one conclusion.

Yes, Martin and Veronica had danced together, but only once, as she had with Paul. Another time the four of them had joined in a rock-and-roll number in a sort of circle, jigging around to the Beatles' hit 'We Can Work It Out'. It had been in the Top Twenty over Christmas and was still being played and sung all over the place. Sandra, noting the covert glances that passed between the two young men, had felt one thing was certain: it would never 'work out' for Veronica and Martin.

'He does like you,' she said now. 'Of course he does. No one could help but like you, Veron – you're such a lovely person. But I'm afraid you'll have to face up to the fact that he doesn't fancy you any more than he fancies me – for instance – or any other girl.' She had decided, however hard it might be and however unpalatable to Veronica, she had to be honest. 'You see . . .' she leaned forward in her chair, 'I think Martin's . . . well, I think he's gay.'

Veronica stared at her. 'What do you mean – gay? I don't know what you mean.'

Sandra thought at first that her friend did not want to know, but she realised, as Veronica continued to look blankly at her, that she did not know the meaning of the word. Surely even Veronica could not be so naïve as not to have heard . . . But then, she supposed, the term 'gay' had not been in common usage all that long. She began again.

'What I mean is, I think he's queer. You know what that means, don't you?'

'Of course I know,' retorted Veronica. 'I'm not stupid. You're as bad as Paul, making out I'm an idiot or something. But you surely can't mean . . . you don't mean . . . that he likes men, and not women? Not Martin. No, I don't believe that. No, you're imagining it. It's just not true. It can't be.'

Sandra sighed. 'I'm afraid it is. At least, I'm almost a hundred per cent sure it is. Just think about it. You're an attractive girl and Martin obviously likes you. And he's certainly not shy, like you tried to say he was. But he's not made any moves towards you. Doesn't that tell you something? And the very fact that he and Paul asked us to go along with them – well, it seems to me that they only asked us so we'd be a sort of foil, a cover, if you like, for him and . . . Paul.'

'Paul!' Veronica almost shrieked the name. 'You mean

Martin and . . . my brother? Oh no, no, I don't believe that.'

'I'm sorry,' said Sandra. 'I don't want to upset you, and I suppose I don't want to believe it either, but it must be true. I'm almost sure of it.'

Veronica continued to stare at her. Sandra would not have been surprised to see her burst into tears, but she did not do so. In fact, after a few moments a different look came into her eyes. 'Yes, I suppose so,' she said slówly. 'It would make sense of . . . what didn't make sense before. But it's disgusting!' She spat out the words, a look of distaste contorting her face.

'Oh, I don't know,' said Sandra reasonably. 'It all depends on how you look at it.'

'What do you mean? There's only one way to look at it, surely. It's awful, it's unnatural.'

'But Paul and Martin do seem to be very fond of one another. And you said they'd been friendly for quite a while, didn't you?'

'Since my brother went to that college, over a year ago, as far as I know. But . . . it's illegal, isn't it, that sort of thing? I mean, they'd be in trouble, wouldn't they, if anyone found out? That is, if it's true. And I'm still not sure it is, no matter what you say.'

'Well, we'll see,' said Sandra. 'Yes, it's still supposed to be a punishable offence, not that I know very much about it. But I think people are a lot more broad-minded today, and if they're quiet about it and keep themselves to themselves, well, who's to know, and what does it matter? It's their own business, I suppose.'

'No, I don't agree with you,' said Veronica heatedly. 'If our Paul is . . . like that, then we all ought to know about it. The family, I mean, especially Mum. Her own son! I'm sure she'd be as horrified as I am, but she has a right to know.'

'No, Veronica, no, you mustn't tell her,' said Sandra. 'It wouldn't do any good. Anyway, she's his mother and maybe she has an idea already. Mothers tend to guess about that sort of thing.' She felt that if Veronica were to tell Doreen it would be, whether her friend realised it or not, out of spite, as a result of her own hurt feelings. Veronica was not spiteful as a rule, but this had come as a shock.

Veronica shook her head. 'I'm sure Mum has no idea.'

'Then leave it that way,' said Sandra. 'She may find out sooner or later, but I don't think you should be the one to tell her. Promise me you won't.'

Veronica looked at her steadily, seeming a little more composed now. 'All right then, I won't say anything. Anyway, we're not really sure, are we? I mean, we're only guessing.'

'Yes, that's true enough,' said Sandra. 'We can't go around telling tales unless we're sure we've got our facts right. And even then, even if we know definitely, it would be best not to say anything.'

Veronica didn't answer. She just stared unseeingly into the dregs of her cup. After a minute she lifted her head. 'I think it is true, though,' she said quietly. 'When you come to think about it, a lot of things begin to make sense. Why our Paul's never had a proper girlfriend; why he always seemed . . . well . . . different somehow.' She sighed. 'Oh, Sandra, why am I so unlucky with fellows? I was beginning to really like that Martin.'

'Never mind, love; there's more fish in the sea,' said Sandra, thinking that already Veronica had scooped up rather a large netful, only for them all to swim away again. 'And one of these days a prize catch will come along, you'll see.'

Her friend smiled sadly. 'Thanks for telling me . . . about Martin and Paul. I'd never have twigged it myself, but then I am rather a nitwit, aren't I? Stupid, in fact.'

'Of course you're not,' Sandra protested. 'Maybe you're a bit gullible sometimes, but that's because you trust everybody and expect them all to be just as nice and honest as you are. It can be a bit of a shock when you realise that not everybody is.' She had really been thinking about Richard, and Teresa too, but she realised her words might be misconstrued. 'Although this situation had nothing to do with not being nice or honest,' she added. 'I'm sure both Paul and Martin are very worthy young men. Neither of them would do anything mean or dishonest. They're just . . . different. Come on, Veron. Let's get off to bed. I'm sure you'll feel tons better in the morning.'

'I'm OK,' said her friend. 'Honest, I am. I'm just not a very good picker, am I?'

As sure as she was in her own mind, Sandra knew that she had to find out if her suspicions were true; and the only way she could do so was by asking Paul or Martin outright. Which meant Paul, of course; she hardly knew the other young man. On the other hand she could leave well alone, which was what she would have preferred to do, but she had a sneaking feeling that this would not be the end of it. She feared that Veronica would be unable to keep the matter a secret and that she might, in spite of her promise, spill the beans to her mother, either intentionally or by accident. And if by some remote chance it happened to be untrue . . . well, they would look very silly.

But how was she going to see Paul on his own? And, if she did, what on earth was she to say to him? Still, nothing ventured, nothing gained. She pondered the question all day, finding it hard to concentrate on the telephone bills, postal orders, pensions and parcels; the hundred and one jobs a post office counter clerk had to deal with. She rang Sunset View from a phone box outside the GPO as soon as she finished work at five thirty. She tried to disguise her voice when Doreen answered, asking if she could speak to Paul and hoping against hope that he would be there. She assumed he would have arrived back from Parklands by now. Luckily Doreen did not ask who was calling and, even more luckily, Paul was at home.

'Hello there, Paul Jarvis here. Who's speaking?'

'It's Sandra,' she replied, almost whispering, although she was not sure why. 'But don't let on it's me, please.'

'OK then. What's up?'

200

'Well, it's Veronica. I'm a bit worried about her, about . . . something. But I can't tell you over the phone. Could you meet me sometime, Paul? Then we could have a chat.'

'Sure. What about tonight? Or are you busy?'

'No, tonight would be fine. I'm usually at the Mountjoy on a Friday – playing the piano, you know – but they're quiet at the moment and they don't need me for a few weeks. I thought I might go and see Mum tonight, but I could meet you first.'

They decided to meet at a pub near Devonshire Square, which was not too far from where her mother and Duncan lived, so Sandra could go there afterwards. 'You will be on your own, won't you, Paul?' she asked tentatively.

'Sure thing. I'm not seeing Martin tonight,' he replied. 'See you later then; about eight.'

He had as good as answered her question already, she thought as she rang off, feeling very guilty for not having told Veronica her plans. She felt even more so later that evening as she set off for the Number Three pub, but Veronica was washing her hair and did not seem to be taking much heed of her friend's whereabouts.

Paul was already there and he quickly rose to get her the pineapple juice she requested, wanting to keep a clear head. 'Now, what's the matter with my sister?' he asked, sitting down on the stool next to her. 'Man trouble again?'

It was just the opening Sandra wanted, and she had already rehearsed in her mind what she was going to say. 'Er . . . yes, it is really,' she replied. 'As a matter of fact, she had a thing about your friend Martin, but I don't think . . .' Oh dear! This was not going to be easy at all. 'What I mean to say is . . . well . . . I don't think Martin is interested in girls, is he? So it's no use, is it? I don't want her to get hurt again, and she really did like him a lot. But last night . . .'

Paul came to her rescue. He stretched out his hand, placing it over hers for a few seconds, in a nice friendly way. 'You've guessed, haven't you?' he said. 'About

201

Martin and me? I thought you might have done, but I knew it wouldn't occur to Veronica. She's so naïve at times it's just not possible. So she fancied Martin, did she? Oh dear.'

'But surely you must have noticed; the way she looked at him and everything? And she said she met him a few times at the hotel, and how well they got on together.'

'So they did, yes. But Martin gets on well with most people; puts them at their ease, you know. And as for Veronica, well, she likes chatting to men, doesn't she? I didn't notice she was particularly interested in him because she's always like that. She tends to go overboard whenever a handsome fellow comes on the scene. So she fancies her chances, does she?'

'Not any more she doesn't,' replied Sandra. 'I said she *had* a thing about him, but she hasn't now, not any longer. She knows; I had to tell her, Paul, but that's why I wanted to see you. To make absolutely sure I wasn't . . . imagining things.'

'My sister knows?' He looked worried, even a touch frightened. 'Oh, crikey! She won't say anything, will she? To the rest of them, to Mum and Dad?'

Sandra shook her head. 'I've warned her not to. But I had to find out myself, to be sure. And I can promise you I won't say anything, not to anyone. But surely people know? They guess, don't they – like I did?'

'Some of them, maybe.' He shrugged slightly. 'It's not unknown at Parklands; there are others, one or two. But we're all very discreet; you've got to be. But I'd die if my mother and father were to find out.' She noticed, as she had before, the slightly feminine timbre in his voice as it rose a few tones, and his exaggerated hand movements. 'I say I'd die, and that's most likely true. My dad would probably kill me! I daren't let them find out.'

'But don't you think they'll realise, eventually? I mean . . . when you don't get married? And when . . . well, Veronica says that you and Martin intend setting up in business together. She told me that a while ago, in confidence, before I knew about the other thing.'

'That's something else Mum doesn't know about yet. She thinks I'm going to be the chef at Sunset View. And so I am, at the moment. I won't let her down just yet. But I have my own life to lead, Sandra, in my own way. I could do what is expected of me, just to allay suspicion. I could even get married, I suppose. Some do, you know, but it often falls apart in the end and I don't want to risk it. It wouldn't be fair, anyway, to any girl. It would just be a sham.' He stopped, smiling at her a little sadly, before continuing. 'Do you know, this is the first time I've talked about it to anyone – apart from Martin, of course – and I can't tell you what a relief it is. Thanks for listening.' He took hold of her hand again and gave it a squeeze. The people sitting near them would, no doubt, think he was her boyfriend, and he was indeed a very nice and suitable young man.

'Thanks for telling me,' she said, 'and for not minding about me being so blooming nosy. I said it was for Veronica's sake, and it is. I wanted to rescue her before she got badly hurt again.'

'Oh dear! Poor Veronica! It's never gone right for her, has it, ever since that carry-on with that priest fellow. It's such a pity. She'd make somebody a lovely wife.'

Sandra smiled. 'She's only twenty. We're talking as though she's on the shelf and there's really plenty of time. I don't want to get married for ages, even though I've got a steady boyfriend, but that's the difference between your sister and me. It's not that she's man mad. I think she just wants to feel – you know – wanted; as though she's really special to somebody – someone who won't let her down.'

'Isn't that how we all feel?' said Paul. 'I know it won't be easy for . . . us, for me and Martin, I mean. But it's the way we've chosen. No, not really chosen,' he corrected himself. 'It's the way it is.'

Paul stayed in the pub on his own for a while after Sandra had gone, alone with his thoughts, whilst he sipped slowly at his second half of bitter. It had been good to talk to her; a relief, in a way, to realise that someone else knew and was willing to listen and not condemn. For Sandra had not seemed at all censorious, as he feared others might be. He had not told her very much, of course, except to admit to the fact that he and Martin were gay, a word that was now coming into more common usage. Come to think of it, he hadn't actually used the word when he was talking to her, but the inference was there. Sandra knew, but he was not sure how much she understood.

But then, how much did he really understand the situation himself and why he should be the way he was? He recalled what he had said to her a little while ago, that it was not, in point of fact, the way of life he had chosen – or that they had chosen, he and Martin. It was just the way it was, just the way they were.

He found himself looking back, as he often did, to a very early age. When had he first realised that he was 'different'? There was not a definite time that he could pinpoint, but certainly, even when he was quite a small boy, he had known there was something that made him not quite the same as the other boys in his class. He didn't understand what it was, neither did he try to talk about it to anyone. It became his secret, a secret he did not, as yet, fully comprehend, but one that he knew he must, at all costs, endeavour to hide from everyone. He realised, also, that he was a quiet and reserved sort of lad, and as he grew older he found that having this secret made him retire even further into his shell. He was quite popular at school, though considered to be studious and serious-minded, and the friends he made were equally conscientious and prepared to work hard to achieve their goals.

It was gradually beginning to dawn on Paul, however, what was the exact nature of his problem. The other lads, aged fifteen or sixteen, were starting to show an interest in girls. 'Girlie' magazines were passed around at break times, though they had to be kept well hidden from the prying eyes of the masters who were, in the main, ordained into the Catholic Church. It was, of course, an all-male school with a reputation for strictness and a high standard of education. Paul looked at the pictures of scantily clothed young women and felt nothing, although he pretended to ogle them and to have a ribald joke or two along with the others.

This was only one aspect of the other sex, however. In the vicinity was the girls' grammar school – not a Catholic one – and the girls could sometimes be glimpsed, over the wall, playing hockey or tennis, or, at the end of the day, walking home in their navy-blue uniforms and porkpie hats. Quite a few friendships, innocent enough for the most part, were struck up between the Catholic boys and the girls from the neighbouring school, although these often fizzled out in the face of parental objections regarding the difference in religion. Paul remembered now that Sandra Horsfall had attended that school. He had seen her a few times in her uniform and had always considered her to be a very friendly and outgoing sort of girl. She had had a boyfriend from quite an early age; that poor lad who had been killed in a car crash. Sandra's family and his own had been friendly for ages – at least their mothers had – and he knew that Sandra would have been an ideal girlfriend for him. She would have helped to bring him out of his shell and he knew he would have got on well with her, as he had done tonight. He thought now what a grand girl she was and how much he liked her. Even the problem of their different religions could have been overcome. But Paul had known, a couple of years ago, as he had looked at Sandra and at all the other girls, that they did not interest him, not in that way.

He made a good pretence, though. One of his friends, Patrick, had a girlfriend called Deirdre and they arranged they would go out as a foursome, Deirdre bringing along her best friend, Daphne, as a partner for Paul. She was a nice pleasant girl – a Catholic too – and Paul quite enjoyed their night out at the pictures. He made no move towards her, though, to hold her hand or anything – not that he would have done so anyway. He was a well-brought-up lad and knew it would not be right, not on a first date, no matter what some of the other lads boasted they got up to. He saw her once more, because he felt it was required of him, and then told her he didn't think it was a good idea for them to go on seeing one another. She had seemed relieved.

It was round about that time that Paul began to throw himself into the game of rugger with more than usual abandon. He did enjoy the game and the rough and tumble, and not because it brought him into close proximity with other males. He had not yet begun to think of that, or, if he did, it was a thought that was quickly suppressed. He had been brought up to be a good Catholic and still attended Mass and, less frequently, confession. But this was something he hardly dared confess to himself, let alone to a priest. To his surprise his prowess at the game led to his being selected for the school's second team. He had been injured in a match towards the end of the season and ended up in hospital with concussion and a twisted knee, quite the hero of the day judging by the friends who came to see him. He remembered how his mother had been away for the weekend, at his Aunt Janey's – or so she had said – and there had been no end of a to-do when his dad had been unable to locate her. That was supposed to be kept from the children, although the older ones had had an inkling about it, and Paul had put two and two together. But his mother was not the only one who had been hiding a guilty secret.

He had always got on well with his mother and had enjoyed helping her with the cooking and baking in their boarding house in Hornby Road, to the amusement of his brother and sisters. Michael had remarked that it was a 'cissy' thing to do and you wouldn't catch him messing about in the kitchen. Paul had assured him that all the best chefs were men, especially in the posh hotels in London, and, more particularly, in Paris and other continental cities. His aptitude, just a casual interest at first, had led to his decision to leave school at seventeen when he had completed a year in the sixth form and enrol as a student at Parklands.

He sensed his mother was disappointed, despite the

fact that he was following in her footsteps and would, eventually, be even more of a help in the larger hotel she was set on acquiring. She had wanted him to go to university, to become a lawyer or doctor, or a master in a grammar school, although he guessed it was largely for her own prestige. Doreen was not a snob, far from it, but she wanted the very best for her children, especially as she had had to forgo any chance of higher education herself, as one of a large and not-well-off family. Paul's own family was quite large, but their standard of living, thanks to the boarding house and his father's steady employment in the Parks Department, was very comfortable. His mother had not objected to Paul's choice of career for long, though, and she had admitted, when she saw how well he had adapted to the college life and the new concepts he was learning, that he had made the right decision.

Parklands had been only five minutes' walk away when the family had lived at Dorabella, and the college hours, nine till four, had meant that Paul still had ample time to help out in the boarding house. There were three terms, the same as the schools, so during the long holidays Paul began to be employed as a chef at Dorabella and, later, at Sunset View. He had found, more and more of late, that he was taking over the responsibility for the catering. His mother was an excellent plain cook, but untrained apart from the night-school class she had attended a few years ago, and Paul was able to introduce new ideas and more novel and tempting dishes to complement the standard fare at the new hotel.

When he'd first started at the college, at seventeen, Paul had been one of the youngest students on the course. There were a few sixteen-year-olds as well, this being the youngest age at which you could enrol. The others were older, even middle-aged, men and women, who had been in the hotel business for quite a while and had decided they would like to add the City and Guilds qualification to their credentials.

There were other courses as well: for waiters, hotel

managers, receptionists and one specially for bakers and confectioners, but Paul's was for general catering, a two-year course that included a bit of everything.

From the very first moment he had known he was going to enjoy it all. He was well aware that he had a talent for the work, but enrolling at Parklands made him feel, for the first time, like a real chef and not just an extra pair of hands in the kitchen. The students were required to wear the correct chef's uniform, known as 'whites': white shirt, white apron, white overall and, the crowning glory, the tall white hat. They were responsible for buying their own uniform and their own set of knives, an expense that Doreen and Norman were only too pleased to meet, especially when they saw the strides that Paul was very soon making in his chosen career.

The trainee chefs were taken, step by step, through a full menu: starter, main course, pudding, cheese and biscuits, coffee and mints. Each course was prepared by the students and, afterwards, served to students who were on other courses. A special menu might include extra courses before the main one: hors-d'oeuvres, soup, a morsel of fish, and then sorbet to clear the palate in readiness for the main dish. This was unheard of in standing boarding-house fare. The starter, if there was one at all, was invariably tinned grapefruit segments, or soup – the powdered variety, which came in large-sized catering tins. But Paul was already toying with the idea of persuading his mother to waken up her ideas. He knew that even the most adventurous of guests would, more than likely, turn up their noses at some of the ingredients in an hors-d'oeuvre dish – pickled herrings or anchovies or fragments of raw vegetables – but he did not see why, in due course, they should not experiment with a few different starters: melon or prawn cocktail or egg mayonnaise. But he knew he would have to go easy with his mother and take one step at a time.

He also learned that the common or garden potato, usually served boiled, mashed, chipped or roasted, could be presented in other, more exotic, ways. The students experimented with Duchesse potatoes, piped into swirling mounds on a baking tray; sauté potatoes; potatoes au gratin; or served with the accompaniment of garlic and herbs or soured cream and chives. He also learned about various sauces that could be served with savoury dishes instead of the good old standbys, rich brown gravy or parsley sauce: hollandaise, béchamel, béarnaise, Cumberland or avocado.

One thing at which Paul excelled and for which he won an award at the end of his first year was pie making. He specialised in hot-water crust, or 'raised' pastry; that is, pastry that is solid enough to stand alone without the support of a dish. His *pièce de résistance* was a Melton Mowbray pork pie.

He had met Martin Wade during the second week of the course. He had found himself working alongside him in the kitchen, and at the end of the morning they had sat together to have their midday meal in the canteen. He had noticed him on the first day; you could not help but notice Martin. He was tall, about the same height as Paul himself, but whereas Paul knew he was quite ordinary-looking, the sort of chap you would pass in the street and not really notice, Martin possessed charisma, a charm which, once you got to know him, you realised was not just superficial. Martin was interested in people and what made them tick, and Paul, normally a quiet and largely reticent young man, found himself opening up and, to his surprise, talking to Martin about his hopes and aspirations in a way he had never done before.

Martin was undeniably handsome, though not in the tall, dark and rugged way. His hair was fair with a sandy tinge to it. He wore it quite long and it flopped across his brow, although when he was working it had, perforce, to be tucked beneath his cap. His eyes were an unusual hazel shade, predominantly green, and their long lashes, darker than his hair colour, was what gave his face a slightly feminine appearance. This was offset, however, by the firm line of his jaw and his wide humorous mouth.

Paul learned he was almost twenty-one at that time,

and until starting at the college he had been working for a firm of solicitors, only to realise he was in the wrong occupation. His father was a solicitor, and it had been taken for granted that Martin would follow in his footsteps, although he had been doing his training with a different firm. Paul gathered that Martin's parents were quite well off and did not mind the change in direction that their son had decided to take. He also suspected that his new friend might be overindulged by a doting mother and father, although he was by no means tied to their apron strings. He had his own flat in Bispham, which was in the same location as his parents' home, and he had lived on his own since he was eighteen. Paul admired him for having taken this confident step. He wondered when he would have the courage to do the same. He felt very safe and comfortable living under his parents' roof and, so far, had had no thoughts of leaving; besides, at the moment he could certainly not afford to do so.

Paul, at first, did not think of Martin in relation to himself. It was only when they found themselves, of their own volition and more and more frequently, being drawn together, that he began to look at him in a rather different light. Yet he was still afraid. How did one know? he wondered. How could you tell? It was easy enough with a member of the opposite sex. If you were attracted to a girl and suspected she might feel the same about you, then you did something about it. And if you were wrong, well then, she would just make it plain that she wasn't interested. You might be disappointed or feel a bit of a fool, but so be it. But as for Martin – Paul, for the first time in his life, was beginning to acknowledge his feelings. Did Martin feel the same? Paul thought so. But there was a chance he might be entirely wrong. He could have misread the signs completely. He could end up getting punched, or, at least, spurned and sent off with a flea in his ear. He decided it was not up to him to make the first move. He would not make a move at all. He would just wait and see.

He did not have very long to wait. It was at the

beginning of October, a couple of weeks after they had first met, when Martin had said to him as, together, they were preparing a dish of cauliflower au gratin, 'Tell me, Paul, do you have a girlfriend? You haven't mentioned one, and I thought, a personable young man like you . . .'

'No, as a matter of fact, I haven't,' replied Paul, his heart giving a leap. 'And you?'

'No, me neither.' Martin shook his head. 'I had a girlfriend once. Jenny – a lovely girl . . . but it didn't work out.'

'Why? Did you fall out with her?'

'No, nothing like that. We never fell out at all. But it wasn't any use. You see, I'm not really interested . . . not in that way.' Martin's luminous greeny-brown eyes looked straight into Paul's. There was a question there and Paul, looking back at him, steadily and quite boldly, answered it.

'Neither am I,' he said. 'I quite like girls. I enjoy their company, but . . . nothing more.' Martin smiled at him. So that was how you found out, thought Paul. It was so simple really. He smiled back, then, feeling suddenly embarrassed and unsure of himself, he dropped his gaze.

'So . . . that's that,' said Martin. 'Don't be afraid,' he added quietly. Then, in a more normal voice, 'I think it's time you came round to see my flat, don't you? I'll give you my address. What about tonight?'

'Yes, why not?' said Paul. 'Thanks. I'll look forward to it . . .'

Chapter 10

Crisis

It had been a highly successful Christmas. The Jarvises' first encounter with guests at Sunset View had been a very rewarding one and several of them had booked up on the spot for a week later in the year, during the late spring or summer of 1966. The hotel was closed now until the Easter weekend when it would open for a four-day break, similar to the Christmas one. And after that, well, it was all in the lap of the gods, Doreen told herself. Many hotels in the town closed down after Easter, opening up again some seven weeks later in time for the Whitsuntide holiday and the start of the summer season. They would remain open then until the end of October when the Lights finished. This extended season, due to the famous Blackpool Illuminations, had been a boon to hoteliers and boarding-house proprietors, who were so often heard to complain, 'We have to live in the winter, you know, after the visitors have gone.' Many hotel owners, indeed, had moved from such resorts as Morecambe, Southport or Scarborough to start again in Blackpool where there was the chance of earning a bit more brass.

Doreen had decided they would stay open between Easter and Whitsuntide if it was at all possible, and that, of course, would depend on the bookings. Now, everything was dependent on the workmen being finished in time for Easter. She sometimes wondered if she had bitten off more than she could chew. Norman, assuredly, believed that she had, although he had kept quiet and let her have her head. The builders had started on the alterations as soon as the Christmas season was over: the reconstruction of two of the first-floor bedrooms so that they would be 'en suite', a term now coming into more common usage. The bathrooms would be rather small – little more than large cubicles – but Doreen had been anxious not to lose any bedrooms, and the front two rooms, she had been advised, were quite large enough to subdivide. The plumbers would be moving in soon, and, fingers crossed, all should be completed then within the week.

So, everything was going according to plan, Doreen was congratulating herself one evening around the middle of March. In a few weeks' time there would be scant opportunity for her to take her ease, she reflected, as she was doing at that moment. She had just finished watching the latest episode of *Z Cars*. She switched off the set and reached, somewhat guiltily, for her packet of Craven A. She did not often indulge, especially as Norman hated her to smoke, but he was out with some friends from the bowling club, discussing the coming season's fixtures.

Her family too seemed to be on an even keel at the moment, she thought contentedly, as she inhaled the hypnotic smoke. They were giving her very little trouble, or 'grief' as Teresa might say. 'Aw, Mum, stop giving me grief!'

Teresa appeared to be on top of the world, although her mother was not sure why, and her policy, with this most volatile of her daughters, was not to ask. The girl was seventeen now and, Doreen supposed, was entitled to privacy and the chance to live her own life without her mother constantly breathing down her neck. She had been sorry when it was all off with Simon Horsfall. Or was it? Doreen didn't know for sure. The lad had not been round recently – neither had any other young men for that matter – but Doreen was sure that Teresa was not dolling herself up the way she did to go out with her girlfriends.

Still, so long as she came in at a reasonable hour, as she had been doing, and continued to work hard at the shop, then her mother was content to leave well alone. It was amazing really how well she had settled down at the Ashcrofts' shop. Doreen was being forced to rethink her policy with regard to Teresa and her work at the hotel. Now she had been taken on as a permanent shop assistant it might be as well if she were to give up her work at Sunset View, apart from a little waitressing, maybe, when they were busy. That was the only part that had been of much interest to her anyway. And now Bernie was almost of an age to step into her shoes.

Doreen smiled fondly at the thought of her youngest daughter. Bernie had never been a scrap of trouble and was as different from Teresa as chalk from cheese. She had been a very clinging sort of little girl, unsure of herself and finding it hard to make friends, and this had led to her spending more time with her mother than any of the others had done. She now had a 'best friend', Maureen, who had helped greatly in bringing her out of her shell. Bernie even looked different now. The brace she had worn on her slightly protruding teeth had done the trick, her spots were dying back and, since turning fifteen, she had started using a touch of pink lipstick, at the persuasion of Maureen, no doubt.

Working at the hotel would be ideal for the baby of the family, Doreen mused, especially waitressing, which would help her to overcome her shyness and insecurity. Perhaps, when she was sixteen, she could go on one of those book-keeping and receptionist courses that Paul had mentioned they ran at the college. The place had worked wonders for Paul . . .

What a godsend he had been over Christmas. Doreen had received compliments galore from the guests about the high standard of the cuisine. What a posh-sounding word that was! One she had picked up from Paul. He was already drawing up menu plans for their Easter opening and had been experimenting, when he was not at college, with all kinds of fancy dessert dishes, which the rest of

214

the family had been delighted to sample. Sometimes Martin came to help him, or he went round to Martin's flat to try out another menu they had learned at college. It was little wonder that neither of them had a girlfriend. There was no time in their busy schedule for girls, although she was sure, one day, that they would each meet someone nice and suitable. Such a good-looking young man, that Martin . . .

Doreen realised, when contemplating her family, that Michael was the one whom she thought about the least. Not that she loved him any less than the others, but Michael, especially of late, had been something of an enigma. He went to school and came back again at the end of the day without any fuss, then disappeared into his room to study. His O level results had been very good, outstandingly so considering he had been a late entrant at his grammar school, and now he was studying for A levels. He seldom went out with his friends, but apart from mealtimes the rest of the family saw very little of him. And knew even less. He did not appear unhappy, though, or worried, and, like his twin sister, Doreen guessed he might resent too much nosing into his affairs. And so, with Michael as well, she decided to mind her own business, trusting that if there was anything on his mind he would eventually tell her.

There was something on Veronica's mind, that was certain. Man trouble again, more than likely, although Doreen knew it would be best not to ask outright. She was not seeing Richard now and seemed to have got over that episode with comparative ease. No doubt she had realised he was not her 'Mr Right'. Doreen had never thought that he was, but she did so wish her eldest daughter could find someone who was just right for her. Relations between the sisters had been strained for a while too; Veronica and Teresa, that was, not Bernie. Bernie, bless her, never seemed to be at odds with anyone. All appeared to be well again now when the two elder girls met, so that could not be what was troubling Veronica.

But something was, and Doreen had an odd feeling – a presentiment, almost – that it was something serious, something she ought to know about. This was her first-born child, and heaven forbid that Veronica should get to the point again where she considered life was not worth living. Doreen had not thought about that traumatic event for ages, but now, as it entered her mind, she was aware of a sense of urgency. Veronica was due to pay them a visit, probably tomorrow. She often called on the evening of her half-day, or she had been doing since she no longer had a boyfriend. She would try and get her on her own, away from the rest of the family.

Doreen reached for another cigarette. Her meandering thoughts, at first, had been pleasant, happy ones. Now, for some unaccountable reason, they had taken a different turn. Doreen was worried.

Veronica had tried to push the thoughts of Paul's – and Martin's – secret life to the back of her mind, but the trouble was they refused to stay there. After a day or two she had almost convinced herself that Sandra had been talking nonsense. She was imagining it; it could not possibly be true. But when she next brought the subject up Sandra told her, to her amazement, that she had asked Paul outright and he had admitted that he and Martin were . . . gay. Veronica hated saying that word, even to herself. She had never heard it used before in that context, until Sandra had told her of its new meaning. It had used to mean joyful, light-hearted; now it was all spoiled.

She had been annoyed with Sandra, peeved that her friend had had the audacity to go behind her back and actually ask her, Veronica's, brother questions about his private life. Just imagine! The boldness of it! Veronica knew she would never have had the courage to do it and that, in some part, may have been why she felt so irritated. On the other hand it was a relief, she supposed, to know for certain, and she could not help but admire her friend for her matter-of-fact approach to it all. She had not stayed cross with Sandra for long. Veronica did not like to be at variance with anyone, and Sandra had proved to be an ideal flatmate ever since she came to live there.

But her uneasy knowledge was having an effect on her dealings with the rest of her family. She felt awkward whenever she went to see them at Sunset View, although it was possible that none of them noticed her discomfiture, except for Paul, of course. She knew that he knew that she knew, although neither of them mentioned it. And Veronica knew that Paul did not want the rest of the family to know; Sandra had insisted that she must not say anything and she had no intention of doing so. It was difficult, though, knowing something the rest of them did not know, and she had been aware of her mother giving her an odd look now and again.

Fortunately she had not encountered Paul and Martin together, not since that evening when they had all gone to the party. Paul, wisely, seemed to have kept his friend away from the hotel whenever he knew his sister might be visiting. She felt even more relieved when Paul was not there either. She hated feeling that way because she was fond of her brother, but the intrusive thoughts of something she did not – could not – understand or come to terms with were marring their brother-and-sister relationship.

Paul was not there when she called at the hotel one evening in the middle of March and she felt herself giving an inward sigh of relief and relaxing a little more. Teresa was there, but she soon left with a cheery, 'Tara, see you later.'

'Where's she going?' asked Veronica as the door closed behind her. 'Is there, er, a new boyfriend, by any chance?'

'I don't know and I've learned not to ask,' replied her mother, to Veronica's surprise. At one time Mum had been so anxious about Teresa – who she was with and what she was doing. 'She's growing up,' she went on in answer to Veronica's questioning glance. 'I've realised I can't always be on to her. It only makes things worse and, well, there comes a point when you've got to let go. You can't watch your children every minute of every day.

You'll know what I mean one day, love. You try to bring them up properly and then you've just got to trust them.'

Veronica saw her mother glance towards her husband, who was engrossed in a Western on the television. Michael, as usual, was upstairs doing his homework, and Bernie had gone to see her friend Maureen. 'Come on,' she said. 'We'll leave your dad to watch John Wayne in peace. Come upstairs with me; I've got something to show you.'

They manoeuvred their way past the building work that was going on on the first floor, and up to the bedroom on the second floor, which her mother and father used. It was a back room, without the sea or sunset view, but the superior rooms had to be left for the guests and Doreen considered it was not worth moving out in the off season, only to move back again later. She opened the wardrobe and took out some garments that Veronica had not seen before, such garments, indeed, as her mother had never worn before in all her life.

'Ta-dah!' she announced in a girlish voice, spreading them out on the bed for her daughter's inspection. 'What d'you think of that, eh?'

Veronica looked in surprise at the black velvet trouser suit. The edges of the jacket, trousers and matching waistcoat were edged with black satin braid. It was certainly very stylish and absolutely up to the minute. It might have seemed too severe and masculine-looking, especially for her ultra-feminine mother, but it would be redeemed by the frilly white silk blouse that lay next to it. This had a lace-trimmed collar and cuffs with a neat red satin bow at the neck, the only touch of colour in the whole ensemble.

'What do you think?' said her mother again, a little unsurely. 'You don't think it's too . . . ?'

'Too what, Mum? Too young? Too modern? Too snazzy? It's all those things, but not *too* much so. I think it's super; you'll look great in it.'

'Thank you, love. I wasn't sure, you see, and you looked a bit taken aback.'

218

'Only because you haven't bought anything like this before. Honest, I love it. I know it didn't come from M&S, though. Where did you get it?'

'Diana Warren's,' said her mother, to Veronica's even greater amazement. Diana Warren's was a very classy dress shop, patronised by folk who were worth a bob or two. You needed to be to shop there. 'Yes, I know I'm pushing the boat out a bit, but I thought, Why not? I can afford it. We did very well at Christmas and I felt like treating myself. It will be nice to wear in the evenings. I was wondering if Sandra would come and give us another musical evening?'

'Sure, Mum; I'll ask her. Are you going to try it on for me?'

'No, not just now, love. Another time, perhaps. I just wanted to have your opinion.' She picked up the garments and replaced them carefully in the wardrobe, then she hesitated before turning to face her daughter again. 'And I wanted to have a little chat with you, on our own, I mean.'

'Why, Mum?' Veronica was instantly on the alert. 'What's wrong?' Surely her mother hadn't found out about Paul?

'There's nothing wrong, dear, as far as I know; not here anyway. But I wondered . . . well, I've felt for some time that there was something troubling you. I don't want to pry. I've just been saying, haven't I, that you've got to let your children get on with their lives, but I don't like to see you looking so worried.'

Veronica shrugged with an air of nonchalance. 'Didn't realise that I did.'

'Well, sort of preoccupied then.'

'I'm not, Mum, honest I'm not. There's nothing wrong; nothing at all.' Veronica was aware that she was speaking too loudly and being too vehement in her denials. She shook her head. 'Perhaps I'm feeling a bit tired, that's all.' She smiled weakly.

'Oh well, so long as that's all it is and there's nothing wrong.' Her mother still sounded a little doubtful. 'I wondered if it was because of Richard, but that was quite a long time ago now and you didn't seem all that bothered when you split up. He wasn't right for you, dear, but you know that, don't you? Never mind; there'll be someone special for you, maybe just round the corner.' A sudden thought seemed to strike her. 'What happened to Martin?' she asked.

The remark was so out of the blue that Veronica heard herself give a startled gasp. 'What . . . what d'you mean?' she stuttered. 'Nothing's happened to Martin, as far as I know. Why should it have done?'

'All right, love. I didn't mean to upset you.' Her mother was smiling understandingly. 'Perhaps I worded it badly. I only meant to say, well, I thought at one time that you and he were getting friendly, then the four of you went to that party. And we don't seem to have seen very much of him since then.'

'Well, it's nothing to do with me.' Veronica was trying to make herself speak calmly now she had had a chance to recover a little. 'I don't know why Martin doesn't come here, but it's certainly not because of me. I'm not interested in Martin Wade. I never have been and I never will be.'

'Mm . . . I see,' her mother answered thoughtfully. 'Perhaps it's Paul then. Maybe he's fallen out with Martin. I know he hasn't mentioned him as much lately and he's been rather quiet. Not that I've taken much notice of that; our Paul's always quiet. Anyway, so long as there's nothing wrong with you; that's what I was most concerned about.'

Veronica sat down suddenly on the bed. She felt as though her legs would no longer hold her. 'Oh no,' she cried. 'Paul and Martin haven't fallen out, you can be sure of that. Paul and Martin are best buddies, aren't they?' She could not keep the bitterness out of her voice. 'They won't fall out because . . .' She shook her head. 'Because they're . . .' She buried her head in her hands and burst into tears.

Her mother sat down beside her. 'Because they're what,

love?' She stroked her daughter's hair. 'Whatever's the matter? What were you going to say? There's nothing wrong, surely, with Paul and Martin being good mates. It doesn't mean that you and Martin can't be friendly. You did like him, didn't you? I can tell.' Veronica didn't answer. Her mother's voice suddenly faltered. 'Veronica, what is it?'

Veronica turned a tear-stained face towards her. 'Paul and Martin,' she wailed. 'I wasn't supposed to say anything. Nobody's supposed to know. But I've got to tell you, Mum; I've got to. Our Paul, he's . . . well, he's what they call . . . gay.' She saw a look of shock and anguish distort her mother's face and she felt so very sorry for her, but it was such a relief to tell her, to share the knowledge that had been burning away at her. 'Paul and Martin; they're a couple, Mum. Do you understand what I'm saying? They're not interested in girls. So it would be no use me liking Martin. Oh, Mum, isn't it dreadful?'

Doreen was not sure what she felt at first. Disbelief, shock, horror, repugnance. These were the thoughts, one following quickly upon another, that seized her in those first few awful moments. Her son was . . . like that; he was the sort of man that jokes were made about, with limp-wristed gestures and a simpering walk. 'You know – he's one of those!' And yet, didn't it all add up, now she had been told about it? There was the fact that he had never had a steady girlfriend, only one or two casual dates, and then, of course, his firm friendship with Martin. She had been aware that it was a close friendship but she had been, oh, so blind. Or had she been hiding from herself, maybe, a truth she had feared all along? His choice of profession; the way he had loved to help her in the kitchen, to the amusement of his siblings. But she realised that that was not an indication. Many of the best chefs, as Paul had often told her, were men, and she was sure that the majority of them were quite normal men. It would be wrong to say they were all tarred with the same brush because they had chosen a career in catering.

These were the thoughts that were to run constantly through her mind for the next few days, giving her no peace and making her moody and irritable. She told Norman it was 'the time of the month', which happened to be true, although it did not usually bother her. She and Veronica had agreed that the truth must be kept hidden from Norman and, indeed, from the rest of the family. She was not sure what her husband's reaction would be; in fact she had no idea at all as to how he would respond to the knowledge. He might be quite calm and philosophical, or he might blow his top. Who could tell? They had never had to face such a situation before.

Doreen had not believed it at first, or had pretended not to, until her daughter had convinced her of the truth of it. Paul had admitted it to Sandra. To Sandra? Then, did her family know? Veronica assured her they didn't. Nobody knew; after all it was not the sort of thing one talked about. It was still a criminal offence, wasn't it? Doreen thought about poor old Oscar Wilde – even she had heard about him – although that was ages ago. She was surprised, when she had got over the initial shock, that she was able to talk about it with her daughter. Poor Veronica! So that was what had been the matter. She had been keeping it all to herself for several weeks and Doreen knew, in spite of her denials, that she had been getting fond of Martin. Poor lass; nothing ever seemed to go right for her.

That evening she had said a hurried goodbye to her father, who was still engrossed in his John Wayne film, making the excuse that she had to go home to wash her hair. Doreen had been left with a burden of anxiety, which, the more she thought about it, the harder it became to bear. She did not understand. Such things were beyond her realm of experience. The next time she encountered Paul, which was the following morning when he was leaving for college, she found she could hardly look him in the eye. She tried to behave normally, but it was impossible. Strangely enough the rest of the family did not appear to have noticed. But Paul had. He sought her out in the kitchen on the Sunday morning. This was nothing unusual; when there were no visitors in the hotel she and Paul always cooked a traditional Sunday lunch for the family. Earlier in the day they had all been to Mass, except for Paul, who said he would be attending later. With Martin, she guessed. She had found out that Martin was also a Catholic, which was a crumb of comfort, she supposed.

'What's the matter, Mum?' His grey eyes looked troubled, as indeed they might, she thought bitterly. She had known there would be a confrontation between the two of them eventually, but she had no idea what she would say to him or how she would act. As she looked at him now her heart ached with love for him, but yet she felt she did not know him. He had become a stranger to her. 'You know, don't you?' he said quietly. 'Veronica's told you, hasn't she?'

'Yes . . .' Doreen let out her breath in a long deep sigh. 'Yes, she told me . . . about you and Martin. I know you didn't want me to find out, but don't start blaming your sister. She's been very upset about it, and having to keep it to herself has made it worse. I knew there was something troubling her and in the end, well, she told me. Oh Paul, why couldn't you have told me yourself ages ago? I'd have tried to understand.'

'I couldn't tell you; I couldn't tell anybody. I didn't understand it myself until . . . until I met Martin, I suppose. It was something that had nagged at me for years and years and I couldn't make sense of it. I just knew that I was . . . different.'

'You mean, even when you were a little boy? You knew?'

'Well, yes. Even then I knew there was something not quite right, but I didn't know what it was, and then gradually I became aware—'

'That you fancied boys instead of girls?' Doreen knew she sounded cynical and that her words and the tone of her voice might be upsetting to her son, but she could not help that. He had upset them badly, both herself and

223

Veronica, and she could not forget that or come to terms with it so very easily. Suddenly she felt angry. 'Why, Paul, why?' she yelled at him. 'Why didn't you do something about it? Get some help or treatment or something? Surely there was something you could have done. You've given in to it; you've been weak-willed. You haven't tried. Oh, I don't understand. I don't understand any of it. I just know it's not . . . it's not normal.'

He stepped towards her and put a hand on her arm. She felt herself flinching, but she tried to keep still. 'I wouldn't expect you to understand, Mum,' he said gently. 'But you must try to accept that it's just the way it is; just the way I am. I can't help it.'

'I'm sure that's what they all say.'

'I wouldn't know about that, because I don't talk about it, not to anyone.'

'Except to Martin?'

'Well, yes, of course. But Martin and I . . . I want you to understand that our . . . relationship . . . that it's only a small part of our lives.' She gave an involuntary grimace of distaste and Paul smiled sadly. 'Yes, I know it's repugnant to you. Try not to think about it. I know you may not believe me, but Martin and I, more than anything else, are really good mates. I've never had a friend like Martin. We like the same things. There's the profession we've both chosen, of course, and lots of other interests as well. We both played rugger at school and we like to watch that rather than soccer; we listen to the same music; we laugh at the same jokes.'

'So it's what you might call a perfect friendship?' Doreen raised a cynical eyebrow, but Paul answered her boldly.

'Yes, we happen to think it is.'

'For how long? How long will it last?'

Paul gave a slight shrug. 'Who knows? For ever, we hope. We're very discreet, you know. One has to be, but times are changing. People are becoming more liberal in their attitudes, more broad-minded.'

'It all depends on how you look at it. Some might say

that our society is becoming far too permissive. It seems as though anything goes today.'

'Oh, come on, Mum. I would never have considered you to be narrow-minded. Try to understand.'

'I am trying, Paul. I'm trying hard, believe me. But all this has been such a shock. You'll have to leave me to come to terms with it in my own way, in my own time. That's all I can say. Now, what about this Sunday dinner? You see to the potatoes; you can do those fancy croquettes, if you like, and some roast as well. And I'll do the veg.'

'OK. Thanks, Mum. Thanks for trying to understand, at any rate. You won't, er, you won't say anything to Dad, will you?'

Doreen looked at him evenly. 'Not unless I have to. But I don't see how you can keep this under wraps for ever.'

'Please, Mum. He mustn't know.'

'All right, Paul.' She regarded him unsmilingly. 'I won't say anything. But your father's not an ogre, you know. He might understand.'

'Pigs might fly! I'm relying on you, Mum.'

'I'll do my best.'

She had not actually promised. Paul had not said the words, 'Promise me you won't say anything', which was just as well because she could not have made that sort of hand-on-heart, solemn vow. She would keep quiet for as long as she could, but she and Norman did not have secrets from one another, not any more. Since that episode when she had tried to deceive him and had had a brief fling with another man they had told one another everything. Her son needed to know he could depend on her and she would try to protect him as much as she was able, but it was her husband who was the more deserving of her loyalty. The truth would out sooner or later, and then she would have to try to make sure that Norman did not completely blow his top. In the meantime she was forcing herself not to think too much about Paul and Martin. This was easier said than done as Paul was now

225

spending more time than ever round at his friend's flat.

Norman noticed this, as he could hardly have failed to do, and commented upon it a couple of evenings later. Doreen wondered why her son, being so afraid of the truth emerging, had not had the sense to keep away from Martin's place for a while. After all, they did see one another during the day at college. But she supposed that was not enough. As always, she tried to turn her mind away from these unwelcome thoughts. All Norman said the first time was, 'Our Paul's round at Martin's again, is he? He spends so much time there I don't know why he doesn't go and live there.'

Doreen's heart almost missed a beat, but she answered casually enough. 'Would you mind if he did?'

'What – go and live at Martin's flat?'

'Well . . . yes. He's nineteen, Norman, and lots of young men have left home at that age.'

'Has he mentioned that he might?'

'No, not really. I know it's convenient for him to live here at the moment, whilst he's at college, but afterwards – well, we'll just have to wait and see.'

'But when he's qualified he's going to be our full-time chef, isn't he? Wasn't that the idea? I don't see how he can go and live somewhere else. He'll be working all hours God sends in the summer; you know what it's like. It's far better to live on the premises.'

'Yes, I suppose so,' said Doreen evasively. 'Maybe he will, maybe he won't. He has his own life to lead.' Feeling that she was getting into deep water and that Norman was looking at her in an odd way she got up and went into the kitchen to make a cup of tea. When she went back he was watching the nine o'clock news and Paul was not mentioned again until another two days had passed.

'Do you know, if I didn't know any better I'd think that son of ours was one of them nancy boys,' Norman said when Doreen joined him in the living room after making a phone call to Abbie. She stared at him, trying to smile, as he was doing, but her face felt frozen. 'He's just gone to

Martin's again,' he laughed. 'Seemed in an almighty hurry an' all.'

'Yes, I've just seen him,' said Doreen weakly. 'He passed me in the hall. He said . . . that was where he was going – to Martin's.'

'Aye, we'd better keep an eye on him,' Norman chuckled. 'Not that I've ever had anything against 'em – them queer fellows, you know – so long as they keep themselves to themselves. Happen we'd better have a word with him, eh? About seeing Martin so much. We don't want folk getting the wrong idea, do we? I know it's not likely they would, not with our Paul, but—'

Doreen sat down suddenly on the nearest chair. 'Norman, how can you be so sure it's . . . the wrong idea? Have you never wondered why they spend so much time together?' She looked at him steadily, watching his face change, his look of tolerant amusement turning to one of suspicion and anxiety.

'What . . . what d'you mean? Paul and Martin? No, never; never in a thousand years. I didn't say they *were*, love. I said we didn't want folk *thinking* that they were.'

'Norman . . .' Doreen gave a long deep sigh, 'they are . . . like that. Paul and Martin; they're a couple. You know – queer, like you just said. An awful word; apparently they say "gay" now.'

'What are you saying?' Norman yelled at her. 'Have you gone completely bonkers, woman? Of course they're not!' Norman had never called her 'woman' before, an expression she hated, but she knew he had said it only because he was so distressed. Anyway, the truth was out now. She had known all along that this would happen. Now she just had to keep him reasonably calm and try to help him to understand something she did not understand herself.

'Norman, it's true, honestly it is,' she replied. 'Veronica found out and she told me. It was when she and Sandra went to that party with Paul and Martin. They noticed – at least Sandra did – and it all came out then. Veronica tried to keep it from me, and I've tried to keep it from you. But I knew you'd have to be told in the end, and I'm glad you know. It's been so hard keeping it to myself. He's our son and—'

'Yes, he's our son . . .' Norman slumped forward in the chair and buried his head in his hands. Doreen wondered if he was weeping. Like many men he thought this was unmanly and on the rare occasions he was moved to tears he tried to hide it from her. But when he looked at her again his face was angry. 'But no son of mine is going to carry on like that. It's disgusting; it's not normal. He's not my son, not any more, if that's the sort of life he wants to lead. I've finished with him.'

'Norman, whatever are you saying? Of course he's our son, whatever he's done, whoever his friends are. It doesn't make any difference – how can it? – to the fact that he's our son. We have to try and understand.'

'Understand? How can I understand something so utterly wrong, so unnatural? Maybe you can, but I certainly can't.'

Doreen narrowed her eyes and looked at him keenly. 'Oh, I see. That's very strange, seeing that you told me, not five minutes ago, that you'd nothing against them – "them queer fellows" – not if they kept themselves to themselves.'

He looked a little abashed. 'Oh, yes; well, maybe I did say that. But I didn't know then that he was one of them, did I? It makes a difference, doesn't it, when it's one of your own? It's no use, I can't get my head round it. I don't think I ever will.' He shook his head sorrowfully. 'I find it hard to believe, Doreen, almost impossible.'

'So did I at first.' She felt sorry for him, but she hoped that after his initial anger had passed he might be able to accept it, as she had tried to do. 'But we can't change things. That's the way it is, and that's the way it's going to continue, whether we like it or not.'

'Not under my roof, it isn't.'

'But it's not going on under our roof, Norman. Martin has his own flat.'

'Then Paul had better go and live there, hadn't he?'

'How can he? You said yourself it was better if he lived on the premises.'

'That was before I knew. No, it's no use, Doreen. He'll have to go.'

She tried to make him calm down. She told him, more or less, everything that Paul had told her, appealing to his sense of reason and trusting that the deep family feeling he had always had would overcome the repugnance he was now feeling towards his eldest son. She pleaded with him to sleep on it, telling him he might feel differently in the morning, but it was to no avail. He was adamant and, what was more, he insisted on waiting up to see Paul that very night.

Doreen went to bed, not wanting to be a part of whatever was going to happen between her husband and son. She felt guilty, partly because she had 'let on' when Paul had asked her not to do so, and partly because she was not supporting him now, when he needed her. But it would be no use. Norman was as angry as she had ever seen him, and hurt too. He had been angry that time she had had her little fling, and rightly so, but he had calmed down in the end and everything had been all right again. Maybe when he actually saw Paul and spoke with him his loving fatherly feeling would prevail.

Their other children were in bed, on the top floor, fortunately, when Paul came in at midnight. Doreen, unable to sleep, had heard the sound of the front door opening and closing from two storeys away. She crept downstairs and crouched halfway down the bottom flight, knowing she should not eavesdrop, but unable to keep away.

'You are no son of mine . . . Your behaviour is despicable and I don't want you under my roof, you and your . . .' Doreen was shocked at the torrent of abuse. She had not thought that Norman would have known such words, let alone used them. 'You'd better go – now – and live with your boyfriend . . .' She was not near enough to hear Paul's reply to his father's outburst, but at the words, 'We don't want you here,' she could listen to no more of

229

it. She dashed into the living room where they were standing, a yard or so apart, like sparring partners in a wrestling match although she knew there would be no blows exchanged.

'Norman, Paul, stop it, both of you!' she cried. 'Norman, what are you saying? Of course we want him here.' They both turned to look at her, Paul sadly and – she feared – accusingly, and her husband with a glance of annoyance.

'Leave us, please, Doreen,' he said. 'I'm dealing with this.'

'Yes, just leave it, Mum,' said Paul quietly. 'It would be best.'

She went back upstairs and it was about fifteen minutes later that she heard the front door open and close again. Norman came into the bedroom and sat on the bed at the side of her. He put an arm round her shoulders. 'I'm sorry, love. I didn't mean to speak to you like that, but I had to deal with it myself, in my own way.'

'In your own way?' She pulled away from his arm. 'All you did was lose your temper.'

'Yes, maybe I did at first. I had to tell him how I felt. It's no use him thinking I condone it, because I don't . . . I can't. But I let him have his say in the end. He said quite a lot actually. He tried to make me understand, but I know I never will.'

'And where is he now?'

'Where do you think? He's gone back to Martin's flat. It was his decision as much as mine.'

'You've driven him away, Norman. And by turning him out you're making it worse, can't you see? He's gone to live with Martin and that's the one thing we don't really want him to do.'

Norman gave a slight shrug. 'He'd have gone anyway; he told me so, and it's better that he and I don't try to live under the same roof. It's too much for me to bear. I feel I don't know him any more – nor do I want to,' he added sadly, 'at the moment.'

'You'll have to see him, though,' said Doreen. 'You'll

have no choice. He's our chef and it will be Easter before we know where we are.'

'You'll have to get another chef, love,' said Norman, quite matter-of-factly. 'Paul won't be with us.'

'What do you mean?' Doreen sat bolt upright in bed. 'You've gone and sacked him, haven't you? How dare you? You know it's up to me—'

'No, I haven't. I'm not saying I wouldn't have done so. I don't want him working here, but he's resigned.'

'Resigned? I don't believe you. And if he has it's because of you, because of what you said to him.'

Norman shook his head. 'No, he and . . . Martin,' he almost spat out the name, 'they're going into partnership. A restaurant or something of the sort. They've been thinking about it for a while. Now it'll probably happen sooner rather than later, that's all.'

'That's all!' Doreen yelled at him. 'We're going to be without a chef at Easter and you say "That's all"? What on earth am I going to do, Norman?'

'You'll cope, love. You always have and you always will. Now, we'd best get some sleep, hadn't we? We'll talk about it in the morning – about his job, I mean. It should be easy enough to get a replacement. Oh, come on, love; I know you're upset, but we'll get over this. And don't forget we've got four other children.'

Doreen turned her back on him, too outraged and hurt to speak. She humped the bedclothes round her and moved as near to the edge of the bed as she could. She could not bring herself to go and sleep in another room. Neither of them had ever done that, but she made no move towards him as he got ready for bed, and for the first time for years they went to sleep without saying an affectionate good night. At least Norman slept, but Doreen stayed awake almost until dawn. She felt sure, however, that Norman could not possibly be as callous and uncaring as his behaviour suggested and that, deep inside, he must be hurting just as much as she was.

Chapter 11

Andy

'Now, you're coming with Ian and me, and I don't want any arguing,' said Sandra. 'It'll do you good to get out for a change and I can assure you it'll be a real smashing do. At the Imperial, and you can't get much posher than that!'

Veronica pouted. 'I'm not bothered about going to a posh do. And you're talking as though I never go out. We went to the pictures last week, you and me, and I came to listen to you when you were playing at my mum's place, and—'

'And that was ages ago,' Sandra replied. 'It was Easter Saturday, and since then you've hardly been anywhere except to go and see your parents. I know you're all still upset about Paul, but life has to go on, you know. Your mum and dad seem to be putting a brave face on.'

'Mum is, you mean. Dad's acting as though Paul never existed. He never mentions him. I feel as though I have to keep going round to see how Mum's coping. I was frightened she'd go to pieces completely that first awful weekend after he'd gone.'

'But she didn't, did she? She's strong, your mother; she won't go under. And they managed to get another chef to help out over Easter, so that was a big worry off her mind. He's still there, isn't he?'

'Karl Robson? Yes, he's still there. They seem very satisfied with him. I suppose my mother still thinks there's nobody like Paul, but she said she'd take Karl on for a trial period and he's proved his worth. They're not all that busy at the moment, till the proper summer season starts. Just ticking over, as Mum says.'

'Then let them get on with it, Veron, and think about yourself for a change.'

'It's very kind of you to invite me, Sandra, but I don't want to play gooseberry.'

'You won't be,' said her friend. 'There'll be a big crowd of us and they won't all have a partner with them. You know some of the girls I work with, don't you? Shirley and Chrissie and Olwen? And the postmen are a jolly crowd.'

'They'll all have their wives with them.'

'Not all of them. There are some younger ones who aren't married.'

'They'll be with their girlfriends.'

'Oh, you! You're determined to be a spoilsport, aren't you?' Sandra took a mock swipe at her with a pot towel and was pleased to see Veronica respond with a smile.

'OK then,' she said, grinning. 'You're nothing but a big bully. But you win; I'll go.'

It was now the middle of May and the event they were discussing whilst washing up the pots after their evening meal was a dinner and dance to be held at the Imperial Hotel on the first Saturday in June. It was being organised by members of the GPO in Blackpool in aid of local charities and, judging by the way the tickets were going, it promised to be highly successful.

'I've nothing to wear, though,' Veronica went on. 'You said it was going to be a posh sort of do.'

'Not all that posh,' said Sandra. 'I only meant the hotel was posh. It's not evening dress or anything like that. Well, I suppose you can wear it if you want to, but Ian and I won't. He'll wear his best suit, I suppose – his one and only suit, actually,' she laughed, 'and I shall wear my trouser suit and a nice blouse, then I can take the jacket off. And you've got your pale blue dress.'

Veronica shuddered. 'I shan't wear that again, not for a

233

while, perhaps not ever.' Sandra remembered it was the dress she had been wearing when they went to that party with Paul and Martin.

'Then buy something new, why don't you?' Sandra said. 'Go on, Veronica. Treat yourself. I was looking at the new styles in Marks and Sparks the other day. They've some stunning clothes at the moment, and you'll get your discount. I'll come and help you choose something if you like.' And then I can steer you away from baby pinks and blues, and on to something more sophisticated, Sandra thought, but did not say.

'All right then; I might.' Veronica still sounded a little hesitant, then: 'Why not? Yes, I blooming well will,' she cried. 'I need cheering up, and a new dress always does the trick; well, partly . . . What I really need, of course, is a new man – the right one.' She looked pensive and Sandra smiled encouragingly. She would have thought her friend might have had enough of men, with her track record, and she was obviously still hurting over the disappointment she had had with Martin. But Veronica, once she shook herself out of the doldrums, was ever the optimist.

'You never know,' said Sandra. 'He might be just round the corner. I'll see what I can do. There must be a few nice unattached men at the post office.'

'Oh no, no.' Veronica held up a restraining hand. 'Don't start matchmaking or trying to introduce me to somebody. I'll be cross if you do. I believe in Fate, I do. What has to be will be.' She burst into a rendition of 'The Man I Love' and Sandra joined in.

She was pleased her friend had cheered up, and considerably so. Sandra believed, however, that sometimes Fate could do with a helping hand.

The postmen at Blackpool GPO, as Sandra had remarked to Veronica, were a jolly crowd. Not that she knew them all, not by any means – there were well over a hundred of them – but the ones with whom she was acquainted were friendly and cheerful, always ready to exchange good-humoured banter with herself and other members of the counter staff whenever they met. She wondered how they kept so jovial, knowing they arose at four o'clock each morning to be in the sorting office by five and out on their deliveries, whatever the weather, by seven o'clock. And then there were the ones who worked at night and snatched what sleep they could during the day. Sandra guessed that might be even worse.

Many of the postmen were older, nearing retirement age, and Sandra did not know this group very well at all, except for a few of them, by sight or just to say hello. The crowd she knew were considerably younger, in their twenties or even late teens; some of them were married and some of them – it had to be admitted – were extremely silly and given to loud, though good-natured behaviour. They said that getting up so early in the morning made them behave like that. It was only the camaraderie they enjoyed in the office that woke them up and kept them going.

Sandra was anxious that her friend should not feel she was playing gooseberry, as she had said she feared, or that she was doomed to be a wallflower. Not that there was much likelihood of that. Veronica was an extremely attractive girl and would no doubt have a lot of dancing partners. All the same . . . She had cast her eyes first at her fellow assistants on the counter. They were mostly women, and the couple of men she dismissed as weedy and uninteresting. The clerical workers in the upstairs office were all married, which led her to consider the postmen she knew. It was tricky, though. Veronica had been adamant that she should not matchmake, although Sandra was inclined to take that statement with a pinch of salt. Her friend was always ready and willing for an introduction to a presentable man. The trouble with Veronica was that she always tried to look too far ahead. The moment she met someone new she imagined she could hear the chime of wedding bells . . . And all Sandra wanted to do, at the moment, was to ensure that she had a good time at the dinner dance. The trouble was that the postmen were, by and large, either too young or too old or married.

She was pondering the problem whilst she was serving on the counter one day towards the end of May. It was almost twelve thirty, the time she was due for her lunch break. She glanced up and noticed Andy Mackintosh in her queue. He was one of the postmen she knew reasonably well, a pleasant, quiet sort of man. He had transferred to Blackpool from the post office in Edinburgh a few years previously as his wife's family lived in the town and she wanted to be near to them. And then, a couple of years ago, just before Sandra had joined the Post Office, his wife had died suddenly as the result of a brain tumour. It had been all the more tragic, not only because it was so unexpected, but because she had been so young and, according to Andy's friends, they had been a devoted couple. She had been only thirty-two years of age, a year younger than her husband. Andy was now thirty-five and doing his best to bring up their two children, Barry and Donna, aged six and eight.

Sandra smiled at him now as he reached the front of the queue. The end of the queue, as it happened, because the two people behind him, noticing there were no customers waiting at some of the other positions, seized their opportunity and nipped across smartly. 'Hello there, Andy; and what can I do for you?' she asked.

'Hi there, Sandra. Just a book of stamps, please, and a ten-shilling postal order,' he replied. He was a softly spoken man and his gentle Scottish accent was pleasing to the ear. 'It's my nephew's birthday and I never know what to buy him. I think lads of ten like the money as much as anything, don't you?'

'I'm sure they do,' she agreed, dealing quickly with his request. No doubt his wife had seen to such things as birthdays in the past; men invariably left such matters to the womenfolk. She caught his eye as he pushed the money across the counter. He was not a very tall man – about her own height with friendly blue-grey eyes and wavy hair of a fairish brown. You only had to look at him

236

to know at once that he was a kindly person, not stunningly handsome, but with craggy, northern sort of features, a trifle weather-beaten and with a few untimely ageing lines across his forehead and around his eyes. A face, however, that you knew instinctively you could trust. On an impulse, as his eyes smiled amiably into hers, she asked, 'Are you going to the dinner and dance next Saturday, Andy?'

'Och, I don't know, Sandra.' The light left his eyes for a moment and he looked a little anxious. 'Some of the lads have been asking me the same thing; trying to twist my arm, you know, saying it would do me good to get out and let my hair down for a change. But I've got out of the way of it, that's the honest truth – going out and having what they call "a good time", if you know what I mean.' Sandra did know what he meant. Some of the younger postmen in their mid-twenties – some married and some not – had befriended Andy, and it was said that when he was with them he could be, surprisingly, the life and soul of the party. He was well known for his dry sense of humour and his droll impersonations of some of the senior staff; amusing, but never meant in an unkindly way. This was only inside the office, however; seldom could he be persuaded to socialise with his colleagues outside working hours.

She nodded understandingly at him now. 'Yes, I know. But you don't have to join in their high jinks if it's not your scene. Anyway, I dare say some of your boisterous mates will have their wings clipped somewhat, won't they, if they have their wives with them?'

'Aye, mebbe you're right,' he chuckled softly. 'I've not made up my mind yet, though, whether to go or not. I'm still thinking about it.'

'Would you be able to get a baby-sitter? Well, someone to look after your children, I meant – they're not babies, are they?'

'Och, that's no problem. Jean's younger sister lives with us and she gives me a hand with the children.' Sandra knew that Jean was the name of his wife who had died.

She had often pondered as to how Andy Mackintosh managed to cope with the odd hours a postman worked, with two children to care for. 'It works out quite well,' he went on. 'Carol – that's my sister-in-law – she's a lot younger than Jean . . . was. She's nineteen – about your age, I suppose – and she felt she needed a bit of independence. So she's got a room – a sort of bedsitting room – at my place, and it means I can leave the house early in the morning and know that the kids are quite safe. And on the very few occasions I want to go out, well, I've got a live-in baby-sitter. She'll no doubt make the most of the opportunity and have her boyfriend round,' he laughed.

'So you've decided you'll go to the dance then?'

'I might; yes, I might well . . . Why?' He gave her a sudden questioning look. 'You'd not be wanting a partner, would you, Sandra? If so, then I'd be only too willing.' His eyes lit up again in a friendly teasing way.

'Oh no, not at all,' she laughed. 'You know I'm not. You've met Ian, haven't you? He's coming home for the weekend.'

'Dash it! Foiled again!' Andy grinned broadly as he thumped his fist on the counter. 'Never mind. You've not got a sister, by any chance, have you?'

'No, but I've got a very nice friend.'

'Och, I see. Yes, I see it now.' He pretended to scowl at her. 'You're trying a wee bit of matchmaking, is that it?'

'No, no, it's not like that at all. Please don't think that.' She glanced around – there was no one else waiting to be served – then at her watch. It was past the time for her lunch break so she put up a notice that read 'Position Closed' before she went on speaking to Andy. 'The thing is, I've got this friend, like I said, and I've had a devil of a job persuading her to go with me and Ian. Eventually she's decided she will, but she was just as adamant as you are that I mustn't try anything like pairing her off with somebody. So I've said I won't.'

'But you will if you get half a chance?'

'No, no. But it just occurred to me, when I saw you, that you might perhaps come and have a drink with us,

238

with Ian and me, casual like, then I could introduce you to her. And you could have a dance with her, maybe, that is . . . if you were going. She's called Veronica,' she added, wondering, at the serious look on his face, if she had blown it. 'She's very nice.'

'I'm sure she is. She must be if she's a friend of yours,' said Andy soberly. 'I'm not promising anything, mind you, but . . . I'll see.' He winked at her. 'Cheerio then, Sandra. Be seeing you. It's been nice chatting to you.'

''Bye, Andy. See you,' she replied. Oh, damn and blast! She hoped she hadn't tried too hard. She didn't think for one moment that Andy Mackintosh and Veronica would fall madly in love or anything like that; in fact, until she had seen him there in the post office queue, she hadn't really thought about him at all with regard to Veronica. Her idea of asking him if he was going to the dance had been a spur-of-the-moment thing. He was a very nice kindly man and she was sure he and her friend would rub along very well together, just for the evening, that was, if he decided to go. Her main objective was to ensure that Veronica did not feel like a fish out of water amongst all the post office crowd.

Ah well, she had done her best and now it was out of her hands. There was no point in worrying any more about it; as Veronica had said, it all depended on what Fate had in store. She, Sandra, could concentrate now on looking forward to the weekend ahead when she would be seeing Ian again. She began to feel a stirring of excitement at the thought of it. It was a month since she had seen him and she found she was missing him more and more when they were apart.

Veronica felt very pleased with her appearance. For once she thought she looked just as sophisticated and suave as her friend, in fact, more so. It was strange how their roles now seemed to be reversed. When she had first got to know Sandra Horsfall – Sandie, she had called herself then – the girl had been a teenager, fifteen or so, and easily impressed by girls older than herself. Veronica recalled how she had shown her how to use a touch of green eyeshadow, which Sandra had considered the height of panache and worldliness. Now it was she, Veronica, who looked to Sandra for guidance as to how she should dress and do her hair.

In the end they had rejected Marks and Spencer's clothes, smart and up-to-date as they might be, because there were too many of them all alike, racks and racks of them. There was nothing worse than turning up at a posh do and finding that half a dozen girls were all wearing the same dress, albeit in different colours and sizes. Instead they had gone to Paige's where Veronica had chosen, with Sandra's assistance, a silky rayon dress in a vivid cerise shade, patterned with huge black spots. It was far too startling, she had at first pronounced, but when she tried it on she could see that it certainly did something for her, making her look extremely chic and striking – but not too conspicuous, she hoped. Her friend assured her it was perfect. The semi-fitted style and boat-shaped neckline suited her admirably, as did the short – but not too short – skirt, which finished a couple of inches above her knees. Sandra had helped her to arrange her blonde hair into a French pleat, fixing a matching cerise bow at the back, and her new Max Factor lipstick toned exactly with the dress.

Veronica had been surprised at the dress that Sandra had chosen for herself, bought specially for the occasion. She had declared at first that she would be wearing her trouser suit, dressing it up with a frilly blouse, but the selection of styles on display at Paige's had proved irresistible, especially as her friend was splashing out. Sandra, also, had decided to throw caution to the winds. In spite of steering her friend away from the pinks and pale blues and lemons, she had, in fact, opted for a dress that was amazingly demure and pretty. It was of cream-coloured crocheted lace, worn over a matching mini-length slip, with elbow-length lace sleeves ending in scalloped cuffs that matched the hem of the skirt. Too young, too fussy, Veronica had thought – but had not said – when her friend had taken it off the rack, but she could see when Sandra tried it on that she looked lovely: young and fresh and vibrant, a girl on the brink of womanhood.

'Yes, I think we'll do,' Sandra said now as they looked at themselves in the full-length mirror in the bedroom. She laughed. 'In fact I think we both look stunning. We'll knock 'em cold, kid! Now, Ian should be here soon to pick us up. It said six thirty for seven on the tickets and he's usually pretty punctual.'

The bar area adjoining the dining room at the Imperial Hotel was filling up when they arrived, but they managed to find a vacant table and Ian went to the bar to order their pre-dinner drinks. Veronica stared round a little anxiously. Sandra knew so many people. Her friend had been greeted with a chorus of hellos from nearly everyone they had met on the way in, the men as well as the women, which was only to be expected as these were her colleagues from work. But, so far, Sandra had not introduced her to anyone. She had insisted, of course, that she didn't want to be part of any matchmaking or anything like that, but all the same she did wonder . . .

'Will we have special places for our dinner?' she asked now. 'I mean, are there name cards telling us where to sit? Because I don't—'

'Because you don't know anybody,' Sandra finished for her. 'Don't worry about it; you soon will. They're a really friendly crowd, I keep telling you. No, I think it's all rather informal; no place cards or anything. I'll find some friends to sit with, Shirley and Chrissie, perhaps, and we'll grab a table, or part of a table. I think they're usually set for about ten or twelve.' She was staring around a little distractedly as she spoke. Then her expression changed as she caught sight of a man who was approaching their table. 'Andy, hello there,' she greeted him warmly. 'Are you coming to join us?'

Aye aye, thought Veronica, a trifle petulantly. She's been up to her tricks, in spite of what I said. She supposed this was to be her partner for the evening, or at least that was what Sandra hoped. But when she looked at him, even before they were introduced, she started to feel that perhaps it would not be such a bad idea.

'The last time I spoke to you, you hadn't made up your mind,' Sandra was going on. 'In fact, I didn't really think you'd come. Are you on your own? You can come and sit with us for dinner, if you like.' The poor fellow couldn't get a word in, and Veronica was still not sure whether or not this was a put-up job. 'This is my friend, Veronica. Veronica, this is Andy – Andy Mackintosh.'

The minute he spoke Veronica knew she was going to like him very much, especially when his blue-grey eyes met and smiled into her own in such a friendly way.

'Hello there, Veronica,' he said, taking her hand in a firm grasp. 'I'm very pleased to meet you. Yes, I'll join you for a wee while if you don't mind, Sandra. I decided to come, as you see, and now I'm very glad I did.'

Veronica smiled back at him as he sat down in the chair next to her. 'You wouldn't happen to be Scottish, would you?' she asked teasingly, and he laughed.

'Och aye, and how did you guess?' He exaggerated his accent which was, in truth, a very gentle Edinburgh one – a joy to listen to, Veronica found as the evening wore on and they chatted together as though they had known one another for ages.

She learned he was a postman and she was surprised to hear how old he was – some fifteen years older than herself – as he looked somewhat younger, apart from the odd tell-tale lines on his face. Lines of strain, she guessed, as he also told her he was a widower with two children. But the lines around his eyes soon became laughter lines as he amused her with his witticisms – she was to learn he was noted at work for his dry sense of humour – and encouraged her to tell him more about herself.

It was not, in point of fact, a particularly memorable meal although it was well cooked and quite palatable. It was the standard fare for a large gathering: mushroom soup, roast chicken with all the trimmings, followed by peach melba or apple pie and cream. But Veronica scarcely noticed what she was eating, she was enjoying herself so much. There were twelve people altogether on their table, including their party of four – already it was obvious that Andy would stay with them for the evening – Chrissie and Shirley, who were friends of Sandra; two young postmen, friends of Andy, who paired up with the two girls; and two more slightly older men with their wives. Andy appeared to be a popular member of the staff, not so ebullient as some of his younger colleagues, but obviously well liked and respected.

After the meal, when they adjourned to the palatial ballroom, the twelve of them sat together in a loosely grouped crowd, laughing and talking with one another. For most of the time, however, Veronica and Andy found they were a twosome, not in need of the company of the others, getting to know one another in a way they both found surprising and quite wonderful.

She could not have said afterwards what they had found to talk about all night, but talk they did; and they danced too, now and again, although neither of them, they admitted, was Ginger Rogers or Fred Astaire. It did not matter about the difference in their ages, nor that Andy had two children. He was going to introduce her to Donna and Barry soon and he was sure they would like one another. Nor that he had a job which required him to work peculiar hours. It seemed as though they had fallen in love at first sight.

Nor did it matter to Veronica that she had been there – or thought she had – many times before. This was what Sandra pointed out to her when they both arrived back at the flat later that night. It was well after midnight when the two girls sat down to drink a cup of tea – over which they could chat – before retiring to bed. They had gone their separate ways when the dance ended, Ian taking Sandra home, of course, whilst Andy offered Veronica a lift in his five-year-old Morris Minor. No one was surprised when she accepted; it had been obvious all evening that the two of them were getting on extremely well.

'Wow! That was quite something,' Sandra remarked, easing her feet out of her high-heeled sandals. 'You and

243

Andy Mackintosh! Who'd have thought it? Come on – tell me all.'

'What d'you mean, "Who'd have thought it?"' Veronica retorted. 'You'd thought about it, hadn't you? It was you who set it up between us, wasn't it? Mind you,' she smiled coyly, 'I'm very glad you did.'

'OK.' Sandra held up her hand. 'I admit I might have put the idea into his head . . . sort of. But I wasn't sure he'd turn up at the dance at all. He wouldn't say yes or no. But I certainly didn't expect the two of you to fall for one another hook, line and sinker. Come on – what happened? Did he kiss you good night? Are you seeing him again?'

'Mind your own business!' replied Veronica, but she could not hide the wide grin on her face. 'No, he didn't, as a matter of fact; kiss me, I mean. Well, only a little kiss on my cheek. And, if you must know – yes – I'm seeing him again, tomorrow.' She glanced at the clock on the mantelpiece. 'Today, actually; this afternoon.'

'Today!' gasped Sandra. 'Good grief! He's not letting the grass grow under his feet, is he?'

'Why should he? Why should either of us?' replied Veronica dreamily. She looked across at her friend, her eyes aglow. 'Sandra, I really think this is it.'

She did not get quite the reaction she had hoped for from Sandra, particularly as it was she who had instigated the whole thing. 'Oh, do be careful, Veronica,' her friend said, frowning a little. 'How many times before have you said exactly the same thing – that this was it?'

'I know I've said it before, but I was wrong all those other times, wasn't I?' said Veronica. 'I admit it. But this time – well – it's different. I know Andy's the one for me. I can feel it in my bones and it doesn't matter what you or what anybody says. I've met him, Sandra; my Mr Right.'

'And is that what he thinks as well?'

'He hasn't actually said so; it's too soon, isn't it? I've only just met him, but—'

'Quite so. You've only just met him.'

'But I know he feels the same as I do. I can tell. He's a

244

widower, though, isn't he? And I know he thought the world of his wife. He said it's the very first time since Jean died that he's met anybody he'd like to see again. So that's good enough for me. I know he's the right one this time; you'll see.'

'Oh dear, I do hope so, Veron, for your sake.' Sandra shook her head bemusedly. 'But I don't want you to get hurt again, can't you see? You've had so many disappointments.'

'Then you shouldn't have introduced me to him, should you, if all you're going to do is nag me about it? But I'm not going to get hurt, I can assure you. Oh, Sandra, I do want you to be happy for me. Do try – it's what I want.'

Sandra smiled at her. 'Of course I'll be very happy for you if it turns out all right – and I'm sure it will,' she added, a little tentatively.

Time would tell, she thought to herself, but she had heard the selfsame thing so many times before that she could not help feeling more than a little worried about Veronica.

Andy lived in a semi-detached house in Marton, in an avenue running off Whitegate Drive. He invited her back there for a cup of tea and a 'wee bite to eat', as he put it, after they had taken a walk around the circumference of Stanley Park lake. He had called for her in his car, as arranged, at two o'clock, parking near to the main gates before beginning their leisurely stroll.

Veronica had to admit to herself, despite what she had said to Sandra, that she was a tiny bit anxious about the meeting. Would she still feel the same way about him in the clear light of day? Would he? But she need not have worried. After a few moments they fell into the same camaraderie and feeling of togetherness that they had both been aware of at their first encounter. To Veronica, on that sunny early June day, the trees had never looked so green, the flowers in the Italian Gardens so brilliant, or the ducks on the lake so amusing. He told her more about his children. This afternoon they had gone with their young aunt, Carol – who, Veronica learned, lodged with Andy – to visit their maternal grandparents.

'We sometimes go for tea on a Sunday,' he told her. 'Not every Sunday, mind you. I don't think it's good for things to become too much of a set pattern; they'd come to expect it and I can't always be there. But I make sure the children see their gran and granddad as much as possible. Losing their daughter was a tremendous shock to them, as you can imagine.'

'And Carol . . . she's your wife's sister?'

'That's right, but a good deal younger, fifteen years or so. Carol was a wee afterthought, you might say. There's a brother as well, Jeffrey; he's married with two children. He lives locally too, so Jack and Thelma – that's my parents-in-law – are not short of family around them.'

'Terrible to lose a daughter, though.'

'Aye, so it was . . .' He looked pensive for a moment and Veronica glanced at him uneasily. He turned to smile at her, taking her hand for the first time that afternoon. 'But life has to go on, doesn't it? I know it's an awful cliché, and I used to get as mad as hell when people said it to me, but it's true. And now, well, I'm so glad I've met you, Veronica.' They exchanged understanding smiles.

'And your children don't mind you not being with them this afternoon? What did you tell them?'

'That I was meeting a friend. They don't mind; they're easy-going kids; you'll see when you meet them. And they love being with Carol. She's tremendous fun.'

Veronica felt a slight stab of apprehension. They might well be so contented with this Carol – a mother substitute? – that they could be resentful about another young woman appearing on the scene. But she decided she would face that problem when and if it arose. For the moment she and Andy were getting on amazingly well, just as they had the night before.

There was a photograph of his wife on the sideboard in Andy's home, as was only to be expected; a pretty young woman with a mass of dark hair. The girl in the photo near to it, eight-year-old Donna, looked the image of her

246

mother, but Veronica did not comment on this. Her younger brother, Barry, looked more like his father.

'A bossy boots, our Donna,' said Andy. 'Like her mother; in all ways, I suppose. Jean was a spirited lass, that's why it was so hard to believe . . .' His voice petered out and he was silent for a brief moment. He tapped at the photo of the two children. 'Donna's taken our Barry under her wing. He's a wee bit of a softie, but she's making him stick up for himself. I'd like you to meet them soon, Veronica.'

'Yes, I'd like to do that,' she answered, but not without a few misgivings. They had obviously been such a happy well-adjusted family.

Tea consisted of tongue and ham sandwiches, prepared beforehand by Andy, Scotch pancakes, copiously spread with butter, and a good variety of shop-bought cakes. She recognised the familiar Danish pastries and cream sandwich from Burton's confectioners; there was a branch of the popular shop not far away. They ate it in the cosy little lounge, from plates held on their knees, then Veronica insisted on helping Andy to wash up. It all felt strange and unreal, as if she were about to wake up from a dream – it had all happened so quickly – and yet she knew that the strangeness of the surroundings would soon become familiar, as they continued to see one another. She was certain they would do so.

She did not overstay her welcome that first time. She was anxious to be away before the children and their aunt returned, and Andy seemed to understand. He ran her home in the early evening, kissing her gently on the lips as they said goodbye. He said he would phone her in a day or two to arrange their next meeting, and not for one moment did Veronica doubt his word.

Their friendship soon developed into a courtship that surprised their friends and respective families, especially Veronica's. But the two of them were not surprised; it was what they had both known would happen from the very first moment they met. It was all progressing so smoothly Veronica was almost fearful that it was too good to last.

Andy's children had taken to her immediately, Barry at first being a little more reserved than his sister, but both of them soon welcoming her enthusiastically whenever she went to their home. Carol, too; Veronica had wondered if the girl might be jealously protective of her brother-in-law, but that was not the case. There was a boyfriend, very much in evidence, and Carol seemed relieved that someone else was now on the scene to help with the children. Veronica soon became fond of them. Donna and Barry were delightful, and she could scarcely believe they had accepted her so readily.

It was not an exciting courtship. Because of the unfavourable hours that Andy worked they usually said good night at around ten o'clock, after spending the evening together at either his home or hers. On a Saturday night they often went to the cinema or had a meal somewhere in the Fylde countryside, at Wrea Green or St Michael's or Skippool Creek on the River Wyre; the following day, Sunday, was the only day on which Andy did not have to rise early. Most Sundays they spent with the children, picnicking at Nicky Nook or Brock Bottoms, or occasionally driving as far north as Kirkby Lonsdale and strolling along the banks of the River Lune.

On some Sundays, however, they went to see the children's grandparents, Jack and Thelma Barrett. Veronica had been very apprehensive before she met them, in spite of Andy's assurances that they would make her welcome. How would they feel about someone stepping into their beloved daughter's shoes, she wondered, especially someone so much younger than their son-in-law? Not that Andy, as yet, had asked her to marry him, but she knew it was only a matter of time. Her fears about Jack and Thelma, however, were to prove unnecessary. When she met them at the beginning of July, about a month after she and Andy had first met, they were just as kind and friendly as Andy had predicted. Nothing definite was said about their relationship, but it was assumed that this young lady was Andy's girlfriend and, more to the point, that she was here to stay.

The only stumbling block was Veronica's own family, that was to say, her mother and father, as her siblings seemed quite complacent, even uncaring, about what their eldest sister was doing. Andy had met Paul – and Martin – and had pronounced them both to be 'real nice guys'. Veronica, ecstatically happy with the new love in her life, no longer felt the need to avoid the pair of them. She had told Andy – it was amazing how she could talk to him about anything and everything – of her brother's friendship and the rift it had caused in the family. Andy tried to explain to her that there were many different kinds of love; no, he did not really understand it, he said, not being that way inclined himself, but it took all sorts to make a world. Her repugnance towards her brother and his friend gradually diminished, and as for Paul and Martin, they seemed glad there were people who could accept them as they were. Veronica realised now that she had been too condemnatory about her brother and his friend. Paul was still, in essence, the same person, the brother of whom she had always been so fond. If he was happy, then it was not her place to sit in judgement.

Teresa had other fish to fry – a shoalful, it seemed – and was taking very little notice of the new man in her sister's life. She had been out with a few young men who had stayed at Sunset View; Sandra had seen her in Blackpool with a crowd of youngsters, both boys and girls.

Michael was living in a world of his own, continuously studying, it seemed, and as for Bernie – well, she was just Bernie, the youngest of the family, the one who, to the rest of them, was still a little girl. No, it was just Veronica's parents who were the flies in the ointment.

She had introduced Andy to them very soon after their meeting. It was hardly surprising, she supposed, that her mother took little notice of her latest boyfriend. After all, as folks continued to remind her, it had all happened so many times before. But now, more than two months later, with the friendship still growing strong, her mother and father were continuing to remain aloof, pretending they had not noticed the deepening affection between their daughter and this latest young man. It could not be said that they were rude or offhand with Andy; they treated him with perfect – possibly too perfect – politeness, as though he were a guest they did not know very well, not someone who would soon be a member of their family. They did not know that yet, of course, but they would find out very soon.

At the end of August Andy asked Veronica to marry him, knowing she would say yes without the slightest hesitation. They went together to choose the ring from Beaverbrooks, a ruby surrounded by a circlet of tiny diamonds, resembling a flower. She was over the moon with joy and had never been more sure of anything in her life. Andy was the man for her, the Mr Right for whom she had been waiting. The other contenders for the role – Dominic, Shaun, Justin, Richard – the memories of them had fast disappeared like mist in the sunshine when she came face to face, at last, with the real thing.

Her friends at work could see the change in her. She was more confident, continually cheerful, and radiant in her happiness. Even Sandra, who at first had been sceptical, could see that this time it was for real. She was relieved that everything had turned out so well. Introducing Veronica and Andy might well have been a mistake, a mismatch of personalities, resulting in her friend getting hurt again. But seeing the two of them together Sandra knew that this was a perfect match. And how wonderful it was that Andy had found such happiness after his time of sorrow.

'I really ought to ask your father for permission to marry you,' he said as they sat together on the settee. They had chosen the ring that afternoon, Veronica's half-day, and had then gone back to his home to tell the children. Donna and Barry had accepted the news with pleasurable smiles, but with no real surprise. 'Can I be a bridesmaid?' Donna had asked, and Veronica had laughingly agreed that of course she could. Now the children were playing out with their friends in the remaining hour of daylight. Veronica was pleased at their casual acceptance of the situation, but at the mention of her father she felt collywobbles starting in her stomach. She had never suggested to Andy that her parents might object to their marriage, neither had Andy made any mention of it, but the knowledge was there between them, implicit but undeclared. If there was to be any opposition at all it would be from this quarter.

'Mm . . . I don't really see why you have to ask my dad,' she answered. 'I'll be twenty-one next month. We can get married then without asking anyone's permission.'

'All the same, it would be the proper thing to do, don't you agree, darling?'

She nodded unsurely, her elation dwindling a little. 'I suppose so . . . I tell you what; let me have a word with them first, Mum as well as Dad. I don't suppose it'll be any great surprise to them. I know they've been burying their heads in the sand, but they must have been expecting it if they're honest.' It was the first time she had spoken to him about her parents' aloofness.

'All right, if you think that would be best. You pave the way for me. I like to do things correctly – I'm a wee bit old-fashioned in some ways – but I would prefer it if everyone was perfectly amicable. But we will be married, darling – and soon too – no matter what anybody says or doesn't say. You can be sure of that.' He kissed her tenderly and she leaned her head against his shoulder, contented again and at peace. Andy always had that effect upon her. He was her rock; the strength, she realised now, she had always needed.

She called at Sunset View the very next evening, choosing a time when she knew the evening meal would be well over and her parents would most likely be on their own. Fortunately her brother Michael and her two sisters were nowhere to be seen. She did not enquire about their whereabouts, but plunged straight ahead with her news, that she and Andy were getting engaged. She did not say they had already bought the ring. She had worn it last evening and had not been able to resist showing it to a delighted Sandra. Now it was tucked safely away in its little heart-shaped box in her underwear drawer, but soon she would be able to wear it all the time.

'You're telling us you intend to marry this man?' Doreen shook her head, smiling sadly. 'Oh, Veronica love, how many times before have we heard this?'

'You haven't,' Veronica retorted. 'OK, I've had a few boyfriends, I admit that, and I suppose I might have thought a couple of them could be the real thing. But I never told you I was going to marry them. And I know now that I was wrong – *they* were wrong. But now I've met Andy I know we're right together, and he wants to marry me. He's going to come and see you.'

'You're not twenty-one yet,' said Norman. 'Why can't you wait a bit? You're only a young lass. You don't want to go off and get wed to someone old enough to be your father.'

'He isn't, of course he isn't! Don't be so ridiculous.' Veronica could feel tears of frustration welling up in her eyes. She hadn't though it would be as bad as this. It was not that her parents were angry. They were not raising their voices and they did not appear particularly surprised at her news. But it seemed as though they were refusing to take her seriously, making out that this was just one more in a long line of boyfriends and that she would, ultimately, change her mind.

'What have you got against him?' she cried. 'Why don't you like him?'

'We haven't said we don't like him, dear,' said her mother, quite reasonably. 'We do like him, as far as we know him. He seems a very nice young man. Well . . . not all that young really, compared with you. And that's one of the main things. He's too old for you. How old is he? About thirty-eight? Nearly twenty years older than you.'

'Actually, he's thirty-five,' said Veronica, 'and I'm almost twenty-one. That's not such a big difference. Anyway,' she looked keenly at her mother, 'how old were you when you married Dad? And how old was he?'

Doreen and Norman looked at one another a little

uneasily. Veronica already knew the answer. Her mother had been only twenty when she was married, and her father about ten years older. 'That's got nothing to do with it,' said Norman now. 'It was wartime and things were different.' They always made that excuse. 'Besides, I hadn't already got a couple of kids, had I?'

'They're lovely kids,' replied Veronica. 'I'm ever so fond of them already and I know they like me.'

'Bound to be problems, though,' said her father, 'taking on somebody else's children.'

'And we were so looking forward to having grandchildren of our own, one day,' said her mother. 'This man may decide he's already got a family and that he doesn't want to have any more.'

'Stop calling him "this man"!' Veronica almost shouted. 'You know very well his name's Andy. And we probably will have children, eventually. We haven't really talked about that yet.'

'No, I don't suppose you have,' said her mother. 'But then, he's not a Catholic, is he?'

'How do you know he's not?'

'Because if he had been you'd have said so, wouldn't you? "He's a Catholic, Mum, so it's all right." That's what you said before about some of the others. But I can tell that this— that Andy isn't.'

'How can you tell?'

Doreen shrugged. 'I'm not sure, but I know he isn't. And it makes a difference, Veronica, you can say what you like.'

'What are you trying to say, Mum? That he's not quite as good as us because he doesn't go to the same kind of church? That's rubbish. It doesn't matter one little bit to me whether he's a Catholic or not. And you're right – he isn't.'

'Mm . . . I see.' Doreen nodded. 'That's very interesting, from someone who used to have an altar in her bedroom; who would never dream of missing Mass or confession.'

'Stop it! Stop it!' cried Veronica. 'That's not fair. Don't

remind me of that. I've grown up since then and I know now that it doesn't matter how you worship, or even if you don't. Not everybody does, but that doesn't mean that they're not good people. Anyway, what about Simon Horsfall?'

'What about him?'

'Well, you didn't seem to mind when our Teresa was friendly with him. And he's certainly not a Catholic.'

'Oh, that was only a boy and girl thing,' said Doreen dismissively. 'I knew it wouldn't last. Anyway, we know the family, don't we? Abbie's my best friend and you couldn't meet a nicer boy than Simon, but it wasn't to be. But this Andy – we know very little about him or his family.'

'They live in Edinburgh, and he's taking me up to meet his parents, and his brother and sister, very soon. And you don't need to worry that he's a heathen, because he's not. As a matter of fact, he's a Presbyterian.'

Her father scratched his head and frowned. 'What's one of them when it's at home?'

'Oh, Norman, don't show your ignorance,' said his wife. 'Even I know that. They're one of that nonconformist lot, aren't they? Like Methodists and Baptists and what have you. Not content with being ordinary Church of England, they've broken away and formed their own little cliques.'

'Not at all,' retorted Veronica. 'You've got it all wrong, Mum. Presbyterians actually belong to the Church of Scotland; that's like the Church of England, except that it's Scottish. Andy used to go there when he lived in Edinburgh, but he goes to the Methodist church now – not all the time, but that's where he goes when he feels like going – because there isn't a Presbyterian one nearby.'

'All right, all right,' replied her mother, obviously miffed to have been told she was wrong. 'We don't want a history lesson about the dissenters, thank you very much. So he's a Methodist now, is he? One of them Bible bashers.' Veronica felt herself seething. Andy was not like that at all. They very rarely discussed religion, but when they did it was all very amicable. He had known from the start she was a Catholic, but it had made no difference. They loved one another, and she knew he was a good man, much kinder and more honest than many of the regular church attenders she knew, whatever their religion. 'At least if he doesn't go regularly he won't try to influence you, will he? You'll be getting married in your own church, of course, won't you? You may not be able to get married at the high altar, with him not being one of us; that is unless he turns for you. He'd be able to take instruction—'

At least her mother had got round to mentioning the wedding instead of scorning the very idea, but she was jumping to the most preposterous conclusions. As if she, Veronica, would even try to persuade Andy to become a Catholic! She had to put her mother straight immediately.

'No, that's out of the question,' she interrupted. 'Andy's not turning. Why should he? As a matter of fact, we've already decided. We're getting married in Andy's church . . .' She was aware of her mother's gasp of indrawn breath. 'Yes, the Methodist one,' she continued. 'It's where Andy's children go to Sunday school, and it's a lovely friendly place. He insists they go there every Sunday morning, even if we're going out somewhere afterwards. They're happy there, Donna and Barry. And they wouldn't feel right in our sort of church; neither would Andy. Theirs is a much simpler kind of service.'

'Oh, I see.' Her father spoke now. 'So we have to fit in with what this . . . this new family of yours want, do we? No matter that your mother and I have always looked forward to our eldest daughter getting married in style. It's important to us, you know; a white wedding and Nuptial Mass and all the trimmings. We love you, Veronica, and it's what we would like to do for you. Your mother and I couldn't have a wedding like that, much as we might have wanted to. Her family couldn't have afforded it, to be quite honest, and the war had only just ended. So we've always said we'd make up for it when you got married.' He looked at her, smiling rather sadly, but his eyes had softened considerably. 'It seems as though you are determined to marry this man . . . I mean, Andy.'

'Yes, I am going to marry him.' Veronica thought she could see a glimmer of sympathy now in her father's eyes. She glanced towards her mother, who was refusing to look directly at her. 'But I would rather do it with your blessing; with the blessing of both of you.'

'In a Methodist church, though,' her mother mumbled. She still seemed unwilling to come to terms with the idea, although her father, during his uncharacteristically long rejoinder, appeared to have calmed down and become resigned to his daughter's news. 'It won't be the same at all.' She sighed, shaking her head sadly.

Veronica felt exasperated. 'For goodness' sake, Mum, stop being so melodramatic,' she cried. 'Anybody would think I was telling you I had to get married. It isn't going to be some hole-and-corner affair in a register office, you know. You'll get your big wedding if that's what you want, but without the Nuptial Mass. Andy's quite willing to go along with whatever I want to do, even though he's been married before. A white wedding; that's important to me, Mum. And I really will be entitled to wear white, if you know what I mean. And bridesmaids: Teresa – that's if she wants to be a bridesmaid – and Bernie, of course, and Sandra. Oh, and Donna wants to be a bridesmaid as well.'

Doreen sniffed. 'It seems as though you've got it all arranged. What's the point of him asking us if you're going to go ahead anyway?'

'Because we want your blessing, I've told you,' said Veronica. 'Do try to understand, Mum. I love him, I really do, and I know we'll be happy together.'

'You could have done better for yourself, Veronica. He's not exactly—' Her mother stopped speaking at the sight of her angry expression.

'He's not exactly what?'

'Oh, nothing, dear. If you're happy and you think it's what you want, then I suppose . . .' Her mother looked up at her and smiled at last, but rather weakly. 'We can't live your life for you. We've got to let you do as you wish, even if it may not be what we would have chosen for you. You've got to make your own mistakes.'

'I'm not going to make a mistake, Mum,' said Veronica firmly. 'This is right. I've never been more sure of anything.'

'Yes . . . I believe you,' said her father, slowly. 'I do believe that this marriage could turn out to be a very good thing. Tell Andy to come and see us, as soon as he likes. We'll put him at his ease, won't we, Doreen.' He sounded as though he would tolerate no opposition.

After a moment's pause his wife nodded. 'Yes. I'm not so convinced as your father seems to be. But, yes; he need not fear that we'll raise any objections.' She sighed. 'We'll do our best for you. We'll try to make it a memorable day. And then . . . well, the rest is up to you.'

Chapter 12

Bombshells

'You changed your tune all of a sudden, didn't you?' said Doreen to her husband, soon after Veronica had departed. She had stayed only long enough to tell them her news and hear their reactions, then she had seemed in a hurry to be off again, to meet that man, no doubt . . . Andy. Doreen knew she would have to start thinking of him as Andy, her future son-in-law. 'One minute you were telling her she wasn't twenty-one yet and why couldn't she wait a while, and the next minute you were encouraging her to marry him. I was flabbergasted, Norman.'

'I wasn't encouraging her, love,' said Norman. 'I could see it was inevitable and there was no point in arguing any further. There was that look in her eyes; it's obvious that she loves this fellow, and if we're honest about it we know he thinks a lot about her. We've just been hiding our heads in the sand, Doreen.'

'Yes, I know, I know.' Doreen tapped her fingers impatiently on the arm of the chair. 'But I still think she could have done a lot better for herself, a clever girl like Veronica. She could have gone to college, you know – university, even – if she hadn't decided to go and be a shop assistant, of all things. And then to tell us she's going to marry a postman . . .'

'So what's wrong with that? It's a perfectly respectable job and a very essential one too. Where would we be without the Royal Mail?'

'But she could have married anyone, our Veronica – a solicitor or a doctor or . . . or . . .'

'Or a Catholic priest?' said her husband with a wry glint in his eye.

'You don't need to drag that up again,' Doreen snapped. 'That's all water under the bridge. But she was a good Catholic girl in those days, you can say what you like.'

'And then we found out why, didn't we?'

Doreen went on as though he hadn't spoken. 'And for a long time afterwards. But now she's throwing it all away. Marrying someone who's a Methodist, of all things. As if it isn't bad enough him being a—'

'A postman,' Norman interrupted. 'Yes, I get the message, Doreen. You don't think he's good enough. I would never have thought you were a snob, but that's what it seems like to me.'

'I'm not a snob! How dare you call me a snob?' Doreen stopped speaking suddenly, however, as a picture flashed into her mind. As clearly as if she were standing there in front of her she could see, in her memory, Mrs Winters, the doctor's wife – Abbie's mother – who had been just about as snobbish as anyone could be. How that woman had hated the idea of her well-bred daughter getting friendly with Doreen, a girl from a poor family, brought up in the inferior Central Drive area. The antipathy had been mutual. Doreen had disliked the woman intensely, but her friendship with Abbie had flourished despite the opposition, and had continued right to this day. She felt a pang of guilt now at her words of contempt about the man with whom her daughter was so clearly in love.

'All right,' she said, holding up her hand. 'I'm sorry. Perhaps that did sound rather snobbish. I didn't mean it to come out the way it did. God forbid that I should ever get above myself.' But maybe that's just what you have been doing lately, Doreen, said a little voice inside her. Sunset View, Gynn Square, all your big ideas . . . 'You know how it is, Norman,' she went on, trying to exonerate herself. 'You want the very best for your children, don't you? I know you do, as well as me. And I did want her to make a good marriage. There are sure to be a few problems with him having two children already, and he's not exactly a big wage earner, is he?'

'There you go again,' said Norman. 'OK, so you'd have liked her to marry a solicitor or a doctor, eh? But it isn't a solicitor or a doctor who's asked her to marry him. And I don't suppose Veronica cares two hoots what he does for a living, so long as it's honest. I think they stand a very good chance. I like Andy, what I know of him, although I've got to admit I was dubious at first. She's had so many young men. But he's pleasant and friendly, he's very courteous to us and he obviously loves our daughter. Yes, despite the difference in religion, I believe they'll make a go of it and be very happy.'

'Yes, I suppose so. I suppose it's possible . . .' said Doreen, still a trifle grudgingly. 'I must confess I was impressed by what she said about a white wedding. You know – that it really would be a truly white wedding in her case; virginity and all that; I took it that was what she meant.'

'Yes, Veronica's a good girl,' replied Norman. 'Have you ever doubted it?'

'No, not really, but you know what girls are like these days. It doesn't seem to matter as much as it used to. And they nearly all get married in white, whether they're entitled to or not. They say it's the purity of the intention that's important, but in our day it meant a lot more than that. Times have changed.'

Norman chuckled. 'You must be getting old, love. Have you forgotten what it was like during the war? There must have been hundreds – thousands – of couples having a night to remember before they were parted. And not all of 'em bothered to get married.'

'Oh well, it's different in wartime, isn't it? There's no excuse now. But I suppose I'm pleased she's decided to have a conventional sort of wedding, not a register office do. She didn't say when, did she?'

'No. I expect it'll be sometime next year. Spring or summer, perhaps.'

'Hm . . . Right in the middle of our busy season, I shouldn't wonder. Still, we'll do our best for her, Norman.'

'You're coming round then, love?'

'I'll have to, won't I? Doesn't look as though I've any choice. We'll do the same for all our daughters, of course, when the time comes.'

'Don't jump the gun, love! Bernie's still at school and Teresa's only seventeen. And from the look of it she won't be ready to settle down for many a long year.'

'Yes, she certainly seems to be doing the rounds. She's been out with at least three of the young fellows who've been staying here – probably more. And I suspect she was friendly with Richard – you know, Veronica's ex, who lives over the shop. I was always suspicious about that. It may have been why they fell out that time. Still, it's perhaps better to play the field than to think every man she goes out with is the one and only, like Veronica used to do.'

'She's found the right one at last, though.'

'Let's hope so.'

'Yes, let's try and be happy for her, Doreen. I must say our children have given us some surprises recently, haven't they?' She knew he was referring to Michael and the bombshell he had dropped recently, and not to Paul. Paul's name was never mentioned, at least not between the husband and wife. It was as though he had ceased to exist for Norman. The situation hurt Doreen tremendously. It meant she did not see Paul as much as she would have liked to, but she did not want to harm her relationship with her husband. 'I thought you might have wanted to tell Veronica her brother's news?' he said.

'All in good time, Norman. She'll find out soon enough,' Doreen replied. 'It may not be any great surprise to her, like it was to us. You know, we should have seen it coming. All that studying and involvement at church. We've been blind, like we've been with Veronica.'

Michael had announced to his parents, only two days ago, that he intended to become a priest. He was due to leave his Catholic grammar school next summer, and in the meantime he was applying for a place at a seminary. They had been stunned, but had both given him their blessing without any show of reluctance. What else could they have done? Was it not the ambition of every good Catholic family to have a son enter the priesthood? Doreen knew she should feel proud, and so she did, in some ways. But there was a part of her that felt a reluctance to let him go, and she suspected that Norman felt the same. The two of them had had frequent discussions at intervals over the last two days, and she sensed in Norman too a tolerance of the situation rather than a definite feeling of pride. Now, of course, they would have something else to talk about. Family life was certainly never dull.

'Yes, I'd never guessed what was in his mind,' said Norman. 'It's amazing how twins can turn out to be so different. And yet Teresa wasn't surprised, was she? She said she'd guessed ages ago, although they've not been close for a long time.' He grinned. 'Not much chance of our Teresa becoming a Bride of Christ, is there?'

'Don't mock, Norman,' Doreen reproached him. 'No, I don't suppose there is . . . thank God,' she added softly. 'I maybe shouldn't say this, but I'd hate it even more if one of our girls decided to enter a convent. That would be worse than Michael deciding to become a priest.' Norman frowned slightly; she could not tell whether he agreed with her or not. 'Yes, I know it's what I should want. I should be rejoicing, but I'm not and that's the honest truth. I want grandchildren, Norman.'

'All in good time, love,' replied her husband. 'You'll get your grandchildren, I'm sure, and plenty of them. We've got three daughters.'

'Yes, I know. But there'll be nobody to carry on the name, Norman. I wanted our sons to carry on the name of Jarvis. I thought it would be important to you; I know it was to your father, with you being the only son. And now Michael's going to be a priest, and as for Paul – well, it's no use hoping for any grandchildren there.' She stole a glance at her husband, noticing a closed look come over his face and the stiffening of his whole body. She hadn't mentioned Paul's name for ages, but they couldn't carry on for ever with the subject of their eldest son a closed book between them. When he spoke his voice sounded strained.

'I've told you before, we've got three daughters. To hell with the name! It isn't as if we're landed gentry, is it? We must try to be proud of Michael and to show him that we are. It's a great honour to have a priest in the family. Hey up, I can hear voices in the hall.' He sounded relieved, as though they were getting into water that was too deep. 'I'll go and see if there are any supper-time drinks required. Come on, love; get your pinny on.'

Once more he had ignored any mention of Paul. But this state of affairs could not go on for ever. Their daughter would be getting married in the not-too-distant future. She would surely want her brother to be at the wedding, and possibly his friend as well. She turned the problem over and over in her mind as she set out the cups and saucers and put the kettle on to boil.

The rest of the family appeared to have accepted the situation – that Paul was no longer living at home, and was no longer their chef – without a great deal of trauma. Doreen had tried to explain to his brother and sisters that he and his dad had had 'a bit of a tiff', but it was nothing to worry about.

'Oh yes, he's gone to live with his boyfriend, has he?' Teresa had remarked with a mischievous grin, but fortunately not in front of Michael and Bernie.

'Yes, he has actually,' Doreen had replied in a casual sort of voice; the least said the better, she believed. 'It's handy for him, with them being at college together.'

'Oh, come off it, Mum. I'm not a kid, you know,' said Teresa. 'I've known about our Paul for ages.'

'You . . . know? What exactly do you know?' Doreen hardly dared to ask.

'That he's – well – what they call gay. He is, isn't he?'

Doreen nodded silently, not looking at her daughter.

'Oh, come on, Mum; this is the nineteen sixties, not the Dark Ages. I guessed ages ago, about him and Martin.'

'Then for heaven's sake keep it to yourself,' her mother hissed, although there were only the two of them in the kitchen. 'Don't go telling Michael or Bernie – or anyone, for that matter.'

'I'm not likely to. It's not the sort of thing you shout from the rooftops. But it happens, Mum, and he's still our Paul, isn't he?'

'Yes, quite so, love,' Doreen replied, very touched by the girl's remark. 'I only wish your father could see it that way. He's really hurt and angry, Teresa; he won't see Paul at all. But I don't want the others to know how serious the quarrel is.'

'OK, they won't hear it from me. They might think it's odd, though, if Paul doesn't come round any more. That is, if they notice . . . Michael's always got his head stuck in his bloomin' books, and Bernie's not really too bothered about the rest of us, so long as she's got you. Don't worry, Mum – I'll keep mum,' she giggled.

Teresa amazed her at times. She would have said, at one time, that she was the most difficult of all the children. She was wilful and unruly, but she had a streak of common sense and the ability to get right to the heart of a problem. The girls of today, of course, knew so much more about the ways of the world than she, Doreen, had known at the same age. It had been much later, after she was married, that she had begun to have an inkling about such matters as homosexuality. It was a word which was hardly ever spoken in those days. Even now she would not have said the word out loud; she could only whisper it timidly, inside her mind.

Her thoughts returned to the forthcoming wedding. Would Norman still persist with his refusal to see or even speak of his son? She pushed the unwelcome thought to one side. It was too disturbing to think of that at the moment.

Chapter 13

Karl

The Illuminations season was well under way and Sandra was now performing one night a week at Sunset View, as her two other appointments had come to an end. The Allenbank had changed hands and the new owners had different ideas, and she had terminated her job at the Mountjoy of her own accord. They had started to attract a much younger, somewhat rowdy, sort of clientele there, and Sandra felt she could not compete with the band who performed there on the Saturday night: the Spidermen, a quartet of local long-haired lads who played guitars and sang – or so they believed – like the Rolling Stones. Her kind of music was much more middle of the road, although she did include some pop songs from the Top Twenty – generally liked by the young and the not so young.

She had needed little persuading from Doreen to take up a regular appointment there each Friday evening during the two months of the Lights season, and then, as Doreen said, 'We'll see how it goes.' It was possible the hotel might close then until Christmas, although she was always ready to take in weekend guests if any should appear.

Sandra was not sure what she would be doing herself, after Christmas. This little job at Sunset View was, in a way, a stop-gap for her, something upon which she could concentrate whilst she decided just what she wanted to do in the future. The truth was, Sandra was restless, dissatisfied even, although she could not have said why, not even to herself.

It could be something to do with Veronica's engagement. Her friend was in a world of her own these days, in a seventh heaven of delight. Sandra was happy for her, but she could not help feeling slightly impatient, at times, at the sight of her sitting there with a moony expression on her face, gazing at the ring on her finger and moving her hand around so that the tiny diamonds glistened in the light.

Sandra could have been engaged herself by now. At more or less the same time as Veronica started wearing her ring, Ian had asked her to marry him. He had been astounded when she had refused, and Sandra herself had not been able to explain to him exactly why she was saying no.

'But, Sandra, darling, why not?' His blue-grey eyes had looked perplexed and slightly hurt. 'You love me, don't you? You've said you do and I believe you. And you must know how much I love you.'

'Yes, I do love you, Ian,' she replied. 'But we're only young, aren't we, and there's plenty of time. I won't be twenty till January, and you've another year at uni. Let's wait until you finish and get a job, and then see how we feel about it.'

'But I know how I feel,' he argued. 'And I'm not going to change my mind. Being young makes no difference; I've known for ages how I feel about you, ever since I started seeing you, in fact. But I didn't want to rush you because of . . . It isn't anything to do with Greg, is it?'

'No, of course not,' she replied, but she knew, in her heart, that it was. It was not that she compared Ian with Greg. The memories of Greg were still very precious to her, but she had known she had to move on. She and Ian had enjoyed many happy times together, they got on well and she was sure she loved him; but she knew she could not, yet, commit herself to him for a lifetime.

She had had only two boyfriends, both of them lads

she had known in their schooldays: Greg, a fellow music student; and Ian, the son of some friends of her mother. She could see the boys still, in her mind's eye, in their school uniform. Poor Greg had died; Ian had matured, of course, and she along with him, but were they mature enough, she wondered. Or was this, in essence, still a boy-girl friendship which they would outgrow?

She said very little of this to Ian that night, as they sat together in her flat, Veronica, as she often was, being round at Andy's place. She just said she needed more time. Of course she wanted to go on seeing him, but she was not yet ready to be engaged. She hoped he would understand. He had said that he did, but their parting that evening had been more restrained than usual. He had continued to meet her for the rest of his summer vacation, and he had been there at her first performance at Sunset View, but the unease between them did not diminish. She was relieved when he went back to university, and she had not believed she could ever feel like that. They had not 'finished'; they were, she supposed, still 'going out' together, but for how long it would continue she did not know. The annoying thing was she knew she still loved him.

She was stuck in a rut, though. There was no doubt in her mind about that. She had the feeling, a lot of the time, that she wanted to spread her wings and fly away. Not too far away, to be sure; not to Australia or Canada or the USA, but to some place other than Blackpool. That was the reason she was considering applying for a transfer to a post office in another town; or a city, preferably, where there was more going on – more life, more excitement. Birmingham? Manchester? Liverpool? She would draw the line at London: too busy, too impersonal. Or somewhere more idyllic or historic, maybe? The elegant city of Bath, or Edinburgh, or York? She had not visited any of these places, only seen pictures and read about them, fancying she might go there one of these days. Perhaps that day had come. But she had not, yet, even got so far as to look at the Situations Vacant in the bulletins at work, or to discuss it with her mother and Duncan, or with Veronica. At one time she would have confided in her friend, but Veronica's head was continually in the clouds these days.

In the meantime, however, she had a performance to give this evening, and some different songs to introduce to her audience. She dressed in the cream lace dress she had worn for the Post Office dinner and dance. It was October now, and the evenings were drawing in and turning quite chilly. It crossed her mind that maybe she should wear something more autumnal, but she knew the dress suited her. It was unlike the majority of her clothes, being much more pretty-pretty and unsophisticated. On a whim she brushed her hair loose instead of fastening it into a French pleat as she often did, then fixed a flowery hairslide to one side.

She pulled a face at herself in the mirror. 'You look like the fairy on the Christmas tree,' she whispered, her brown eyes twinkling back at her. Still, she knew the audience of mainly middle-aged folk would approve of her appearance: young and sweet and innocent. No one looking at her would guess how rebellious and troublesome she had been a few years ago. Her friendship with Ian had done a lot to temper the unruly side of her nature. She knew he was a good influence upon her, but did she want someone sitting on her shoulder, as it were, prompting her as Jiminy Cricket had done with Pinocchio? The feeling that had been creeping up on her gradually over the past few weeks – that she must be her own person and not be afraid to make some changes in her life – was intensified now. She grinned back at her reflection. 'Go for it, girl,' she said.

She put on her coat and rang for a taxi to take her to Gynn Square. She knew that another thing she really should do was learn to drive. Her mother was always trying to persuade her to take lessons. The self-willed girl she had once been would not have hesitated, but at that time she had been a schoolgirl and too young to learn. Since Greg had been killed in the car accident all desire to drive had left her. For a while afterwards she had even felt nervous in a passenger seat. But now her confidence had returned maybe she could afford a little run-about, a Mini Minor or a Hillman Imp. She was sure she would find the driving no problem; a few lessons and she would be well away.

The lounge bar was fairly full when she began her first spot of the evening at eight thirty. Twenty or so people, at a rough estimate, she thought, as she took a quick glance around; mostly married couples. That would be almost the sum total of the guests, most of them staying for a long weekend although some made a week of it. The weekenders would have arrived earlier that day and enjoyed their first evening meal. Friday was a good time for a musical evening during the Illuminations season. It was a time for settling in to the hotel and maybe taking a short saunter along the nearby cliffs to see the tableaux. The full viewing of the Lights, however, was usually left till the Saturday evening, when the road along the prom-enade would be packed, bumper to bumper, with cars and coaches. The best way to travel was by tram or, for the more energetic, by Shanks's pony.

Sandra started her performance with some familiar, although not all very modern, songs. This first group were on a travel theme: 'Trains and Boats and Planes', 'Around the World', 'I Love Paris', 'Tulips from Amsterdam' . . . Some she sang, with the audience singing along with her, but for the haunting melody 'Where is Your Heart?' from *Moulin Rouge* she let the notes of the piano alone convey the poignant lyricism of the music.

She saw Karl Robson, the chef who had been appointed in Paul's place, enter the bar during the medley, sitting down on one of the tall bar stools, slightly away from the guests who were grouped around the small tables. He nodded and smiled in her direction, applauding enthusiastically when she had finished her first selection. She was aware of him throughout her first spot, watching her with interest, though only in a friendly sort of way, as he sipped his glass of beer. The only person he spoke to

269

was Norman, on duty behind the bar. Later, no doubt, as people realised this was the chef, out of his whites, he would receive a goodly number of compliments on his cuisine. Sandra had not sampled any of his dishes, but she gathered, mainly from what Veronica had told her, that Doreen was very pleased with the young man. She would not go so far as to admit he was as good as Paul, but Sandra guessed that that was the truth. That must be one weight off Doreen's mind – finding someone to step into the gap left by Norman's hasty dismissal of their son. Poor Doreen, she was certainly experiencing some problems with her family, but she appeared, to a casual observer, as cheerful and friendly as ever.

'Long, long live love . . .' Sandra sang with gusto, playing along to her vocal rendition, then smiling and nodding to acknowledge her applause, before taking a seat at an empty table at the back of the lounge. Karl Robson slipped off his bar stool and came over to her.

'May I join you, Sandra?' he asked, placing his half-empty glass on the table. 'And may I get you a drink?'

'Yes, and yes, thank you,' she smiled. 'Just a pineapple juice, please. I like to keep a clear head.'

'Okey-doke; be back in a minute . . .'

'That was a superb performance,' he remarked on his return, sitting down on the long seat next to her, 'especially the last song, although I enjoyed it all. Sandie Shaw'll have to watch out. You're just as good as she is. Better in fact, in my opinion; not quite so strident. Come to think of it, you look a bit like her.'

Sandra laughed. 'It must be the hair, that's all. I did use to call myself Sandie, funnily enough, when I was a kid. Nothing to do with her; but then I decided Sandra sounded more grown-up. Perhaps I should start singing barefoot, eh? No – maybe not; I like to do my own thing.'

'Yes, I dare say you do,' said Karl, smiling at her. 'Leave the bare tootsies to Sandie Shaw. You are your own person, Sandra; I can see that. You don't need to imitate anyone. Have you another spot tonight, or is that it?'

'No, I'm on again in about half an hour. I usually finish about ten thirty.'

'And then what? You drive straight home?'

'No. Well, I do go straight home, but I don't drive. I usually get a taxi, or sometimes Norman runs me, but I don't expect him to.'

'I thought you might have had your own car?'

'No. I'm not exactly loaded, you know; I'm only a post-office clerk. But I was thinking of getting a little runabout, a Mini or something of the sort. It would make life easier, not having to wait for buses and trams, although I can walk to work at the moment.'

She told him she shared a flat on Park Road with Veronica, but he seemed to know that already. He too lived in a flat, on Warbreck Hill Road, only a few minutes' walk from the hotel. So his car was not required for his work, but was useful, he told her, for nipping over the Pennines, as he did every so often, to visit his family in York.

She learned that his parents had a small hotel there, not far from the Minster. They were kept pretty busy all the year round with tourists, both from home and abroad. Karl had grown up with the idea of becoming a chef, like his father, and had never veered from his childhood ambition. His parents had encouraged him to spread his wings, however, and not become too tied up in the family business. There was, in fact, no need for him to remain at home, as his father, still only in his early fifties, was an accomplished chef and intended to carry on working for many years. It was understood that Karl would, eventually, inherit the business, but at the moment he was a free agent. He had trained at Gleneagles, in the Scottish Highlands, and had had various appointments in Scarborough and, more recently, in Blackpool. This was his first position as senior – or the sole – chef.

'Mr and Mrs Jarvis seem very satisfied with me,' he told Sandra. 'In fact Doreen has asked me if I'll stay on a permanent basis. She told me to call her Doreen; nice friendly woman, isn't she? But I guess she's the one who wears the trousers in this house!' he added in a quieter voice.

'Sometimes, yes,' agreed Sandra. 'It's virtually her business, of course. She's the kingpin, you might say, and what she says usually goes. But she doesn't always get her own way.' She was thinking of Paul and his summary dismissal by his father. 'Norman's a stronger character than you might imagine. He's not a typical landlady's husband who won't say boo to a goose.'

'No. I gather he sent their son off with a flea in his ear. That's why I got the job, of course.'

'Where did you hear that? Not from Doreen or Norman, I'm sure.'

'No, but there are rumours flying around. I've heard blokes from some of the other hotels talking about it. Not that it's any business of mine. I've never met this Paul, and I'm not going to ask you about it. That wouldn't be fair. You're a family friend, aren't you?'

'Yes, our families go back a long way; our mothers were friendly ages ago. Paul's a very nice chap and a talented chef, so I hope things go well for him. He's only young – well, about my age – and I'm sure he'll go a long way. He's got a restaurant now; a part-share in one anyway. He and Martin – that's the young man he shares a flat with – opened up in August when they both left Parklands. It's on Hornby Road, quite near to Parklands, actually. They've called it Two's Company, and I hear they're doing very well. It's near enough to the town centre to be convenient, but far enough away to escape the exorbitant rents.'

Karl made no comment, nor did he move a facial muscle at all at the mention of Martin. No doubt the rumours he had heard had been about the nature of the friendship. Sandra, indeed, had raised her eyebrows when Veronica had told her the name of the newly opened restaurant. Rather blatant, surely, for a couple who were trying to be discreet about their true relationship? But Veronica insisted the name was because they were concentrating on couples wanting to celebrate a special occasion

– engagements or wedding anniversaries, although family bookings and small receptions were catered for as well.

She was glad of Karl's tact and disinclination to gossip. She did not tell him – as it was not his business, or anyone else's, for that matter – that although Paul was thought of as a partner in Two's Company, the enterprise virtually belonged to Martin. Paul had little capital of his own and, under the circumstances, had been unable to ask his parents for any financial help, whereas Martin came from a well-off family where money, it seemed, was no object. No doubt the situation would be remedied in time when Paul had managed to acquire some money of his own.

The two of them had given up their flat in Bispham and now lived in the upstairs rooms above the restaurant. The building, in its original state, had been a double-fronted house dating from the Edwardian era. It had been easily renovated downstairs into a dining room and separate bar lounge, with a largish kitchen at the rear. Sandra and Ian had intended visiting the place for an evening meal, but with the slight cooling off of their relationship they had not got round to it.

Sandra found Karl was very easy to talk to and she soon felt as though she had known him for ages. She had, previously, only spoken to him briefly a couple of times after they had been introduced. He was not the sort of man you would notice immediately. He was of medium height and a stocky build, with wavy hair of a fairish brown, which he wore rather long, but as it was covered by his white cap when he was working that did not matter. He could not be called handsome, as his nose was a shade too long; his mouth turned up at the corners, an indication of good humour, and his grey eyes were bright and alert. He had a very pleasing smile, and he did smile quite a lot, always showing an interest in what other people were saying.

He listened keenly to Sandra and appeared surprised she had never visited York, his hometown and a city he quite clearly regarded as second to none. She told him she had been born and had lived for several years in

Wymondham, a small town near Norwich, which, also, she assured him, was a beautiful and historic city.

'Mm . . . so it is,' he agreed, frowning a little and pursing his lips thoughtfully. 'I've been to Norwich. I think it's quite impressive, but it's not a patch on York. You really should see York, Sandra: the Minster and the Shambles and the River Ouse; there's nowhere like it, not anywhere.'

She laughed. 'You wouldn't, perhaps, be a tiny bit prejudiced, would you, as I am about Norwich? Although the truth is I've not been anywhere very much. I once went to Brittany with my parents when my brother and I were quite small; and we went to London as well to see Buckingham Palace and the changing of the guard, and so on. Apart from that, nowhere; the odd visit to the Lake District since we've been living here, and to Manchester to shop.'

'You surprise me,' said Karl. 'You sang those songs with such feeling. "Far away places with strange-sounding names", just as though you'd been there. Or was it a case of wishful thinking?'

'Yes, possibly. I'd like to travel,' she replied wistfully, 'if I ever get the chance. I sing songs about Paris in the springtime and all that, but I've never been. I'd love to go. Have you been to Paris?'

'No, I haven't. Don't get the wrong impression; I'm probably not much more widely travelled than you are. The only time I saw a bit more of the world was when I did my National Service. I was fortunate to be sent abroad.'

'Oh, really? I didn't realise you were old enough to have done that. The last call-up was in nineteen sixty, wasn't it? I thought you might have missed it.'

He laughed. 'You're fishing, aren't you? I'm twenty-five, if that's what you want to know, and I was in one of the last batches to be called up. I'm flattered if you think I don't look old enough.'

Actually, she thought he did. His face held a certain maturity; he was a man, not a boy. 'And did you want to go,' she asked, 'or did it mess up your training?'

'It interrupted it for a while, but I didn't mind. It was an experience and it was a good opportunity to go overseas. I was in Germany for a while, near Cologne, and then I had a spell in Trieste in northern Italy. I was in the catering corps – I rose to the dizzy heights of corporal, working in the officers' mess – so I was able to keep my hand in with the cooking and all that. Anyway, enough about me . . . You're a post-office clerk, you say? In the main office on Abingdon Street?'

'Yes, that's right; for the moment. To be quite honest, I'm thinking of applying for a transfer to another town. York was one of the places I had in mind, as it happens, but I'll have to see where and when a vacancy arises.'

Karl nodded. 'Getting itchy feet?'

'Something like that. I know I'll have to rethink when Veronica gets married; get another flatmate or move to somewhere less expensive. So I suppose that's one of the reasons I thought of making a change.'

'What about your boyfriend?' He looked at her just a shade searchingly. 'You are seeing someone, aren't you?'

'Yes . . . Ian; but he's away at university in Leeds. I don't see him all that often.'

'You'd be able to see him more often if you worked in York, wouldn't you?'

'Yes, I suppose I would, but that wasn't the reason I'd thought of going there.' Strangely enough, that fact had not occurred to her. 'Ian finishes there next summer. Anyway, it's not all that serious with him and me. It's just that I've grown up with him, sort of, you know. My mother knew his parents, that's all.' Straight away she felt a little guilty, knowing how hurt Ian would be, and quickly tried to rectify her remark. 'I'm very fond of him, but I know he's his career to think about. He'll need to get settled into that before we start thinking about . . . anything else.'

'And what is his career?'

'He wants to be a pharmacist. At the moment he's planning on coming back to Blackpool.'

'I see. Well, time will tell, won't it? With you and Ian and with all sorts of other things. All I would say, Sandra, is this: if there's something you really want to do, then do it while you've got the chance. Go for it, girl!'

Those were the selfsame words she had whispered to her reflection earlier that evening. She smiled confidently at him. 'Yes – you're right. Thank you, Karl. I do believe I will.'

They had chatted for so long and so easily together she had scarcely noticed it was time for her next spot. ''Bye for now, Karl,' she said as she stood up to take her place at the piano again. 'It's been nice talking to you.'

She fully expected him to finish his drink and leave, but at the end of her session he was still there. He rose and stepped forward to meet her. 'Well done,' he said. 'I was wondering – would you like to take a little stroll along the cliffs? It'll blow the cobwebs away and we can have a look at those magnificent tableaux I've heard so much about.'

'Yes, that would be great,' she agreed readily. She always needed some time to unwind after a performance. 'Don't tell me you haven't seen the Lights yet? Shame on you!'

He laughed. 'I've seen some of them in passing, when I've happened to drive along the prom at night, but I've not been up as far as Red Bank Road.' That was the point at which the famous series of tableaux ended. 'What about you? You've seen them all, have you?'

'*Touché*,' she grinned. 'I'm just as guilty. When you live in Blackpool you don't bother to sample its attractions. We really should. It's the greatest free show on earth, isn't it? Well, one of them at any rate.'

'Come on then; let's go and take a dekko at them. Put your coat on, but you can leave your music here, can't you? We'll pick up all your belongings later, then I'll run you home.' Sandra didn't protest. She would be grateful, indeed, for the lift, and she knew instinctively she could trust Karl; he would have no ulterior motive.

They did not cross over to the sea side of the promenade, but walked along the side where the hotels were situated: the Savoy on the corner of Gynn Square, and, further along, Uncle Tom's Cabin, the Cliffs and the other larger establishments, which catered for the more well-heeled visitors. The tableaux could be viewed at a greater advantage from this side – in between the flow of traffic, of course – and they were, indeed, quite splendid. Sandra felt like a child again as she exclaimed in delight at the circus scene: animated clowns, jugglers tossing balls and trapeze artists swinging to and fro, all appearing to move at the on and off turning of the multicoloured lights. There were scenes from fairy tales, an underwater theme with mermaids and the wreck of a ship, a jigsaw puzzle with each piece lighting up in turn, and every lamp standard was decorated with gleaming coronets and crowns. Illuminated trams went past, one shaped like a rocket and another resembling a Mississippi paddle steamer.

They did not talk much as they walked northwards, except to comment on the scenes they were viewing. When they reached Red Bank Road, the promenade ahead looked dark and gloomy in contrast to the wonderland they were leaving behind.

'Time to turn back,' said Karl. 'Let's walk back on the other side, shall we?' He took her arm as they crossed the busy road, then still held on to it as they walked along, neither of them so enrapt now at a second viewing of the scenes at their right hand.

'I'll take you out for a few lessons when you get your car,' said Karl suddenly, although the subject had not been mentioned since Sandra's casual remark earlier in the evening. 'You are going to get one, aren't you?'

'Yes, I suppose so,' she replied. 'Don't rush me, Karl. I need time to think about it, but thanks for the offer.'

'No time like the present,' he observed. 'You'll need it, won't you, when you get your new job? In York, or wherever.'

'Goodness! I wouldn't have the confidence to drive so far; not at first, anyway,' she laughed. 'But aren't we getting ahead of ourselves? I haven't even looked for a car yet, or a new job. All in good time. But you've helped me to look at things more positively. Thank you, Karl.'

'The pleasure's all mine,' he said, pressing her arm briefly as they arrived back at Sunset View. 'Now, if you pop in and get your things I'll go and get the car. It's only just up the road. I shan't be a jiffy . . .

'I've enjoyed your company,' he said as he parked the car outside her flat. 'Thank you, Sandra.'

'So have I,' she agreed wholeheartedly, as he leaned across and kissed her on the cheek.

'Good night then, and God bless.'

'Good night, Karl.' She opened the door and stood on the pavement. 'Cheerio then.'

'Cheerio; see you soon,' he said as he started the car up again. 'Very soon, I hope. Now remember what I've said about the driving lessons. I really mean it.'

'Yes – thanks. See you, Karl,' she replied.

He was a very nice young man and she had not enjoyed an evening so much for ages, she thought as she got out her key and opened the door. Veronica, it appeared, had already gone to bed and Sandra was rather relieved as she did not want to tell her about the time she had spent with Karl. Her friend was so apt to leap ahead and imagine things that were just not there, whereas she, Sandra, had her feet firmly on the ground.

Karl was a friendly, very pleasant and attractive young man whose company she had enjoyed for an evening. That was as far as it went and as far as she intended it to go. He was more mature than Ian; she had noticed that at once, but she did not intend to start making comparisons. Karl had helped her to look ahead more positively. She did not know what the future held – did anyone? – but she knew she must make some changes, starting right now. Not everything could be left to fate; sometimes you had to make things happen.

Chapter 14

Old Friends

Simon was at a loose end. Melanie had gone off to training college in Staffordshire and he was surprised, now she had gone, at how fed up he was feeling. Not that there was anything serious between them, but he had become quite fond of her and he was used to having her around. His mum liked her, and Melanie's parents seemed to like him too. They had spent quite a lot of time at each other's houses, playing records or just chatting and watching television. He had kissed her, many times, but there had been nothing else. Simon had heard some of the lads at school boasting about their exploits with their girl-friends; how far they had gone and all that. If it was true, well, they were just stupid, taking such a risk; but Simon didn't really believe them.

Anyway, Melanie wasn't that sort of a girl. She would be horrified, he was sure, if he were to try anything on. She was very sensible; a little too serious at times, maybe. She had been looking forward to starting her college course and eventually becoming a teacher, like her sister. She was older than Simon, of course, nearly a year older and she liked to remind him of it at times.

Still, he missed her and he was now trying to pick up the threads of the life he had lived before she had come along – the match at Bloomfield Road with the lads on Saturday, and the odd game of snooker or darts. Simon would not be eighteen until early next year, but neither would some of his pals who had invited him to join them at their local. They just enjoyed the facilities and did not drink; well, maybe the odd half, that was all, when the landlord was willing to turn a blind eye.

A pub near Devonshire Square was a favourite with a group of lads in Simon's sixth form. He was enjoying a game of darts there on a Friday evening in late October when he heard a familiar voice behind him.

'Good shot, Simon. Go on now – let me see you score a bull's-eye.' He turned round to see Teresa grinning roguishly at him. He had hardly seen her at all since last Christmas, certainly not to have any conversation with her; and when he had caught a glimpse of her she had usually been with a lad, a different one every time, it seemed. He was surprised at how pleased he was to see her again now.

'Hi there, Teresa,' he said. 'How're you doing?'

'Oh, I'm OK; top of the world. How about you?'

'Yes, I'm OK. Er, can you wait a bit, till I've finished this game, then p'raps we could have a drink and a chat? Unless . . . you're with somebody else?'

'No, nobody I can't get rid of. OK – see you, Simon.' She gave a cheery wave and disappeared round the corner of the bar.

The encounter seemed to have put him off his stride, and although he had been winning, he lost the game.

'Hard luck, Si.'

'His mind's on other things; and we know what, don't we?'

'Who's the smashing bird, Simon?'

He laughed good-humouredly at his friends' ribbing and tapped his nose. 'Wouldn't you like to know? See you later, lads.' He winked at them and went off in search of his former girlfriend.

She was sitting by herself at a small table in the far corner. 'Hey, what are you doing, all on your owny-own?' he asked, sitting down on the seat alongside her. 'You didn't come by yourself, did you?'

'No; I'm with a friend, Steve . . . but he doesn't seem

bothered whether I'm here or not. I came with him, but that doesn't mean I have to leave with him, does it?' Her big blue eyes looked tantalisingly at him. He remembered that glance of hers very well. She cocked her thumb sideways. 'He's over there playing snooker. He wouldn't notice if I did a bunk. Don't suppose he'd care much either.'

'Steve? Is he your boyfriend, then?'

'No, as a matter of fact, he's not,' she said. 'I've seen him a few times, but it's more off than on at the moment. He's getting rather too demanding, but I'm not playing. I'm not that sort of a girl.' She grinned and nudged his elbow. 'You know that, don't you, Simon?'

'Er . . . yes,' he mumbled, not sure whether he could believe her – if she meant what he thought she meant. 'Can I get you another drink? What are you having?'

'A shandy, please.'

'OK, and I'll have the same.'

'Really? You shouldn't be drinking, you know.' She tutted exaggeratedly. 'You're not eighteen yet. Does your mum know you're here?'

'Leave it off, Teresa,' he said a trifle irritably. 'If I'm not eighteen, then neither are you. And don't remind me I'm still at school or I'll . . . I'll . . .'

'You'll what? Do tell me.'

'I'll be annoyed, that's all.'

'Oh, Simon, don't be cross. I wasn't going to say you're still at school, honest I wasn't. Come on, hurry up and get that drink, then you can bring me up to date on what you've been doing.'

There was very little they both did not know of family news, with their mothers being such close friends – Veronica's engagement; Michael's decision to become a priest; how the first season at Sunset View had gone very well; but Paul was hardly mentioned. Simon knew he had gone to live with his friend and that they had opened a restaurant. He had not been told the reason for Paul's sudden departure from the hotel, but he had reached his own conclusion. Honestly, his mother still treated him like a child at times. He told Teresa he was intending to go to college in September, a physical training college, after which, hopefully, he would be a teacher. He did not make too much of it, however, knowing she could be scathing about such things.

'Are you still seeing that girl?' she asked. 'What was her name? Melissa or something?'

'Melanie,' he answered, quite sure she had not forgotten the name. 'She's gone to college.'

'Ooh – another clever-clogs, eh? But are you still seeing her?'

'I can't see her when she's away, can I? But – yes – I'm writing to her, and I'll probably see her during the holidays. But that doesn't mean I can't see anybody else . . . if I want to.'

'And do you want to?'

'I might . . . I tell you what, Teresa. When we've finished our drinks why don't we have a walk into town? Then we could have a look at the Lights – I've not seen them yet – then I could take you home. You're still living at your mum's place, are you?'

'Yes, I'm still there. OK, Simon.' She quickly drained her glass. 'Let's go.'

'Hadn't you better tell Steve you're going?'

'No; why should I? I've told you – he'll never notice. Come on – what are we waiting for?'

Simon could not understand why he had, so suddenly, felt a surge of happiness at seeing Teresa again. He had told himself it was all over between them – not that there had been all that much going on in the first place – and that it was better that way. She was a dreadful tease and she had behaved very badly with that Richard fellow, making him, Simon, feel no end of a fool. Anyway, he had Melanie now and she was a much more suitable friend for him. His mother thought so . . . and so did he. But she was not nearly so much fun as Teresa. If he were honest, he had been getting rather bored with her, although he had not realised the fact fully until he had seen Teresa again.

When Melanie came home from college for the Christmas holiday he would, no doubt, see her again; but in the meantime there could be no harm, surely, in seeing Teresa? She was an old friend – a friend of the family too – and, from what he could tell from his conversation with her, she seemed . . . different, somehow. Gentler and nicer, and obviously wanting to be friends again.

He took hold of her arm, smiling at her, as they left the pub, and they started to walk towards the town.

It had been good to see Simon Horsfall again, Teresa thought, as she snuggled contentedly beneath the bedclothes. Truth to tell, she liked him very much and she had been as mad as anything when she'd heard he'd starting seeing that Melanie girl. That had been her own fault, though, she remembered. She had been flirting with Richard, trying to make Simon jealous, and it had all backfired.

She was seeing him again next week – Simon, that was – although she wasn't sure she wanted to get all that involved with him, much as she liked him. He was going to college next year, so there was no future in that, not for her. What a pity!

Besides, next weekend Tony was coming over again for the last chance to see the Lights. He had been over twice already, he and two other lads from Bolton, to spend the weekend at Sunset View. But this time he was coming on his own as he said he wanted to spend more time with her. Tony was good fun.

She had decided she would not see Steve again. He would probably have got the message with her walking out on him tonight, but what did he expect when he spent nearly the whole of the evening playing snooker? If he did happen to ring she would tell him to get lost. Besides, as she had hinted to Simon, he seemed determined to make her give in to him, and Teresa was not having any of that. She had learned her lesson with Richard and, since then, had played hard to get. When she did go the whole way she wanted it to be with someone she really cared about; with someone who cared about her.

It was Simon she was thinking of as she fell asleep. It was a pity he was so far out of her league . . .

Chapter 15

A Change of Scene

Doreen had been very pleased at the success of their first full season at Sunset View. They had been booked up for most of the time, and even during the two autumn months of the Illuminations season they had been full at weekends and had had only a few vacant rooms for the rest of the time.

She knew that the move to Gynn Square had been a propitious one. This was generally considered to be a more select area, away from the hurly-burly of central Blackpool, with its amusements and sideshows and often rowdy behaviour of the crowds; although when thoughts such as this entered her mind Doreen warned herself that she must guard against snobbery. All would agree, however, that it was much quieter up here at the north end of the town, although there were attractions in plenty, especially for those whose tastes were slightly more genteel and who did not wish to be part of a boisterous crowd.

Its delights were many and varied. Right in front of Sunset View were the Gynn gardens, a sunken rock garden with flowerbeds and shrubs and pleasant walkways. There were seats where parents and grandparents could while away a peaceful half-hour or so whilst the children explored the playground or the crazy golf. There was a small snack bar too, selling pop, crisps and cups of tea, and across the promenade, at the bottom of the slope which led down to the lower prom, there was an ice-cream parlour.

There was another pleasant rock garden on the main promenade and, a little further along and lower down, the boating pool. This was a constant delight to children – not only visitors, but residents as well – although its attractions were simple and few in number. Gaily painted paddle boats, small enough for a child to handle; an automated ride with all kinds of chunky wooden zoo animals – zebras, lions, tigers, and for the more adventurous, tall giraffes and wide-backed elephants; and a stall with a striped awning which sold fizzy pop and ice-cream. Deck chairs, too, where the grown-ups could snooze while the children enjoyed themselves in perfect safety. A strict eye was always kept on the boating pool and the boats were called in by the attendant, number by number, when their time elapsed.

A little to the south, nearer to the town, was the famous Derby Baths, Blackpool's pride and joy when it had first been built in 1939. It boasted an Olympic swimming pool where national finals were sometimes held, a learners' pool, sun lounge and various diving boards. Its cream-coloured tiled exterior was considered to be a classic example of art-deco architecture. Like the Odeon cinema, built in the same era, it had been the last word in modernity.

Bispham, however, had its own cinema, the Dominion, on Red Bank Road. The films shown there appeared somewhat later than the box office hits acquired by the Odeon, the ABC and the Princess, but it was a cosy little cinema, frequented by both visitors and residents. Bispham village itself, though it was now being affected by modern-day planning, afforded a pleasant little half-day visit for the holidaymakers staying at the north end of the town. It still boasted a few thatched cottages, and All Hallows church, with its picturesque graveyard and rustic lich-gate, was a photographer's dream.

The cliffs at Little Bispham and Norbreck provided bracing walks and the beach at this far end of the resort had the advantage of being far less crowded. It was at times almost deserted, ideal for those families who wanted a more restful holiday. Here the children could paddle in the rock pools, gather shells and pebbles, and build sandcastles without the fear of them being demolished by overexuberant neighbours.

If the visitors so wished, however, Blackpool town centre was only a twenty-minute walk or a short tram ride away. But there were plenty of shops on nearby Dickson Road selling rock and postcards and inexpensive presents to take back home. The area known as North Shore was a little world of its own and Doreen had no regrets at all about moving there.

The only setback they had experienced, of course, was Paul's departure. Doreen still agonised over this, although she tried to hide her heartache from the rest of the family. Paul did visit the hotel occasionally, but usually when he knew his father would not be there. Norman was still being recalcitrant in refusing to speak to his son. It was Doreen's opinion that having adopted this stubborn attitude he was now finding it impossible to back down. Maybe the forthcoming wedding might afford an opportunity to let bygones be bygones? She hoped so. She hated even one member of the family to be at odds with another.

The wedding had been arranged for the Saturday before Christmas. So much for Veronica's desire to have a springtime or June wedding, thought her mother. Obviously she couldn't wait to become Andy's wife – Mrs Mackintosh – and she was now throwing herself joyfully into plans for what she was calling a 'real Christmassy wedding'. Doreen had decided, after all, that she liked Andy very much. She had known she must try to do so, for her daughter's sake, but she did feel, in all fairness, that he was a genuine and agreeable young man who would make Veronica very happy. The children too, Donna and Barry, were pleasant, likeable kids who appeared to have taken to their father's fiancée without any misgivings. Doreen was still disappointed, of course, that the wedding was to be at a Methodist church; the one on Raikes Parade, near to the town centre, where the children attended the Sunday school. It would feel strange, almost alien, she thought, to be in such a church, but it was her daughter's choice and she had made up her mind not to do anything to spoil her day.

One thing she could do was to make sure they had a splendid wedding reception, one worthy of her eldest daughter. And where else should they hold it but at Sunset View? Karl had already started planning the menus, but the ultimate choice would be Veronica and Andy's. There would be around fifty guests, which was all the hotel could comfortably accommodate in the dining room and lounge. Normally, of course, it was much less crowded than that. Thirty resident guests was the most Doreen had provided for, but there was sufficient room for a few extra tables and chairs. And Karl Robson, thankfully, had proved to be an excellent chef who would be well able to plan and cook a meal for a larger number.

Doreen had been very apprehensive at first. The young man's references were very good and she had taken to him straight away on sight, but it was such a risk, whichever way you looked at it, taking on someone you did not know for such an important position. She had believed – or had she only wanted to believe? – that Paul would be impossible to replace, but she had been proved wrong. Karl Robson was, indeed, excellent, and she had had no qualms about offering him the permanent position after his initial trial period. The hotel was closed now for the winter, although she was not averse to opening for an odd weekend or few days, should it be required, and they would, of course, be opening for four days at Christmas. She was paying Karl a retainer which, he said, suited him fine. He would keep himself occupied with bar work, casual helpers always being in demand in the larger hotels, or an occasional job as temporary chef.

Doreen had been watching with interest, recently, the young man's growing friendship with Sandra Horsfall. Not that the girl had said anything to her – neither had Veronica – but she could not help but notice that they enjoyed one another's company. She did not see as much of Sandra now – nor of Karl – as the musical evenings had ended with the close of the season. What of Ian? she wondered. She had thought he and Sandra were most definitely a 'couple' – Abbie certainly thought so – but the lass was only young when all was said and done, and it could do no harm for her to look around a bit before she settled down. It was very odd, though. Apparently Sandra had now got a transfer to another post office, and that had happened soon after she had become friendly with Karl. Veronica said she would be starting at the Harrogate office after the New Year.

So the flat they had shared would be vacant. Maybe that was why Sandra had decided to leave? Doreen mused. The two girls had got on extremely well, just as she and Abbie had always done; but now, at exactly the same time, they were to about to start new lives.

'Happy, darling?' asked Andy, squeezing his new wife's hand beneath the table.

'Do you need to ask?' replied Veronica, smiling back at him. 'Blissfully so; happier than I ever imagined I could be.'

'Good; then so am I,' said Andy.

It had been a memorable day so far: a simple, but moving service at the church, with her own and Andy's friends and relations gathered around them. Veronica was sure that all the guests could not help but have been impressed by the sincerity of the minister – she must remember not to refer to him as a priest, or even a vicar – who had conducted the service, or by the service itself. Unless it was the very simplicity of the worship that some might have objected to; those more accustomed to the ceremony and panoply of the Roman Catholic Church. Anyway, it was her, Veronica's, day – hers and Andy's – as even her mother had admitted. Doreen had gone along uncomplainingly with everything her daughter had suggested.

'I want it to be a real Christmassy wedding,' Veronica had declared at the outset. 'OK, I know I've always said

I'd like a June wedding – happy the bride the sun shines on, and all that – but I'm sure a winter one can be just as happy an occasion.

She had planned the wedding of her dreams, albeit a December one. Christmas Day fell on a Sunday that year, so their 'big day' was Saturday, 17 December. A little inconvenient, maybe, as they were going away on honeymoon – to a destination unknown to Veronica as yet; Andy's secret – and would not return until Christmas Eve. But no one had had the heart to disappoint Veronica by telling her the date was less than ideal. The children would be well cared for in their absence by Mr and Mrs Barrett, Andy's former parents-in-law, and Veronica had made sure she had done her Christmas shopping well in advance.

Her sisters had both agreed to be bridesmaids, although Teresa had needed far more persuading than Bernie. Teresa was in a funny mood at the moment. At times she appeared very down in the dumps, unusual for the normally high-spirited girl. Veronica put it down to boyfriend trouble – again. She seemed to have several strings to her bow at the moment, although that should make her happy, surely, rather than depressed? At any rate, she had snapped out of her dismal mood today and she looked lovely in her bridesmaid's dress of dark green velvet, as did the other three attendants: Sandra, Bernie, and little Donna.

'Dark green for a wedding? Surely not, love,' Veronica's mother had said at first. 'Too sombre.'

'Trust me, Mum; it'll look terrific for a Christmas wedding,' she had replied. 'I know it will.'

Sandra had agreed with her that it would look very stylish, and they had gone together to the posh material shop near Talbot Square to choose the dark green velvet and also some bright red satin ribbon for trimmings. Her friend had demurred a little about that, fearing it might look too garish; but today, dressed in all their finery, the four bridesmaids looked beautiful. The simple princess line suited them all, and the red bow at the back of each dress – a detail that could not be missed by the guests as they walked down the aisle behind the bride – and the tiny red headdress in the shape of a poinsettia, worn by each girl, added a strikingly seasonal touch.

Veronica's dress was simplicity itself. She had taken Sandra's advice and had chosen a semi-fitting dress in white textured heavy silk, with long tapering sleeves and a stand-away collar. With it she wore a tiny pill-box hat in matching fabric from which flowed a short silk tulle veil. She carried an all-white bouquet of small chrysanthemums, carnations and orange blossom, while the bridesmaids' posies were composed of tiny red flowers to match the trimmings on the dresses.

It was a cold day, as was only to be expected, but a pale sun had shone, though somewhat fitfully, as they came out of the church, mid-morning, and posed for the photographer. Then, after the customary shower of confetti and rose petals and shouts of 'Good luck!' from the onlookers who had gathered, they had all gone back in cars or taxis to Sunset View, where Karl and one or two extra helpers, hired for the day, had prepared a most appetising and sumptuous meal. It consisted of salmon mousse for a delicate and somewhat unusual starter – unusual, that was, for most of the guests; roast duckling with orange sauce, or turkey for the more conservative diners; followed by an exquisite ice-cream flavoured with mincemeat and brandy.

Seamus, one of Andy's postman friends, who was acting as best man, proposed the toast to the bridesmaids. He was clearly very nervous at such an ordeal, but not nearly so much as her father must be, thought Veronica, as Norman stood up to make his speech of congratulations to the bride and groom. To her surprise and relief he acquitted himself very well, and there was no doubt about the pride and love that shone from his eyes as he looked across at her. Veronica was touched and she felt a little tearful. Poor Dad. Like her mum he had not been too happy about the marriage at first, but he had put aside all his misgivings for Veronica's sake. She really believed now that both her parents would welcome Andy into the family without any reservations.

She glanced across to one of the side tables where Paul was sitting with Martin. He had not looked at her father, she had noticed, throughout the speech, but had stared down at his wine glass, idly twisting it round and round. As far as she knew, he and his father had still not spoken to one another, but it had been Veronica's view – and Andy had agreed with her – that it would be unthinkable to invite just Paul and not Martin to the wedding. The family had known Martin for ages, long before their secret had become known and all this trouble had arisen. If her father wanted to continue with his pig-headed ostracism of his elder son and his friend then there was nothing she could do about it. It was the only minor blemish in an otherwise perfect day.

They cut the cake and drank the champagne, and Andy made a fitting little speech of thanks to everyone, 'on behalf of my wife and myself'. Veronica smiled and blushed a little, then they went and mingled with their guests. It would not be for long, though, as they had a plane to catch later that afternoon. Andy had booked a taxi to take them all the way to Manchester airport; Veronica had gasped at the expense that must be, but he said it didn't matter and that he would do anything to make her happy. And then they were flying off to . . . somewhere warm, he said; a few days' escape from the English winter.

'Veronica, isn't it time you were getting changed? You haven't much time.' She turned to find Sandra at her side. 'Come on, and I'll help you to get into your going-away gear.'

This consisted of a warm trouser suit, dark green, like the bridesmaids' dresses, and a round hat of brown fur. She had packed a variety of clothing – woollen sweaters and skirts as well as summer dresses, as she couldn't imagine anywhere could be all that warm at this time of the year; except for Australia, of course, or Africa, but they couldn't possibly be going anywhere like that.

'It's been a wonderful day, hasn't it?' said Sandra as she unzipped the wedding dress and helped her friend to step out of it. 'I'm so happy for you, Veronica. Everything's gone so well, hasn't it?'

'Yes.' Veronica beamed delightedly. 'It's all been wonderful, as you say, and the best is yet to come.'

'Oh yes?' Sandra raised her eyebrows expressively.

'Oh, I don't mean that!' Veronica felt herself blushing a little. 'Well, I'm sure that will be . . . wonderful as well. But I meant the holiday; flying off somewhere. It's so exciting.'

'Hasn't he told you yet where you're going?'

'No, he says he'll tell me when we get to the airport. He'll have to, won't he, before we get on the plane? I'm ever so nervous really, Sandra, 'cause I've never flown before, but I haven't told Andy I'm scared. He was so full of it all, getting me a passport and everything. I hadn't the heart to tell him.'

'Don't worry; you'll be OK. Have a brandy before you get on the plane. Andy'll look after you. I'm quite envious actually. It's something I've not done either, and now you're doing it before me. Oh . . .' she put her hand to her mouth and laughed. 'Flying, I meant; not . . . anything else.'

Veronica laughed too. 'Honestly, your mind!' She gave her friend an odd look. 'Are you telling me you have done . . . something else?'

'No, as a matter of fact I haven't.'

'Well, I'm very glad to hear it,' said Veronica, rather primly. 'About flying, though. Didn't you fly when you went to Brittany, when you were a little girl?'

'No, we went on the cross-Channel ferry; I was sick, I remember. I expect flying's much easier. Perhaps I'll get the chance one of these days.'

'I'm sure you will. Er, how's Ian? Have you made it up with him? He looks a bit lost today, if you don't mind me saying so.'

'Oh, he was all right, sitting with my mother and Duncan and Simon. I couldn't sit with him, could I, being the chief bridesmaid and on the top table and all that. What do you mean anyway – have I made it up with him? We've never fallen out, not really. I didn't want to get engaged, and I've told him perhaps we'd better, well, cool it a bit, you know. But we're still good friends.'

'And now there's Karl,' said Veronica, looking at her quizzically.

'Karl's just a friend too,' Sandra sounded a little wistful, 'at the moment.' She gave a casual shrug. 'Anyway, I'm off to Yorkshire in a couple of weeks, so I've been too preoccupied to think about fellers. All in good time, eh?' She grinned. 'Come on now; are you ready? Let's go and get the farewells over with. You look stunning, kid, by the way; really radiant.'

'That's how I feel,' said Veronica.

'Malta – a captivating island in the heart of the Mediterranean which basks in all-year-round sunshine.' So it said in the holiday brochure that Andy gave Veronica to read once they were airborne. She was surprised and quite intrigued – she had hardly heard of Malta – but not disappointed. She was sure that Andy would have made a good choice and she trusted his judgement in this as in everything.

Her nervousness had dissipated somewhat once they had arrived at the airport. It was Veronica's first experience of such a place, and the bustle of the crowds, the queues at the check-in desks, and the departure boards informing the travellers of flights to far-off destinations made her forget for a while that she was scared. After all she told herself, all these other people – hundreds of them – were flying off somewhere as well. Some of them might be experienced travellers, feeling very blasé about what was, to them, a common occurrence, but there were sure to be others, like herself, who were flying for the first time. She took hold of Andy's hand and smiled confidently at him, willing herself to enjoy every second of this new adventure.

She felt a moment of sheer panic as the jet plane

speeded along the runway with an almost deafening revving of the engines; and then, so easily, so gently that you were scarcely aware of it, the plane left the ground. They were in the air, going up, up, up; over the airport buildings, over the rooftops of the houses and the dark streets with the lights shining like rows of glittering beads on a necklace. It was too dark to see very much, but Andy told her that on the way back, on a daytime flight, she would be able to see much more. Would she want to, she wondered. It had taken all her courage to peer out of the small window into the blackness of the night sky. She hoped the pilot knew where he was going in all that darkness. She let her breath out in a deep sigh, and placed her hand over Andy's.

'I was scared, Andy,' she told him. 'I didn't like to say, in case I spoiled it for you. But I'm OK now. If you don't think about it too much, that you're thousands of feet up in the air, you can imagine you're on a bus, can't you . . . sort of?'

Andy chuckled. 'Yes, I thought you might be a wee bit nervous. To be honest, so was I.' Although she knew he had flown before and was probably just saying that to make her feel better. 'I'll get you a brandy and ginger when the hostess comes round. How about that? Then we'll be having a meal.'

The novelty of it all intrigued her. The smiling hostesses in their smart red and navy uniforms and peaked hats, all so very obliging; the miniature bottles of spirits and the plastic beakers which fitted into a hole in the tray in front of you; and then the meal itself, which arrived in a sealed box, one for each passenger. It was nothing to write home about, Andy remarked, just standard airline fare, but Veronica opened each little packet with all the excitement of a child at Christmas; the potato salad; the bread roll and minuscule pat of butter; the portion of chicken breast; and the fruit and jelly, topped with a blob of cream. The hostess came round with the coffee to which you added the packets of powdered milk and sugar contained in the box. And then, afterwards, all the debris was collected up in an enormous sack and the passengers settled down to enjoy the rest of the flight. Or to snooze, as many did.

Veronica read the brochure about their destination, thinking it all sounded very exciting and different – not at all what she had expected when Andy had told her they were going abroad. But then, what had she expected? The island of Capri, maybe – she had heard of that; or the south of France; or one of the Spanish resorts that were now becoming popular? She had certainly not thought of Malta.

It was late when they arrived at Luqa airport and the difference in the time zone made it later still. That night Veronica's first impression, as they were driven in a coach to their hotel in Sliema, was of a barren landscape and then a not-very-attractive-looking hotel – from the outside at any rate. Inside, however, it was considerably more appealing, with marble floors, Turkish rugs, and furniture which was a mixture of old and new. Their bedroom contained a huge double bed covered with a heavy woven cotton quilt, the design and colours of which –red, green, blue and black – matched the rugs at either side of the bed. The wardrobe was immense and made from ornately carved, almost black, teak wood, matching the chest of drawers and the two chairs with red plush seats. It all looked so foreign, thought Veronica, as she gazed round apprehensively, and much more old-fashioned than she had imagined. But the adjoining bathroom was the last word in modernity. There was a shower as well as a bath – even a bidet – and a washbasin with gold-coloured taps and a toilet, all in gleaming white porcelain.

'It all looks a wee bit strange, doesn't it?' said Andy, sitting next to her, where she had flopped down on the bed. He put an arm round her. 'Never mind, darling. I can tell you're feeling a bit lost; wondering what we've come to, eh?' He squeezed her hand. 'I understand. You'll feel better in the morning; it'll all look different then. And I know you're tired tonight, but there'll be plenty of time tomorrow, for . . . everything.'

'Of course there will, Andy,' she replied, blinking away a stray tear. How silly she was, feeling tearful when she was really so very happy. 'We've a lifetime ahead of us, not just tomorrow.' She realised, as soon as she had spoken the words, that they were, maybe, unwise. Jean, Andy's first wife, must have thought she had a lifetime ahead of her, but it was not to be. Poor Jean. If Andy had noticed, however, he did not comment and Veronica decided to let it go and not to apologise. But she must learn to guard her tongue. He just kissed her tenderly that night and urged her to have a good sleep.

So she did, surprisingly. It was often hard to sleep in a strange place, but she had been truly exhausted after the events of a long and exciting day. She awoke to see the bright sunlight filtering through the shuttered windows. On flinging them back she gazed out on to a long promenade – not unlike Blackpool, was her first thought; certainly no natural beauty here – and beyond, a stretch of golden sand and then the intense blue of the Mediterranean Sea. She gasped involuntarily as she stared out at it. Never had she seen such a blue: deep, deep turquoise with here and there a shimmer of paler sapphire as the sunlight played on the waves. This was, indeed, truly beautiful, and she felt in that moment that it was worth coming all that way just for a glimpse of that unbelievable sea.

Andy appeared behind her. 'Good morning, darling,' he whispered as he kissed her. 'Quite spectacular, that sea, isn't it? Are you glad you came now?'

'Of course I am, Andy,' she replied. 'I'm sorry if I was a bit ... well ... less than enthusiastic last night. I feel much better now. I know it's all going to be ... wonderful.'

'Come back to bed,' he said quietly. 'Let me show you just how wonderful it can be.'

He was a gentle and considerate lover, and although, in a way, she was rather jealous of his experience in such matters – she would have liked to have been the first – she was glad of his know-how, because she was quite naïve.

She was pleased, however, that she had waited for this until she was married. Andy would teach her all she needed to know. At the end of the week she knew she was far more in love with him than she had been on their wedding day; and judging from Andy's tenderness and care for her, as well as the heights of pleasure and rapture they had reached together, she guessed it was the same for him.

It was an enchanting week, and Veronica felt, at times, that she was in the middle of a fairy-tale dream from which she would awake with a sickening jolt. She had to confess that her first impression of the island, that of a barren landscape with little natural beauty, stayed with her for a little while. But gradually the place grew on her and she became captivated by the various facets of its rugged charm and absorbing history.

'How yellow it all is,' she remarked the first day, when they walked along the sea front at Sliema, then took a bus to the nearby capital city of Valletta. 'There don't seem to be many trees; hardly any vegetation at all.' The characteristic yellow sandstone buildings were part of the appeal of Valletta, rising high above the finger of land on which it was built above its two vast natural harbours. They wandered along the crowded narrow streets of the town, they paid a visit to St John's Cathedral, which dated back over four hundred years to the time of the knights of Malta, and then ended up at the Barracca Gardens, which afforded a breathtaking panorama of the Grand Harbour.

Another day they went to St Paul's Bay, the place where the writer of the epistles had been shipwrecked. It had a picturesque fishing harbour, as did the quaint village of Marsaxlokk, to the east of the island. Veronica loved the colourful fishing boats; red, blue, green and yellow, with a prow, seemingly, at the back as well as the front.

They travelled around on the local buses; oh, so very slowly – but that was the way life was in Malta, unhurried and serene. It had seen much conflict, though, and the inhabitants were proud of the honour that had been bestowed upon their island by King George after the Second World War. Malta, GC; the George Cross island which had been so ravaged by the horrors of war.

Now the island was peaceful once again. In the more isolated villages it seemed to Veronica that she was stepping back in time, not just a hundred years or so, but almost two thousand, to Biblical times. The flat-topped houses, hewn from greyish-ochre sandstone, clustered close together, almost touching one another across the narrow streets. Strings of washing stretched between the houses; dark shirts and dresses and undergarments hanging limply in the warm air. Occasionally you would see an old woman wearing the black headdress – Andy told her it was called a *faldetta* – which had once been worn by all the women, but which was now mainly traditional. Some of the older women, however, liked to adhere to the old ways, and the men, too, herding their flocks of sheep and goats as their forefathers had done, hundreds of years ago.

They visited the walled city of Mdina, known as the Silent City; and on the last afternoon of their stay they took a boat trip over to the neighbouring island of Gozo. The sea was a little choppy, but Veronica forgot her queasiness at the sight of the magnificent cathedral built on a pinnacle of rock in the harbour. It dominated the skyline, looming ever larger as they drew nearer.

'But it's such a small island,' she remarked. 'I can't imagine why they need a cathedral like that. It's massive.'

'Built to the greater glory of God, no doubt,' Andy replied. She glanced quickly at him, wondering if he was being a mite cynical, but he didn't appear to be. 'You're a Catholic, love,' he went on. 'You should understand their reasoning more than I do, but I have to admit it's a splendid building. Built since the war, I believe.'

Veronica, on reflection, did understand, having been brought up in the traditions and doctrines – some might say dogmas – of the Catholic faith. They believed in more outward show – more magnificence and pomp – not only in their worship, but in their churches as well, than did many of their Protestant contemporaries. She knew that the inhabitants of Malta and Gozo were almost a hundred per cent Catholic in belief. Little wonder then that they should build such an edifice thanking God for their deliverance from the hands of the enemy.

'Come on; let's go and explore,' said Andy, seizing her hand as the boat reached the quayside.

The narrow streets of Gozo wound upwards through the little town. They came across a herd of goats wandering through the street, even climbing on to the steps of the church, with no sign of a goatherd anywhere near. In the doorways of the houses old women, clad in their traditional dress, were crocheting the dainty Maltese lace, their fingers moving busily in and out of the clicking needles. Veronica, fascinated, bought several lace-edged handkerchiefs to take home for presents. Already at the market in Valletta she had bought some locally made handicrafts – filigree jewellery, leather purses, glassware, and dolls in Maltese costume for Donna, Teresa and Bernie – marvelling at how cheap everything was. An added advantage, of course, was that they used English notes and coinage on the island.

The weather had continued agreeably mild, like a warm spring day back home. The locals, however, must have thought it was cold as many of the women wore heavy winter coats. The radiators were turned on in the hotel bedrooms, and in the lounge, in the huge old-fashioned fireplace, a log fire was burning every evening.

All too soon it was time for their flight home. As the plane rose above the sheet of vivid blue sea Veronica, not at all fearful this time, looked down to see the whole panorama of the greyish-ochre island spread out beneath them, with the two smaller islands of Gozo and Comino nestling to the side like a smaller brother and sister. It looked just like a map in an atlas. They soon left it behind as they flew up the length of Italy, although they could see little except the masses of banked cloud above which they were flying. It seemed as though they almost touched the top of the snow-capped Alps, glistening silvery-white in the rays of the sun. Then at last, they were home again, back to a damp and dismal England, although, way up above the clouds, the sun had been shining.

Veronica remarked on the fact to Andy as they stood by the carousel awaiting their luggage. 'It's like a parable, isn't it? The sun's always shining somewhere, even though you can't always see it.'

He smiled lovingly at her. 'You're a grand wee lass, Veronica; did you know that?' He grabbed hold of their suitcases, one in each hand. 'Come on; let's go and see if our taxi's waiting for us. I can't wait to get home.'

Home was a semi-detached house in an avenue off White-gate Drive, nearer to the centre of Blackpool than the house Andy had previously lived in. Veronica had felt a slight unwillingness to move into the Marton house where Andy lived with his children, but she had not been able to tell him how she felt for fear he might misunderstand or be hurt. After all, it was his home, and Donna and Barry's too; but she did not want to start her married life surrounded by memories of Jean. Neither did she think this would be a good idea for him and the children. As it turned out, she did not need to say anything, as Andy guessed, without being told, exactly how she might be feeling. Of his own accord, he had put the house on the market – a highly saleable residence, it had soon been snapped up – and then, together, they had looked for a new home.

The one they chose was, in point of fact, very much like Andy's previous house – Blackpool semis differed very little in design – but the important thing was that it belonged to both of them. Andy had insisted on joint names on the mortgage book, and Veronica's bits and pieces of furniture, as well as his, were transported to their new abode. With Veronica's homely touches here and there – she had the ability to make each place she lived in feel like home – it seemed already as though they had occupied it for ages.

At the start of their new life together, Veronica felt as

though she was experiencing for the first time what it meant to live life to the full. Until now, contented as she thought she had been, she had been merely existing. Now, at last, she was really living.

Sandra was pleased to see Veronica so happy. In fact, she was positively bubbling over with delight as she showed her friend around their new home.

'This is our room, mine and Andy's,' she announced with obvious pride, and just a trace of smugness. Sandra guessed that the furniture, standard G-plan in light oak, had been Andy's, but the finishing touches were, without doubt, Veronica's: the billowing pink eiderdown, the lace-edged pillows, rose-patterned curtains, and the deep pink carpet, which looked new, but quite inexpensive.

'We've had all new carpets,' Veronica went on. 'Only rubber-backed ones, of course – it was all we could afford – but it's nice to have new and they are very hard-wearing. Donna's got the back bedroom – she chose a blue carpet, see . . . and Barry's in here. It's the boxroom really, but it's not a bad size. Lads always end up in the smallest rooms, don't they? It was the same with our Paul and Michael. Of course, we slept all over the show, living in a boarding house.'

So it had been with her and Simon, thought Sandra, as Veronica chattered on about the children and about Carol, Jean's sister, who had now gone back to live with her parents, but was wanting to move in with her boyfriend. Simon had always been allocated the smallest room until she, Sandra, had got a place of her own. He had then moved gleefully to the room she had vacated. Now she was living back home again with her mother and Duncan, and it was her turn to sleep in the small room. Which was only fair, as next week she would be taking up her new position in Harrogate. The flat that had been hers and Veronica's was unoccupied at the moment. It had been sad to see it looking so forlorn and soulless when all their possessions had been moved out. But time did not stand still, as Duncan, in particular, kept reminding her;

and Sandra knew it was time for her to move to 'pastures new'.

Her parting from Veronica that night was rather tearful, not only on her friend's part, but on hers as well, although Sandra had believed she was made of sterner stuff.

'We must keep in touch. You will write, won't you?' begged Veronica. 'And you must come and see us whenever you come back to Blackpool, mustn't she, Andy?'

'Good gracious; I'm only going to Yorkshire,' said Sandra, sniffing back her tears. 'It's not the other side of the world – only across the Pennines. And I don't know how long I'll be there. It might only be temporary; I'll have to wait and see. I'll write, though, I promise.' She could not ring because her friends had not yet got a phone. 'Cheerio then. Take care of yourselves . . . and be happy. I can see you are, though,' she said, as she kissed Veronica on the cheek, and then Andy.

'We are indeed,' he replied, with the contented smile he always wore these days. 'And we have you to thank for that. God bless, Sandra, and you take care of yourself as well. You've been a wonderful friend – to both of us. Cheerio, then. Be seeing you.'

She gave a last wave, then brushed away a stray tear as she got into her Mini and started the engine. It fired first time, fortunately; she was still inclined to panic whenever it stalled. She depressed the clutch, engaged the correct gear and drove off homewards; a little gingerly, but her confidence was increasing every time she drove out on her own.

She had surprised everyone, most of all herself, at the speed at which she had, first, bought her car – a dark red Mini, four years old – and then learned to drive it. She had taken her test just before Christmas and, to her delight, had passed the first time. Those who knew her best, however, had to admit they were not really all that surprised. It was typical of Sandra; she tackled all new challenges with the positive attitude that she was going to succeed.

303

She knew, though, that she was still not confident enough to drive the car over the Pennines to Yorkshire. It was more than likely the hills would be covered in snow, so she had taken heed of the warning of others – particularly her mother – that she must not try to run before she could walk. She was leaving her precious little car for the time being outside the house, covered with a tarpaulin sheet. The double garage was already full with Duncan's car and her mother's; they both needed vehicles for their work.

'Gosh! We're not only a two-car, we're a three-car family,' Simon had remarked. 'Just wait till I get mine, though. It'll be bigger and better than any of yours.'

'Oh yes? And what do you fancy?' asked Sandra, fully aware he was only joking. Simon was never envious of anyone; he was a very easy-going and contented lad. Besides, he could afford very little at the moment, although he took odd jobs during the school holidays to augment his allowance.

'Oh, I dunno; a Jag, maybe, or a Bentley,' he replied airily. 'I haven't quite decided yet. But a Mini'll do very nicely to be going on with. You will let me have a go at driving it, won't you, sis?' He had asked before, and she didn't really see the harm, provided Duncan was with him. But she pursed her lips doubtfully; it didn't do to give in too easily. 'I'll see; I'll let you know before I go to Harrogate.'

Karl Robson had said he would drive the car over to Yorkshire for her in a few weeks' time, when there was the promise of better weather, but her mother did not know about that yet. Abbie was a little disapproving altogether about Sandra's friendship with Karl, although that was all it was: a friendship. She had tried to explain she was not 'two-timing', as her mother seemed to be implying.

'So Ian knows all about Karl, does he?' she asked.

'Well . . . yes. He knows that Karl has given me a few driving lessons. What's wrong with that? Ian couldn't teach me, could he? He's not here.'

'But you've not been seeing him as much when he is here, have you?'

'No, no, I haven't actually. But I've told you, Mum, we're still friends, Ian and me. But we've decided we don't want to be too involved, not at the moment. Ian's still at uni, anyway.'

That was what Sandra had decided, and Ian had had no choice but to agree. It was the issue of the driving lessons, and the fact that Karl had gone with Sandra to choose the car, that had sparked off the only row – heated argument, at any rate – that the couple had ever had.

She had been forced to tell him, when he had come home for a weekend at the end of November, about the driving lessons, as he had seemed amazed at the speed with which she was learning to drive.

'Oh, it's not just BSM,' she had replied easily. 'I've had a few extra lessons . . . with Karl Robson; you know, the chef at Sunset View.'

'You've been out with him?'

'Only driving; nothing else. Although he did go with me to choose the Mini.' A perverse streak had suddenly made her want to get Ian aroused. 'He knows a lot more about cars than I do.'

'And so do I. Why couldn't you have waited and asked me?'

'Because you weren't here, were you? And I wanted to get moving. You know me, Ian: when I get an impulse to do something, then I want to do it straight away.'

'That didn't involve getting engaged to me, did it? Now I know why, of course. It's this Karl fellow, isn't it? You've been seeing him.'

'I haven't! I wouldn't lie to you, Ian, and I've told you the truth now about the driving lessons. I'm not seeing Karl; well, I am, but not really "seeing" him in the way you mean. I didn't want to get engaged because, well, like I said, there's plenty of time. You're still at college, and now I've got this new job to think about.'

'So you've no time for me. I can see that; I know I'm very low on your list of priorities, aren't I?'

'Oh, for goodness' sake, Ian – don't be so selfish!'

'Selfish! Well, I like that! You know very well, Sandra, that I put you first in everything, all the time.'

'Sorry, Ian. That was rotten of me. I know you do, but that's what I'm trying to say. I wish, sometimes, that you wouldn't. We mustn't get tied to one another, not so soon, not until . . . we see how things go.'

He had looked at her imploringly then, in the light of the streetlamp outside the gate of her flat. They had been to the Regent Cinema, walking there and back as it was only a short distance away. She felt sorry for him. She did love him, and he was one of the kindest people she knew.

'Come in and have a coffee,' she said. 'Veronica's out with Andy. Oh, Ian, we mustn't fall out like this.'

They had made it up, although Ian's kisses had been far more restrained than usual. The next day, Sunday, he had taken her out for a driving lesson, but she did not tell him he was not as adept a teacher as Karl.

When he came home for the Christmas holiday he seemed in much better spirits, especially at the news that Sandra's new position was in Harrogate. 'Couldn't be better,' he said. 'It's less than twenty miles from Leeds. We'll be able to meet quite often, er, darling. You will come and see me, won't you? Or, better still, I can come and see you in Harrogate.'

She assured him they would meet, once she had settled in her new environment. She did not go out with him very frequently, however, during the vacation, making the excuse that she was busy preparing for her move. They met on Christmas Day, when, as she had done the year before, she gave an evening performance at Sunset View. Although he was not mentioned, Karl Robson – the figure in the background, serving drinks and mingling with the guests – was on both their minds.

When Harrogate had appeared on the list of vacancies Sandra had decided to go for it. It was not all that far from York, the place she had first had in mind – only twenty miles or so – and, as Ian had reminded her, only the same distance from Leeds. So, if she should desire a taste of city life, both places were near at hand.

She felt at once that she would like the town, dignified – quite staid, in fact – and genteel as it was, and certainly not part of the swinging sixties scene. She loved being surrounded by so much greenery, something which was missing, by and large, in Blackpool. In the spa town of Harrogate, there were two hundred acres of grassland, known as the Stray, which bordered on the very edge of the town. Here, distinguished-looking old gentlemen and ladies clad in fur coats exercised their dogs; but it was a pleasant walk for anyone, young or old, on a crisp winter afternoon. Sandra looked forward to seeing it in the spring or summer, though, when the flowerbeds around the cenotaph at the end of the Stray would be in full bloom. She was learning, as she had been warned, that the Yorkshire winter was very cold, far more so than breezy Blackpool, with a raw wind blowing across the Pennines.

Opposite the cenotaph, at the corner of a main street, was the famous Betty's Café, frequented by the well-to-do and tourists who did not mind the experience of paying over the odds for their coffee. And at the other end of this street, which led down from the town, were the Valley Gardens. This was another delightful stretch of greenery, surrounded by shady, though now leafless, trees, with walkways leading between flowerbeds and water cascades and terraced gardens.

It was in one of the smallish guest houses, in the row opposite the bottom gate of the Valley Gardens, that Sandra, for the time being, was staying. The terms were very reasonable out of season, and the GPO had agreed to subsidise her for a few weeks until she found lodgings for herself. A few people knew her address: her mother and Duncan; Veronica; Ian; and Karl, who had promised to bring her car over.

She was a little surprised, but very pleased, to receive a letter from him in the middle of January. No, he was not bringing the car, not yet, but he would be coming to York the next weekend to visit his family. Could he come and see her? He did not have her phone number, but would she please ring him? He gave her the phone number of the house – his parents' house, she presumed – where he would be arriving on Friday night. How fortunate, she thought to herself, that Ian was going to a football match on Saturday afternoon. Leeds United were playing at home and it was an important match he particularly wanted to see. In fact, she would not be seeing him at all that weekend, and she had no other plans.

Chapter 16

A Second Crisis

Teresa stared at her reflection in the dressing-table mirror. Did she look any different? An anxious little face stared back at her. There were slight shadows beneath her eyes, but that could be with worry, and she was rather pale, but not so much that anyone would notice. She turned sideways, pulling the fabric of her miniskirt tightly across her stomach. There was nothing to be seen there, but then there wouldn't be, would there . . . not yet? Maybe, after all, she was mistaken. Maybe it would happen soon; today or tomorrow. She tried to convince herself she could already feel the niggling little pain starting deep inside her, but she knew it was only 'kidology'. She would have to face the fact that she was pregnant.

But how could she be? It had only happened once. You couldn't get pregnant the first time, could you? How could anyone possibly be so unlucky? Besides, she wasn't even sure they had done it properly. She had been nervous, naturally, though she had pretended not to be, and it had all been such a rush.

She had been due the week before Veronica's wedding, but nothing had happened. It was most unusual; she was normally as regular as clockwork, but she had had a cold, so she had tried to tell herself that was the reason she was late. But it was now nearly the end of January and her second period should have started over a week ago. But it wasn't going to start now; she knew it wasn't. She could feel a slight tenderness and tightness in her breasts; she touched them gingerly now. She did not feel sick, not yet, but she was sure that would happen soon. Perhaps she should pluck up courage and tell her mother before anyone heard her in the bathroom or noticed she was off-colour.

She would say it had been a mistake – well, of course it was; no one would get into such a pickle as this on purpose – and that it had only happened once. But who would believe that? Her mother might; mothers always liked to believe the best of their children. But nobody else would believe her; not Veronica or Sandra, or her friends she had boasted to about all the boyfriends she had had. And which of her various male friends would believe her when they found out – which they would, inevitably? Oh heck! Soon everybody would know and she would be branded a trollop, or, at the very least, a good-time girl, one who didn't have an 'aporth of sense. It just wasn't fair. She had gone on and on saying no to them all – except just that once.

Oh well, there was no time to fret about it now; she would be late for work if she didn't get a move on. Besides, it was too late; the damage was done and could not be undone, certainly not in her case, being a member of such a staunch Catholic family. Unless she didn't tell her mother, and made her own arrangements, very soon; then nobody would be any the wiser. But she knew, deep down, that she would not be able to do this. The thought had crossed her mind a couple of times, only to be hastily dismissed. It was too risky, she had no idea who she could turn to for help, and – the most significant fact – her conscience would not allow her to go ahead with something she knew in her heart would be wrong and contrary to everything she had been brought up to believe in.

She put on her coat and grabbed her shoulder bag, then shouted a brief, 'Tara,' to her mother before dashing off to catch the bus. Whatever she decided to do, she knew this was something she had to face up to on her own . . . when she felt she was ready.

She waited another fortnight and then she knew she could keep it to herself no longer. They had finished their evening meal, her mother was on her own in the living room, her father at a darts match, and Michael and Bernie busy with their homework.

'Mum,' said Teresa. 'I've got something to tell you . . .'

Doreen had guessed as soon as she heard the words just what it was that Teresa was about to tell her. She had been watching the girl closely for a week or two and she knew she was a little out of sorts, pale and listless and more inclined than usual to snap at her brother and sister. Until round about Christmastime the three of them, Teresa, Michael and Bernie, had appeared to be getting on unusually well, with Teresa more than normally pleasant and cheerful. Then, gradually, there had been a change in her. Doreen was not the kind of mother who checked up on her daughters, knowing exactly when they were due for a period and then worrying herself frantic if it didn't occur. Abbie's mother, Eva Winters, had been of that ilk, but thankfully not her own, Doreen's, mother. She did not know for certain that Teresa was overdue, possibly a couple of months, but all the signs were there. She supposed, if she were honest, she had only been waiting for the girl to tell her.

And was she really all that surprised? She had to admit to herself that she wasn't. If this was going to happen to one of her daughters, this thing that all mothers dreaded hearing, then it was bound to be Teresa, in spite of all the 'talkings to' she had had. Doreen mused, in the few moments it took for Teresa to impart her news, that there were, in fact, two things that mothers most feared hearing. One of them was what Paul had already divulged, the question of his confused sexuality; and the other was this.

But she knew there was no point in being outraged or shocked, and she must certainly not let it show on her face. Teresa, to give her her due, was not being flippant or brazen about it. Rather, she looked lost and frightened; a little girl again, appearing much younger at that moment than her eighteen years. It had been her birthday, her and Michael's, the week before.

Doreen sat next to her on the settee and put her arm round her. 'I'm glad you've told me, darling,' she said. 'That was very brave of you. Now, you are sure, are you? You're not just panicking because you're late?'

'No, Mum; I've missed two,' said Teresa. 'And I feel sort of . . . all peculiar; and I was sick this morning, the first time. That's when I knew I'd better tell you.'

'And have you any idea when it's . . . when the baby's due?'

Teresa nodded. 'August, I think; about the end of August.'

'And . . . who is the father? Do you know?'

Doreen realised as soon as she had said them that she should not have uttered those last few words. Teresa's reaction was instantaneous.

'Of course I know! What do you think I am, Mum, a trollop or something?'

'I'm sorry, dear. I'm very sorry. Of course I don't think that. But you must admit you've had a lot of boyfriends, haven't you? And I just thought you might have . . . that you might not be very sure, that's all.'

'Well, I am sure. I'm sure I'm pregnant – worse luck – and I'm sure of who the father is. You thought I'd been playing around, didn't you? You thought I'd been going with all of them, one after the other.' Her face was no longer pale, but quite pink with anger, and her blue eyes were blazing mad. 'Well, I haven't! If you must know it only happened once and now look what a mess I'm in. And nobody'll believe me that I'm not like that. Even you don't believe me.' She burst into tears, burying her head in her hands and sobbing hysterically.

'Hush, love, hush. Of course I believe you. I've told you always to tell the truth, and I'm sure you are doing now. Now, come along; stop crying. I know it's a mess, but I'm here to support you all the way, and your father will as well.'

Teresa lifted a tear-stained face to stare at her mother.

'What, like he did with Paul, you mean?'

'That . . . that was different, dear,' said Doreen, feeling uncomfortable. 'Your dad didn't understand – neither did I, really – and he still can't come to terms with it. Anyway, never mind all that now. It's you we're concerned about, and I can assure you your dad will support you just as much as I do. After all, you're not the first girl in the world to make such a mistake and you certainly won't be the last. It was a mistake, wasn't it?'

'Of course it was. You don't think I wanted to get pregnant, do you?'

'No, I suppose you just got . . . carried away, was that it? I haven't forgotten what it's like to be young, Teresa, although in my day parents tended to make a great hue and cry about that sort of thing. So I suppose we knew we had to . . . well . . . watch what we were doing.'

'Yeah.' Teresa nodded glumly, seeming a little calmer now. 'I knew we shouldn't have, but I suppose I thought it wouldn't matter, just that once, and so . . . we did.'

'You and . . . who? It takes two, Teresa.'

The girl shook her head fiercely. 'I can't tell you.'

'Oh, come on, love. You've got to tell me who the father is. I mean, who is going to be the father. And then we can perhaps decide what we're going to do about it.'

Teresa still shook her head. 'I can't say, and I'm not going to say, ever.'

'Why? Is he married?'

'No; of course he's not married. I don't go out with married men. What do you take me for?'

'All right, dear. Then why can't you say?'

'Because . . . because I don't want him to know, that's why.'

'You mean to say that he – the young man who's responsible – doesn't know? You haven't told him?'

'No, I haven't and I can't. I know what you'd all say, all the lot of you – that we'd got to get married. But he wouldn't want to marry me; he couldn't anyway. And I don't want to get married neither. It wouldn't work. Don't try to make me tell you, Mum, 'cause I won't.'

313

'Very well, love.' Doreen smiled at her sadly. 'But what about the baby? You'll want to keep it, won't you? And you know you mustn't even consider trying to—'

'Trying to get rid of it? Honestly, Mum, surely you know me better than that. I'm a good Catholic girl, aren't I?' There was just a hint of sarcasm in her tone. 'I'll have the baby, and then . . .' she shrugged, 'I suppose I'll see how I feel. I may want to keep it; I may not.'

'Adoption, you mean?'

'Maybe; I don't know, Mum, do I?'

Doreen felt a pang of heartache even though this baby, this unasked for baby, was still months away from being born. No, she could never allow her daughter's baby – her first grandchild – to be given away for adoption, even if she had to look after it herself.

'I don't think you'll feel like parting with it, Teresa,' she said gently. 'Anyway, that's all a long time ahead, isn't it? At the moment we've got to make sure you're all right and that you keep well. The first thing is for you to see a doctor. You haven't, I suppose?' Teresa shook her head. 'No, well, we'll have to make an appointment. And you mustn't worry about anything, love. I'm here for you, now you've told me, and that's the important thing. A trouble shared is a trouble halved. But we must try not to look at it as a trouble, Teresa love. A new baby; that's always a reason for being happy, whatever the circumstances.'

'Thank you, Mum,' said Teresa, so meekly that Doreen could scarcely believe it. 'Thanks for being so understanding. And I'm sorry I flew off the handle. You'd be sure to think that I'd – you know – been with a lot of lads. That's what everybody'll think. But I haven't. I like lads, though. I enjoy their company, more than girls, I suppose. And they like me an' all. That's the trouble, isn't it?'

'And this particular one. You like him, do you? Well, I suppose you must have done.'

'Mm . . .' Teresa nodded. 'Yes, I do, actually.'

Doreen decided not to push her any more for the moment. Perhaps, in a day or two, Teresa might be more willing to divulge who was the father of the child. She told Norman later that night, unable to keep news of such enormity to herself. Her husband, as she had anticipated, was a little taken aback, but came to terms with it quite readily. After all, this was quite a normal sort of occurrence – one you might easily expect when you had three daughters – not like ... the other shock they had received. He did not say all this – Paul's name, still, was hardly ever mentioned between the two of them – but Doreen knew how his mind worked. He asked, of course, who the father was, and she had to tell him that Teresa would not say. Doreen had her own ideas about that, however.

What about that lad she had gone out with in the summer, Tony, from Bolton? He had been over a couple of times since then, Doreen recalled, once on his own. That had been at the very end of October. She counted quickly on her fingers. No; the timing was not quite right – Teresa had said the end of August, at least that was what she thought – unless she had met him again somewhere, unbeknown to her mother.

She was well aware that Teresa did not tell her everything, only those things she did not mind her knowing about. Doreen knew she had been seeing a lad called Steve, but that had not seemed to last very long. There might have been others, though. She was out nearly every night.

It was last November too that she had met up with Simon Horsfall again. She had said she was going to the pictures with him. She had been quite open about it, knowing that her mother liked him, but as far as Doreen knew she had not seen him much since then. That was a ridiculous thought, though; Simon Horsfall. Anyway, Abbie had told her he had a girlfriend, a girl called Melanie, who was away at college.

Doreen knew there was one person in whom she must confide about this disturbing news, although the more she thought about it the less disturbing it seemed to be. And that was her friend Abbie Hendy. After all, Teresa had not said she must not tell anyone, and, as the girl had said, everyone would know before long. How then, Doreen pondered, did she expect to keep the knowledge of her pregnancy away from the one who was responsible for her condition? If he lived in the same town he would be sure to find out, wouldn't he? So on reflection Doreen realised it was more likely to be that Tony – Tony Hibbert, that was his name – from Bolton. It was not very likely he would be coming to Blackpool again for several months, if at all. Whoever it was, though, he ought to be told of what had happened and made to face up to his responsibility for the mishap. But Teresa continued to say that she did not want that at all; she seemed determined to go it alone.

'She's got us behind her, though, Norman and me,' Doreen told Abbie a couple of days later, 'and we're trying to make the best of it. Actually, I'm quite looking forward to it, in a way. Well, I've got to, haven't I? It's there and there's nothing we can do about it. The poor lass needs some support, even though she has been a very silly girl. Honestly, though, Abbie; it never rains but it pours, doesn't it? First that business with our Paul, then Michael, then Veronica getting married – mind you, we like Andy well enough now we've got used to the idea – and now this. It's a good job we don't know what's round the corner. If we knew what troubles lay ahead we'd never be able to face them, would we?'

Poor Doreen, thought Abbie when her friend had gone. She had certainly had more than her fair share of problems over the last year. And she had hoped that once they had settled into Sunset View everything would turn out fine. But you never knew what Fate had in store for you.

Doreen confided in Abbie about all her family problems, and vice versa; that was what friends were for, the two of them often remarked to one another. They had been close friends now for more than twenty-five years. Abbie knew that Doreen had been badly shaken by the news of Paul's proclivities. She had tried to put herself in the same position. How would she feel if she were to discover that Simon was gay? The very thought of it filled her with repugnance, which was what Doreen must have felt at first. But, as her friend had explained to her, he was still her son and she still loved him just as much as ever. And Abbie realised that she too would forgive her son, and her daughter, whatever they might do. Sandra, indeed, had caused enough trouble in the past, but she had come through it all and was now a much stronger person. That was what parents did, particularly mothers: they went on forgiving and trying to understand. As Doreen so prosaically had said, Paul had not suddenly become a different person, just because she had found out something she would rather not know. He was still the same Paul, her son, under the skin, still needing her love and support. It was a pity that Norman, as yet, was not able to face up to the reality of his son's way of life.

Then, hard on the heels of that disturbing news, had come their second son's announcement that he wanted to become a priest. A cause for rejoicing maybe in many Catholic families, but Doreen had had very mixed feelings. Abbie knew how much her friend wanted grandchildren, particularly ones who would continue the male line, but it was not to be. It was ironical that there should now be news of a coming grandchild from a totally unexpected quarter. Abbie, however, had not been surprised when Doreen had told her the news, although she had pretended to be. She had always thought that Teresa Jarvis was a little madam and she was relieved that Simon was no longer seeing her. Doreen had said that the girl knew who the father was – because 'it' had only happened the once! What was more, she said she believed her, but it was Abbie's view – unspoken, of course – that Teresa did not know for sure and that was why she could not say. At all events they seemed to be making the best of a bad situation, which was all you could do, Abbie supposed, once it had happened.

'Well, at least your Veronica's happy,' she had consoled her friend. She and Duncan had attended the wedding and they thought Andy Mackintosh was a most suitable husband for Veronica. 'And she'll be presenting you with a grandchild before long, you'll see.'

Doreen was not so sure; Andy already had two children of his own, and Veronica had her hands full looking after them, and her home, and with her job at Marks and Spencer. She was still harping on about the fellow not being a Catholic. Abbie had been quite sharp with her and told her that if ever there was a girl head over heels in love, then it was Veronica.

'Mm . . . I suppose you're right,' said Doreen. 'And I must confess I do like Andy. You have to let them make their own choice, haven't you? At least I've still got Bernie,' she had added. 'She's a good girl, never a minute's trouble. I can't see her ever giving me any grief.'

Abbie was in a contemplative mood after her friend had gone home. She was pondering that she, Abbie, had very few – if any – worries at the moment. Her home life was happy, she and Duncan were blissfully contented, and Simon was working hard at school, studying for his A levels. He was hoping to go to a physical education college in September, to train as a teacher of games and PE. It was not all work and no play, however, for the lad. He was still friendly with Melanie Holt; he wrote to her and went out with her when she was home from college. Abbie often found herself thanking her lucky stars that her son was 'normal', though not without a pang of guilt that she should feel that way . . . Poor Doreen.

She was a little concerned about Sandra and her love life. She realised, however, as she and Doreen had just been saying, that she had to let the girl make up her own mind. On no account must she interfere. It would have been so fitting, though, if Sandra and Ian Webster had made a go of it. It had looked that way at one time, but now Karl Robson was very much in the picture. Sandra had been at home at the end of last week for a flying visit. And then she and Karl had driven off together on the Sunday, back to Harrogate, in Sandra's Mini. Karl had been at the wheel and Sandra, at his side, had looked like the cat who had got the cream. It was plain to see the way things were heading there. Mind your own business, Abbie told herself. The girl had to live her own life, even make her own mistakes, if needs be. And she, Abbie, could find nothing to object to in Karl – except that he was not Ian. Ian had been a good friend to Sandra; he had been there when she needed him. Maybe she needed him no longer?

Abbie was contented at school now, particularly since she had settled her grievances with the awkward teacher, Mrs Bell; or, rather, the woman's grievances with her. It had been the second week in January, not long after they had returned to school after the Christmas holiday, that Abbie had gone into the staffroom to find Mrs Bell on her own in there. To her discomfiture the woman was sitting in an armchair with her head in her hands, quite obviously weeping.

'Oh . . . oh, I'm sorry,' Abbie had said, taking a step backwards. 'I didn't realise anyone was in here. I've got a free period and I've some books to mark, but I can go somewhere else. I'm sorry if I disturbed you.'

'No, it's all right.' The woman looked up and, to Abbie's amazement, tried to smile a little through her tears; a sheepish smile, as her next words revealed. 'Come in, Mrs Hendy, and don't say you're sorry.' She sniffed audibly. 'I should be the one that's saying I'm sorry. I've been wanting to say it for ages, but I've never got round to it. I'm stubborn, that's my problem.'

You can say that again, thought Abbie, but what she actually said was, 'There's no need, Mrs Bell. I know we haven't always seen eye to eye, but if you're ready to bury the hatchet now, then so am I.'

'You're a nice person, Mrs Hendy,' said Mrs Bell. 'Everybody says you are, and I know it's true. Oh dear . . .' To Abbie's embarrassment she started crying again.

Abbie sat down on the chair next to her. 'Come on, now. It's nothing to get upset about. But surely that's not what you're crying about, is it, because you and I didn't get on very well? There's no need; we can sort it out.'

'No.' Mrs Bell shook her head. 'It's not just that, but seeing you come in made me realise what an absolute cow I can be sometimes.' Abbie did not know how to answer, because that, unfortunately, was all too true. 'My husband's ill,' she went on, twisting a damp handkerchief round and round in her hands. 'He might be very ill. He has to have an operation . . . tomorrow. I haven't said anything to anyone, apart from Mr Knighton, of course. I don't talk about my private life at school. I suppose I think it's nobody else's business and – well – I've never found it easy to get on with any of them. The trouble is, you see, I'm in the wrong job. I hate teaching; I always have done, and there's nothing I can do about it, not now; it's too late.'

Abbie was astounded. She had considered Mrs Bell to be one of the most dedicated teachers on the staff, albeit old-fashioned and set in her ways. 'Oh dear,' she said, feeling that the words were somewhat ineffectual. 'I'm sorry to hear that; I'd no idea. But I'm even more sorry to hear about your husband. I can understand how upset you are. What is the matter with him?'

'Oh, something internal – you know,' said Mrs Bell evasively. 'They won't know properly until they operate tomorrow. I'm just praying that they don't find . . . anything.'

'And I'll say a prayer too, I promise you,' said Abbie.

'Thank you. My Dougie means everything to me,' said Mrs Bell, staring into space. 'I can't imagine how I'd carry on without him. It suddenly came over me when I was in the classroom, and I had to get out. Luckily I've got a student in, as you know, so I've left her to cope. And I don't want anyone to see me like this.'

'They won't,' said Abbie. 'Don't worry. It's half an hour off playtime. Listen, I'll make us a cup of tea, shall I? To heck with these books! I'll take them home to mark tonight.' She busied herself with the kettle and mugs and tea bags while the other teacher sat in silence. 'Do you take sugar, Mrs Bell? I'll put it in, shall I?'

'Just a small one, dear. You're very kind. And . . . my name's Doris.'

'Yes, I know,' said Abbie, handing her the cup of tea. 'And I'm Abbie, to most people.'

'Yes, I know that as well,' said Mrs Bell. 'I've been a fool, not getting to know you sooner. I've wanted to, but—'

'But we got off on the wrong foot,' said Abbie.

'Maybe,' said Doris, 'but that was my fault. As I've just said, I don't like teaching, but I don't think anyone else realises how I feel. And then when I see enthusiastic teachers, like you and young Jacquie Holt, joining the staff, I feel, well, jealous, I suppose, because I don't feel the same.'

'But why,' asked Abbie, 'did you become a teacher if you didn't want to do it?'

'An overpersuasive mother,' replied Doris, grimly. 'You could say a domineering one.' Abbie nodded; she knew only too well about mothers such as that. 'She was determined her daughter should go to college – I'm an only child, worse luck – to have the chance she'd never had, she said, and all that, and how I had to make the most of my opportunities.' Abbie did not interrupt with disclosures about her own mother. Mrs Bell seemed to want to go on talking.

'I finished college the year before the war started. I taught in Preston for a couple of years. A really rough school, that was; not the best sort of introduction for a young teacher, but I thought it might be better when I got a job in Blackpool.'

'This is your home town, then?'

'Yes. I taught in Marton at first and then I came here. I've been here twenty years now.'

'But why put up with it for so long if you don't like it?'

Doris pursed her lips. 'Habit, I suppose. Maybe I'm too lazy to look for anything else, although it's not easy when you've been trained for teaching. I can't do shorthand or typing or anything like that. The pay's not bad, and my husband's not a very big wage earner. He's a garage mechanic, but he works for someone else, not for himself. We always thought we'd have children, you see – we intended to – but none ever came along and so I just kept on and on in the same old rut.' She sighed. 'Dougie and I are so happy, though, and that's all that really matters to me. I don't know what I'd do if anything were to happen to him.'

'Don't think like that,' said Abbie. 'Try to be positive; he'll need you to be, won't he?' She had never looked all that closely at Doris Bell before; she had only seen her as a rather nondescript, sallow-faced woman who seldom smiled. She noticed now, however, that the woman had lovely eyes, deep brown, like Abbie's own. They were sad now, but Abbie could see the depth of feeling there and she realised that this ordinary, even dreary-looking, little woman must love her husband very much indeed.

'I met him during the war, you know,' she said now. 'In the Tower ballroom. He was in the RAF, stationed in Blackpool; he was only ground crew, so I never had that awful fear that he might not come back.'

'Well, fancy that,' said Abbie. 'I met my husband – my first husband, that is; he died about twelve years ago – I met him in the Palace ballroom. He was in the RAF too.' She did not add that he had been a flight sergeant. She smiled. 'It's amazing how many girls met their future husbands in a Blackpool ballroom. So we do have something in common, you see.'

'Yes; amazing,' replied Doris distractedly. 'I found it amazing that he should fall for me. I always used to be so shy and I never thought I was very pretty, like some of the girls. I'd never been encouraged to go out with boys – my mother was very strict – but a friend persuaded me to go to the Tower with her, and that was that.' She actually smiled a little. 'Of course my mother didn't approve of Dougie at first.'

'Same here,' said Abbie. 'My mother was a real tartar. She thought Peter wasn't good enough for me.'

'Yes, the same old story.' Doris nodded. 'Anyway, I was old enough to please myself. I was twenty-seven when the

322   ·

war ended, so Dougie came to live here – he's from Sheffield originally – and we got married. We've been so happy.' Her lip quivered slightly again. 'Being contented at home is all that I've ever bothered about. The job is . . . just something to do.'

'But surely it would be better if you tried to enjoy it,' said Abbie. 'Duncan and I are tremendously happy, but I enjoy my job as well. I wouldn't like to drag myself here day after day, feeling that I hated it.'

'Perhaps hate is too strong a word, then,' said Mrs Bell. 'I tolerate it, as something that has to be done. You'll find that a lot of teachers of my age feel the same, if they're honest. And then we see the young ones coming in and getting promotion and it makes us annoyed – even though we've never wanted the extra responsibility ourselves.'

'I'm not young,' said Abbie.

'No; but you're keen; I can tell that. And you don't mind all these new-fangled ideas that Philip Knighton has. He's a good head, mind you, full of enthusiasm.'

'But you're strictly a three Rs teacher?' Abbie smiled wryly at her. 'Well, that's what matters in the end: knowing how to read and write and do sums; you can't get very far without that. And you certainly get the best out of the children in your class; we all know that.'

'Thank you, dear. That's very kind of you. You'll forgive me, then, for being so horrid to you?'

'There's nothing to forgive, honestly,' Abbie leaned across and patted her hand briefly, 'not now I understand how you feel. And I'll be saying a little prayer for your husband tonight,' she added in a quiet voice as she heard footsteps approaching the staffroom. 'Try not to get too upset; I'm sure he'll be OK.' But Abbie knew that such words sometimes proved to be futile; her mother-in-law had died from cancer a few years ago.

Doris Bell's husband, however, had recovered from his operation. Whatever the surgeon had found – Doris was very reticent about it – had proved not to be life-threatening. She was a much nicer person now, trying to be on good terms with the other members of staff, but still as rigid in her approach to teaching. At all events, it meant that school was now a pleasanter place for Abbie. She had hated being at cross-purposes with the woman, especially as she had not known the reason.

'Hello there, love.' Duncan poked his head round the door, interrupting her wandering thoughts. 'I thought I'd leave you and Doreen on your own for a while to have a chat. She's feeling a bit better, is she, now she's told you about it? Poor Doreen . . .' He had stayed just long enough to hear her tale of woe, and then had gone to visit a man down the road with whom he had become friendly; they both enjoyed classical music and swapped gramophone records. He came and sat down opposite her, leaning forward with his elbows on his knees. 'Are you going to tell Simon about – you know – Teresa's news?'

'I don't think so,' replied Abbie. 'At least . . . not yet. I wouldn't want him to think I was tittle-tattling. He was friendly with the girl at one time – not any more though, thank goodness – and he might think I was getting at her. No; I'll leave it. He'll find out soon enough.'

'Yes, maybe you're right,' said Duncan. He looked deep in thought for a moment. 'Yes, I'm sure you are. Least said, soonest mended, eh? I'll go and make us some cocoa.'

Sandra was enjoying her new job in Harrogate. The work was very much the same as it had been at the Blackpool office, but the surroundings were much pleasanter – something she would not admit to her friends and relations back home, many of whom thought there was no place in the world like Blackpool – and it had been good to make a new set of friends. She had stayed in the guest house opposite the Valley Gardens for only a couple of weeks, then she had had the offer of a flat to share with one of the girls with whom she worked. It was in a quiet tree-lined avenue leading off the Stray, some fifteen minutes' walk from the centre of Harrogate. She and her new friend Amy walked to work if the weather was fine, but if it was very cold – as it so often was – or raining heavily, they went in either Amy or Sandra's car. Both were Minis: one pale blue and one dark red.

Sandra was driving with more confidence now. Karl had been driving at first when they set off from Blackpool to take the car to its new home, but when they were more than halfway there, through Skipton and on to Blubber-houses Moor, he had said it was time for Sandra to take the wheel. There had been little on the roads that winter's day and she had felt quite composed and pleased with herself. The roads around Harrogate, indeed, were quieter than those in Blackpool – far hillier, though; her driving lesson experience of hill starts was soon put to the test – and she felt that she might, before long, be able to attempt the drive back home on her own, or over to York when Karl came to visit his family. She did not want to attempt the journey to Leeds; the amount of traffic there and the busy roads and roundabouts and one-way systems would be too much for her, especially as Ian's flat – he was now sharing with a friend – was near to the university, almost in the centre of the city.

Besides, she no longer saw Ian quite so frequently. She had seen him only three times since the start of the year, and it was now the beginning of March. She had travelled to Leeds, just once, on the train. They had had a meal in town and then gone to see a show at the famous City Variety Theatre, after which she had stayed in Ian's flat, his friend being absent for the weekend. Ian had slept on the settee whilst she had occupied one of the two single beds. He had not suggested that she should do otherwise. Since she had refused to become engaged to him there had been a certain reserve between them, although neither of them would go so far as to say they wanted to end the friendship. Maybe that was all it had ever been, Sandra often pondered; a very loving friendship – it had assuredly been that – some-thing they had both needed at the time. But when she had been faced with the question of whether or not she wanted to spend the rest of her life with Ian, she had

325

not been sure. Surely, she told herself, that was answer enough?

She had seen Karl much more frequently, and she had decided at the outset that she should not be secretive about their meetings. She had told Ian and he had seemed not to mind too much. She had a sneaking feeling that he too was seeing someone else, although he had not actually said so. He was rather evasive, however, about his social life at the university. He must, surely, have met and even become friendly with some of the young women students; he was an attractive young man. But perhaps he was loath to tell her, after saying so often that she, Sandra, was the only girl for him. But anyone could change their mind, as she was beginning to realise had happened to her.

She knew that the reason she was enjoying her new life so much in this very sedate and genteel town – just about as different from Blackpool as one could imagine – was because of her developing friendship with Karl Robson. His home, originally, had been in York, where, as he had told her, his parents kept a small hotel. She had not remembered him visiting the place all that much when she had first known him in Blackpool, even during the late autumn when Sunset View had closed down, but now he seemed to be over in Yorkshire almost every weekend.

He was taking only casual work now – bar work and an occasional temporary chef's job – and he always tried to leave the weekends free. It would be different when the holiday season started. The hotel would be open at Easter and by Whitsuntide the summer season would have begun in earnest. Karl would be expected to be there more or less all the time. He would be entitled to a day off, but he would be obliged to work on Saturday and Sunday. It would be quite a problem and Sandra, for the first time, was beginning to wonder if her decision to move to Yorkshire had been a wise one.

She and Karl had spent several weekends together, enjoying one another's company more and more each time they met. The weather at first had been bitterly cold, but wrapped up warmly against the biting wind and the flurries of snow, they had visited such places as Ilkley, Bolton Abbey, and Grassington, a charming village in the heart of the Yorkshire Dales. Sandra's favourite place was Knaresborough, only five miles away from Harrogate. They had spent a few pleasant afternoons there, wandering along the narrow streets of Georgian houses, then down the steep alleyways that led to the River Nidd. The ruins of a fourteenth-century castle stood on the clifftop above the town, affording a splendid view across the valley to the viaduct.

They stood there one cold but bright day in early March. In the distance they could see a train crossing the viaduct, looking like a child's toy from so far away, and below, the silver ribbon of the river meandering along the valley bottom. Karl put an arm around her shoulders.

'I think you're growing to like Yorkshire just as much as I do, aren't you?' he asked. 'I said you would, but I don't think you believed me.'

Sandra turned to face him, half frowning, half smiling. 'I didn't want to commit myself too soon; I wanted to be sure,' she said, knowing her words were ambiguous. 'Yes, I do believe I've fallen in love with Yorkshire.'

He put his hands on her shoulders. 'Sure about the place, or about . . . the company?' he asked.

'Both,' she replied. 'Yorkshire's a beautiful county, but I've come to appreciate it so much more because of . . . the company.'

He kissed her gently, then again, more deeply. He had kissed her in a friendly way before, but now it was far more meaningful, as though it were a seal of assurance upon their relationship. 'Sandra, I've fallen in love with you,' he said. 'I'm not going to ask you if you love me. I don't think that would be fair. I mustn't rush you. I know about Ian and about . . . the other young man.' She had told him about Greg. 'I want you to be very sure, you see, because – well, this isn't just a casual thing. I hope it will be for ever.'

Sandra nodded. 'Thank you for being so understanding, Karl,' she said. 'It isn't a casual thing for me either. I really care about you. But there's Ian. I must tell him . . . first.'

'Of course you must, darling,' said Karl. 'And then, next weekend, I was wondering if you would come to York to meet my parents? You could stay Saturday night at the hotel, then I'll take you back to Harrogate on the Sunday. They're looking forward to meeting you.'

'They've heard about me, then?'

'Of course. It might be almost the last time we'll have, for a while, to spend a weekend together. It will be Easter before we know where we are, then summer, and then I'll be working all hours God sends at Sunset View. Oh dear, why ever did I persuade you to apply for a job in Yorkshire?'

'Because neither of us knew, did we, Karl, what was going to happen? Never mind; we'll find a way, I'm sure. I'm due for a week's holiday in the spring. I can spend it in Blackpool. And, yes, I'd love to come to York next weekend.'

But before that happened she knew she must confront Ian. She felt it would be cowardly to write to him, and so she phoned him at his flat, asking him if he could come over to Harrogate one evening during the following week. She felt sad, knowing that she still cared a lot for him. She could find in him nothing to dislike or disapprove of, but that was not enough. She had not felt able to commit herself to him for a lifetime, but she knew, without any doubt, that if Karl were to ask her to marry him she would say yes without the slightest hesitation. The reason she had not yet told Karl that she loved him was because of her still tender feelings for Ian. She recalled a time when they had stood together in the gardens at Gynn Square and declared their love for one another. She felt mean now, and sorry it was ending like this.

Ian did not seem surprised when she told him it would be better if they 'called it a day'. She did not say she had fallen in love with Karl, only that it was not fair to go on seeing Ian knowing that her feelings had changed. Ian agreed, and admitted that he too had become friendly with a young woman in his year at university. Sandra said she was glad for him and wished him well; but at the same time she wondered why she should feel a little peeved. They parted on the very best of terms.

On the grassy banks sloping down from the city walls of York, purple and bright yellow crocuses and early daffodils were blooming. Sandra had visited the city only once, in the company of Ian. Now it was Karl's turn to show her the delights of his home town: the Shambles; the awe-inspiring Minster; the medieval gates – known as bars – leading into the city; and the Castle Museum with its reconstructed cobbled streets and shops of the Victorian and Edwardian era. They walked on the ancient walls surrounding the city, then climbed up to the dizzy heights of Clifford's tower. It was truly a magnificent city, as Karl had boasted.

Mr and Mrs Robson, Karl's parents, made her very welcome in their unpretentious but very comfortable guest house near to the Minster. After a hearty Sunday lunch of roast beef and Yorkshire pudding, followed by apricot crumble, Karl drove Sandra back to Harrogate. He came into her flat for a few moments to say goodbye, before driving on to Blackpool. He had a temporary job for the following week at a South Shore hotel whilst the permanent chef was on holiday.

'Thank you for a lovely weekend,' said Sandra. 'I can't tell you how much I've enjoyed it.'

'Same here, darling. The first of many, I hope.'

She looked into his clear grey eyes, seeing herself mirrored there in their luminous depths. 'I love you, Karl,' he said simply. 'I want you to know . . . I'm sure. I love you . . . so much.'

'That's wonderful,' he replied. 'That's just what I wanted to hear.' He gathered her into his arms again and kissed her. 'See you soon, darling. Next weekend, maybe; I'll phone you. Take care now. Love you.'

'Love you, too. Drive carefully now . . .'

When the phone rang on the following Wednesday

evening, Sandra was sure it would be Karl, making arrangements for the weekend. She was surprised to hear her mother's voice.

'Sandra? Oh, Sandra, love; I'm so glad you're not out.'

'Mum? What's the matter? You sound all hot and bothered. There's nothing wrong, is there?'

'Well, yes, there is, love.'

'What is it, Mum? Come on – tell me.'

'I can't, not over the phone. I was wondering . . . could you come home this weekend? Please, love; do try.'

'Yes, of course I will. I'll come on Friday night, after I finish work. But what is it? It's not you and Duncan, is it?'

'No, of course not, dear; nothing like that.'

'Nobody's ill, are they? Nobody's . . . died?'

'No, no. I'll tell you when you come home. I need to talk to you, Sandra.'

But apart from that, her mother would say nothing.

Chapter 17

Simon

'Mum . . . I want to tell you something.'

Abbie looked up from the pile of books she was marking to see Simon standing there. She could tell at once that he looked extremely worried, although, when she thought about it, he had not been his bright and breezy self for several days now. She had put it down to pressure of work, knowing he had his mock A levels coming up soon.

'Yes, love; what is it?' She put down her red Biro and patted the settee next to her. 'Come and sit down.' He did sit down, but on the opposite chair and not at her side.

'Mum . . .' he said again. His brown eyes looked at her appealingly and then quickly looked away again, down at his hands, which were clenched tightly together. 'You know . . . you know Teresa's having a baby?'

'Yes . . .' Abbie could scarcely find the breath to utter the word as an awful thought occurred to her. But it couldn't be . . . Simon couldn't possibly be about to tell her that. 'Simon,' she asked, 'what is it?'

'I'm sorry, Mum, but . . . well, it's mine.' He did not look at her, but continued to look down at his hands. He was clenching and unclenching them now, the knuckles white with the pressure. 'I know I've been stupid. Well, we both have, but it was my fault, Mum.'

Abbie was too flabbergasted to speak at first. She stared at him in silence for several seconds, unable to take in what he was saying. She had heard him, sure enough, but this . . . it was impossible to believe. He looked up at her as the silence got to him. 'Mum . . . ?'

At last she found her voice. 'Yes, Simon,' she said, as calmly as she could. 'Teresa's having a baby, and you think you might be the father. Why? Has she said so? Has she told you?'

'No. I haven't seen her since Christmas. I think she's been avoiding me. After we'd . . . well, you know . . . after we'd done . . . that, we both felt a bit embarrassed, sort of, and I didn't go out with her again. Well, only once and it didn't work. And then, a couple of weeks ago, someone told me she was pregnant, and I knew it must be me.'

'Who told you, Simon?'

'Oh, just somebody who knows both of us. It doesn't matter who. But it's true, isn't it? I overheard you and Duncan saying something the other day.'

'Yes, yes, it's true enough. Doreen told me about a fortnight ago. I knew you'd find out sooner or later, but I never dreamed . . . Simon, listen to me. You are not the father. Whatever put that idea into your head?'

'Because Teresa and I have . . . been together; I told you.'

'Simon, Teresa has had lots of boyfriends. Surely you know that? Why should it be you? It could be anybody.'

Simon's brown eyes blazed with indignation. 'That's an awful thing to say, Mum. I know she's had a lot of boyfriends, but she's not like that. When she went with me, well, it was the first time, ever. She told me.'

Abbie would have laughed if she had not felt so distraught. 'And you believed her?'

'Of course I believed her. Why shouldn't I?'

'And it was the first time for you as well, I take it?'

'Mum!' The one word said it all. 'Surely you can't think—'

'No . . . no, I don't think that at all, not really.' She was just so blazing mad, now that the news was beginning to sink in, that that little minx Teresa should have duped him like that. 'But I know Teresa,' she went on. 'I've known her ever since she was a baby, Simon, and I know what she's like. She led you on, didn't she?'

'She didn't, Mum. I've told you. It was my fault. And it was the first time, for both of us. I could tell.'

Abbie gave a deep sigh. 'OK, OK, Simon, if you say so. But if what you say is true, then why hasn't Teresa been to see you, to tell you that it's your baby?'

Simon shrugged. 'Dunno. P'raps she doesn't want me to know. She knows I'm still at school and I'm going to college in September and— Oh heck, Mum. What a mess! What on earth am I going to do?'

'You should have thought about that before,' said Abbie, grimly, although she still could not believe it was her son who was responsible for Teresa's dilemma. 'And when did it all happen, with you and Teresa?'

'The end of November, thereabouts.' Abbie did a quick sum in her head. Oh hell! The dates fitted if what Teresa had said was correct about the baby being due at the end of August. 'I met her in the pub one night when I was with the lads. And then I saw her a couple of times afterwards.'

'You didn't say anything to me.'

'No, well, I know you don't like her very much.'

'It isn't that I don't like her, Simon . . .'

'Well, anyway. You were out one night, you and Duncan, and she came back here, and we played some records . . . and all that.'

' "And all that", indeed! In your room, you mean?'

'Well . . . yes. Oh heck, Mum, what's the use of going on and on about it? It's happened, hasn't it, and . . . and I don't know what I'm going to do.' To her horror he burst into tears.

'Oh, come on now, Simon. We'll sort it out, don't worry.' She went and sat on the arm of his chair, gently stroking his dark hair. 'At least we know Teresa's from a nice family, and we'll all try to help as much as we can . . . when we decide what we're going to do,' although she was not sure whether it made it better or worse that she and Doreen were such close friends. 'The first thing we must do is see Teresa, and Doreen, of course. The girl has to be made to tell the truth. It's no use her going on refusing to say who the father is.' Abbie was still clinging to the vain hope that Teresa would admit it was someone else – Tony or one of the other lads she had been friendly with – when she saw that Simon was taking the blame.

'A family consultation? Oh gosh, Mum! Not that.'

'How else are we going to sort it out? Look, love, it's the only way; we have to get things out in the open.'

'What will Aunty Doreen say?' He sounded like a little boy who had been caught with his fingers in the biscuit barrel.

'She knows Teresa, doesn't she, only too well?' But Doreen had said she believed the girl's story about the one and only time. 'She will just want to sort it out, like I do, and to do what's best.'

'She'll want Teresa and me to get married, won't she? I . . . I don't mind. I would do, Mum. I love her, really.'

Over my dead body, thought Abbie. But what she said was, 'Let's not be too hasty, love. I'll phone Doreen later tonight, and then perhaps they can come round tomorrow evening. The sooner, the better.'

'OK, if you say so. I'll go and finish my homework now.' He got up and slouched dispiritedly towards the door.

'Simon,' Abbie smiled at him as he turned back to look at her, the very picture of misery, 'try not to worry too much.'

'OK, Mum. Thanks . . .'

'The silly young fool,' said Duncan when she told him later that evening. 'I would never have thought Simon's brains were all in his trousers. Still, what's done is done. No use locking the stable door and all that.'

'It might not be him, you know. I still can't believe it.'

'What did Doreen say?'

Abbie had rung her just before Duncan came in, telling her of Simon's surprising confession. 'Oh, she seemed quite relieved to think it was Simon. Well, she would be, wouldn't she? So long as she doesn't come up with the crazy idea that the pair of them should get married.'

'Oh, come on, love, let's not cross our bridges till we come to them. And the last thing we want is you and Doreen falling out about this. She's coming round tomorrow, you say?'

'Yes, her and Teresa, and I dare say Norman will come as well. You will be there with me, won't you, Duncan, to support me?'

'Of course I will. Oh crikey! A family conference, eh?'

'Yes – that's what Simon said.'

'Poor kids. You can't help feeling sorry for them.'

Simon and Teresa looked sheepishly at one another. They were not sitting together on the settee. That was occupied by their two mothers and Duncan, whilst Norman was pacing the floor puffing spasmodically at a cigarette. The two young people regarded one another from opposite armchairs.

'So, Simon, you say you're the father of the baby Teresa's having?' said Norman, stopping his pacing for a moment. 'It's all right, lad; we're not angry with you. It's too late for that. We just want to know, that's all.'

Simon glanced at Norman, then at Teresa. 'Yes, I am. Oh, come on, Teresa, tell them. It is me, isn't it?'

'Yes . . . yes, you are,' replied the girl. She looked up at her father. 'It's true, Dad. It's Simon's baby.'

'Then why didn't you say so before, you silly girl?' said her mother. 'If we had known it was Simon—'

'Because I didn't want him to know,' said Teresa. 'Because he's going to college. I didn't want to mess it all up for him. So I thought if I didn't say anything—'

'Don't be so daft,' said Simon. 'You must have known I'd find out. And I'd know it was me because . . . well, because there hasn't been anybody else, has there? Not like that.'

'No, that's true.' The girl shook her head. 'I wasn't thinking straight.'

'But you are now, aren't you?' said Abbie. 'And you're

quite willing to let Simon take the blame, is that it? That's very convenient . . .'

'Here, hang on a minute,' said Doreen. 'That's not fair . . .'

At the same time Teresa was saying, 'It's true, Aunty Abbie. I'm not making it up. I know what you all think about me, but I'm not like that, honest. What me and Simon did, it was the only time. I know we shouldn't have, but we did. It was my fault.'

'No, it wasn't. It was mine.'

'For heaven's sake, the pair of you!' snapped Doreen. 'Stop trying to take the blame for one another. You're in this together, that's quite obvious.' She glared at Abbie. 'Now do you believe her?'

'I suppose so,' said Abbie grudgingly.

'And now we have to decide what we're going to do about it,' Doreen went on. 'Teresa will have the baby, of course.'

'Of course,' murmured Abbie.

'And Teresa and I will get married,' said Simon calmly and very firmly. 'I've decided. I'll get my A levels and I'll be able to get a good job and . . .' He glanced round at all their surprised faces, some of them shocked rather than merely surprised. On Doreen and Norman's there were glimmers of relief as well. Duncan looked stunned. As for his mother, her eyes had opened wide in horror, although he had hinted to her before that he would not mind getting married. Teresa looked more amused than anything. It was she who spoke first.

'Hey, come on, Simon. What do you mean, you've decided? What about me? I haven't decided. I don't want to get married, do I heck as like! What's the point? We've just made a mistake, but you're going to college and—'

'What's the point?' Simon interrupted. 'The point is . . . I love you, Teresa; honest, I do. And I think it's only fair—'

'Now, hold on a minute,' said Duncan quietly. 'Just think about what you're saying, Simon. Your words do you credit, but you're only just eighteen; so is Teresa. You are both far too young to think of committing yourselves to one another for a lifetime. Good heavens – you haven't even been going out together seriously. I know this has happened and it's unfortunate, but—'

'No, it's out of the question, Simon,' said Abbie. 'Besides, Teresa has said she doesn't want to get married.'

'Excuse me a minute,' said Doreen, 'if I may be permitted to speak. It's my daughter who will be left holding the baby, bringing it up without a father, and it isn't the sort of life we want for her . . . is it, Norman?'

'Er, no, love,' said Norman. He had sat down now, on an upright chair as all the easy chairs were occupied, and he slumped forward looking extremely dejected.

'Simon has agreed to marry her and we appreciate that,' Doreen went on. 'We were relieved to know it was Simon and not . . . someone else, so what we'll have to do now is go ahead with our plans and make the very best of it all.' She smiled at Simon, then at Teresa. 'I'm sure they'll be happy together; they've known one another for ages.'

Abbie could feel herself getting crosser and crosser. Hints of *Pride and Prejudice*, she thought. Doreen was behaving for all the world like that insufferable Mrs Bennet. 'Simon is going to college in September,' she said, aware that the remark was peremptory, but she could not help herself. 'He's already been promised a place there. It's all arranged.'

'Provided I get my A levels, Mum,' said Simon in a quiet voice. 'But I've said I don't mind not going if—'

Abbie went on as though she hadn't heard him. 'Anyway, he's not a Catholic, is he?' She looked meaningfully at Doreen, raising her eyebrows.

'There's no need for sarcasm,' retorted Doreen. 'It doesn't matter whether he is or he isn't. Teresa is and the baby will be and—'

'It mattered when your Veronica wanted to marry Andy, didn't it?' said Abbie.

'Of course it didn't matter. We like Andy and anyone can see how happy they are. That's a mixed marriage that's turning out perfectly well.'

'That's not what you said at first. You made a heck of a fuss when you knew they were engaged.'

'Stop it, you two!' said Duncan, in an unusually severe voice. 'It's not doing any good, bickering like this.'

'Yes, shut up, Mum,' said Simon quietly, whilst Teresa said, in a much louder voice, 'Shut up, both of you! Sorry, Aunty Abbie, but honestly! Will you stop going on and on about Simon and me as though we're not here? I don't want to get married. In fact, I flatly refuse to, and I don't think Simon wants to either, not really.'

'It's my baby,' said Simon, 'and I want to do what's right, that's all.'

'Yeah, I know,' said Teresa. The look she gave him, so understanding and so – suddenly – mature, made even Abbie admit to herself that perhaps she was not such a bad kid after all. 'I'm sorry, Si, but it wouldn't be right. It wouldn't work, you and me. As Duncan says, we're too young. Well, it's not just that – lots of people get married at eighteen, I suppose – but we don't want to make another mistake, do we? We've already made one. Anyway, you're going to college – deffo! I'm not going to mess that up for you.'

'I don't have to, honest—'

'Simon,' said his mother quietly, 'just listen to Teresa, will you? She's talking a lot of sense. Thank you, Teresa.' She smiled at the girl, aware that Doreen at her side was bristling.

'An' I'll look after the baby myself,' Teresa continued. 'I 'spect I could still work part time. I know I've messed up, but, well, that's the way it goes, i'n't it?' She shrugged her shoulders and grinned at Simon, much more like her old self. 'We can still be friends, Si. You can come and see it – the baby, I mean – he or she. I don't want to push you out or anything like that. I just don't want to marry you.'

'Simon will face up to his obligations – that's when he's able to,' said Abbie evenly. 'It will be a few years before he's earning a proper wage. In the meantime, this will be our grandchild as well, and we're not going to turn our backs on it, are we, Duncan?'

'Mine by proxy,' said Duncan, 'but I agree with Abbie. It's up to all of us to see that the baby has the best start in life.'

'Thank you,' said Doreen stiffly. 'I suppose there's nothing more to be said, if Teresa is so determined.'

'It's probably for the best, love,' said Norman soothingly. 'Anyway, we all know one another, don't we? It's a real family thing.'

'I'll go and make some coffee,' said Abbie, retreating with great relief to the kitchen.

Sandra had arrived home late on the Friday evening after a train journey involving two changes, having been unwilling to face the drive over the hills in the darkness. She had been stunned at the news that Teresa was expecting a baby. Not so much at that – she might have expected that – but that her 'little brother' had admitted he was the father.

At first she had insisted, as her mother had done, that Teresa must be pulling a fast one. OK, it might be Simon, but in all probability it was someone else. But Abbie had convinced her, eventually, that it was true. Teresa had had sex – although her mother did not put it quite so bluntly – only once, with Simon, and now a baby was on the way.

'So, what's the great problem now, Mum?' Sandra asked. 'He's faced up to it; so has she; but they're not going to get married. Sounds like a sensible solution to me. Teresa will have her wings clipped, I know, and that's hard luck, but considering the way she's carried on—'

'She says she hasn't, love.'

'No, maybe not; she's not a bad kid at heart. But it might turn out to be a disaster if they got married.'

'Very likely; but when I was a girl they would have jolly well had to get married, and no messing. You were scarred for life if you had an illegitimate baby.'

'Never!'

'Well, that's what it seemed like. There were some, of course – quite a lot, actually – because of the war; but

339

unmarried mothers were frowned upon.'

'Thank goodness times have changed.'

'Er . . . yes. I was quite adamant that Simon should not marry her, but I can't help feeling rather guilty now that Teresa will be left holding the baby – quite literally. She'll have her wings clipped, as you say, but Simon will be getting off scot-free; able to go to college, meet other girls if he wants to.'

'What about Melanie?'

'Oh, crumbs! We've hardly given that poor girl a thought. I expect it will all be over when she finds out.'

'So Simon's not going to have it all that easy,' said Sandra. 'He won't be able to escape either, with our families being so involved with one another.'

'I don't suppose he'll want to escape,' said Abbie. 'He's a conscientious lad and he'll face up to his responsibilities. After all, he did say he would marry her. That's what worries me, Sandra: that it's too much of a family thing; that they both might succumb to pressure, eventually, and feel that they've got to try and make a go of it. We're too close for comfort, sometimes, our family and Doreen's.'

'And how is it with you and Aunty Doreen? You've not fallen out, have you?'

'No, not exactly. There's a certain coolness, but we'll get over it. We've had fall-outs before, but we always come round in the end.'

'Well, there you are then. Don't worry, Mum. We've had worse problems to face than this, haven't we?'

'Yes. And there was I feeling sorry for poor Doreen with all her problems. Congratulating myself, I was, that everything was going smoothly for us. Well, pride goes before a fall, I suppose.'

Sandra had told Karl of her unexpected visit home, so he had stayed in Blackpool that weekend. They shared a quick snack of spaghetti bolognese in his flat on the Saturday evening, then he listened attentively as she told him of Simon's dilemma. Karl was a very good listener.

'What do you think he should do, Karl?' she asked.

'Mum thinks it's all decided that he's going to college as planned, but Simon's still wavering; he's told me so. He's so anxious to do what's right, and he thinks he might be able to persuade Teresa to marry him. Her mother would support him, that's for sure. Well, you know Doreen, don't you?'

'No – definitely not; he mustn't marry her,' said Karl, so vehemently that Sandra looked at him in surprise. 'There's no point in letting one mistake ruin your whole life. I know Teresa and I know your brother – not as well as you know them, of course – and I can see it would be a disaster for both of them. Anyone can make a mistake,' he stared unfocusedly across the room for a moment, 'but it doesn't have to be the end of the world.'

'But what are her chances, of getting married, I mean, if she doesn't marry Simon? Who would want to take on someone else's child?'

'Lots of people do,' he grinned. 'Duncan, for instance.'

'Oh, that was different; we were older.'

'But not much less trouble, from what you've told me.' He raised his eyebrows.

'Never mind all that! A young child, I meant – a baby. She would find it difficult.'

'She might not want to get married, but Teresa won't be short of followers, whatever her circumstances; you can be sure of that. Tell Simon he must insist on seeing the child, though, even if Teresa moves away. It's important; he'll regret it if he doesn't. I remember—' He stopped abruptly, shaking his head.

'You remember what, Karl?'

'Nothing . . . Well, I suppose I might as well tell you. I was going to say I remember how it affected . . . a friend of mine; a school friend, actually, in York. He got this girl into trouble, as they say. There was no question of them getting married; it was a very casual sort of boy-girl thing. Anyway, she got married, to someone else and moved away; and that was that.

'You mean, he never sees the child?'

'Hardly ever; once in a blue moon. I know it hurts him;

341

it was his child, when all was said and done.'

'We're looking too far ahead,' said Sandra. 'We don't know, do we, what's in the future for Simon and Teresa? But I'll try to persuade him to carry on with his plans for college. Come on, Karl, you're getting all broody. We'd better get a move on if we don't want to miss the start of the film.' *West Side Story* was on again in town and she was looking forward to seeing it for the third time.

'Sandra, I have something to tell you,' said Karl, the following day. They had been to her mother's home for Sunday lunch, Abbie at last having grown more used to the idea that Karl, and not Ian, was now her daughter's boyfriend. Sandra had said her goodbyes to her family; she was catching a late afternoon train back to Yorkshire, and she and Karl had planned to take a walk along the cliffs before it was time for her to leave.

As they drove northwards along the promenade he half turned to glance at her. 'I should have told you ages ago, but . . . I didn't. But now . . . I know I must.'

'That sounds ominous, Karl,' she replied, looking at him quizzically. He had turned back to the wheel and his unsmiling face caused her to feel a stab of fear. Surely he was not about to tell her it was all over between the two of them? Not after he had said he loved her and she had said the same to him. Surely there could not be someone else? She had realised recently how much he meant to her and the sudden thought that she might lose him made her feel wretched.

He parked the car on the promenade at Norbreck and they crossed the tram-track to the path that led along the clifftop, high above the sea.

'What is it, Karl?' she asked. 'You're making me feel quite scared.'

To her relief he turned to smile at her. 'There's no need to be, darling,' he said. 'I'm the one that's scared, about what you will say, although I'm hoping – praying – that it will make no difference.'

He stopped, and she stopped too, leaning on the

railings and looking out across the expanse of sand and the grey-blue sea. 'I haven't been entirely honest with you,' he said. 'At least – I haven't told any lies, but there is something I have omitted telling you.' He turned to look at her. 'Sandra . . . I have a son; he's called Luke and he's seven years old.'

She could not speak for a moment. It was a shock, sure enough, but not the one she had dreaded hearing. 'You mean, you've been married?' she breathed. An awful thought struck her. 'You're not . . . still married, are you?'

He shook his head. 'I've not been married at all. And I expect you can guess why I'm telling you now, can't you?' She half nodded. 'Yes, it's because of Simon. It gave me quite a jolt hearing you tell me about him, because the selfsame thing happened to me.'

She gave a gasp as she recalled Karl's words. 'Your friend,' she said. 'The one who doesn't see his child – you mean it was you?'

'Yes, I'm afraid so,' he said. 'Oh, Sandra, I do hope you will forgive me for not telling you sooner.' He took hold of both her hands, holding them tightly in his own. 'I would have done so eventually, of course, but when I heard about Simon I knew I had to tell you now.'

'Yes. Tell me about it,' she said.

It had happened just before he was called up for his National Service. Wendy was 'just a girl', he said; someone he had been out with now and again, but he had no intention of marrying her or even going out with her seriously. However, the night before he left York for his two-year stint in the army they had got 'rather carried away'. Wendy had written to him two months later to say she was pregnant. He had been horrified, but being a dutiful sort of lad he had quickly obtained a forty-eight-hour pass and had gone home, offering to marry her. Wendy had refused. There was no point, she said; they didn't really love one another; it would not work, as they were totally unsuited. It was at her parents' insistence that she had written to Karl, otherwise she might not even have bothered to let him know. Karl knew that what she said was true: for them to marry would just be spoiling two lives.

Another two months later – Karl was by this time in Germany – she had written to him again saying she was about to be married; to Raymond, a man several years older than herself who had always been 'sweet' on her and was only too happy to bring up the child as his own.

'There was nothing I could do,' said Karl, quite calmly, but Sandra could detect a trace of sadness in his eyes. 'They went to live in Coventry; her husband had got a job down there in the car industry. They are very happy, I believe. I know she wouldn't have been happy with me, or I with her. She was rather – I feel awful saying this, Sandra, but it's true – rather empty-headed, always after the bright lights, the *dolce vita*, you know. I'm surprised she's settled down so well.'

'Something like Teresa, in fact?'

'Yes, very much so.'

'And are you sure the child was yours?'

'Oh, yes. I saw him when he was two years old, when Wendy came back to York to see her parents. There was a look about him that was unmistakable. My sister, Clare, had a little boy about the same age. The likeness was uncanny.'

'And did you never feel like . . . well . . . claiming him as your child?'

'There was no point, was there? Raymond's a decent bloke, by all accounts, and Luke regards him as his father. It would be unsettling for the poor kid if I were to stick my nose in.'

'You must have felt sad about it, though.'

'Yes. It's odd to feel you have a child that you can't lay claim to. The last time I saw him was about two years ago. He was five: a grand little lad, growing to look more like his mother, though, which was perhaps as well. Wendy told him, "This is Karl – he's an old friend of mine." We chatted a bit; he was a bright, friendly little boy . . . but that was that.'

'Oh, that's sad,' said Sandra.

344

'Then . . . it makes no difference to you and me?'

'No. Why should it? I'm glad you've told me, though. Did your parents know all about it?'

'Yes, of course. I came in for a lot of censure, but they knew it would have been a mistake for me to marry Wendy. They're sorry about Luke, but my sister has three children now. And who knows what may happen in the future?' He smiled rather wistfully at Sandra.

She smiled back. 'Who knows?' she repeated.

'I feel so much for your Simon,' he continued. 'That's why I think he should be involved with the baby – his son or daughter – even though I think it would be a mistake for him to marry Teresa. He's a caring sort of lad and I should hate to see him pushed out . . . like I was.'

'I shouldn't imagine there's much chance of that,' said Sandra, 'with both our families being so involved. But we can't plan their lives for them, Karl.'

'Very true, darling. We have our own plans, haven't we? The rest of our lives to look forward to.' He put an arm round her and drew her closer to him. 'Thank you for being so very understanding. I think the reason I didn't tell you, right at the start, was because I was afraid of losing you.'

'There's no fear of that, Karl,' she replied, with absolute conviction. His revelations had made no difference to the way she felt about him. Karl was the man she was going to marry. She was only waiting for him to ask her.

'Well, that's a bit of good news, anyway,' said Doreen to her husband, soon after the Easter weekend. 'Karl and Sandra's engagement. Mind you, I've been expecting it. He's had that look in his eyes for ages; so has she.'

'Strange she should decide to go and work in Yorkshire, though, isn't it,' said Norman, 'just when things were getting serious between them?'

'She'd already decided she wanted a change, before she and Karl got friendly. And I'm sure that is what she needed – to get away from Blackpool and all its memories for a while. Poor lass; she was ever so brave when that terrible thing happened to Greg. She deserves all the happiness she can get.'

'How does Abbie feel about it? She was quite set on her making a go of it with Ian, wasn't she?'

'At one time, yes. But she realises now that maybe the families were too close; hers and Jim Webster's. She was engaged to him once, you know, ages ago. It would be somewhat . . . incestuous – well, not exactly that, but you know what I mean – her daughter getting together with his son.'

Norman looked at her curiously. 'You mean like it would have been if our daughter were to marry her son?'

She shook her head impatiently. 'That was different, Norman. Yes, I know our families are close, but it would have been a solution; the ideal one, in my opinion. But we can't force the lass.'

'No, indeed we can't and we mustn't. I'm glad you and Abbie have sorted out your difference of opinion, anyway. And there's another piece of good news, don't forget, as well as Sandra's engagement. A grandchild to look forward to – another one, I mean. A legitimate one.' Veronica had recently announced, very proudly, that she and Andy were expecting a baby in December, almost exactly a year after their marriage.

'Yes, that's wonderful news,' Doreen agreed. 'She's really happy, isn't she, Norman? At least one thing is turning out all right. We've certainly had our fair share of troubles.'

'True enough, but then all families have troubles – well, problems, anyway – of one sort or another, don't they? You must get things into perspective, love. At least, nobody has died.'

Doreen, all of a sudden, felt herself go cold, as though a goose had stepped over her grave, as her mother used to say. No, it was true that nobody had died. And nobody will, she told herself; they were all in the best of health.

'Yes, we've had our problems,' Norman went on, seemingly unaware that she had suddenly gone silent. 'But there's not one of them that can't be overcome . . . with a bit of tolerance. I know I haven't always been as – what shall I say? – as open-minded as I might have been. However, wrongs can always be righted – in time.'

She pulled herself together, realising he must be referring to the on-going hostility between him and Paul. Maybe, at last, his attitude was beginning to soften, but she knew she did not dare to mention it.

'Anyway, I'm off to bed,' Norman said abruptly, aware, possibly, that he might have committed himself too readily. 'I'm dead beat. See to the doors, will you, love? I may be asleep when you come up.'

'Yes . . . OK, Norman. I'll be up in a little while. I'm going to have a nice quiet read. Good night, love.'

She picked up her *Woman's Own*, but when Norman had gone it lay unopened on her lap. There was something niggling at her, although she knew she was being stupid. There was something else her mother used to say, besides the thing about the goose and the grave; that troubles always came in threes. Doreen knew it to be an old wives' tale, but it was strange, through life, that things seemed to work out that way.

She had had two troubles to face, for sure: Paul's disclosure, and then Teresa's unwanted pregnancy. But could she be said to have experienced a third? She knew she was being superstitious, downright ridiculous in fact, but she hoped so. Veronica's marriage, though she had not approved at first, had turned out to be a blessing; the girl was happier than she had ever been. Michael's startling news, however; his decision to enter the priesthood – she could not call that a trouble, not when she knew she should really be rejoicing, but it was certainly a problem she had had to face, one that had given her a great deal of heartache and soul-searching.

Yes, Doreen managed to convince herself that her three problems, or whatever you wanted to call them, had already arrived and had been dealt with. The only real worry on her mind was that of Norman and Paul. When would they start speaking to one another again?

Chapter 18

Bernie

'I'm going to miss you, Maureen,' said Bernie to her best friend as they walked home from school one Friday afternoon in May. 'I don't know how I shall manage when you've gone. You know what they're like, all the others; I think they only put up with me because of you.'

'Don't be silly,' said Maureen. 'They like you, honestly they do. You shouldn't have such a low opinion of yourself, Bernie.'

'I can't help it. You know how shy I am. Well, I used to be till I met you. And I'm scared I will be again when you're not there.'

'There's no need to be scared of anything. You're part of our crowd now; you have been for ages: you and me, Susan and Linda, Sheila and Val.'

'Val's OK. I like Val. She's always nice to me. But the others – they hardly take any notice of me. I know they were fed up with me at first, tagging along with you.'

'Well, they're not now. I've told you, you imagine it, Bernie. You'll be all right when I've gone, really you will. Go and join in with them, just as though I'm there.'

'But you won't be there, will you? That's what's worrying me. You will write, won't you?'

'Course I will.'

'And come and see me when you come to Blackpool?'

'Sure.'

'You could come and stay at the hotel, in the winter,

perhaps, when we've no visitors in. We've loads of room and I know Mum won't mind.'

'That's a great idea, kid. You'll be helping to run the place by then, won't you? Second in command to your mum, eh?'

Bernie cheered up a little at the thought. 'Yes . . . yes, maybe I will. I'll be at Parklands, though, like our Paul used to be. The book-keeping and receptionist course, though, not catering. I don't mind helping out in the kitchen – we have to muck in anywhere when we're busy – but Mum wants me to take over all the office work from her and do some waitressing as well.'

'Super! I bet you're looking forward to leaving school, aren't you, and being a proper working girl?'

'You bet! I can't wait to leave, 'specially now you won't be there. You lucky beggar! You've left already, haven't you?'

'Yeah . . . There's only half a term left and it's not worth starting at a new school in Ipswich. That's why they're letting me leave early. You must come and stay with me an' all, when you're not too busy at the hotel. Don't worry, kid; we'll see one another again soon . . .'

But Bernie wondered if Maureen was just saying that. She was the sort of girl who made friends easily, just as she had done when she first came to the school in Blackpool. Maureen's father had a good position in the Ministry of Pensions and they were moving now because he had been given another promotion. Maureen too had been promised a job in the same department, on the bottom rung of the ladder, of course, and she would be attending night school to obtain the necessary qualifications. Bernie feared that her friend, all too soon, would be so engrossed with her new job and new associates that she would forget all about her.

The girl had been a saviour, almost, to Bernie when she had joined the school a couple of years ago. Bright and bubbly and outgoing, she had seemed the very antithesis of the quiet and retiring Bernie Jarvis. Nevertheless, the two had become close friends and Bernie had been encouraged to gang up with a group of girls, whereas, previously, she had always been a lone figure on the sidelines. The fact that the two of them were Catholics, in a school that was largely non-denominational, may have had some bearing on their friendship, but whatever the reason Bernie knew she would miss Maureen very much indeed.

She said goodbye to her on the corner of Maureen's street with a brave attempt at cheerfulness. She did not want to let herself down by being tearful or else her friend would think she was a real old misery-guts. She ran nearly all the rest of the way home, then let herself into the house and darted upstairs to her bedroom without saying her usual hello to her mother. It was only then that she let a sob escape and allowed the tears to spill over. She did not cry for very long, however; she told herself she was being silly, and at least she had the weekend at home before she had to go back to school and face up to life without Maureen.

She peered at herself in the dressing-table mirror to make sure her eyes were not red before she went down to have a chat with her mother. After she had changed out of her school uniform, which she loathed, she dabbed her blotchy face with a little Pond's powder and then applied a touch of pink lipstick. There, she thought; she didn't look too bad at all, and it was Maureen she had to thank for the subtle change – you could hardly call it a transformation – in her appearance. She had been dull and dowdy and insignificant, or so she had considered herself to be, when Maureen had first appeared on the scene. Now she was doing what she could to improve the way she looked, although she knew she did not possess the sparkle and vivacity of some of her friends, or her two elder sisters. But that would only come when she had more confidence in herself, and that was something which, at the moment, was sadly lacking in Bernie.

But she knew there had been an improvement of sorts. Her straight dark hair, which had used to hang limply round her neck, had now been professionally cut and

350

styled. Her mother had been only too pleased to pay for her to visit Maureen's hairdresser, and now her feather cut gave a new lightness to her appearance. She was thankful, too, that she had got rid of that awful brace on her teeth. It did seem to have done the trick, straightening her two enormous front teeth so that she no longer had to suffer the nickname of Brer Rabbit or Bugs Bunny. And her spots had gone, too, thanks to some ointment from Boots, recommended by Maureen. She knew she would never be pretty, though, like Veronica or Teresa. But look what had happened to Teresa! If that was what came of being pretty and vivacious then perhaps it was as well to be plain and boring.

Bernie sat down on the bed and for several moments she was deep in thought. She knew it wasn't just Maureen leaving that was troubling her; it was things at home as well. Everything seemed to be in such a turmoil these days. Bernie's anchor had always been her mother; so long as Mum was there then she knew everything would be all right. Mum was still there, of course – she and Bernie were as good friends as they had always been – but Mum was preoccupied with all sorts of problems and Bernie felt she did not confide in her as much as she might have done. She still treated Bernie as the baby of the family, as they were all inclined to do.

She had told her, as she had more or less been obliged to do, that Teresa was expecting a baby. Bernie was not stupid; she knew where babies came from, but she had felt quite disgusted with her sister that she had done 'that' before she was married. She was so embarrassed that she could scarcely look Teresa in the face, let alone speak to her, for about a week. And Teresa, oddly enough, seemed to be equally discomfited. When she had found out that the father of the expected baby was none other than Simon Horsfall Bernie had been even more shocked. For a long time she had had quite a 'thing' about Simon. He was tall and nice-looking, good at sporting activities and so popular with everyone. When they had met on family occasions she had gazed at him covertly, worshipping him

351

in secret – no one had any idea about how she felt – and she had been over the moon with delight when he actually spoke to her. Not that a lad as outgoing as Simon would ever want to have much to do with her, Bernie; but she had been content with a few friendly words. Now, alas, she had found that her idol had feet of clay.

Then there had been that business of Michael deciding he wanted to be a priest. Bernie had thought that was terrific and could not understand why her mother was so downhearted about it. The priest at the church they attended, where Michael for a long time had been an altar boy, had been thrilled to bits to hear the news. Bernie, with great pride, had told Maureen, and her friend had agreed that it was terrific news. The others had overheard her, though, and she had come in for a good deal of ribbing, especially from Susan and Linda. So she had kept quiet about it after that and had not mentioned it for ages.

She had heard her mother saying to Veronica that she felt she was losing both her sons, and that was something Bernie could not understand at all. What was troubling her most was the thing that had happened first; that had seemed to be the beginning of all her mother's problems. Paul had suddenly left home and had gone to live with his friend Martin; and not only had he left home, he was no longer their chef. All her mother would tell her was that he and his father had fallen out about something.

'About what?' Bernie had asked, only to be told, 'Oh, don't worry your head about it, love. It's nothing you need to know about. All families have rows now and again. Paul and your dad will make it up one of these days. They're both stubborn, that's the trouble . . .'

But time had gone by and still Paul and her dad did not speak to one another. Paul came round only when he thought his father would not be there; and he was . . . different, somehow, no longer the nice and easy-to-get-on-with big brother she had admired so much. She and Paul had been the only ones in the family who had shown a real interest in Sunset View. Veronica had never worked in the hotel, Teresa had done so only under duress, and Michael had his sights set on higher things. Bernie, however, had always maintained that when she left school she would work in the family business. It had been, and still was, her sole ambition: to work at Sunset View, and then, perhaps, one day to be a hotel proprietor, like her mother, with her own establishment. Paul had encouraged her, telling her how much he enjoyed Parklands and he had persuaded her to enrol for a course there as soon as she left school. He had been a wonderful chef, everybody had said so, with such clever ideas. Then, suddenly, he had gone and the next news was that he and Martin had opened their own restaurant. Bernie missed him very much. It almost seemed as though he didn't want to be bothered with any of them now he lived and worked with Martin. Bernie could not understand it at all.

Soon they would all have gone, except for her and Teresa. Goodness knows what Teresa would do. She was still working at the newsagent's shop although she was now six months pregnant and what her mum called 'showing'. For that reason Mum had said it might be as well if she didn't do any more waitressing, but Teresa had said, 'Why not? I'm not ashamed of it even if you are.'

Mum said, 'Don't be silly. Of course we're not ashamed of you, but I don't want you to get tired, carrying heavy trays.'

But Teresa had insisted she was OK and, as usual, she had got her own way. Nothing had changed there. She served the meals and cleared away, chatting to the guests just as animatedly as she had always done. Bernie did not try to emulate her. She, Bernie, had her own style. She was quiet and efficient, and friendly, but with a more respectful approach than her sister's chummy one. To her surprise she seemed to be just as popular with the visitors as Teresa was, receiving just as many tips at the end of the week.

Although Teresa's pregnancy did not prevent her from waitressing, Bernie had noticed that it *did* prevent her from setting the tables and helping in the kitchen.

Admittedly, she had another job and was often tired when she came home at the end of the day. Bernie, on the other hand, enjoyed helping out where she could, although her mother had said she did not expect her to do so whilst she was still at school.

She shook herself out of her doldrums now and went downstairs to find her mother. Doreen was setting out the cutlery and glasses ready for the evening meal and Bernie started to help her.

'Hello, love. Have you had a nice day?' her mother asked, as she always did.

'Not all that nice, Mum. Maureen's left school today, you know. They're off to Ipswich tomorrow.'

'Oh yes, I remember now.' Doreen smiled at her sympathetically. 'You'll miss her, won't you? Never mind, though. You'll be leaving yourself before long, and you'll make lots of nice new friends at Parklands. Like . . . like Paul did.' Her mother's voice suddenly went quiet and sort of guarded. Bernie wished she dared ask, again, what had gone wrong between her dad and Paul, but her mother's face had that closed look and she guessed she would get nowhere at all; so she kept quiet.

Two's Company, Martin and Paul's restaurant on Hornby Road, was proving to be a very popular place for eating out. They had enjoyed a moderate success at first, but now, some nine months into their venture, business could be said to be flourishing. Word had got round about the excellence of the cuisine and the friendly ambience of the place: homely, but with those finishing touches, both to the food and the décor, which denoted real classiness.

They had deliberated for quite a while before Two's Company opened, about the menus they would present. French cuisine was all the rage; they had learned a lot about it at Parklands, but they both agreed that a more down-to-earth approach might be better for the clientele they expected in this largely unsophisticated seaside resort. They did not hope to attract many of the holidaymakers who stayed in the town for a week or –

more unusually nowadays – a fortnight. These people would make the most of their full-board or half-board at their guest houses and could rarely be tempted to spend their holiday money on eating out. Some of the hotels, however, had been converted into holiday flats; not all hotel proprietors were doing as well as they had hoped. Some people now preferred a more 'do-it-yourself' type of holiday, catering for themselves and occasionally, to make a change, going out for a slap-up meal somewhere. Martin and Paul intended to capture some of this trade, but in the main they were concentrating on the locals: those Blackpool residents who wanted to treat themselves to a night out for a special occasion.

Chinese and Indian eating places were springing up; you could get 'pub grub' – chicken in a basket, scampi and chips, and that sort of thing – at any number of pubs, and there was a fair sprinkling of posher places out in the Fylde countryside. Paul and Martin aimed for something different, but not too exotic or overelegant. They decided, between them, on the idea of dishes, not from around the world, but from around their own British Isles. Good and wholesome – some might say plain – food, excellently cooked and with an added piquancy in the ingredients, a touch of wine or spice, perhaps, which would lift it out of the ordinary.

Their menu was wide-ranging and suited all tastes. There were dishes from no particular region in the country: pot-roasted beef, roast duck with a tangy gooseberry sauce, toad-in-the-hole, and an extra special bacon and egg flan – which would later come to be widely known as quiche. Their specialities were Fidget Pie, from Shropshire – this had originally been a harvest home supper meal, a sweet-sour dish made with gammon, apple and onion, finished off with a short-crust pastry topping; beef and tomato pie from Devon; Welsh lamb pie, consisting of lamb cutlets, leeks and kidneys; and, of course, the traditional Lancashire hot-pot with layers of lamb, potatoes, mushrooms and onions.

The pudding menu was quite extensive too – ordinary enough dishes, but given an added appeal when presented as coming from elsewhere in the country: Bakewell pudding from Derbyshire; Yorkshire curd tart; butterscotch tart from Scotland; old English trifle, said to be originally from Suffolk; also summer pudding, and baked pears in cider, which were not from anywhere in particular, but were popular specialities on the menu.

Several of their friends and relations had dined at the restaurant, some returning for a second visit. Paul and Martin had entertained some of their former fellow students from Parklands; Veronica and Andy had been; so had Sandra and her new boyfriend, Karl; and Abbie and Duncan Hendy. Paul had been very surprised to see them, but Abbie, and Duncan too, had been as charming and friendly as ever. Martin's parents had visited several times. Paul was amazed that they appeared to accept Martin, and Paul as well, just as they were without any recriminations or disapproval, or even a curious glance at the pair of them.

Paul's parents were conspicuous by their absence. He had the feeling that his mother would love to visit the restaurant she had heard so much about, but that she felt it would be disloyal, or even deceitful, to do so without her husband accompanying her. And there was no chance of that whilst Norman remained resolute in his antagonism to his elder son's lifestyle. Just recently, however, Paul had noticed what might be the slightest thawing in his father's attitude. He had actually nodded and said hello the last time Paul had visited his former home, instead of totally ignoring him. Paul had expected him to be out at a bowls match. He had, indeed, departed soon after his son's arrival, making the atmosphere much less strained. Paul and his mother were now closer than they had ever been. There was no longer the restraint between them, brought about by Paul's secrecy regarding his sexuality, that had marred their former relationship. It was possible that his mother would never entirely understand but she was doing her best to live with what she now realised was an unchangeable part of her son's life.

Paul was talking to Martin about it late one night towards the end of May. They had had a busy evening – Friday was usually one of their best nights – the last group of people, celebrating a silver wedding anniversary, having departed at eleven thirty. The two young men, students at Parklands, who helped out as waiters, had gone home, and now, having stacked the dishwasher and cleared the tables, Paul and Martin were enjoying a relaxing beer before retiring for the night.

The bar lounge was a pleasant place where the diners could sit both before and after the meal. It was there that the final course of coffee and Elizabeth Shaw mints was served. The armchairs were comfortable, the sort you could sink into and appreciate the friendliness and warmth of the surroundings. The curtains and the silken flower arrangements – Veronica's handiwork – echoed the same colours. On the walls were prints of beauty spots and places of interest around the British Isles, and a further selection was to be seen in the dining room. They ranged from fishing villages in Cornwall to the grandeur of the Scottish Highlands, not forgetting the sepia prints of Victorian Blackpool in its heyday.

'Well, that was a successful evening if ever there was one,' said Martin, raising his glass to Paul. 'Cheers, mate. I think that is going to be our forte: silver wedding parties. We might get a few more bookings when word gets round. Mr and Mrs Edge seemed delighted with everything; the older folk seem to like us.'

Paul laughed. 'I don't know that they'd like to hear you call them older folk. They're about the same age as my parents, I reckon. Well, younger if anything, because Dad's quite a few years older than my mother. Mum certainly tries to hang on to her youthful image and I don't blame her.'

'Yes, she's still a very attractive woman,' said Martin. 'They'll be celebrating their silver wedding soon, won't they?'

Paul frowned thoughtfully. 'Let me see . . . I think they

got married towards the end of the war. It must have been a year or so before the end because our Veronica was born in 1945 and I'm sure there wasn't any – you know – hanky-panky. Yes, it'll be their silver wedding in a couple of years or so.'

Martin chuckled. 'D'you think they'll celebrate it here? Will your father be speaking to us by then?'

'I certainly hope so,' replied Paul. 'I thought when I was round there the last time that there was a slight – ever so slight – change in his manner. At least he managed to say hello to me.'

'But he's not ready yet to meet the two of us?'

'Give it time, Martin. My mum was saying that she's sure he'll come round in time. Apparently he has admitted to her that all quarrels could be mended with a bit of tolerance, and that he knows he's stubborn.'

'You can say that again! He forgave your Teresa readily enough though, didn't he?'

Paul gave a wry smile. 'Perhaps he was relieved she was normal – what he considers normal at any rate. It's the boys in the family that are a worry to our parents. First me, and then Michael. Bang go their hopes of continuing the male line.'

'Not to worry,' laughed Martin. 'The girls are sure making up for it. I'm ever so pleased about Veronica's news. When did you say the baby was due?'

'Oh, not for ages yet – December. Trust Veronica to tell everybody as soon as she knew herself. She could only just have found out when she told Mum. That's what she's like, though. She can't keep anything a secret.'

'She's a grand lass, isn't she? I really like her, you know, Paul. I would have hated to see her get hurt again by getting the wrong idea. I'm so glad she met Andy.'

'Yes, she's certainly had a few chaps, but I'm sure Andy's the right one. You mean, if you'd been straight you might have fancied her?'

'I'm jolly sure I would. I much prefer the females in your family to the males – present company excepted, of course.'

'I should damn well hope so!'

Martin winked at him. 'Your Michael's rather an odd bod, isn't he? I never felt as though I'd got to know him properly.'

'Neither did I; now I know why. The lad had a secret, the same as me; well, not the same secret, but you know what I mean. And before long we'll be calling him Father. Father Michael, just imagine that!'

'Yes, your family are a mixed bag all right. Colourful characters, the lot of them. How's your Bernie? I've always thought she was a nice sort of kid. Shy, though, isn't she?'

'Yes, she's reserved, not very sure of herself, but she's getting better. Being a waitress has helped, and I'm sure once she gets to Parklands she'll be much happier. She'll meet people with the same interests and ambitions. She's never been too happy at that school, and now her best friend's left she's out on a limb again. She's finding it hard to mix with the rest of them without Maureen alongside her; that's what Mum says.'

'Poor kid. Perhaps we could invite her to come and have a meal here. She could come with Teresa – she's never been here either – or with Veronica and Andy. It would give her an insight into another side of catering. We could even ask her to do a bit of waiting-on for us. What do you think?'

'I'm not sure,' replied Paul. 'I feel I've neglected her lately, since I've not been living at home. We used to be quite pally, with us both taking an interest in the hotel. But now she seems – I dunno – a bit cagey with me.'

'Do you think she knows?'

'I shouldn't think so. Mum won't have told her, that's for sure.'

'Your Teresa might have done. She's a knowing little madam, that one. I'm pretty sure she's guessed about us even if she hasn't been told.'

'I don't think she'd say anything to Bernie, though. We've all tended to treat Bernie like a little girl.'

'She's sixteen, isn't she?'

'Yes, but she's still very naïve; still very sweet and innocent, really.'

'Nobody stays like that for ever, Paul.'

'No, more's the pity. But I wouldn't want to do or say anything that would upset her. I dare say she'll learn about it – about you and me, I mean – gradually; just part of the growing-up process.'

'Parklands should help. You meet all sorts there!'

'You're not kidding!' Paul laughed, raising his glass again to his friend. 'Here's to us, pal.'

'Now, you're coming with us tonight, aren't you?' said Val to Bernie as they made their way out of school on Friday afternoon. 'You'll enjoy it, honest you will, and we all want you to come with us.'

'You might . . . but I don't suppose the others do,' said Bernie, feeling very unsure. Part of her badly wanted to go to the cinema with them, but she didn't want to feel like a fish out of water. If they had been going to a nice musical like *The Sound of Music* or *South Pacific* she wouldn't have hesitated, no matter who else was going. But she didn't think her mother would approve of the choice of film and she wasn't sure that she did either. She had seen a crit in the paper and judging from that and the posters she had seen outside it sounded as though it was very racy; even sexy.

'Anyway, it's an X film, isn't it?' she said. 'They might not let us in.'

'Is it heck!' replied Val. 'It might be an eighteen and over, but who cares? Slap on a bit of lipstick and look confident and they'll let us in. How do they know how old we are? Oh, come on, Bernie. Don't be a spoilsport. It'll be great. Peter Sellers is a real scream.'

'OK then, I'll come,' said Bernie. 'You'll sit next to me won't you, Val? I feel a bit of an odd one out now Maureen's gone. You know – you and Sheila, Susan and Linda.'

'Of course I'll sit with you,' said Val. 'Don't be daft. And you don't need to feel like that. The others are OK

360

they just like a bit of fun, that's all. See you outside then, seven o'clock. Tara for now.'

They just like a bit of fun . . . Bernie turned Val's words over in her mind as she walked home from school. She knew the others thought she was a bit of a misery and a prude because she didn't always laugh uproariously at their comments and jokes. The truth was that often she didn't 'get' them and she would stand there looking puzzled while the others were laughing their heads off. Then, 'Oh, for Christ's sake, explain it to her, somebody!' Susan or Linda would say, and she would end up feeling a fool. She didn't like the way those two girls blasphemed either, and used quite awful swear words, not just damn and blast, which everybody said sometimes. Maureen had agreed with her about that and the two of them had usually made themselves scarce when the rest of the crowd were passing round a dirty book. Linda had brought a copy of *Lady Chatterley's Lover* to school, which had been very well thumbed.

Bernie sometimes wondered how she had got involved with this particular set of girls. There were other much nicer and quieter girls in the class; but it was, of course, because of Maureen. Her friend had palled up with them when she had first joined the school and they hadn't been too bad then. Now they seemed to have become rather common and loud, given to making fun of everything and everybody; all except Val Wilcox. Val had befriended her this last week since Maureen had left, and it was mainly for this reason that Bernie had decided to go to the pictures with the rest of the crowd.

Her mother didn't ask which film she was going to see. She just seemed glad that Bernie was going out for a change. 'Have a nice time, dear,' was all she said, kissing her on the cheek as she always did. She did not tell her not to be late. Bernie knew that she was expected to be home by half-past ten, quarter to eleven at the very latest if there was no school the next day, and she had always abided by the rule.

The girl in the box office scarcely looked at them as

361

Susan, judged to be the oldest looking, asked for 'Five back stalls, please.' *Only Two Can Play* was a rerun of the classic Peter Sellers comedy. It was really very amusing and Bernie found herself laughing, in parts, just as much as the others were doing. She need not have worried; there was nothing too shocking, just a few bedroom scenes with Peter Sellers pursuing somebody else's scantily clad wife. Bernie told herself she would have to grow up and not be so narrow-minded. He was playing the part of a dissatisfied librarian who worked with an odd little Welshman, a religious sort of fellow, who was a dreadful prude. Bernie couldn't help feeling sorry for the Welsh fellow at times.

'Wasn't that a hoot?' screamed Linda as they all poured out into the street. 'Honest, I thought I'd wet myself, I laughed so much. Come on, girls; where are we going? What about that pub round the corner? They'll serve us there, no problem.' Linda and Susan set off arm in arm along Talbot Road with the other three following behind a little more slowly.

'A pub?' said Bernie. 'D'you think we should? I haven't been in one before – have you?' She looked warily at Sheila and Val.

'Course I have, loads of times,' said Sheila, but Bernie didn't really believe her. Sheila was OK, though not as nice as Val. She liked to exaggerate and pretend she was as worldly-wise as the two girls who were the leaders of the gang. 'They take no notice of who they're serving, 'specially when they're busy. Come on, Bernie; don't be so soft. Val and I are going, aren't we, Val?'

Bernie was still unsure; besides, it was getting late and she knew she would have to get her bus home before long.

'It'll be OK; honest it will,' said Val. 'I've not been in a pub before either,' she added in a lower voice, 'but I don't want the others to know. You can just have an orange juice or a lemonade. That's what I'm going to do.'

Bernie let herself be led along to the pub halfway down Talbot Road. She glanced at her watch: it was a quarter to ten already. Probably the rest of the girls' mothers did not insist on them being home before eleven, but Bernie was

362

relieved that it would give her an excuse to have only one drink and then leave. She tried to convince herself that going into a pub was no big deal; Teresa had been doing it since she was younger than Bernie was now. And look what has happened to her, came the next thought. But that was a different thing altogether. Bernie didn't even know any boys yet, not properly, nor, to her amazement, did Val or Sheila. It was only Susan and Linda who boasted about their various escapades with the opposite sex – to be taken with a pinch of salt, Bernie suspected.

Susan and Linda went to the bar for the drinks whilst the other three procured a table in the corner where, luckily, there were five seats. The little round stools were covered in red plush that was wearing thin, and the table was ringed with beer stains. Bernie sniffed; the place stank of beer and cigarette smoke and was busy with Friday night revellers. She wondered what on earth her mother would say if she knew she was here.

'No problem,' said Susan, coming back with a laden tray containing an orange juice, a lemonade and three shandies. 'We got served as easy as anything.'

'Oh, come on, Sue, be honest,' said Linda. 'He asked how old we were.'

'So what? I said we were eighteen and he believed us. You don't have to show 'em your birth certificate or anything. Here y'are, girls. Get this down yer necks.'

Susan and Linda very quickly gulped down their shandies and were soon ready for a refill. Bernie decided she would drink her orange juice quickly while the two ringleaders were at the bar, and then sneak out. The bus stop was only just round the corner on Dickson Road and she was not worried about being out on her own after dark. But it was not to be. Bernie and Val and Sheila started talking about the film they had seen and some of Peter Sellers' other comedies and so she was delayed. She was just picking up her bag and putting on her cardigan when the other two returned.

'Oh, don't say you're going so soon, Bernie,' said Susan. 'What's the matter with you? Don't you like it here?'

'Yes, it's all right,' said Bernie, 'but I'll have to go because—'

''Cause Mummy says she has to be in by half-past ten, doesn't she, Bernie?' jeered Linda. 'What'll happen if you're late? I 'spect you'll have to go and confess to that priest fellow, won't you?'

'Hey, leave off,' said Val. 'There's no need for that.' But Susan and Linda, once started, would not be stopped. They had had only one shandy each so they could not be drunk, but they had been in a giddy mood before they entered the pub.

'She won't need to go to the priest,' said Susan. 'She can just go and confess to her brother, our Michael.' She started to giggle uncontrollably. 'Forgive me, Father Michael, for I have sinned. I've been led astray by some wicked girls. We went into a pub and I had . . . an orange juice!' Her cackle of laughter made the people at the next table turn and stare at them.

'Shut up,' said Sheila. 'People are looking at us.'

'And just leave Bernie alone,' said Val. 'You're dead mean, both of you. I wouldn't have come if I'd known.'

'If you'd known what?' sneered Linda. 'I bet I know something you don't know . . . about her brother.' She pointed her finger accusingly at Bernie.

'Of course I know,' retorted Val. 'We all know that her brother's going to be a priest, and I don't see anything to laugh at neither. I expect they're very proud of him,' she added loyally, putting a hand on Bernie's arm.

Bernie was longing to get up and walk out, but she did not know how to make her escape with those two awful girls making fun of her.

'I don't mean *that* brother, you idiot,' said Linda. 'Everybody knows about Father Michael. But she's got another brother, haven't you, Bernie?'

Bernie nodded. 'Yes, our Paul.'

'Yes, our Paul,' mimicked Linda in a silly sing-song, gloating sort of voice. 'Well, I bet you don't know what Susan and I know about "our Paul", do they, Susan?'

'No, I bet they don't,' said Susan.

'What are you talking about?' asked Bernie.

'Yes, what the heck are you on about?' said Val. 'Whatever it is, just leave it out. And leave Bernie alone. She's not done anything to you. Why are you being so nasty?'

'Because she's a little Goody Two-Shoes,' jeered Linda. 'And she's no need to be, 'cause her sister's having a baby before she's married . . . and her brother's gay!'

At the last word, which was almost shouted, the crowd at the next table turned and stared again. 'Shut up!' hissed Val. 'For goodness' sake, keep your voice down, Linda. You're talking rubbish, anyway.'

'Oh no, I'm not,' retorted Linda. 'You ask her.' She turned to Bernie. 'Your brother's got a friend called Martin, hasn't he?' Bernie nodded numbly. 'Well, my brother knows him. And he's . . . one of those, you know.' She made a limp-wristed gesture, waggling her shoulders expressively. 'A nancy boy, that's what Martin is, and her brother is an' all. They live together.'

Bernie stared at her aghast, only dimly understanding what the girl was saying. She knew very little about such things, only that there were some men who preferred other men, instead of women. And Linda was saying her brother was like that; Paul, the big brother that she loved so much. No, it couldn't be true . . . But she found herself remembering things she had not understood at the time: Paul's row with her dad, and how she had never discovered what it was about; Paul's sudden departure to live in Martin's flat; a snide comment of Teresa's that had puzzled her; and the way her mother and Veronica would stop talking suddenly when she entered the room.

She stood up, facing Linda and Susan. A sudden spurt of anger was making her feel braver. 'Shut up!' she yelled. 'You nasty horrible girls! It's not true . . . but what does it matter if it is? He's worth a hundred of you, any day. I hate you and I never want to see you again, any of you.' She turned and fled from the pub, elbowing her way through the crowds of drinkers and out through the swing door. Without even glancing to her left or right she shot across the side road, straight into the path of the car that

365

was turning out of Talbot Road.

'Bernie, Bernie, wait . . .' Val, with Sheila close behind, was chasing after her. They were just in time to hear the squeal of brakes and a sickening thud, and see Bernie lying in a heap at the side of the road. They were too stunned to move for a moment, then they dashed over to her.

'Don't touch her,' said a man who had just got out of the large Morris Oxford car. He looked shocked and his arms were trembling. 'I couldn't stop; I didn't stand a chance. She ran right in front of me . . . We'd better get an ambulance.'

'And the police,' said another man who had now arrived on the scene. 'I'll go and phone.'

Linda and Susan had now joined the other two, and they stood in a forlorn little group, staring at the unconscious, unmoving form of Bernie.

'Gosh! I didn't mean . . . I'm ever so sorry,' said Linda.

'D'you think she's . . . dead?' whispered Susan. 'Honest, we never meant . . .'

'Let's hope not,' said Val. 'We'd better start praying. That's what Bernie would do.'

'What about her mum and dad?' said Susan. 'Somebody will have to tell them.'

The ambulance and a police car arrived very quickly. One of the policemen, a sergeant, looked through her handbag, which was lying a few yards away, and shook his head at the other policeman. Then he noticed the little crowd of girls and came over to them. 'Do you know this young lady?' he asked.

'Er, yes, we do,' said Val. 'We were with her. There was a bit of an argument and she ran out.'

'Shhh,' hissed Susan. They might be in for a load of trouble if it was known they had been in the pub. The policeman gave her a calculating look, then turned back to Val.

'Who is she then?'

'She's called Bernie . . . Bernadette Jarvis, and she lives in Gynn Square; Sunset View, the hotel's called. D'you want us to go and tell her parents?'

'No, thank you,' said the sergeant. 'We'll see to all that. I take it you'd all been in there?'

'We are eighteen, officer,' said Linda. He narrowed his eyes, looking at her searchingly. She knew he didn't believe her, that he was aware she was lying. She began to feel afraid and, for the first time, a little guilty about her behaviour towards Bernie. But it wasn't her fault; how was she to know that the stupid girl would take to her heels and run? A sideways glance at her three friends told her that they were feeling just as bad as she was.

'I am going to take all your names and addresses,' said the police sergeant. 'And your ages – your correct ages, if you please,' he added with another probing look.

They all knew they had to conform. It was the first time any of them had had a brush with the law. In subdued voices – even Linda was chastened now – they told him who they were, where they lived, and that they were all sixteen.

'Hmm . . . I thought as much,' he said. 'We will be seeing the landlord of the pub and the person who served you. And then . . . you will be hearing from us. Our main concern at the moment is to see to your friend, Bernadette.'

'Bernie didn't have a drink,' said Val. 'Well, none of us did really. Not . . . not proper drinks. But Bernie's a real good girl. She didn't want to go in the pub in the first place. Is she . . . will she be all right?'

'Let's hope so,' said the police sergeant curtly. However, he glanced at them all in turn, not unkindly. 'You've had a shock, I know, so let's hope it teaches you a lesson. You'd better get off home now, the lot of you. We'll take care of your friend.'

Meanwhile Bernie, still not moving, had been lifted on to a stretcher and into the ambulance. The four girls stared after it dazedly as it turned into Talbot Road, its sirens blazing.

'Gosh!' said Linda again. 'This is awful. What are we going to do?'

'We're going home, that's what,' said Val, a sob catching in her throat. 'And then I'm going to ring the hospital.'

'They won't tell you anything.'

'They might. I'll say I'm her best friend.'

'It's easy to say that now.'

'Shut up, you, Linda Morris! I was never horrid to her like you were. It's all your fault she got knocked down, saying all those terrible things about her brother.'

'But they're true,' said Linda, not very convincingly.

'Well, even if they are true, you didn't need to say them, did you? Bernie knew nothing about it, you could tell; about her brother being – you know – like that. She must have had an awful shock.'

'Yeah . . . I know,' admitted Linda. 'It was a bit mean of me.'

'A bit! A heck of a lot, I'd say.'

'Well . . . anyway, I didn't know she'd react like that, did I? But I'm sorry, honest I am.'

'Yeah . . . so am I,' said Susan. 'I didn't mean to upset her either. But she used to annoy me; she was always so goody-goody and I . . . Oh heck, what have we done?' Susan burst into tears.

They all stared at her in surprise, but with sympathy as well. Susan was a cool customer – as was Linda – and not given to tears. But they all felt like crying now. 'Come on, Sue,' said Linda, putting a hand on her arm. 'Don't get upset. That's not going to help Bernie, is it?'

'No, it's no use any of us falling out about it now,' said Sheila. 'It doesn't really matter whose fault it is. The main thing is to hope and pray that Bernie recovers. Come on, Val; let's go and get our bus. Tara, you two,' she added dispiritedly.

'Yeah . . . Tara. See you Monday,' said Val.

They walked away leaving Linda and Susan looking at one another in silence for several moments. Susan was still sniffling. 'Oh, crikey,' she breathed. 'What on earth have we done, Lin?'

'I don't know,' replied Linda. 'It doesn't bear thinking about.'

'D'you think he'll get in touch with us, like he said, that policeman?'

'I dunno; he might. But I should think he'll be more keen on talking to the pub landlord. They're not supposed to serve us.'

'And we're not supposed to be there. Are you going to tell your mum and dad?'

'I suppose we'll have to,' said Linda. 'I'll get into awful trouble, though.'

'So will I,' sniffed Susan.

'But it would be even worse if . . . if anything happened to Bernie,' said Linda in a small voice. 'Come on . . . We'd better go home.' Two disconsolate little figures walked up Talbot Road towards the bus station.

Chapter 19

The Family

Doreen sat silently, studying the face of her youngest daughter, as she had been doing for the last few hours, willing her to open her eyes. She lay there so still and pale, the stark white sheet making a hump over the leg that was encased in plaster. She had a few cracked ribs as well as intensive bruising on her body, and a gash on her arm that had required a great number of stitches, but her face was unmarked apart from a purplish bruise on her temple. She was still unconscious and the doctor said he did not know how long she would remain so; the concussion was quite severe. But she had been lucky, he said; as far as they could tell there were no internal injuries; it was just a matter of time.

Why Bernie? Doreen asked herself over and over again as she and Norman sat, most of the time in silence, at her hospital bedside. Bernie was the member of the family who had always been the least trouble, so obedient and good-natured and willing to help. She remembered the 'goose walking over her grave' a couple of weeks ago, when Norman had made the remark that nobody had died. That had been her immediate thought when she had seen the policeman standing on her doorstep the previous night. Half-past eleven and Bernie had not come home. Doreen had already begun to fear that something awful had happened, and when she had heard his words, 'Bernadette Jarvis . . . are you her mother?' she had almost fainted with the shock, believing her daughter was dead and that Norman's words had been a terrible omen. But the police sergeant, a kindly and understanding man underneath his rigid stance, had quickly assured her that Bernie was not dead, only injured; but they did not yet know the extent of her injuries. Would her parents come at once to Victoria Hospital?

Doreen had wakened Teresa and Michael, telling them the awful news and then informing them that they were now in charge of the hotel until such time as their parents were able to return. Sixteen guests were due to arrive the next day, and the fourteen departing guests would all require a full English breakfast before they went on their way. To give them their due, the twins had not quibbled; they had been concerned only about their young sister. Doreen knew that Teresa and Michael would pull out all the stops in an emergency, and extra responsibility would be good for the pair of them. Karl Robson was due to come in early in the morning to cook the breakfasts, and Doreen's sister, Vera, always came on a Saturday for 'change-over day' to see to the bedlinen and towels. Doreen had phoned her at once, and Vera had promised to bring a friend to help out and had urged her sister not to worry about the hotel.

Bernie had been in the theatre when they arrived at the hospital. Now she was in a little side ward on her own. Norman had dozed fitfully in one of the – comparatively – easy chairs, but Doreen had remained wide awake, myriad thoughts racing through her mind; mainly about Bernie, but about her other children as well. She recalled a quotation she had heard from way, way back, but she did not know the source of it. 'Children bring certain sorrow, and uncertain joy.' That was how it went, and she reflected now that it was very true. But balancing the one against the other, sorrow and joy, their children, all five of them, had probably brought just as much joy as sorrow to their parents.

But why Bernie? she asked again, knowing she would not receive an answer. Since she had heard the news she had been praying inside her mind, over and over again, the same words: please, God, let her be all right; Holy Mother, please listen to me; Lord Jesus, take care of her. She had railed against God as well, feeling that somehow He had let her down. Hadn't she had enough problems already, for goodness' sake? And with a son about to train for the priesthood, willing to give his life over to the service of God, you would think that He would be more considerate. Then she chastised herself, knowing in her heart that the ways of God should not be questioned. It was hard, though, so very hard not to ask why, why, why?

Norman, who had dropped off again for a few moments, woke with a snort of breath and a sudden start. He blinked confusedly. 'What time is it?'

'Eight o'clock,' replied Doreen.

'She's still not . . . ? She hasn't moved at all?'

'No, not yet.'

A nurse brought them some tea and toast, which they did their best to eat. A doctor came and looked at Bernie, feeling her pulse and nodding in what Doreen hoped was a satisfied way. And they continued their vigil.

'They say it might help if we talked to her,' said Doreen. Norman shook his head. He seemed unable to find any words, but Doreen started to chat to her unconscious daughter about all sorts of trivial things. About what a nice day it was – the early morning sun was streaming through the windows, as though unaware that it had no right to shine when people were feeling so sad; about Teresa and Veronica and how lovely it would be when there were two new babies in the family; about Sandra and Karl – wasn't it nice that they were planning to get married next spring when Sandra was twenty-one?

The fingers of Bernie's right hand, on the arm that was not injured, fluttered slightly, then tried to pluck at the sheet. 'She can hear me, Norman,' said Doreen. But the girl did not open her eyes.

It was mid-morning when Michael arrived in the ward, his crash helmet under his arm. He had recently passed his motorcycle test and was the proud owner of a BSA motorbike. 'We had to come,' he said, 'Teresa and me. We can't stop thinking about our Bernie.' He looked down at his sister. 'How is she? Will she be all right?'

'We think so; we hope so,' said Doreen. 'She's just moved her hand. That's a good sign.' She glanced questioningly at her son. 'The hotel . . . ?'

'Don't worry, Mum. It's all under control. Karl's there, and Aunty Vera and her next-door neighbour. And Karl's rung Abbie and she says she'll go and lend a hand. Teresa will be here in a few minutes. I've just dropped her off at—'

'Teresa?' said Doreen. 'Don't say you've brought Teresa on the back of your motorbike? And her six months pregnant! Honestly, you two; have you no sense?'

'Calm down, Mum,' said Michael. 'She's OK. She had a crash helmet on; I made sure of that.'

'Where is she then?'

'She had to see somebody. I've told you; she'll be here in a few minutes.'

Norman looked across at his younger son. 'Thanks for coming, son,' he said, the first words he had spoken for what seemed like hours. 'Your mum and I appreciate it.'

'We're a family, Dad,' said Michael. 'We stick together, don't we?' His father nodded gravely.

'Aye, that's right, son. At least, that's what we ought to do.'

'Hey, Bernie – it's Michael. Hello there . . .' Her brother leaned over her, touching her hand, but she did not stir.

'I've come to see me sister.' They all looked up at the sound of a familiar voice in the corridor. Teresa! And then the nurse's voice, 'She's in here. She has three visitors already. It's not really allowed, but under the circumstances . . . Don't stay too long though.'

Teresa entered the room in her usual uninhibited manner, going straight over to the bed. 'Bernie, oh, Bernie! Please wake up! She's going to be all right, isn't she, Mum?' She turned a tearful face towards her mother.

But Doreen was staring at the person who had entered

the room behind her, more diffidently than his sister. It was Paul. He also approached the bed. He scarcely glanced at his parents, or at the twins, only at his kid sister. He took hold of her hand. 'Hi, sis,' he said. 'It's me – it's Paul. Come on now, aren't you going to say hello to me?'

Norman made a move as if to say something, but Doreen put a restraining hand on his arm. 'Leave it, Norman,' she said quietly. He turned to look at her, sighing gently.

'I was only going to say hello to him,' he whispered. 'Surely you didn't think . . .'

'Norman, look . . .' Doreen spoke again, more loudly. 'Look . . . I think Bernie's opening her eyes.'

Paul was looking lovingly down at Bernie as though willing her to wake up. Her eyelids, indeed, were flickering. 'Bernie . . . Bernie . . . Come on; it's me, Paul,' coaxed her brother. But the girl's eyelids were still again and she appeared to be retreating back into unconsciousness.

'Try again, lad,' whispered Norman. 'Go on – make her wake up,' he added, a note of desperation evident in his voice.

Paul leaned over and took hold of his sister's hand. 'Hello, Bernie,' he said. 'We're all here waiting for you to wake up. And we all love you very much.'

Bernie's eyelids flickered once again. Her fingers moved beneath his, then, after what seemed ages, but was really only a few moments, she slowly opened her eyes. She blinked as though in a daze, and then, her gaze resting upon Paul, she gave a tiny smile.

There was silence in the room for several seconds, then Norman rose to his feet. The father and son looked at one another, the first direct glance they had exchanged for many months, then Norman walked round the bed and put his arms round his son, holding him close. 'Thank you, Paul,' he said, his voice gruff with emotion. 'Thanks . . . son.'

Paul, too, tightened his hold on his father, enveloping

him in a loving hug. 'It's OK, Dad,' he said. 'Everything's going to be OK.'

Doreen, watching them, was too overcome to speak. The tears streaming down her face, she smiled at them and then at her youngest daughter. Bernie's face held a puzzled frown as if she were thinking, What's happened? Where am I? But the frown disappeared and was replaced by a tentative smile as Doreen took hold of her hand.

'Hello, Mum . . .' she said.

They were all there at Sunset View on the last Saturday in August for a double celebration. Teresa, just two weeks ago, had given birth to a seven-pound baby girl, Deborah Jane, and mother and daughter were now out of hospital and doing fine. And Bernie, at long last, had had the plaster removed from her leg, her cuts and bruises had healed and though she was still pale and shaky she was well on the road to full recovery and looking forward to starting her course at the catering college.

It was a lunch-time party because the work had to go on. Eighteen guests had already arrived at Sunset View and would require an evening meal, and Paul and Martin were fully booked at Two's Company that evening with a golden wedding celebration.

Two's Company was going from strength to strength. It had had a mention in a prestigious guide to good restaurants and was starting to become *the* place to eat, not only for the more well-heeled residents of Blackpool, but for those from Lytham St Annes – the somewhat posher resort to the south of the town – as well.

Doreen looked round at them all with a feeling of pride and an intense joy such as she had not felt for ages. Her family; now an extended family. She felt a little sad as she looked at Michael. He was on his own, as he so often was, but this did not seem to worry him. She knew it was something he would have to get used to in the future. The life of a Catholic priest could be a lonely one, having to forgo, as he must, the love and companionship of one special person. But Michael seemed happy and resolute in the path he had chosen and was already developing a maturity beyond his years.

His twin sister, too, had matured greatly of late. Even before the birth of Deborah Jane, Teresa had started to grow up, and now, with her baby daughter asleep in her arms, she looked the very picture of serene motherhood. She was a wonderful mother, there was no doubt about that, and had not once grumbled about sleepless nights or feeding problems or the chore of changing dirty nappies and the endless washing – which she had undertaken all on her own. Maybe the girl was finding her true vocation, mused Doreen. Simon was at her side now, and Doreen saw the two of them look at one another and smile a little shyly as they then looked at the sleeping baby. They were obviously proud parents; and Doreen knew that Norman shared her own pride in this, their first grandchild. Whatever the circumstances of her birth, Deborah Jane was a very precious gift. Who could tell what the future might hold for the three of them; Teresa, Simon, and baby Deborah. But it was certain that Simon as well as Teresa would face up to his responsibilities, whatever they might be.

Doreen's glance rested on Bernie, the baby of the family, who had caused them so much anguish not so long ago. Doreen had feared, through one dreadful night, that she might lose her, but God had been good and she had pulled through. She looked happy and relaxed now, her usually pale cheeks pink with excitement. As a special privilege – because the celebration was Bernie's as well as Teresa's – she had invited along her new friend, Val. It was Val's friendship that had helped Bernie to regain her confidence. Maureen, too, the friend who had moved away, had been to stay at Sunset View for part of the summer holiday. Those two, and Paul, bless him, had lifted Bernie out of her depression and Doreen knew her youngest daughter was looking forward eagerly to starting her course at the catering college.

Doreen and Norman, before the end of the year, would have a second grandchild. Veronica was delighting in her pregnancy and now, with her devoted husband, Andy, and the two children, Donna and Barry, she looked more contented than Doreen had ever seen her.

Abbie and Duncan Hendy were there, too, holding hands; Sandra and Karl, looking forward to their spring wedding; and Paul . . . and Martin, accepted now by them all, including Norman, as Paul's companion.

Norman stood and raised his glass of champagne. Doreen could almost see his chest bursting with pride as she watched him standing there, his eyes resting briefly on each of his children in turn. Finally he looked at Doreen, the love shining from his eyes, and she felt the answering look in her own as she smiled back at him.

'Here's to us – to the family,' he said.

'To the family . . .' they all echoed.

Now you can buy any of these other bestselling
books from your bookshop or
direct from the publisher.

FREE P&P AND UK DELIVERY
(Overseas and Ireland £3.50 per book)

The House on Lonely Street	Lyn Andrews	£5.99
A Glimpse of the Mersey	Anne Baker	£5.99
The Whispering Years	Harry Bowling	£5.99
The Stony Path	Rita Bradshaw	£5.99
The Bird Flies High	Maggie Craig	£5.99
Kate's Story	Billy Hopkins	£5.99
Taking a Chance on Love	Joan Jonker	£5.99
The Jarrow Lass	Janet MacLeod Trotter	£5.99
All or Nothing	Lynda Page	£5.99
A Perfect Stranger	Victor Pemberton	£5.99
Where Hope Lives	Wendy Robertson	£5.99
Better Days	June Tate	£6.99
A Rare Ruby	Dee Williams	£5.99

TO ORDER SIMPLY CALL THIS NUMBER

01235 400 414

or visit our website: www.madaboutbooks.co.u

Prices and availability subject to change without notic